R

Modern War

Anatiposi

Randal Roberts

Modern War

Reprint of the original, first published in 1871.

1st Edition 2023 | ISBN: 978-3-38211-380-3

Anatiposi Verlag is an imprint of Outlook Verlagsgesellschaft mbH.

Verlag (Publisher): Outlook Verlag GmbH, Zeilweg 44, 60439 Frankfurt, Deutschland
Vertretungsberechtigt (Authorized to represent): E. Roepke, Zeilweg 44, 60439 Frankfurt, Deutschland
Druck (Print): Books on Demand GmbH, In de Tarpen 42, 22848 Norderstedt, Deutschland

MODERN WAR.

MODERN WAR:

OR THE

CAMPAIGNS OF THE FIRST PRUSSIAN ARMY, 1870-71.

BY

SIR RANDAL H. ROBERTS, BART.

SPECIAL MILITARY CORRESPONDENT TO THE 'DAILY TELEGRAPH.'

LONDON:

CHAPMAN AND HALL, 193 PICCADILLY.

1871.

TO

THE MOST NOBLE

THE MARQUIS OF DONEGAL, K.P.

THIS BOOK IS DEDICATED

BY

THE AUTHOR.

CONTENTS.

six potatoes. This was our dinner, breakfast, and supper. But the general occasionally sent me over a bottle of Kirsch and a lump of sugar; so that in the evening we had a sip of hot grog, if the rain permitted our fire to burn.

of the troops, although dysentery is still very much felt; but provisions are getting more abundant, through the medium of the railway to Ars from Saarbrück. The Crown Prince has said that the war is seven-eighths over.'

the French generals had the opportunity of commanding large masses—and the result is but too well known.

As we rode through the camp of Châlons—so often described by others, that it is superfluous for me to attempt what has already been done so much better—I was amused by the various inscriptions which appeared on the houses of the permanent barracks. "*Vive la Famille Impériale!*" "*L'Armée de Reconnaissance!*" "*L'Honneur, la Gloire, et la Patrie!*" and suchlike mottoes, stood out in bold relief upon the walls; but, as if in mockery of the sentiments, the flowers of which they were composed hung dead and mournful-looking from the strings. The whole camp was a miserable dreary waste; and as we rode on, we wondered that the efforts of *la grande nation*, with such splendid opportunities, had been in a military point of view so grievously wasted. Politically speaking, I should like to know when France will learn anything conducive to solidity or contentment?

On the 15th of November the Prussian troops marched into the ancient town of Rheims. I hardly think that it is necessary for me to go over old and well-trodden ground—to describe a city which from time immemorial has held so large a place in history, as the scene of the coronation of so many French kings—except that the city of Rheims bid fair to experience disorders as great as any that visited many of the other towns of *la belle France;* so much so, that the inhabitants were particularly anxious to retain a German garrison, as the workmen, who numbered some twenty thousand, threatened the place with disturb-

dalous way upon the unfortunate soldiers, whose honest, good-natured faces, as they paid their money like men, was a study for the pencil of Frith or Ward.

The good city of Amiens had to pay dear for its resistance, and the possession of the citadel enabled the general to take far more troops with him than he could have otherwise done. A German préfet and sous-préfet were appointed, whose office commenced immediately, and under whose auspicious rule things, much to the astonishment of the mayor, came tumbling into their places. Next day the shops were all open, and the streets lined with inhabitants, watching the march of the troops out of the town.

while the boiling of the potatoes went on un superintendence of a staff-officer. In an hour n was supposed to be ready; cooked or uncool could wait no longer. Each man brought h plate. Shall I ever forget the frozen cabbage. nothing of the half-boiled fowls, or the way ii we swallowed the hot water, salt, and pepper. w tried to fancy soup? But we dined; and the who had cigars smoked, and those who had n and growled at those who had, until we got u horses and rode back to Combles, to find our l gone—for it had been sent on to Hérbecourt. ever dreaming that we should be able to main position. Fatigue, however, makes all thin *leur de rose:* we stabled our horses, fed the selves, and in two minutes each one of us wa asleep wherever he could lay his weary bones.

On arrival at Dompierre more specific info as to the movements of the enemy was r They were in full retreat upon Arras and followed by the cavalry in hot pursuit. T cuirassiers (Rhenish) had ridden down two ba of the enemy to the north of Sapignies, takin prisoners. The German losses were heavy killed and wounded, with 24 officers. Out of t 33d regiment lost 7 officers killed and 4 w with 228 men killed and wounded. This regiment had now lost 47 officers and exactly strength, or 1500 men. There were now o officers with the regiment, or one for each co Péronne still held out; but the town was heap of ashes. The cavalry were within fou

the campaign after the fall of Metz in the north of France, there is grave food for reflection. In it we find a great country suddenly called upon to continue a struggle with her reserve forces which her regular army had failed in. And not only to do this, but to make the attempt under the most trying circumstances, viz. without cavalry and indifferently supplied with artillery. That the reserve forces of France in some instances fought well, there can be but little doubt; but that the fatal mistake of want of organisation and military knowledge too often robbed them of victory at the moment it was in their hands, is also apparent. Had this not been wanting, at Pont-Noyelles the Prussians would have been beaten, and at Bapaume they would have been driven back and the siege of Péronne raised. But in the moment of victory General Faidherbe *dared* not trust what may be said to have represented the volunteers of France.

THE END.

LONDON: ROBSON AND SONS, PRINTERS, PANCRAS ROAD, N.W.

PREFACE.

It is hardly my province in these pages to discuss the political aspect of affairs at the outbreak of the war, or to attempt to unravel the tangle of diplomatic secrecy which seems to shroud this view of the matter. Mine is to chronicle, to the best of my ability, the principal military events—the achievements on the one side, the faults on the other; to note the organisation here, and the want there; which, thanks to the facilities which my position on the staff of General von Göben, the modern Wellington of the day, gave me, I have been enabled to do.

In the contents of this history I have occasionally quoted from letters which I supplied as 'Special Military Correspondent to the *Daily Telegraph*' during the war, and which have appeared in its columns. I believe that I am an isolated case of one who followed the fortunes of one of the armies engaged from the beginning to the end without a change: and therefore I cannot refrain from noticing a circumstance, which must be patent to every one, and which the English army must ever consider as a gross mark of neglect and injustice—I allude to the fact that little or no opportunities were given to the officers of our staff or army to watch the events of this important campaign.

Never, since the Peninsular War, have we had a fairer opportunity of improving our military organisation, or of gaining knowledge for the benefit of the service; and yet with five exceptions no other representatives were on the spot, where so much was to be learnt, so much experience to be gained. General Walker has not yet given to the public his experiences, which is the more to be regretted inasmuch as such matter never improves by keeping. Poor Colonel Pemberton, as *Times* correspondent, was killed at Sedan; Colonel Fielding was with General Chanzy's rabble on the Loire; Captain Hozier never came out until after the fall of Metz; so that there remained but one English officer who went through the campaign from end to end. It is true, that here and there a favoured few did come over for two or three days; but their opportunities were scarce, and even these were much curtailed. Although no longer in the regular army, having been compelled to leave it from unfortunate circumstances over which I had no control, I have ever devoted myself to a profession which I consider to be second to none in the world; and in publishing these pages I throw myself upon the generosity of my military readers, hoping that the object which I have in view may atone for any shortcomings, descriptive or otherwise.

The position of Reserve forces is one that will

also be found treated upon in this volume; and as a Volunteer I strongly recommend those who take an interest in the movement to mark well the painful experience herein detailed, which has been gained through the mobilisation of the French Reserve forces for the defence of their country. Continuous as has been the cry for organisation, Government is permitting the golden opportunity to slip. Every one cries out against the absurd mockery of so-called instruction, which the Volunteer learns at the Easter scramble, called a sham fight, or the profitless fourteen days' shooting at the Camp at Wimbledon, and yet no one seems to come forward or to legislate upon so grave a matter.

May the experiences of the last campaign, as I have endeavoured to describe them, together with the frowning uncertainty of Europe, teach us the necessity of prompt action! English infantry are the finest in the world—as were the French, and are still: for no one will for a moment pretend to detract from the splendid material which, without leaders, destitute of proper battalion officers and non-commissioned officers, and often without ammunition or commissariat, fought the battles of Spiecheren, Colombey, Mars-la-Tour, and Gravelotte. Something more is wanting than material; let us hope it may be found, and that quickly.

R. H. ROBERTS.

London, June 1871.

MODERN WAR.

CHAPTER I.

GOING TO THE FRONT.

It was a rude awakening, that morning in July 1870, when Prussia's King, wearied of imperial insolence, turned his back upon the representative of *la grande nation*. It was a severe shock, that awoke continental Europe from fancied security, and taught countries and ministers the value of generals, soldiers, and military organisation. Modern war has so metamorphosed the appliances for inflicting wounds and scattering death broadcast, that the fate of nations is no longer a question of years, but of months. The Austrian campaign of 1866 first opened the eyes of every one to the fact of the superiority of breech-loading arms; but the struggle was so short, that the world had scarcely time to judge upon the merits of the question.

Upon leaving England to join the Prussian army, I felt fully convinced in my own mind that the campaign about to take place would be one where the issue, as both armies were supplied with breech-loaders, would depend more upon organisation, generalship, and endurance than the superiority of the weapons used; and in this belief I was fully borne out by the rapid events that followed one another.

If France, as is asserted, was unprepared for war, Germany certainly was equally so; and as I took my passport in Downing-street, not without certain misgivings, I confess that I felt no little anxiety to see the unusual sight of a large kingdom suddenly mobilised, and sending her troops to protect her frontier or invade the enemy's, as the case might be.

But a few short months ago and the autumnal journey to the Rhine was a matter of no difficulty: a few short hours reduced the trip to a state of melancholy uncertainty. Last July, when you took your ticket at Charing-cross, it was not so much a question of your reaching the destination you had booked for, as to how far you could get upon your route; and if uncertainty had a charm, it was to be found in a ticket to Cologne.

In vain on the passage from Dover did one look for French men-of-war, although before starting you were confidentially told by a friend that the probabilities were we should 'hear guns:' the journey, however, was safely accomplished, and Ostend pier sighted and gained. It is true that on the journey a smart-looking French corvette gave undeniable chase to a screw collier steering Balticwards; but as they both lay out of our course, no one knew what was the upshot.

A more melancholy-looking place than Ostend at this time it is hardly possible to imagine. The old woman whom we have all known for years, and from whom we have purchased our *Daily Telegraph* at the railway-station, sat in her corner without moving at your approach. The porters who put your luggage into the train looked melancholy, the passengers suicidal. As I passed through this fertile country, never so fertile as last year, I listened to the hopes and fears of two gentlemen holding a very distinguished position in their country as to the probability of reaping this harvest. From what I heard and from what I saw, it appeared as if none but women were left to accomplish this; for almost every available man had gone to the front. One gentleman who had just returned from St. Petersburg described a scene that took place at the railway-station of that city. It appeared that some dozen Germans living there had been recalled to serve during the war; about the same number of Frenchmen happened to be collected at the station at the same time, evidently with the same object. No sooner did they become acquainted with each other's nationality, than they immediately commenced a campaign on the platform, the result of which was, that three Frenchmen were placed *hors de combat* by the time the train started.

On my arrival in Brussels I found the streets solitary, and the whole city pervaded by a heavy and gloomy atmosphere. The Belgians seemed to build their hopes upon English assistance, and looked upon both the French and Prussians in the same light. The next morning I tried to book to Cologne, but this was impossible. I could only take a ticket to

Verviers. In the railway-carriage I met with a Belgian colonel, in command of a regiment encamped upon the frontier. At first, taking me for a Frenchman, he steadily refused entering into conversation; but, after mentioning the Belgian Volunteers at Wimbledon, and satisfying him as to my nationality, all reserve vanished; and from what he told me and what I saw myself, I fancied that Belgium, so far as she could be, was ready for any emergency. As we came in sight of Tirelemonde, I saw a regiment of Lancers marching in; the men looked well, but their cattle might have been better.

Arrived at Verviers, my miseries commenced. There were only two trains for passengers to Cologne; but after a great deal of difficulty and a few thalers I at length got a seat in a luggage wagon. On the frontier I had another fight to get through, Lord Granville's signature not sufficing to grease the wheels of the 'Eisenbahn;' but I had a flask of Irish whisky in my pocket and plenty of cigars, which, in the end, proved more efficacious than my Foreign Office passport. Between Aix-la-Chapelle and Cologne, what a melancholy scene!—fields of barley, wheat, and oats, ripe and over-ripe, left to take care of themselves, for want of some one to reap them. I do not think that I saw twenty men between the two places. As we neared Cologne the platforms were crowded with Landwehr, their wives and sisters clinging to them, and the men vainly endeavouring to keep up a nonchalant air. Arrived at Cologne, my miseries commenced afresh. Upon showing my passport, I was cross-examined, and told that 'this was no time for a journey of pleasure,' my only excuse to the stern official who interrogated me; but after a great deal of consultation I was at length permitted to enter the town.

Cologne was under the command of General von Falkenstein, a gentleman who was not likely to be behindhand in anything, and was strongly garrisoned. The trees were all felled in front of the fortifications, and everything was ready to receive an invader. Within a period of fifteen hours after my arrival, no less than sixty trains, containing 80,000 men, went through Cologne; and the only intimation you had of their entrance and exit was the cheers with which each train was welcomed. I saw a battalion of rifles go through, and, although they were spoken of as a very crack corps, they seemed to me not to be quite up to the mark. Great excitement prevailed when a report was spread abroad that Baron Rothschild had received a telegram to the effect that Marshal Bazaine had crossed the Prussian frontier; but this being contradicted, people took refuge in the King's proclamation, posted all over the town, in which he told his people that he was leaving for the seat of war, that he and his ministers had done all in their power for the protection of the country, and that he left the issue of 'Fatherland' in their hands.

Unlike the French, all the Prussian troops that I saw—some 120,000 about this time—showed a steadfast determination, quietly exhibited, rather than a giving way to uproarious enthusiasm. They seemed by no means confident of the result, and were fully aware that the enemy they were going to meet was one that would test their powers to the utmost. Where they thought they had the superiority was not in their numbers, but in their generals; for they seemed to hold the French military leaders in the utmost contempt. Whilst writing, the sanctity of my room was invaded by a couple of 'Polizei' (police), who again requested to look at my passport, and who objected to the very un-English way I had of pronouncing French: to get on, however, was my principal object, and no amount of Polizeis seemed for the moment to offer a sufficient excuse as an impediment to my progress.

When, indeed, at Cologne, I mentioned Kreuznach as my destination, people merely laughed at me; and when I said Saarbrück, they thought I was mad. Under these circumstances I thought it advisable to have an interview with the commandant of the town, inasmuch as that freemasonry which exists amongst soldiers is to be found in every continental nation. Manifold were the warnings I had given to me as to the imprudence of my proposal; but having always found that straightforward dealing, in a soldierly manner, generally succeeds with soldiers, I determined to beard the lion in his den. I confess, I was not prepared to meet with so much military bluntness; but inasmuch as I met it with a like behaviour, and got all I wanted, I cannot complain.

The railway station, when I arrived there, presented an unusual appearance. In addition to the military bustle and crowd of soldiers, some hundred nuns were collected on the platform; each one wearing a white badge, with a red Maltese cross upon it, sewn round the left arm—the emblem of the Geneva Convention, afterwards fated to be the cloak for so many sins. Besides these, there were about a hundred gentlemen wearing similar badges, who, I discovered, were going to the front for the purpose of nursing the wounded soldiers and attending as nurses in the hospital. There was the strictest watch kept at the railway station by the officials and the police. Each platform was in the charge of an officer, whilst the whole station was commanded by a field-officer. The 'Wartesaal' would have furnished Mr. Frith with a subject worthy of his talented pencil. Here an old Prussian officer, with hair and moustache as white as snow, embracing his son; whilst hanging round his neck is a lovely girl, down whose cheeks the tears are rolling, although she is evidently striving to restrain them. There a great strapping Landwehrman is supporting the tottering steps of his aged mother towards the platform, that she may see the very last of her boy. Seated in a group round a table are five or six nuns, their hands crossed before them, not uttering a single word. Leaning against the doorway, with his arms crossed upon his breast, is a tall fair-haired young man, quietly noting everything that goes on, and paying particular attention to the military trains as they go by, with their freights of 1050 men in each. Suddenly his observations are disturbed by the rude grasp of a police inspector, and immediately he is surrounded by a gaping crowd. His arms are seized by a couple of soldiers, and he is dragged off; he is a Danish spy.

One more sketch, and I have done. Walking up and down the platform is an officer in the uniform of a dragoon. On either arm he carries a little child, boy and girl, of the respective ages of four and five. They are both dressed in deep mourning; they have just lost their mother, and their father is now leaving with his regiment for the front. Poor fellow! in vain he tries to laugh as the little fingers are twined in his long moustache, and the boy, with a crow of delight, places a glove on the top of his helmet. It is a sad melancholy smile that flits across his manly countenance. But now the bugle sounds—the moment has come—he must part with the two little ones God has given him to remind him of his dead wife. He places them carefully on the platform, a nurse takes them by the hand, and, without another look, he darts into the nearest carriage.

My train was now ready. There were only two passenger trains from Cologne southwards during the day-time. I get into a carriage with two officers going to Mainz. We stop at Coblenz, where the King had passed an hour before on his way to Cologne. At this time there were a large body of troops in Coblenz, and nearly 500 French prisoners. After a fatiguing journey, lasting from 11 A.M. till 6 P.M., I get to Bingenbrück. Here the rail branches off for Kreuznach, Kaiserslautern, and Saarbrück. I am obliged to change, and I find a battery of artillery about to start. The wagons each hold six horses, who are loaded with their heads looking inwards; the men stand beside their horses. Away rolls the train, and immediately behind it comes a forage train. Into this I manage to get, and I arrive at Kreuznach at 8 P.M.

On the platform of the station the first signs of the stern reality of war greet me in the shape of some 120 French prisoners taken at Saarbrück. Some of them were slightly wounded. They were waiting for a train to take them to Coblenz, and seemed very unlikely to play any farther part in the war. They were sullen and silent, and very little pleased with the jokes which the country people were making at their expense. When I got to the hotel, I tried to get some information on the subject; I could, however, hear nothing. Kreuznach was the rear of the centre of the Prussian position, their right resting on Trèves, and their left upon Rastadt. There were only two regiments there—a rifle corps and a dragoon regiment, and both went on to the front the next day; but trains were continually pouring through laden with troops and stores, and after that day no more passenger trains were to be permitted to run. I was therefore just in time. Great want of forage was felt there, the hay being all bought up for the troops. If ever there was a city of the dead, Kreuznach at that moment was one; the Kursaal and shops were closed, and the hotels shut up. There were but few people moving about in the streets; and I was heartily glad when I was out of it.

It was here that I first listened to reproaches upon the course which the English Government had thought fit to adopt. There were murmured whisperings and mutterings against a policy that prescribed neutrality on the one hand, and supplied war material on the other. Had not Prussia and England ever fought side by side to uphold peace, and the proper balance of power in Europe, against the grasping, overbearing conduct of France? I was asked. And now, when civilisation had made such strides, was trade, the arts and sciences, social and political economy, and the Continent to be upset by the same *irritamenta malorum*, when England's influence could have turned the scale? It is true our army was not a great one; but the moral effect of even 40,000 men, to say nothing of the fleet, *on either side*, would at that moment have saved much bloodshed, and have maintained England in her proper position. If our sympathies had been with France, an English army and an English fleet would have caused Prince Bismarck to pause; whilst if, on the other hand, our ancient alliance with Prussia had been revived, the catastrophes of Sedan and Metz would perhaps have never been chronicled. The fault was, we did nothing; we were unjust to France and truculent with Germany; and the time is not far distant which will prove that by this milk-and-water policy we have lost all. The same story has again been played by a ministry harassed by an active opposition; once more common sense has not entered into the military policy of Great Britain; and as it was with the Walcheren expedition, so it was last July, with the exception that we have now no Iron Duke to save us from the contempt with which England and Englishmen are now looked upon.

The only apparent way of accounting for the lack of troops upon the frontier seems to be found in the utter surprise with which the Prussians received the intimation that war was declared. In fact the 40th Regiment was hastily ordered up from Trier to protect this important point, and the 7th Uhlans were marched at a rapid rate across the 'Eifel' to watch the proceedings of General Frossard, who was massing his troops at Forbach, evidently awaiting the coöperation of the Metz troops on his left and M'Mahon on his right flank. Some idea may be gathered of the unprotected state of this portion of the Prussian frontier at this time from the fact that the 7th Uhlans used to vary their facings with different-coloured paper in order to let the French imagine there were more cavalry regiments than one on the frontier. Again, only on the 16th of July did the intendant of the 8th army corps receive orders to prepare for the march of General von Göben's corps over the Hunde Rücke, one of the poorest and most barren districts in Germany. Upon this famous march I shall hereafter expatiate, showing as it does the perfect system of Prussian organisation in connection with their commissariat.

After innumerable difficulties and all sorts of adventures, I managed to reach Saarbrück in time to witness the first engagement worth mentioning between the French and Prussian forces; and although it was only an affair of outposts, yet it will not easily be forgotten as the commencement of the Franco-Prussian war of 1870. When I arrived in Saarbrück, I found the town occupied by the 40th regiment of Prussian infantry, with two guns, and the 7th regiment of Prussian Lancers or Uhlans. It may be as well, before proceeding to describe this partial collision between the contending forces, to take a glance at the relative position of the two armies.

By referring to the map, it will be seen that the French army was scattered between Thionville and Strasburg, the principal formations being naturally towards the centre of this line, upon which the Prussian frontier takes a somewhat encroaching position. The Prussian forces lay between Trèves and Rastadt; the outposts at Forbach and Saarbrück representing the advanced central posts of either army—the French at Forbach, the Prussian at Saarbrück. Saarbrück is one of the frontier towns of Prussia, occupying a most important position on the railway, being in a direct line of communication with Bingenbrück—that Clapham Junction of the Rhine. It was therefore a somewhat important post; and it is strange that the Prussians had not a greater force to hold a place giving such ready facilities for communication with the interior. Here, too, are situated the far-famed collieries of the Saar, which were about to cost France so much money and so many lives. The town of Saarbrück lies in a valley, the greater portion of it lying on that side of the river towards the French frontier, whilst the suburb of St. Johann is on the other.

On Sunday sounds from the French camp gave token of great excitement. The bands played, the men shouted, and there seemed to be a general rejoicing. On Monday all was quiet, except that the trains plied between Metz and Forbach. On Tuesday morning, at 9 A.M., the pickets and vedettes were driven in, and the French commenced advancing upon Saarbrück, covered by skirmishers, with artillery on the flanks, and cavalry supporting; two strong columns of infantry brought up the rear. The town was entirely undefended by any sort of defence, and the bridges crossing the Saar were quite unprotected. The first man killed was a Prussian lancer; he was shot through the head, and he fell instantly under the tree where he had taken up his position. Two English gentlemen immediately rushed out and endeavoured to bring his body back; but a Prussian lancer is a heavy fellow, even when he is dead, and they found it difficult to accomplish. They had managed to get him some two hundred yards, when one of the gentlemen received a wound; the other dropped the Prussian lancer, and carried his friend in. Meanwhile the Prussian outposts retired, and the 40th regiment deployed into an irregular line of skirmishers along the drill-ground. No serious fire was opened until they were within three hundred yards of one another; the French had by that time advanced their attacking columns in rear of their artillery, and poured in a heavy fire, driving the Prussians back through the town to the bridges crossing the Saar.

Here they made a stand, and formed up in some sort of order; and it was then that the mitrailleuses opened fire. The sound was like that of an exaggerated policeman's rattle, and it certainly had a most serious effect upon the opposing force massed upon the bridges, across which a barricade of casks filled with stones had been erected. They divided as if a wedge had parted them—some going to the right and some to the left. The French then opened a heavy fire of shells upon the town, smashing the houses in St. Johann, and driving the troops who had taken refuge in them still farther back into the town. The Prussian troops behaved with the utmost coolness. I never saw men steadier under fire. By some extraordinary arrangement, not more than 500 or 600 men of the 40th regiment were engaged. One company, No. 7, Baron von Rosen's, deserves particular mention. At one time they were left nearly unprotected to bear the fire of two French regiments, and the company lost very heavily. Notwithstanding the heavy fire these gallant fellows were exposed to, they refused to retire until they received an order to do so, leaving many on the field.

The position of the people in the town during the shelling was anything but pleasant; the Hotel Hagen suffered most, for it was in rear of this that the broken Prussian regiments formed before evacuating the place. In this hotel were comfortably seated four English gentlemen, some of them connected with the press, playing at whist. A shell coming through the roof, and bursting in the room above, disturbed the equanimity of one gentleman who had been carefully playing for the odd trick; whilst a shriek from below was accounted for by the appearance of the landlord, who informed them that a shell had spoilt the beefsteaks; and before the house was left, the façade had been severely damaged. Meanwhile the Prussian troops made good their retreat through a tunnel under the railway embankment, into which the French poured mitrailleuse and shell with wonderful accuracy, sending one or two parting shots over the embankment. The French had now gained possession of the town, and the Prussians retired into the woods to the north, falling back upon Groswald. It is impossible to estimate the loss on either side, but the French were decidedly the sufferers in numbers; for the Prussian guns were admirably served, and they played upon the unprotected masses of the French exposed on the drill-ground above Saarbrück.

On the 3d of August the French still held possession of Saarbrück, their patrols moving about the suburbs of St. Johann, and advancing as far as the road to Dudweiler. Upon this road were the advanced posts of the Prussians, composed of cuirassiers and lancers. Upon venturing into Saarbrück, I found the French in possession of the town. They had helped themselves to beer, sausages, and bread. The loaves they carried stuck upon their bayonets, whilst sausages gracefully festooned their belts. A rather clever thing was done by a Prussian lancer who was patrolling near the suburb of St. Johann, on the Dudweiler road. Whilst standing at the top of one of the streets, the landlord of an hotel beckoned to him; and on his coming up, told him that there was a French non-commissioned officer upstairs, who might perhaps be taken; but the Frenchman, hearing hoofs, happened to look out of window, and, seeing the lancer, tried to make his escape, undressed as he was, up the street. Some women, seeing how matters stood, opposed him in a body, and throwing themselves upon him, held him fast till the lancer came up. A cord was then found, and being securely bound by the ladies, the Frenchman was hoisted on the lancer's horse, and carried off in triumph.

The main road through the valley of the Saar was meantime in the possession of the Prussian cavalry of the eighth army corps, commanded by General von Göben. The 6th cuirassiers held the line of communication open between the railway at Saarbrück and the village of Dudweiler. On going down to see the French position and to take a look at the battle-field, I met a squadron of the 6th cuirassiers, commanded by the Graf von Montz, at the bend of the road leading into Saarbrück. I was somewhat disappointed with the horsing of this crack regiment of Prussian cavalry. The men were fine big fellows; but their horses, with very few exceptions, were not up to the weight they had to carry, and were a very weedy-looking lot. It was surprising to see a cuirassier regiment employed for vedette or patrol duty; inasmuch as a polished cuirass and headpiece, with a bright sun shining upon them, present an object like a looking-glass, not easy to miss with a chassepot at five hundred yards. A fatigue party of the 69th regiment were sent to destroy the railroad about half a mile from the station, in order to prevent the French from making a flank movement, and to protect the railroad communication which was bringing up Von Göben's Rhinelanders.

Certainly the strange inactivity of General Frossard at this moment was greatly to be blamed. Whether he had news of M'Mahon's calamity or not, is hard to say; but certain it is, that had the French advanced up the valley of the Saar, the position of General von Göben and the 8th Corps would have been far from a pleasant one. However, Frossard contented himself with considerably reinforcing his centre, and certainly not less than 10,000 men were at this time behind the rise of ground on the French side of Saarbrück. The position that the Prussians held in the affair of Saarbrück might even, with the handful of men who disputed it, have been made good with a little more prudence.

I am not going for one moment to impugn the military stratagem, necessitated perhaps by the unfortunate want of artillery, that dictated the plan of defence; but to the most casual observer it must have been easily perceived, that had the ridge in rear of the town and railway station been defended with guns, and the trees cut down upon the crest of the hill over which the French advanced, they never could have obtained possession of Saarbrück without a very heavy loss. Again, supposing the Prussians to have been forced to retreat from their first position, the guns, as well as the troops, would have had a sort of natural covered way through which to retreat, formed by the peculiar nature of the valley, and, the woods on either side of the railroad being lined, incredible loss might have been inflicted upon a force which would have had to advance over an open space exposed to a murderous fire from men under cover. The men of the 40th Regiment behaved nobly; their name should never be forgotten by their brothers in arms; and had they been better handled, the French loss would have been doubled.

Turning my glass upon the heights opposite, I found the disposition of the French troops considerably altered. A fresh camp seemed to have sprung up on the right and left of Saarbrück, stretching from the village of St. Arnoul to Forbach. Running my eye to the left, I found that the heights above Sarreguemines were occupied by a very large camp. This I ascertained eventually to be the division of the French General Lavallière, whilst the troops in the attack upon Saarbrück of the previous day had been those only of General Frossard's division.

Returning to the village of Dudweiler, I met an officer commanding a squadron of Cuirassiers bringing in a baggage wagon full of accoutrements belonging to the 40th Regiment, which in their retreat from Saarbrück they had been forced to leave behind. The arms, it appears, the French had collected, placed in a cart, and given into the charge of the Mayor of Saarbrück, who naturally gave information to the nearest Prussian outpost. Amongst the accoutrements of various kinds two chassepots were discovered, which created an immense sensation. They were passed from one to the other with exclamations of wonder, and eventually deposited in a barn.

After the taking of Saarbrück it has ever been a mystery to me for what reason the French attacked it, inasmuch as they neither blew up the railway station, nor made any effort to advance up the valley through which the railway from Bingenbrück runs. Probably General Frossard was awaiting a simultaneous attack by M'Mahon and Bazaine; but certain it is, that one of the great mistakes of the campaign was made here. The mistake is the more apparent from the fact, that two divisions were echeloned to Frossard's right rear, and that, supposing M'Mahon even to have been beaten, which he was at that time, Frossard's advance up the valley of the Saar would have checked the Crown Prince in his pursuit of M'Mahon, and compelled General Steinmetz to retreat.

The Cuirassiers—who by this time had the shine taken off their gorgeous cuirasses, which, covered with rust, looked more like old iron coal-scuttles than anything else—were still in the valley in small parties, with their vedettes thrown out nearly as far as the suburb of St. Johann, and the French soldiers were still encamped above the drill-ground, where they had thrown up some earthworks between the trees. When I entered St. Johann, I found it occupied by a company of the Prussian 69th Regiment of the line, who had just taken a French prisoner. The poor fellow was a private of the 60th line, and as I passed he took off his hat to me, with a 'Bon jour, mein Herr'—happy mixture of French and German—and walked along with that devil-may-care swagger a Frenchman knows so well how to adopt. In the main street of St. Johann I found some Hussars and also some Lancers, who galloped up and down, taking care to get across those openings commanded by the French pickets as quickly as possible. The right-hand portion of St. Johann, or that situated in front of the railway station, seemed to have suffered most from the enemy's fire; but the town of Saarbrück and the left-hand portion of the suburb were not touched. I visited the hospital, and saw the French and Prussians who had been wounded in the affair of the 2d; and it was here I first learnt that the fearful nature of a wound stated to be caused by a chassepot bullet was a mere fallacy; it certainly inflicts a much smaller and less grievous wound than the Enfield.

Whilst I was in the hospital a smart fire of musketry commenced. I ran down, and when I got out into the streets I found that the French pickets were engaged with the Prussian outposts in exchanging shots across the river. To illustrate the cool courage of the Prussians, I will relate what I witnessed. A lancer rode across the bridge, evidently with the intention of seeing if there were any tirailleurs in the vicinity of its entrance. He had got about half way, when three shots were fired at him, which brought his horse down, giving the man a bad fall; he got up, shook his fist at the French, and was going back to his comrades, when a French officer rushed out and tried to make a prisoner of him. The lancer allowed him to come within five yards; then, drawing a pistol from the holster of his saddle, he shot him dead. Four French soldiers then rushed out; but some men of the 69th poured in a volley, killing two and wounding one. During this diversion in his favour the lancer made good his escape. After this, a sort of guerrilla warfare commenced along the bank of the Saar, which then formed the boundary between the French and Prussians, and, the river being only sixty or seventy yards wide, the contending parties were at pretty close quarters. It appears that General Frossard and his staff ran a narrow escape of being captured one evening. They were riding through St. Johann about ten o'clock, and had just got across the bridge within the line of their own sentries, when a strong body of Prussian lancers trotted through the street. There were many French soldiers from the province of Alsace, who came across from the camp into St. Johann, went into the cafés, and, hanging up their arms, remained quietly drinking until they were captured by the Prussian patrols. The general feeling amongst these fellows appeared to be that they were good Frenchmen, but equally good Germans. Forty soldiers of the 40th Regiment were so badly wounded, that they were made prisoners by the French, and taken into Forbach, where, it is said, they were surrounded by a crowd, who would have maltreated them, but that the old French chivalry did not permit such barbarism. The troops turned out and surrounded the wagons, and with the utmost kindness and attention marched the men up to the hospital.

On the 5th of August the intelligence arrived that the 11th Prussian Army Corps had advanced beyond the frontier, and that the French troops had retreated towards Haguenau. Then came the news of the fatal battle of Weissenburg, causing Frossard to detach the two divisions echeloned to his right rear to the assistance of M'Mahon, and withdrawing the main body of his troops to the heights of Speicheren, leaving only a small force to occupy Saarbrück and to watch the Prussian movements. Here again another fatal mistake occurred, namely that of isolating a corps with a beaten army retreating in its rear, with no communication kept up between the other corps that had been shifted to restrain the advance of the Crown Prince, and with a badly organised staff. General Steinmetz could hardly fail to see the advantage. The railway trains, crammed to suffocation, hurried battalion after battalion to the front; squadron after squadron, and battery after battery, passed through the valley of the Saar, on their way to Saarbrück. On the 5th the news arrived that the French had abandoned Saarbrück, and that Frossard had taken up his position on the Speicheren Berg, to protect M'Mahon's flank; and on the 6th the decisive battle of Speicheren was fought, which was one of the hardest, and made more moral impression than any other in the campaign.

The morning of the 6th of August 1870 dawned, one of those lovely ones which this season in the south of France so often gives birth to. All night the busy trains kept pouring in their living freights. General Zimmerman's cavalry were patrolling from St. Arnoul on the left to the woods of the iron foundries on the Forbach road on the right. The French fires glowed all night along the heights above Forbach, and their advanced chain of sentries lay in the valley beneath.

As morning dawned both armies were under arms; but the attack was delayed, inasmuch as General von Göben did not think himself strong enough. General Steinmetz, however, telegraphed a peremptory order to attack, and to General Kameki, commanding the 14th division of the 7th Army Corps, was intrusted this important duty. At 8.30, under a scattering fire, the French outposts retreated to the right and left of the Speicheren Berg, some retiring into Forbach, others being lost in the heavy woods above St. Arnoul. At 9.30 the first gun boomed across from a battery above Saarbrück. Between the Speicheren heights and those above the town of Saarbrück lies an undulating valley, broken on the one side by a dry water-course and a thick copse of undergrowth, and on the other by a deep irregular ravine. As the boom of the guns, quickly followed by others, told that the action had commenced, General von Sastrow and General von Göben, with the 7th and 8th Corps, formed up and faced the French position.

On ascending the heights on the Saarbrück side of the valley, the French position became distinctly visible; and as I gazed at the seemingly impassable barrier, stretching across, glittering with bayonets, and then looked at the plain across which the German troops must advance before they even arrived at the base of those heights that must be stormed, I confess I thought the attack not only rash, but ill-advised, inasmuch as the corps were weak and had not as yet received their full complement. But there was nothing for it now; and the 39th, 40th, and 12th regiments, covered by a cloud of skirmishers, deployed from column into a long irregular line, and commenced advancing across the plain, heavy masses of cavalry to their right and left rear, and the artillery sending their shells shrieking over their heads. As they advanced, the murderous fire of the chassepots at 2000 yards even then began to tell; a horse here, a blue uniform there, and the hurrying up of the ambulance, told that the work of destruction had begun. The French, holding the lower portion of the valley, retired sullenly upon Forbach, covered by two batteries of artillery; and the 14th division, with a rush, gained the bottom of the hill, whilst in their rear heavy masses were forming as quickly as the trains could disgorge them. Meantime the cavalry took ground to their left, and formed up under a protecting spur.

All this time nothing but rifle-fire came from the Speicheren Berg, and beyond the batteries by Forbach; the French seemed to have no artillery. It was now the Prussian artillery commenced to show its superiority over that of the few French guns. Captain Stumpf actually managed to drag two of his guns up an old broken road, and as the two first lines of defence were gallantly stormed, he opened fire on the left flank of the 39th, at about 150 yards from the French infantry. It was a gallant deed, and one that told well upon the fortunes of the day. But now the Prussians waver, a murderous fire is poured upon them, and their advance slowly retires, the French infantry doubling up and taking up their old position again. Things were critical—the second line, composed of the 8th Brandenburgers, the 70th, and the 65th, owing to the steepness of the ground, and the galling fire from the woods, took a considerable time to reach the foot of the heights; it was 4.30, the battle had raged all day, and Speicheren was still in the hands of the French.

Meantime, on the right flank, the 13th division was deploying to attack Forbach, whilst all along the line the powerful Prussian artillery thundered away with fatal accuracy. At length the second line attacked and retook the second line of rifle-pits, and just as night was falling the French abandoned the crest of the hill, after one of the most gallant resistances upon record. I say it was gallant, because the heights were held by a weak French division—7000 infantry, with scarcely any artillery, no supports, and after 5 P.M. no General. Is it to be wondered at, therefore, that the Speicheren Berg was stormed? It is a lasting shame and disgrace to General Frossard that these brave men were left unsupported, and, what is worse, *without ammunition.*

Thus ended the battle of Speicheren; the French retreating during the night, the Prussians sleeping on the field of battle. All night long the groans of the wounded filled the valley and the surrounding woods. The ambulance worked hard; but where so many lay it was impossible to do everything, and many a poor fellow died of exposure, having done his best for Fatherland and for France.

On the morning of the 7th I wended my way to the heights of Speicheren, the scene where the sanguinary conflict between the contending armies finished with the darkness of the previous evening. The battle-field to a soldier, be he the victor or the vanquished, is a sad retrospect. It is here that he learns what he is, and what a few hours may make him. It is here that, if he have any of those noble feelings that the soldier should ever possess, his nerves are more terribly tried than under showers of shot or shell. The battle-field, after an engagement such as that of Speicheren, is the true place for the soldier to learn his duty, both to God and to his fellow-man.

Until one reaches the base of the heights upon which the French had taken up their position, you can have no idea of the steepness of the ascent; and, had I been asked if any infantry in the world could storm those heights under the fire of a force posted upon its advantageous ridges, I should have scoffed at the idea as utterly absurd. Nevertheless, the battalions of Germany accomplished what must ever remain a wonder to their brothers in arms. The ascent to the Alma was a farce to this position, as an old Crimean officer and I both agreed. The French had three lines of defence, one above the other, each one of which was more formidable than, and commanded, the other. Their flanks were protected by thick woods, and the country was open for them to retreat in rear. Everything was in their favour, had they been properly supported; but, notwithstanding this, the Prussians gained a most decisive victory, for at sunrise next morning there was not a French soldier within miles of the Speicheren heights.

I ascended from the plateau exactly in the centre of the Prussian attack; the hill is covered with brushwood, and rises to a height of some 800 feet above the plain below. As I passed on my way the Prussians were burying their dead, and I stood by and listened to the simple funeral service that was pronounced over the bodies of a lieutenant and sergeant of the 39th Regiment, who were buried where they fell in one grave. As the bodies, rolled in their cloaks, were lowered, an audible sob by my side made me turn round. I found that it came from a fine handsome-looking fellow, who apologised to me for his manly grief by saying, 'Ah, sir, I can't help it; he was the kindest friend and the best lieutenant in the regiment.' Proceeding up the hill, I found the Prussians lying thick, whilst every here and there the gray coat and red trousers of the 24th French infantry appeared. On the top of the first ridge there were little heaps of French and Prussians mixed; whilst on the second ridge the French uniforms lay thickest.

Upon reaching the brow of the hill a heart-rending sight met my eye. It had evidently been the last stand of the 24th; for their uniforms, mingled with the Prussians, lay to the number of seventy-five in a very small space. Facing the road, with a smile on his face, lay the major of the French regiment. In one hand he clasped a sergeant's hand, and in the other a lock of hair wrapped in a bit of paper. Both the sergeant and he must have been shot at the same time. The woods to the left were, as I anticipated, filled with wounded, whose piteous cries were heart-rending to hear. On the crest of the hill the Prussian uniforms lay very thick. I counted more than 150 to about 30 of the French. This was the hard-fought-for point, and where all the slaughter took place—I say advisedly slaughter, for it was nothing less. At twelve o'clock next day the wounded were still being transported into Saarbrück; and I leave any one to imagine their sufferings all night long without a drop of water. All branches of the service seemed to have suffered; for I picked up a lancet and some surgical instruments close to the body of a doctor, who had evidently been shot whilst employed in attending to a wounded man. Here I saw a French soldier of the line, his face still bearing a stern determined look upon it even in death, while close by his side lay the protector of his Fatherland, with his face to the enemy and his helmet in his hand.

The gallant behaviour of the Prussian troops is beyond all question; and it was then that I wrote home and said, that after taking such a position, defended as it was with the greatest gallantry, France would have enough to do to keep them out of Paris.

The Prussian loss in killed and wounded was about 2700; the French must have lost also very heavily, but not nearly so many as the Prussians. Their victory—for a victory it was—cost them dear, and the battle of Speicheren for the moment eclipsed that of Königgrätz. After the storming of the heights, it appears that in the evening the 13th division of the 7th Army Corps took the French town of Forbach, and the advanced posts of the Prussian army might be said to be almost in sight of Metz. The Crown Prince also sent a telegram to say that he had driven back Marshal M'Mahon; so that the French were retiring in every direction, and the Prussians steadily advancing on their road to Paris. The 3d, the 7th, and 8th Army Corps now formed a junction, and their outposts were already a long way over the French frontier. The regiments that suffered most in the sanguinary conflicts at Speicheren were the

39th, the 40th, and the 12th; the 39th had only forty men left in one company, and no officers. This loss is something too awful to contemplate, if you consider that their companies are 250 strong instead of 100.

After Speicheren the Prussian army was, I need hardly say, in the greatest spirits. They were not over confident, but they believed in their generals, and they cordially hated the French. Here, too, let me note there was not a tent in the whole of the Prussian army; they marched with their kit on their backs, and bivouacked on the ground where they halted. These men, who marched without stockings, many in new boots of untanned leather, would have done some of our generals' hearts good to see. Their feet are wrapped in a greasy cloth, two pairs of which, with a bottle of grease, comprise a portion of each man's kit in his knapsack; and certainly, if proof positive upon trial were required, the experiences of this campaign would teach that this system is eminently and practically successful. Here, too, the Government would have another chance of exerting that military economy that seems so necessary to their legislation.

The way in which the people of Saarbrück behaved to the wounded will ever be remembered as one of the great features in the struggle for Fatherland. The women were absolutely running about on the field of battle, giving drink to the wounded, and every house in the town at once turned itself into a hospital. Country carts, with wine and eatables, lined the road to Forbach, and all possible means to alleviate suffering were employed. The wounds were almost all chassepot bullet wounds, and were much less dangerous and ugly than those made by the larger Prussian bullet. Most of the wounds from the chassepot were in the head and feet, whilst those from the needle-gun were in the body.

The town of Saarbrück was filled with troops, who marched on into French territory from morning to evening; trains of artillery, ammunition, and forage for the horses, with batteries of artillery and heavy battalions of infantry, formed the principal impedimenta. The dust and heat were fearful, but I did not see ten stragglers on the line of march.

Can we glean no lesson of usefulness here? or are we still and for ever to be hampered with that long incubus of baggage wagons that are required to carry the tents of a British brigade on the march? Is it true that our soldiers are unable to bear exposure, and are therefore inferior to continental troops? The Crimean campaign is a sufficient answer to such a query. But that is not precisely the question. It was owing to this immense saving in transport that the German troops were able to make those marches, the rapidity of which not only astonished the world, but paralysed the movements of the enemy. To each regiment of infantry but three wagons were allowed, to each one of cavalry but one. Why not the same with our troops, who can bear it equally well, if not far better than any in the world? It is the immense trains of baggage blocking up the roads, that render the retreat of an army in the face of an enterprising enemy a matter not only of extreme danger, but of great uncertainty. It was these long trains that impeded M'Mahon and paralysed Bazaine; and it will be the same incubus that will encumber the movements of our soldiers when we take the field, unless we reduce the amount which 'red-tape' and 'pipeclay' conservators of old landmarks would have us believe are necessary to the British soldier. The baggage of a British infantry regiment on the march is as much as that of a Prussian brigade.

On the morning of the 8th of August, being forced to return to Neuenkirchen for the remainder of my baggage, which the rapid advance of the Prussian army had compelled me to leave behind, I was enabled to witness a strong contrast to the scene I had looked upon but a few hours before. Now the train was filled to the number of 850 with wounded soldiers, and when I got to Neuenkirchen, the station, hitherto so full of troops, was crammed with provision trucks and oxen for the invading army—for such we must now call it. I arrived in time for the *table-d'hôte* at the Hôtel Joclum, and was much amused with the difference in the persons of those who surrounded it. There were, first of all, a few civilians who had just returned from Saarbrück, and who regaled the audience with stories of horrible wounds and inconceivable feats of individual heroism; then there were officers just going to the front; and last, though not least, was the chaplain of the army, who, I am free to confess, drank one more 'schoppen' than his clerical position ought to have sanctioned.

When I got back to Saarbrück, the whole town was hung with flags; the King was expected, but his

Majesty had not arrived. As I passed the crest of the hill so long held by the French, I paused to look upon a scene that was both interesting and curious. I stood upon the frontier of Germany, whilst about half a mile in front of me blazed the bivouac fires of the Prussian troops upon French territory. The evening threatened rain, and the cheerless prospect, without tents, was for the Prussian troops anything but agreeable; nevertheless, the soldiers were gathered round their fires, chatting and smoking in the greatest spirits, the only damper being the volleys from the Forbach heights fired over the dead bodies of their comrades, who were being buried on French ground.

The fulsome report that the Emperor sent to the Empress, which was published in a French newspaper, stating that the town of Saarbrück had been taken, although defended by a body of 20,000 Prussians—the troops in Saarbrück being actually only 952 strong—now reached the head-quarters of the 1st Army, and afforded immense amusement to every one. This was the commencement of those tissues of falsities that misled the people of France and emanated from the French press.

At this stage of my narrative I cannot do better than refer to some of my letters published in the *Daily Telegraph*.

'*Speicheren, August* 9.

'A walk of four miles, and again across the Waterloo of the day, brought me to the head-quarters of the 8th Army Corps. The battle-field presented a more orderly appearance; little mounds surmounted by wooden crosses marked the resting-places of the defenders and assailants of the Forbach heights. The graves were studded with sword bayonets, to the number of the men the grave contained, stuck upright in the ground, and upon each was placed the helmet of the soldier. In one place I counted ninety-six piles of arms, most of them being needle-guns; knapsacks, cloaks, boots, and shakos also strewed the field in every direction, whilst that never-to-be-mistaken odour of the battle-field filled the moist and heavy atmosphere. It had rained hard all night, and the effect upon some of the faces of the dead was anything but pleasant. The bells in the neighbouring villages rang the assembly of the inhabitants for the forming fatigue parties to bury the dead.

'Upon my arrival in Spiecheren, I found it a very small French village, of the poorest description. The troops, as was their custom, were bivouacked outside, although many of the officers had installed themselves in the French *tentes d'abri*, which their hasty retreat had caused the enemy to leave behind; but, notwithstanding the drenching rain, the troops were in the best of spirits. The Prussian loss in officers at the battle of Saarbrück was 200, and their total of killed and wounded larger than was originally stated.

'After a great deal of trouble, I discovered a refuge for myself in the cottage of an old peasant, who was too old and too poor to attract attention. He was seventy-four years of age, and his wife seventy; they lived alone, and were, I need hardly say, miserably poor. When I entered the house, the poor old man burst into tears, whilst the wife hastily hid some cooked beans and potatoes in a saucepan underneath the bed. After reassuring the luckless wretches, they told me that the French army had lain there for at least four weeks, and that they had left them absolutely nothing; neither did they know what they were going to do during winter. Poor creatures! it was the same thing everywhere. There was literally nothing left, and eating or drinking became a matter of very grave consideration. After establishing myself in my anything but agreeable quarters, I turned out to take a walk to the front. On my road I met Colonel von Witzendorff, Chief of the Staff, on his way to visit some French prisoners who were wounded, and had sought the shelter of the village in the retreat.'

I cannot help remembering these poor fellows. They were certainly in a most wretched state; for the Prussians, although most willing to do so, could not feed them, the troops being in need of provisions themselves; in fact, so short was everything in the shape of eatables or drinkables, that it was apparent to everybody that the army must advance within a few hours. The villages of Kerbach and Etzling, in the immediate neighbourhood, were full of French wounded, unable to get any farther. From them I learnt many interesting facts regarding the battle of Saarbrück; and my former opinion that the French had no large force and no reserve to assist them was fully justified by the account they gave me.

It appeared that the Emperor inspected the position himself, and pronounced it, as well he might, impregnable; and so it would have been, if common prudence or the simplest laws of military tactics had been observed. But General Frossard, over-confident in his position, permitted a division to occupy this post on the heights, entirely isolated and unsupported. He never dreamt of being driven from it, and consequently echeloned the other divisions of his corps d'armée so far away, in order to assist M'Mahon, that when their assistance was claimed at Spiecheren, they were unable to reach the battle-field, and when sent for arrived within two miles of it, to find their comrades in a hasty retreat. The Prussians, however, knew the fearful struggle before them. Regiment after regiment kept coming on the ground, even up to nightfall; and fresh troops were sent continually against the worn-out men who had been fighting for more than eight hours. The French were dreadfully deficient in artillery, and an old corporal told me that many of the soldiers were so young that they could scarely charge their rifles.

In the village of Kerbach I saw a cart with four wounded men upon it; they had been sent out of the village because there was nothing for them to eat. As the cart stopped in the street, I took them my flask to give the poor fellows a drink. Whilst talking to them a smart-looking jaunty fellow in the 24th got a bit of bread and some wine from a Prussian. 'Monsieur,' said he, 'you are very kind; but, notwithstanding this kindness, if I were free, I would still have the honour to *tirer un coup de fusil* upon you.'

In one thing they were unanimous, which was that they were badly handled on the Spiecheren heights.

The Prussian 7th army corps was now sent in advance, and its camp or bivouac was a model of neatness. The men cooked in messes, if they had anything to cook; but provisions having run short, I cannot say much for their fare. Their horses, too, were beginning to look thin and worn, and the forage was desperately scanty.

Not a single reporter was now permitted in camp, except by the express permission of the King, who arrived in Saarbrück on the morning of the 11th; he expressed his intention of visiting the field of battle on the next day, and there were strong suspicions that a great battle would shortly take place somewhere in the neighbourhood of Metz. With the advance of the Crown Prince, Prince Frederick Charles, and General von Steinmetz, and the massing of their forces together, it seemed absolutely necessary that the fortunes of France and Prussia should be decided somewhere in this neighbourhood. The various corps expected orders to move forward on the morrow; and the sooner the better, inasmuch as there was not an egg or fowl for miles round to be got for love or money. The enthusiasm of the French troops had greatly abated; and, as an indication of their feelings at this time, I can only mention what a wounded officer said to me when I asked him how he felt. 'As to the pain,' said he, 'I suffer but little from it; my real agony lies here,' placing his hand on his heart; 'for,' he added, 'the Prussians are fighting in a good cause, whilst we are fighting for a *vaurien* and a boy!'

It will be perceived that the prognostications above alluded to as to the fate of France being settled somewhere in the neighbourhood of Metz proved correct by the battles of Colombey, Mars-la-Tour, and Gravelotte, which were, I may say, fought under its walls: although no one was prepared for the separation, as it were, of M'Mahon's, and the Crown Prince's, army to another scene of conflict.

For the rapid advance of the Germans after Spiecheren, I must again quote from my letter to the *Daily Telegraph* on the 11th of August:

'*Spiecheren, August* 11.

'Yesterday, finding I was short of provisions, I left Spiecheren to walk into Saarbrück. When I got there, I found that the King, with Count von Bismarck, and their staffs, had taken up their quarters in the town; and after purchasing some stores, I made my way back to Spiecheren, the then head-quarters of the 8th army corps, under General von Göben. I got there at 10.30; and to my utter astonishment, of all the 35,000 men I had left twelve hours before, not one remained. Where had they gone? that was the question. On my way thither, I met a division of troops marching towards Forbach—though what division I am not at liberty to mention; so I shouldered my bundle and started for Forbach, one hour's march, and on my way I met his Majesty the King, with a large staff, riding over the line by which the French had retreated.

'When I got to Forbach, I found that not only the 8th army corps, but the 7th, the 1st, and the 3d, had all marched off to Lauterbach. A glance at the map will show that this village is on the Prussian frontier, and lies to the right of Forbach, twelve miles distant. The French town of Forbach is one of some little importance in these parts; it lies on the extreme edge of the French frontier, close to the enormous iron manufactory of Stiering. The French troops laid here for about four weeks, and had absolutely eaten and drunk everything. The shops were all closed, so were the private houses; and I was also told by a French gentleman that they had robbed the town of 10,000 francs' worth of tobacco. The people were in the greatest possible distress, and how they were to keep starvation from their doors during the winter, I could not conceive. The country looked desolate and bleak, the corn was trampled and carried off, the potatoes were dug up in the fields, and everything looked like a desert. The road was choked up with two endless rows of baggage wagons carrying food for the invading army; for they were forced to take everything with them, the French having left nothing behind, except a store of meal and grain at Forbach, which the Prussians took.

'To increase my troubles, about four o'clock it began to rain heavily, and when I got to Lauterbach it was quite dark. It was hopeless to look for my baggage at that time, for I had sent it with the baggage wagon of the 33d regiment; I therefore bethought me where to lay my head. The troops were bivouacked in the open, without a tent to shield them from the pitiless rain which was now driving in torrents over the undulating plain. After stumbling along the road up to my knees in mud, I reached a small wayside inn, crowded with Prussian soldiers. All the accommodation I could get was a bundle of wet straw in a corner, which I shared with a friend who accompanied me. There was nothing to eat and nothing to drink, but I had brought some provisions, and there was a fire; so I did not much care.

'Meanwhile the poor soldiers were in a most fearful state; the rapid marches of the last four days had so put them in advance of their baggage, that they had had nothing to eat except a small piece of bread for two days. They were wet to the skin, and many of them were ill; for even tobacco, that mainstay of the German, was denied them. I did not know how to refuse when they came and asked me for a bit of my bread, which they devoured ravenously; but what could I do among so many? Just as I was settling my bundle of straw in a corner, an order came through a sergeant from his Excellency General von Steinmetz that every soldier was to join the bivouac of his regiment. Out they went immediately into the pitiless drizzling rain, and laid themselves down in the mud, hungry and thirsty, without a murmur. "Immer vorwärts!" was their cry. The sufferings of these men through the night of the 10th are quite indescribable. Early in the morning I was aroused from my bundle of straw by a good shake of the shoulder. It was just daybreak, and I was called upon to give up my bundle of straw to a sick man who had just been brought in; half an hour after, he was dead.

'The 1st army corps marched farther on next morning; but the 7th, 8th, and 3d army corps still remained encamped at Lauterbach and Lutweiler. I found my baggage after a trudge of a mile, and shared the tent of the major of the 33d regiment—a fact which enabled me to write these few lines. The encampment or rather bivouac of the 33d lay in a wood about a mile from Lauterbach. The poor fellows were making themselves as comfortable as they could; but the rain, pouring down in torrents, put their fires out; I am thankful, however, to say that food had come, and they at least had something to eat.'

The Crown Prince lay at St. Avold, whilst the 1st and 3d army were massed in the direction of the Metz road, and a great battle was expected shortly somewhere in that neighbourhood. Count von Bismarck evidently calculated upon a short war, or he never would have exposed his troops, without tents, to the weather they were enduring. The horses were also suffering dreadfully from want of forage; it seemed therefore utterly impossible for us to remain where we were more than twenty-four hours.

Upon joining the head-quarters of the brigade to which I was attached, I found that they had removed out of the potato fields, which were now nothing but swamps, and had taken shelter in the woods; and as it may not be uninteresting to the reader, I will endeavour to describe how the Prussian army bivouacked on this march.

A Prussian regiment of infantry is composed of three battalions, each battalion has four companies, and each company is supposed to be 250 strong. The regiment has one colonel, and each battalion is commanded by a major with an adjutant. When the regiment is halted the arms are piled, the battalions being drawn up in line of contiguous columns at battalion distance; the men then take off their helmets, and each man places it on his rifle, which acts as an effectual protection from any wet getting down the barrel; they put on their forage-caps, and the companies then break off by subdivisions to the right and left of their arms, the knapsacks are placed in a row, the camp kettles taken off, and the fatigue squad falls out from each company to draw water. Meantime the remainder dig small oblong holes in the ground for their fires; a couple of sticks at each end, and another resting across, completes the simple but practical arrangement. On this stick hang the camp kettles, generally speaking by twos—one for the potatoes, and the other for the soup and meat. At night big fires are got to burn, and, if near a wood, screens of boughs are erected to protect the men. Their cloaks are then spread upon the ground, and in ten minutes the bivouac is complete. At Lauterbach 300,000 men encamped in this way.

The officers—with the exception of the commanders, most of whom had tents—were exactly on the same footing as the men, and quite as much exposed. Upon coming on the ground where it is intended to halt for the night, the officers commanding battalions tell off an officer and twelve men to bring up provisions for the troops. There was no pillaging of the villages permitted; the strictest orders protected the inhabitants everywhere; although it was naturally hard to prevent the cavalry from making free quarters in any village they came to, inasmuch as they are in the advance of every column of troops. It seems hard that in a conquered country one was not allowed to dig the potatoes; but the general's order was strict, and a speedy punishment awaited the offender. Upon the first halt of the German armies in France, provisions were very short, and one's supper consisted of potatoes and the fattest of bacon. At first we were subjected to constant alarms. One evening, just as we were going to turn in, an engineer officer, with a very grave face, came to report that some Frenchmen had been seen some five hundred yards from the bivouac. Now, as the night was dark, and the whole camp illuminated by the bivouac fires, the chances of a chassepot were anything but lively. It turned out afterwards that the Frenchmen were a fatigue party of the 3d rifles coming for water.

One of the most imposing features in this bivouac in the woods was the 'Zapfen Streich,' or the last Post, played by the band of each regiment. First of all, a roll on the drum called your attention, then the Post was magnificently played, and lastly the evening hymn. I shall certainly not easily forget the impression made upon me as I listened for the first time to the beautiful strains of holy music, and gazed upon the forest, lit up by the light of ten thousand bivouac fires, surrounded by the soldiers. From Lauterbach the 1st and 2d army marched upon Oberwisse, and on the 12th August, at nine o'clock, the 1st army commenced its march into France. The battalions paraded, the arms were rigorously examined, and, notwithstanding the wet of the two previous days and nights, the rifles were in perfect order. We heard at Oberwisse that the Crown Prince's loss was 5,000 killed and wounded, and that the French had about the same, and had lost six mitrailleuses, 100 officers, and 2,000 prisoners at the battle at Bitsche. We were certainly badly off for provisions, inasmuch as my breakfast, and indeed the breakfast of every one, consisted of coffee, without milk or sugar, and no bread. But the intelligence that the French had taken up a position on the river Nied, and intended disputing our advance to Metz, cheered every one up. It is hardly possible to describe the utter destitution of the inhabitants in the French villages through which we marched, and if the Prussian army had retreated with their commissariat as it was then supplied, the consequences would have been fearful.

The effects of the severe exposure on the night of the 10th now showed themselves upon the men—a great many of them falling out before they got half-way to the end of the day's march. It was therefore perhaps as well that the French were not followed, after the battle of the Spiecheren heights. We reached Oberwisse at 4 P.M., after a tiring march, a large division of cavalry having gone to the extreme front. The 1st and 7th army corps were bivouacked in front of us; so that for that night, at any rate, the 8th corps could sleep in safety.

We have now arrived at, perhaps, one of the most important periods of the campaign—a time when the French leaders showed more apparent ignorance of manœuvring than at any time during the whole of the war. Although the campaign was prolonged by the siege of Paris, there is no one that will dispute that the fortunes of France were virtually settled by the events which took place between the 2d and 30th of August. His Imperial Majesty the Emperor had assumed the command of the army; his programme of the campaign, win or lose, was to be carried out intact; and his instructions were followed by the rash and brave M'Mahon, and by the weak, vacillating, diplomatic Bazaine.

It is useless for military historians to throw any blame upon the material of the French army, for it perhaps was never finer than at this moment; but it was now, more than at any other time, that the men wanted confidence in their leaders and in their officers to keep them together. There is nothing so easy as to call upon victorious troops to act; nothing so difficult as to inspire fresh confidence into a beaten army, more especially one with a temperament like that of the French. They had been taught that *la grande nation* was invincible; that French soil was so sacred, that should an enemy perchance invade it, fire from heaven would of a surety fall and destroy them. The battles of Wörth, Wissenburg, and Spiecheren rudely destroyed this belief, and tore away, with no gentle hand, the veil that had been so carefully thrown over their eyes. The enemy was there; the best soldiers of France had been *attacked* and beaten in positions which they had chosen, strengthened by nature and art; and there was a wavering and despondency which was not allayed by the conduct of their generals.

CHAPTER II.

THE ADVANCE OF STEINMETZ UPON METZ.

The events of the next few days were indeed momentous, and the rapid movements so great on the part of the Germans, that the French, beaten at Wörth and Wissenburg, defeated and pursued at Spiecheren, now withdrew into Lorraine, falling back upon the fortress of Metz. The troops marched from six in the morning until seven or eight in the evening, giving little or no time for anything but necessary repose.

At two P.M. on the 14th instant, the 13th division of the 1st army corps, under General Manteuffel, engaged the enemy about four miles from Metz, at a place called Colombey, a few miles to the north of that city. Here the French held a strong position with two divisions, under the command of Generals Andremont and Frossard. General Steinmetz followed on the retreating steps of the French troops, with the rest of the 1st army (care must be taken not to confuse *army corps* with *army;* for a Prussian *army*, such as the 1st for instance, is composed of two or more *army corps;* thus, the 1st army was composed of the 1st and 8th army corps).

Meantime Prince Frederick Charles marched with the 3d and 7th corps upon the Moselle, crossed it on the 14th at Noveant, and marching up the valley of Gorze, he bivouacked on the afternoon of that day within one English mile of that town. To return however to General Steinmetz: that intrepid old soldier, finding the French inclined to accept battle in their position at Colombey, at once attacked them, for reasons which I shall assign hereafter. The action occurred thus:

The French had, it appeared, employed 1,000 labourers to strengthen their already strong position, by digging rifle-pits. The patrols of the Prussian 43d regiment of the line became first engaged with the enemy, and were supported by the 1st battalion of the 1st Jägers and one battery of artillery; but the fire from the French decimated their ranks, and the 3d regiment was sent to the support of the corps engaged. The French fire was hot, and their artillery well served: the 1st Jägers lost 400 men, and it was necessary that the rest of the corps d'armée should engage. The artillery fire was tremendous on both sides, shells bursting in every direction. At six P.M., the action having lasted four hours, and the 1st army corps having been dreadfuly handled, the 7th corps, on the left, was called up, and its guns opened a heavy fire of six-pounder shells. The French then gradually retired, and at about eight P.M. abandoned the position. The troops then returned to their bivouacs. The Prussian loss was very heavy, though it was impossible at the moment to state the exact extent, but it was supposed to be at least 2,000 *hors de combat;* but I do not think the French loss could have been so great, inasmuch as the men were completely protected by the rifle-pits which had been dug. Eventually the loss of the Prussians was ascertained to be 1700. The French retired upon Metz, and General Steinmetz ordered the 8th corps to march on Arry *viâ* Orny, and cross the Moselle. The 43d regiment, the corps that distinguished itself so much in the Austro-Prussian war of 1866, suffered very severely in this action. In two companies all the officers were either killed or wounded, and one company had only 57 men left out of 250.

Again the French generals appeared to have made nothing but a succession of the most puerile mistakes, which the Prussians never failed to avail themselves of. The country between Saarbrück and Metz contained a series of positions which, if vigorously defended, would have cost the invading army dear before it got even to the valley of the Moselle, and have given time to pull the shattered legions together; but all these had been abandoned, and the Prussian troops advanced almost unmolested.

Whilst the action in the neighbourhood of Metz was being fought, two movements were made, one of which perhaps influenced the result of the campaign in no small degree. The Prussians, having engaged the attention of the French by the attack upon Colombey, crossed the Moselle under the command of Prince Frederick Charles at Noveant, as I above explained, without resistance. The importance of this movement is at once apparent, inasmuch as it prevented a junction between the troops of General M'Mahon, who was retreating before the Crown Prince, and Marshal Bazaine's army at Metz. The

Crown Prince's advanced posts were on the 16th August at Nancy. Meantime, the 8th army corps by a rapid march relieved the 1st army corps, and threw itself on to the Moselle, between Metz and Pont-à-Mousson. The object of the attack on the French position at Colombey was therefore now apparent, inasmuch as whilst General Steinmetz engaged the attention of the French at Colombey, Prince Frederick Charles's army was permitted to cross the Moselle unmolested, and prevented the junction of the two French armies under M'Mahon and Bazaine. The 15th of August being the fête of Napoleon I., a movement was anticipated, but nothing of importance occurred until the 16th.

In the mean time, the 8th army corps (Prussian) had, as I said, relieved the 1st. The villages through which they passed were entirely deserted by the male inhabitants, who had all gone to join the Garde Mobile, and none but women, children, and old men were to be seen. On the evening of the 5th, the 8th army corps, after marching from six A.M. till nine in the evening, had to turn out to extinguish a fire in the village of Orny in which they were quartered. The poor fellows never got to bed until 3.30, and marched again at six. A glance at the map will show the position of the contending forces at this particular moment. The Crown Prince at Nancy, with M'Mahon retreating before him; Prince Frederick Charles having crossed the Moselle at Pont-à-Mousson and Noveant to cut off Bazaine; Bazaine, in the neighbourhood of Metz, with General von Steinmetz before him—and the outline of the battle-field is before you. If the French could not keep the line of the Moselle, the Marne and Châlons it was thought would be their next standing-point, and the fate of France be decided there. Each advance of the Prussians cost them a fearful number of men, for when they did meet the enemy, they found them well worthy of their best attention; but the pluck and endurance of the troops were beyond all praise.

The strictest attention was paid to the inhabitants, and the soldiers were not permitted to plunder anywhere. One man was caught taking a piece of bacon, for which venial sin he was tied to a tree for three hours. A young Englishman who was travelling with me very much astonished the Prussians by his method of proceeding whilst the village of Orny was on fire. He had found a bit of bacon somewhere, and a few potatoes, and, being very hungry, he had commenced cooking them in a room next to the one that was in a blaze; and, notwithstanding the entreaties of the men, nothing would induce him to leave his much-cherished food until it was cooked.

To give you an idea of the discipline of a Prussian regiment, I will relate a circumstance which occurred on the march. A soldier of the 2d battalion, 33d regiment, had evidently gone somewhere without leave; the major calls him up and asks for explanations, which not being satisfactory, he gives him a tremendous box on the ear, and bids him rejoin his company; upon which the man, who has four decorations on his breast, and whom a hundred French bullets would not have turned back, burst into tears and sobbed like a child.

At this time there was little or no sickness in the Prussian army, at least that part to which I was attached; and if we had only had more to eat and a little more sleep, we should have done very well.

On the 16th of August, hearing that Bazaine was on his march for Verdun, General Moltke ordered Prince Frederick Charles to attack him, and, if possible, drive him back upon Metz. This determination brought on the battle of Mars-la-Tour, the most bloody of the whole war, and I must again refer for my description of it to my letter to the *Daily Telegraph*, dated the 17th of August, from the village of Gorze.

'*Gorze, August* 17.

'Another great and fearful battle has just been fought in this continental duel. Yesterday I wrote to you, on our way to intercept the junction of Bazaine's with M'Mahon's troops; and I told you that Prince Frederick Charles had crossed the Moselle at Pont-à-Mousson on the morning of the 14th at eight A.M. The eighth army corps, under General von Göben, crossed the same river at Arry, and advanced upon the town of Gorze. The previous evening we had heard heavy firing in the direction of Metz, and to-day all was explained. I should have seen the beginning of the engagement, but unfortunately, whilst reconnoitring the French position the day before yesterday, the French chasseurs-à-pied did me the honour to wound my horse, and he died that night, so that I had nothing but my feet to depend upon. When I arrived in Gorze the engagement had already commenced; and, in order to explain to you the manœuvres, I must give you a short sketch of the ground and of the plateau upon which this—as yet the most sanguinary—engagement of the campaign took place.

'Gorze is a town about ten miles from Metz, containing some 1,500 inhabitants. It is surrounded by high hills, which in the direction of Metz are covered with a thick fringe of woods. About two miles from the town of Gorze a sort of undulating plateau extends to the villages of Rezonville and Gravelotte, through which passes the high road from Metz to Verdun. This plateau was the scene of the fearful carnage of yesterday, and on its outskirts in the direction of Metz, the dropping fire of the outposts still tells that the morrow's sun may rise upon another bloody field. Due south of the ground upon which the action of Mars-la-Tour took place is a deep valley, through the middle of which winds the road to the Moselle, and up which Prince Frederick Charles advanced unmolested and even *unknown* to within a mile of Gorze.

'It is, perhaps, incredible and will scarcely be believed, when I here state that, although the French army was encamped in the villages of Mars-la-Tour, Vionville, Rezonville, and Gravelotte, along the Verdun road, and at right-angles to the Gorze road, with their flank consequently exposed, and that although but three English miles from the Prussian corps lying in the Gorze valley, they were positively unaware of their close proximity or even of their presence. Strong in cavalry, it was one of the most monstrous things upon record. It appears, that on the morning of the 16th, the French cavalry were sent to reconnoitre; they returned and reported that there were *a few Uhlans* in the valley of Gorze, and at 8 A.M. their bugles sounded unsaddle, and the men began to breakfast. The first intimation that General Battaile, who commanded the infantry brigade at Rezonville, had of the enemy's presence, was the sudden appearance of the Germans on the Verdun road, leading from the town of Gorze: a glance at the map will explain this.

'Prince Frederick Charles commenced his attack with cavalry between Mars-la-Tour and Vionville, sacrificing nearly the whole of the dragoons of the guard to a mad impetuosity. The colonel of this gallant regiment, when ordered to attack, turned round to his regiment, saying, "Remember, children, this is no fault of mine, and I hold myself blameless." Poor fellow! he never returned; the regiment was cut almost to pieces. The action commenced by the attack of the 3d corps on the French advance, whilst the 7th corps, marching out of Gorze, attacked in flank towards Rezonville.

'The intention of the French, it would appear, was to march upon Châlons, and in this movement they were checked by the rapid advance of the 3d corps d'armée, under Prince Frederick Charles. The 11th regiment (Prussian) deployed in front of the wood surrounding Gorze, having marched up the road from that town to Metz; whilst the 35th regiment and the 72d continued the line to the left. The French batteries immediately opened with shells, and in a few moments the woods which covered the advance of the Prussian troops seemed to be in a perfect hurricane of bursting shells, telling severely upon the advancing Prussians. No sooner did the right battalion of the 11th emerge and deploy than the French chasseurs and line opened fire at 700 yards; and fearfully effective was the discharge—so much so that this gallant regiment lost their colonel and five officers, besides a considerable number of men. They then retired into the wood until the whole line could advance together, the French shells meanwhile inflicting fearful loss upon the troops advancing, although under a screen of foliage.

'Whenever the Prussian advance appeared, the French troops opened a crushing fire, the assailants falling, literally, in heaps; but "*Immer vorwärts!*" was the cry, and, under a storm of shot and shell, the gallant 3d division, led by the troops I have above mentioned, advanced to meet the foe. For full an hour they fired at one another from a distance of fifty paces, the French, who had not until now suffered much, losing many men. The first line of the French troops then gradually retired, and three regiments of the Garde Impériale for the moment stood the brunt of the Prussian advance, almost alone in their glory. Here the Prussian line was strengthened thus. General von Göben, hearing the heavy firing, long and continued, and knowing the weakness of the Prince's command, took upon himself to order up the 16th division of the 8th corps, under General Barnaekow. This body of troops, composed of the 40th and 70th regiments, the 9th hussars and the artillery, marching through the town of Gorze and up the Metz road, deployed to the left of the 7th corps, just at the moment when the guard had gained a slight advantage. As the leading files of the 40th emerged out of the wood, they faced the premier Grenadier de la Garde, who poured in such a fire, that the leading companies were almost swept away, the adjutant and many officers wounded, and the colonel killed. But Major Hohleben led on the 2d battalion, the 3d followed close upon its steps, and at twenty to thirty paces the fire was something fearful; at length the guard had to give way, and fell back to the village of Gravelotte.

'The action had now lasted some six hours; the dead, the dying, and the wounded encumbered the field in every direction; while the blazing rays of a hot autumnal sun fell with fearful force upon the unprotected wounded. The Prussians now disentangled some batteries of artillery from the Metz road, and plied the retreating but still stubborn French forces with shells, inflicting the most frightful wounds. Up to nine at night the French guns still sullenly rolled forth their fearful music, until darkness wrapt the scene of carnage in obscurity. Then rose the moon, and the plain awakened to the awful cries of the wounded—so piteous, especially to the soldier. The Prussian loss and that of the French in this action is something too awful to contemplate in so small a space; for in an area of one and a half square miles quite 10,000 men had been put *hors de combat.*'

That night I returned to Gorze. What a scene!

Every house a hospital, the streets lined with wounded, the gutters positively running with blood. Who was to answer for this seemed a question that demanded an answer, and let them look to it who can give no satisfactory explanation.

By the battle of Mars-la-Tour, the Prussians occupied the main road to Verdun, Châlons, and Paris, and effectually prevented any junction of Bazaine's army with that of M'Mahon, driving the former general back to Metz, and giving him the option to cut his way through or shut himself up in Metz for a better opportunity.

It has been asserted that at this battle the contending armies came to the bayonet; this is quite a mistake—they never came nearer than from thirty to forty yards of one another.

You who live in your homes at ease, think of the plain of Gorse, and those who were wounded in the middle of the day, and who lay out all night unable to move, without a drop of water to moisten their lips, their wounds untended, and no one to say a cheering word. If you can realise a scene such as this, follow me to the battle-field.

As I leave the wood already mentioned, and come upon the plain, the dry soil seems covered with heaps of blue uniforms; but not a single French soldier is to be seen. About half a mile from this the French dead and wounded commence. There is a small house on the roadside which the French held. It was evidently used for cattle, and now contains thirty-six French bodies, with only one soldier alive. In the rack, where he has crawled for shelter, lies a veteran of the 24th regiment of the line, his hair and moustaches white as snow. As I advance up the road to the village, a white rag tied to a ramrod attracts my attention; and upon arrival I find a chasseur-à-pied, with three medals on his breast, lying with a fearful wound through his right lung, through which his laboured breath comes in fitful gasps. '*Monsieur*,' said he, '*faites-moi seulement une service, donnez-moi un coup de pistolet.* He had lain there for twenty-three hours.

How shall I go on? It was a scene too awful to describe. I have seen many battle-fields; but never one like this. To my left, on a small knoll, I see a group of conveyances, with a red cross. I know what it means—if that ghastly row of mutilated humanity close by were not sufficient to tell me that it is a hospital ambulance detachment. I go up to see what I can do, and I find four Prussian doctors hard at work, *not on their own men*, but on French. They have been there since 10 A.M. the day previous, and have had nothing. I offer one a tin cup of wine, which, instead of drinking himself, he takes to the French wounded. Two priests are there—one a prince—ministering in their holy office amongst the dying. There was a mutilated soldier of the Garde Impériale, with both feet shattered and his cheek taken away; when I told him that he need not alarm himself about the amputation, he answered, '*Qu'est ce que ça me fait ça? donnez-moi un cigare.*' The doctors were tired out, their assistants were weary, and still the groans of the wounded were heard in every direction.

Now a new sound causes me to look in the direction of Metz. It is the roll of the mitrailleuse, and the scattering fire of the outposts—more bloodshed, more misery, more agony! When I return from my sad walk, I find that Prussian discipline has turned Gorze into something more orderly. As I pass down the street, the general kindly asks me to have a glass of beer. Since the day before, at 12 A.M., I had had nothing but a tumbler of red wine. We discuss the war, and he tells me that England has lost all influence in Europe. I agree that she has.

When I got into the town, a Prussian soldier begged a bit of bread. It is but too true: these troops who had won the bloody field of Mars-la-Tour—fed upon half-cooked potatoes and rice the night before, then marched fourteen miles and attacked a determined enemy—were without food. The nights, too, were raw and cold, but the Prussian soldier had nothing but the heavens and his military cloak to cover him. What would happen the next day no one knew. Bazaine would, perhaps, once more try to cut his way through to Châlons. France had but one chance left, and that was the Marne and Châlons.

After the engagement of the 17th the Prussians held the village of Rezonville, which was occupied by the outposts of the 8th army corps. The French held a position on the ridge above the road between Metz and Thionville, still keeping open the road to Paris, their right resting on St. Privat-la-Montaigne to the right of Gravelotte, about two miles distant, and their left upon the road into Metz above the village of Rozerieulles. The position of the Prussian army was as follows: Their centre, consisting of the

8th and 9th army corps, was massed in rear of the village of Gravelotte; their right, composed of the 7th army corps, lay concealed in the woods between Gorze and Gravelotte; whilst their left, formed by the 3d and 4th army corps, with the division of guards and the 10th corps, occupied the woods to the left of the latter place, stretching away to Marie-au-Chêne. Against this force the French had about five corps and a half and the strongest position, with Metz in their rear.

Behind the Prussian army lay the bloody battle-field of Gorze, the dead still unburied, and some of the wounded still uncared for—the French having left theirs to the tender mercies of strangers. The sun struck hot and sultry upon the fearful plateau, and the stench from the dead bodies was almost insupportable; but more important matters attracted attention. The Prussians were desirous of cutting off the retreat of the French from Metz, whilst the French were, of course, anxious to make good their road to Châlons. In order to effect their plan, on the 18th of August, the Prussians, having got their left wing into position, at about 11.30 engaged the French right, in the hopes of inducing them to extend their forces more in this direction, and thus allow the Prussian right—which, as I have already said, was concealed in a wood—to get between Metz, and to overlap their left: this brought on the battle of Gravelotte.

The fire commenced in a brisk manner, the thundering reports of the mitrailleuse sounding above the roar of musketry. The Prussian left then retired, but to no purpose; for the French general, evidently perceiving the intention, maintained his position. The 8th army corps then advanced through the village of Gravelotte, supported by a heavy fire of artillery, and led by the three battalions of the 33d regiment, an enormous mass of cavalry taking up a position in rear of their centre. The French opened their batteries on the ridge of the hill, situated at St. Hubert and Point-du-Jour, and, with their front covered by tirailleurs protected by rifle-pits, rained a tremendous fire of shot and shell upon the advancing Prussians. Now, to the left of the village of Gravelotte and in front of the French position there lay a small hamlet called Malmaison—no inappropriate name for such a locality. Here the Prussians suffered severely, the French shot and mitrailleuse cutting them down, and, after setting a house on fire, compelling them to retire and take ground to their left. A regiment of Prussian lancers, hoping to make some prisoners, now charged down the front of the Prussian advance, but were beaten back with severe loss.

After three hours' hard fighting, the Prussians gained some half-mile in advance of Gravelotte, and occupied the now smoking hamlet of Malmaison, with the farms of St. Hubert and Moscau. At 4.30 the cavalry division advanced to the front, and the 7th division made good their ground to the right, but not one inch did they gain upon the French. Battalion after battalion was sent to the front, only to be shot down by the French in their, so to say, artificial position. The village of Gravelotte presented a frightful spectacle—the dead, the dying, and the wounded filling the houses and cumbering the roads. Meantime the attack on the French right had again commenced, the Prussian guards taking the village of St. Privat-la-Montaigne with fearful loss, the 3d, 4th, and 10th corps making good their advance also, and forcing the French back towards Plappeville from Amanvilliers and Roncourt. A demonstration on the French left upon Ars-sur-Moselle had not proved successful; but the Prussians still held the farms of Moscau, St. Hubert, and the hamlet of Point-du-Jour; in fact their centre had not budged, both sides firing at one another doggedly from their respective shelters. At 5.30 a fresh supply of ammunition was borne to the front, the clattering train galloping through the badly-paved street of Gravelotte, and adding to the din of the bursting shells and rattle of musketry; and so the sanguinary conflict continued until 6.30, when the cannonade slackened and eventually subsided into a dropping fire, from which the Prussians suffered worse than their opponents.

This pause in the fearful fire which had been going on all day gave one breathing time to ask after friends, and anxious questions, replied to by most unsatisfactory answers, were heard on all sides. I found that a very dear and kind friend, one who had been most anxious to give me every assistance, lay with two wounds in an old mill some half mile from Gravelotte and about 150 yards from the French line.

I had got about 200 yards from the old mill, and

was talking to an officer, when a tremendous fire of chassepots and shells was opened, and by the light of the blazing shells I could see a French column advancing upon the Prussians. In a moment the state of affairs seemed changed. Two Prussian guns were deserted, their men flying to the rear. The front line of the Prussians gave way; there was no order; for in the engagement of the afternoon the regiments had got so mixed together that it was impossible to distinguish them; and a confused mass of wounded soldiers, hussars, doctors, artillerymen, and hospital conveyances came flying back through the streets of Gravelotte. The French advance was splendid, and had they gone on, the village of Gravelotte would have fallen into their hands. The Prussian guns on the right and left of Gravelotte however stood firm, and poured a rapid fire upon the French; but it did not seem their object to come any farther, for, after clearing the front of their position, they retired.

The 2d division, which had remained in reserve all day, now came up, their bands playing and the men hurrahing. In compact masses they advanced, relieving the worn-out troops who had been fighting all day, and taking Moscau, Point-du-Jour, and St. Hubert with a rush, driving the French from their position, and forcing them back upon Metz by way of Longeau, Lissy, and Rozerieulles. At this point of the conflict the French artillery fire was quicker than that of the Prussians, as also their infantry fire; but, although their artillery was beautifully served, the fire from the chassepot was all luck, inasmuch as the men scarcely ever put the butt of the rifle to the shoulder. My experience of the chassepot is, that from 100 to 500 yards it is an inferior weapon, but from 600 to 1,000 yards it is very effective. The recoil is dreadful.

My horse having been shot and myself severely wounded, I was unable to see the last of the day. I lay just below the farm of St. Hubert, to the left of the main road into Gravelotte, for some time, until about 11 P.M., when I was carried back to Gravelotte, and fortunately found a heap of straw in a room with six officers, where a doctor kindly dressed my side for me. Imagine a room 15ft. by 12, the floor spread with straw and blankets, mostly covered with blood. I am in a corner which was vacated for me by an officer of the 67th regiment, who was shot through the foot. To my right was a captain in the same regiment with the bones of his leg shattered to pieces below the knee; to his right was a lieutenant, shot through the knee; whilst on my left lay three others, more or less dangerously wounded. Here I remained till the break of day, listening to the continual firing of the French and Prussians. At daybreak I was put into a cart, and sent back to Gorze.

Thus ended the second great battle in front of Metz, which has been called the battle of Gravelotte. Its result was to force Bazaine into Metz, and to prevent most effectually his junction with M'Mahon.

Early on the morning of the 19th, the 2d Prussian army corps took possession of the French position at Malmaison, or rather the ruins representing that fatal spot, which had cost the Prussians in the combat of Gravelotte between 7,000 and 8,000 killed and wounded. The French retired, and took up a position under the guns of Fort St. Quentin, protecting Metz on the east side.

The King telegraphed on the morning of the 20th to Berlin, to announce that the French army under Bazaine was entirely surrounded in Metz—which was no more than the truth—and that the Crown Prince was on his way to Paris. Reports also came that the French had abandoned Châlons, but these were not believed; certain, however, it was that the Crown Prince, with seven army corps, was four days' march from Nancy on the road to Paris. The 1st, 2d, 7th, 8th, 9th, and 10th army corps, under the command of Prince Frederick Charles and General von Steinmetz, kept watch over Metz, and their outposts were in sight of the French, who were seen to be hard at work strengthening the works of Mount St. Quentin. The disposition of the different army corps who remained to watch the French army in Metz was pretty much in the order I give them. It was arranged that no attempt should be made on the part of the Prussians to attack the French in any way, but simply to prevent their breaking through either to join M'Mahon or to get to Paris. Such was the state of things as far as the opposing armies were concerned in this locality after the battle of Gravelotte.

Referring to my letter in the *Daily Telegraph*, dated from before Metz on the 20th of August, the battle-field is thus described:

'This morning I went up from Gravelotte to look

at the field of battle of yesterday, and to inspect the French position. Bazaine had strengthened himself along the road between Metz and Thionville by a succession of rifle pits, and had also thrown up small works to protect his guns. The walls of the gardens and the houses of the hamlets were also made as defensible as possible, and had evidently been lined with skirmishers, who could pour an incessant cross-fire upon any troops advancing up the road from Gravelotte, the distance of this village from the French position being about an English mile. Exactly halfway between Gravelotte and the French ground, a deep ravine, lined on either side by a thick undergrowth of hazel and oak, made the advance of troops still more difficult, whilst upon emerging beyond this sunken coppice the soil made a gentle ascent up to the French rifle pits.

'The peculiarity of the situation, which the French had taken up with extreme judgment, was, that almost every movement the Prussian troops made was distinctly visible, even to the shifting of the position of a single man; and this accounts for the fearful slaughter the French were able to inflict, and the comparatively small loss they suffered, their killed and wounded being about 600 or 700. For the first time since the commencement of hostilities, I saw not a single French body; but in the ruins of Malmaison some twenty or thirty of the more severely wounded French lay. From them I learnt how fearfully they had punished the Prussians; and if more evidence was wanting, the houses, stables, and barns of the village of Gravelotte were quite sufficient.

'I cannot describe to you my feelings upon looking over the spot where—if I may so call it—the Balaklava of the day upon a small scale took place. The road from Gravelotte to Malmaison runs due east and west; about a quarter of a mile from Gravelotte it dips into the ravine I have already described, and in the bottom of this dip stood the squadron or two of Prussian lancers who made the charge. It appears that they saw some French skirmishers creeping forward, in order to throw a cross-fire into a regiment of Prussians who lay partly concealed in a stone quarry on the left of the road. In the hope of capturing these they dashed up the opposite hill, and when they reached the brow received the fire of a mitrailleuse battery which swept the road. Thirty-two dead horses marked the first discharge and the fatal mistake. Fortunately, they were able to make good their retreat before any farther serious loss was inflicted on them. The 60th regiment of Prussians, which lay on the right of the road, lost twenty-four officers and 1154 men, and the other regiments engaged all sacrificed from 500 to 600 each, with a very large proportion of officers.

'The French have still the road open to Luxemburg, if they choose to take it, and, the inhabitants being favourable to them, I cannot see what better movement they could make, unless, as I said before, they can break through our position and make good their way to Châlons; in which case they would place themselves between the army of the Crown Prince and our own, with a very faint hope of effecting a junction with M'Mahon.

'On my return to Gravelotte, I found a French ambulance corps had arrived from Metz, with many French civilian doctors, all wearing the Geneva cross, sent out to look after their own wounded. They were accompanied by two priests, but they did not seem to obtain much assistance from the Prussians. A proclamation, signed by General von Göben, commanding the 8th army corps, was posted on the walls of the village, to the effect that any one assisting the French, by giving information as to the disposition of the troops of his majesty the King of Prussia, or serving against the King of Prussia, or in any way aiding or abetting the escape of French prisoners, would without trial be shot upon the spot. The feelings of the French peasants of Lorraine are by no means inimical to the Prussians. They speak of his majesty the King as their *nouveau Roi;* and they universally deplore the *plébiscite*, which they affirm is the principal cause of the war. They do not blame the Emperor in any way; but they say that it is the French people who wished for war, and not their ruler. The troops have had meat served out to them to-day; and when I returned to the camp of the 8th army corps, I found the poor fellows busily cooking, previous to marching forward in order to take up the position, from which I now write, assigned to them in the blockade of Metz.

'The particular regiment with which I am associated more than with any other is the 33d Fusiliers, whose fearful loss I stated to you in my letter of yesterday. It has had one major killed and two others severely wounded. Some of its companies I found without officers, and others commanded by lieutenants. The colonel, with his adjutant, was sitting at an improvised table writing a report of the action, and a melancholy mention of the losses. A shake of the hand, with a mournful look in the direction where his shattered regiment lay around their piled arms, while the tears welled up into his eyes, was all that passed between us. The officers stalked about, not speaking a word; but the men laughed, talked, and smoked, seemingly in excellent spirits.'

I must now say a few words about the Prussian arrangements for the wounded, which, like all the rest of their organisation, were perfect, from the simplicity and ease with which the system was carried out. Each regiment had a party of men told off, who wore the red cross upon the left arm as a distinguishing badge. They numbered about a hundred, and were unarmed, except with most useless-looking horse pistols. It was their duty to follow in rear of the regiment, and when the corps went into action stretchers were distributed to them, which were carried in the staff ambulance wagons belonging to the brigade. In addition to this corps there were six doctors to each regiment, and a regimental medicine wagon upon two wheels to each battalion, which always followed in rear of the column, containing medical comforts and surgical instruments. This regimental ambulance is more for the use of the troops on the march than for succour in the battlefield, for which purpose the staff or brigade ambulances are used.

The latter are perfection itself in their arrangements. They consist of a large wagon upon four wheels, drawn by four horses. On the top, under oilskins which form tents for the hospital corps, are packed the stretchers. The back part is opened by folding-doors, and a perfect apothecary's shop is exposed, commencing with drawers containing surgical instruments, bandages, and cordials of every description, and ending with chloroform and medicines of every sort and kind that can be useful in the field. My space will not permit me to give a detail of what these wonderful carriages contain; suffice it to say that nothing is lacking. These ambulances are under the charge of experienced staff doctors, who have also a corps of assistants similar to that attached to the regiments. I may here add, that the surgeons found the plaster-of-paris splint a most useful thing in cases where the bone was shattered, and it was almost universally used.

In addition to the very efficient medical staff that follows the Prussian army, there is a 'Sanitats Corps,' or volunteer medical and nursing society, which renders all the assistance in its power to the sick and wounded. The most perfect order regulates everything, and the attention paid to the wounded French by the Prussians was quite beyond praise. The only people who gave me the least idea of being not quite up to the mark were a few of the stretcher-carriers, who never failed to rifle the pockets of the dead whilst on their melancholy search for the wounded.

Shortly after my return to Gravelotte the 8th corps

marched up to the position assigned to them in front of Metz; and a truly miserable site for a camp it was. They were placed to the left of the Metz road, about fifty yards from the two battered houses which formed the centre of the French position, in whose ruins some twenty badly wounded Frenchmen lay. I had read in past days with delight of the fertile plains of Lorraine and their beauty; but the present situation reminded me of the plateau before Sebastopol, where I spent some miserable months of my existence, more than anything else. The worst of the position was, that there was little or no water to be got, and that the artillery at Gravelotte, in rear of us, had to go some three miles for theirs. Wood, with the exception of what was green and would not burn, was also wanting—two necessaries without which an army of occupation cannot exist. The only weak point in the Prussian organisation at this time was the Proviant Colonna, or commissariat train, which never seemed to me to come up with the division until a few moments before they were going to start on their march.

After the regiment had bivouacked—for encampment it was not, except that a few of the officers had managed to secure some French *tentes d'abri*—I determined to return to Gorze, some six miles from where we lay, as my wounded side was somewhat painful, and I thought the luxury of sleeping in a bed might perhaps do some good. Accordingly off I trudged; the worst part of the journey being that which took me across the battle-field of the 16th, where the odour from the still unburied bodies of horses and men was anything but pleasant. The town seemed to me to have put on a more orderly appearance, which arose from the fact that about an hour from Gorze the railway was opened to Saarbrück, and consequently all the wounded who could be moved had been sent off. I soon arrived at my old quarters, and had the inexpressible luxury of sitting down to some *bouillon* and a salad, with a bottle of red wine. I found that all sorts of reports were scattered about the town; one being, that the Prussians had taken Strasburg.

At that moment Gorze presented a fair specimen of what a town suffers whilst occupied by an enemy's forces. The inhabitants were afraid to leave their houses, or even to move about in the streets with baskets in their hands. The red cross even did not protect them from seeing what they were carrying to the sick taken by the half-famished soldiers. As to cigars or tobacco, if you smoked anything in the streets, you ran the risk of having it snatched from your mouth. Those who closed their shops and houses fared worse; those fared best who gave what they had got. I had been invited to supper one evening by a rich citizen of Gorze, who told me that he would give me *some meat* in all probability, and who was ready to do anything for an Englishman. He was a wise man in his way, and having foreseen certain clouds in the horizon, he had collected his most precious goods and buried them in the ground. Nevertheless he always kept a good glass of wine for a friend and brother.

When I made his acquaintance, I was shown into a room where mine host was eating *bouillon* with a German or Prussian priest. As soon as my nationality became known to him, he took me into another room, and asked me what I wanted. I told him simply a good bottle of wine. He explained to me that he had plenty, although circumstances had compelled him to hide it; but that he thought one or two bottles still remained, and that if I would go into another room, we would drink a bottle together. Accordingly, after some little time my friend appeared, a bottle hid under his coat-tails, and down we sat to about as good a bottle of Moselle as I ever tasted. As the bottle waxed low, so the conversation warmed, and I was enabled to glean some useful information, by which it would appear that the French army were at that time by no means so utterly demoralised as had been imagined, although the generalship had hitherto been of the most mediocre description.

The unusual cessation of hostilities—that is to say, of any actual engagement about this time—gave time to mark what was going on. The 22d was, *mirabile dictu*, the fourth day on which we had no thousands slaughtered and tens of thousands wounded. Three weeks had elapsed since the war opened, or rather since the first serious collision between the contending armies took place, and in that short time from 60,000 to 70,000 Prussians had been placed *hors de combat*. What the losses of the French were, I was unable, of course, to compute; but judging from what I saw and heard, I imagine they suffered less dreadfully. Each victory had cost the Prussians very dear; so much so, that his majesty, as I before said, deemed it prudent to withdraw the command of the first army to a certain extent from General von Steinmetz, and place it in hands less regardless of the value of human life. General von Steinmetz, however, remained in command of the first army, assisted by Prince Frederick Charles. The stories that flitted about were as curious as they were diverse. It was rumoured that the Crown Prince was bombarding Paris, and that the Emperor had gained a victory; that Strasburg had been taken by the Prussians; and that a French corps d'armée had succeeded in cutting its way through the blockading troops around Metz. One circumstance seemed, however, to meet no contradiction; and that was, that there had been a conscription for the purpose of recruiting the French army—not from the Garde Mobile, but out of all those who were capable of bearing arms between the ages of 25 and 35 years. This ought to have furnished a reserve which should have stood France in good stead in her moment of peril—for at least eight-tenths would be educated soldiers—if only the authorities could find weapons to give them.

On the 22d of August the Prussian army of observation, or rather the blockading force, still held the same uninteresting position; and to add to its inconveniences, provisions were anything but plentiful. Hitherto the fertile province of Lorraine and the valley of the Moselle had supplied food for the invading army; but Prussia had over-estimated the resources of the country through which she was marching, and a single halt of two days at any one place at once realised the impossibility of obtaining a sufficiency of subsistence. The Prussian commissariat made superhuman efforts to meet the emergency, as the shortening days and the coldness of the temperature warned them what to expect.

At this time there were above 1,500 severely wounded soldiers in the small town of Gorze. The inhabitants could scarcely find food for themselves, and yet were asked, or rather compelled, to furnish it for perhaps twenty wounded who might be quartered upon them. Besides these, there were some 450 French wounded and prisoners, who served to add to the general inconvenience. The state of things in this little town was as follows:

Gorze contained some 1500 inhabitants. Like most of the places in the neighbourhood of the Moselle, its staple commodities are wine and spirits. The shops in the town are merely equal to supply the wants of its inhabitants, any farther demand having always been met by the larger and better-furnished town of Metz. My readers will, therefore, imagine the consternation of the inhabitants when an invading army of some 600,000 men marched through the streets, and took up their quarters in and about their vicinity. This was not all; the army which marched through was able to shift for itself; but scarce twenty-four hours elapsed before the very gutters of Gorze—not to use too far-fetched or extravagant an expression—positively ran with human blood. What was the consequence? Those who closed their houses had them broken into; the wounded were bundled in pell-mell until proper attention could be paid them; the soldiers, athirst and hungered, as I have already described, by reason of their indifferent commissariat, quartered themselves somewhat roughly upon the unfortunate inhabitants; those who resisted, or attempted to hide their little all, had their furniture thrown out of windows, their cellars broken open, and their persons maltreated; while those who offered what they had were merely put to inconvenience and a certain amount of personal loss. Bread there was little or none, meat ditto; the potato-fields were ransacked all round; but of wine and horribly bad spirits there was plenty. Meantime the unburied dead and the festering wounded added to the miseries of a town situated in a sort of crater, where there was little or no air to drive away the pestilential atmosphere which seemed to hang over it. Disease already stalked about the streets, and fresh relays of wounded added to the miseries around. Such, then, was Gorze at that moment.

I had occasion to go to the Château St. Catherine, whose proprietor was an ex-French officer of engineers, who, for some motive or another, had not removed his family on the approach of the Prussian troops, although his residence was situated scarce a quarter of a mile from Gorze. Since the loss of my horse in the action of the 14th, and also the loss of what is somewhat more trying to an Englishman—animal food—I had vainly endeavoured to remount myself. The Prussian army had too few to be of any assistance to me, one battery alone in the action of the 18th having left sixty-two horses on the field; the country people had all their animals taken in requisition; so that my chance of obtaining anything to carry me was but small. By a great piece of good luck, however, I managed to pick up a farmer's brood mare, strong, slow, and excessively ugly, but infinitely preferable to the prospect of having to walk some sixteen or eighteen miles upon an empty stomach. Having obtained my prize, the next thing was to come by saddle and bridle. This seemed even more difficult than a horse; but having heard that the seigneur of the Château of St. Catherine might perhaps possess such a thing, I went there.

The château was much the same in point of architecture as those which are so plentifully scattered over Southern France, and dated back to about the beginning of the present century; but, alas, the beautiful grounds which surrounded it had been the site where a division of Prince Frederick Charles's army camped previous to the action of the 16th. Trees were cut down, gates unhung and broken to pieces for firewood, potatoes dug up wherever a patch was to be seen, arbours turned into shelters for the night, and the parterres broken, destroyed, and strewn with the débris of bottles or littered with straw. The court-yard of the house had become a hospital; 1600 wounded had left its gates during the previous three days; but the château itself was still inhabited by the proprietor and his family. There were, it is true, forty-two severely wounded soldiers in and about the out-houses; but some sort of order had been reëstablished.

The proprietor of the château shortly made his appearance, the ribbon of the legion of honour in his button-hole; himself a fine specimen of the French country gentleman, who had considered it his duty to serve his country for a certain number of years, and who had now retired, as he supposed, to end his days peacefully in his lovely château in Lorraine. I made known to him who I was, and what were my wants; whereupon immediately the only saddle and bridle in the house were at my orders. 'Sir,' said he, 'the Prussians have taken twenty-five horses, they have pillaged my fields, they have broken, spilt, and drunk 6500 bottles of wine, they have killed my cows, they have slaughtered my sheep, and have burnt my gates for firewood; and I am therefore grieved to be unable to offer you that hospitality which I should wish to have shown.' We spoke of the war, but with caution; and it was then that, after warming to the subject a little, I found from him that my surmises as to the many retreats of the French and their want of success were but too well founded.

It is neither my province nor my desire to put forward too strongly my own opinions upon this subject; but the world will know before long, that whatever reverses the French troops suffered have arisen, not from want of courage among them, but through the consummate ignorance of their generals. I cannot refrain from mentioning a fact which even the simplest soldier could not but have wondered at. I allude to the entirely unopposed passage of the Moselle by the Prussians. In the spot where the crossings were effected, one single division of infantry might have disputed it, causing fearful loss to the Prussians, as, from the nature of the ground in the valley of the Moselle, most people will readily understand. The French commanders can offer no excuse for this egregious blunder; the more so, as the passage of the Moselle was effected between Nancy and Metz.

That the French received no intelligence of the Prussian movements, is a thing which no one could for a moment believe, inasmuch as those movements took place in their own country, and were seen by their own people, even supposing they were destitute of cavalry. In no single instance had the French, upon being attacked, any reserves upon which to fall back, or fresh troops to make good any numerical losses. They fought until their ammunition failed them, and were the admiration even of their adversaries.

Not so the Prussians. Their cheap army did more than was ever expected of it. Badly fed, worse housed, and indifferently clad, but splendidly armed, with excellent officers and first-rate generals, it accomplished what no modern army has ever yet been known to do. Its rank and file lost cruelly in every action; they endured fatigue, hunger, and want of shelter; and yet under all these trying circumstances there was no murmuring, the discipline was most perfect, and the campaigning beyond praise. One thing was, however, clear, that unless Prussia was prepared to feed her enormous army in the coming struggle, this region would not. The Moselle country was devastated, gutted; and it was now a race against time. Should winter overtake the Prussian armies, woe betide them, for at that moment one could not see how they were to exist. Already the rib-marks upon the Prussian cavalry showed the want of forage, and the three or four miles they had to go for water twice a day did not improve the condition of their horses. It is true that most of the regiments were on outpost duty; but they were gradually eating their way forwards, and leaving nothing behind them. The artillery was suffering even more than the cavalry, inasmuch as it was forced to remain with the divisions of infantry.

A sketch of my quarters at this time may perhaps interest the reader. They were situated under the remains of the garden wall of Malmaison, and were formed by two French *tentes d'abri*, into which I crawled every night, and considered myself excessively lucky. When it rained hard, my situation was not exceedingly lively; for I was obliged to sit on a bundle of straw four days old, and smoke some stumps of cigars, out of which I had improvised an exceedingly nasty mixture to fill my pipe, which, with my tooth-brush, and saddle-bags containing nothing but some mementoes of the fields of Saarbrück, Forbach, Colombey, Mars-la-Tour, and Gravelotte, my sketch-book, and, I am thankful to say, my invaluable Ulster coat, formed the whole of my baggage. A friend who was with me *en amateur* struggled daily with some very wet and very green sticks to light a fire, over which a soldier's camp-kettle was to be suspended, containing a piece of pork, some onions, two carrots (for which we had to walk three miles), and

CHAPTER III.

BEFORE METZ.

On the 24th August the sun shone, and the miserably oppressive weather of the previous few days disappeared. The muddy plateau above Gravelotte—for it was already reduced to that—was getting gradually dry, and you could walk from one camp to another without carrying ten pounds of clay upon each foot. But the miserable shelter the Prussian troops had against the cold and wet of the last few days, together with the insufficiency of food, already told its tale. Diarrhœa and dysentery began to be severely felt by the troops, and a screen of leaves on the damp ground is not the sort of shelter calculated to improve the health of an exhausted frame. About this time it was determined to take Metz; but whether this determination would be actually carried out or not, still seemed to remain an open question. The operations would not be commenced until some certain news was heard from the Crown Prince, who was said to be at Bar-le-Duc on the 23d; at any rate the French were hard at work strengthening their position in the direction of Mont St. Quentin, whilst their outposts were continually coming into contact with those of the Germans; and outpost duty on a dark night is by no means an agreeable occupation, especially in front of an active enemy.

One morning I waded across the half-dry plain, where the horses killed by the French in the Prussian cavalry charge lay still unburied, to the ruins of St. Hubert. In one wing of the house the head-quarters of the division had taken up their uncomfortable quarters, whilst at the other end, in the stable, where half the roof still afforded some shelter, and the shell-holes in the walls had been stopped with dead men's coats, lay some ten or a dozen Frenchmen too seriously wounded for transport. Amongst these unfortunates I found an officer of the 26th regiment of the line. He had been shot through the knee, and, whilst lying on the ground between the two fires, he had received another bullet through the arm. So severe had the wound been in the knee, that the doctors found it necessary to remove a portion of the knee-cap, and when I went to see him, the poor fellow was suffering most exquisite agony. His sufferings, I am sorry to say, were not lessened in consequence of some unfortunate circumstances which very naturally incensed the Prussians.

A Saxon officer, very severely wounded, sought shelter, it seems, in the house of a peasant in the neighbourhood of St. Marcel. The unfortunate man, exhausted from fatigue and loss of blood, threw himself upon a bed and fainted. Whilst in this state of helplessness the woman to whom the house belonged deliberately gouged his eyes out with a fork, and then left him to die a horrible death. He lingered long enough to tell his fearful story to a Prussian ambulance train. Again, after the battle of the 18th instant, a cuirassier officer, with a trumpeter conveying a flag of truce, approached the French lines in front of Metz, for the purpose of requesting them to send assistance to their wounded. The trumpeter was fired upon and shot through the head, and the officer returned to tell a tale that roused universal indignation. Truly *la grande nation* has degenerated as much in morality as in leaders.

But to return to the wounded French officer: a more interesting conversation I could scarcely have had; and as a man at the point of death, and suffering the most fearful agony, is scarcely likely to exaggerate, I will give the substance of his conversation with me. He had served at the battle of Spiecheren, and he informed me that they had neither artillery nor mitrailleuse upon the heights; that they were but one division; and that at half-past seven in the evening they found themselves still in possession of the heights, without general and without ammunition. Furthermore, they had no supports to fall back upon, and no one from whom to take orders. In the morning before the action this officer breakfasted with the general commanding what artillery they possessed, who told him that he could not go into action, inasmuch as he had no ammunition. This entirely bears out what I before stated, that had the French been properly supplied with artillery and ammunition, and had the French generals in rear moved up their supports, the Spiecheren Berg would have been impregnable.

Passing on from this melancholy scene, I proceeded towards the left of the Prussian position; on my way I met some 200 peasants from the neighbouring villages, whom the Prussians had at length compelled at the point of the bayonet to turn out and bury the now putrid corpses. I also met wagons containing sick men, all more or less suffering from dysentery or diarrhœa. The usual spitting fire of the outposts was going on, varied by an occasional shell from Mont St. Quentin. The Prussians cut off some of the water-supply from Metz; but I don't think this affected the enemy much, as the Moselle gives a plentiful supply. No appearance of a siege train or heavy guns of any sort had as yet come to the front, but as the railway was open within a distance of two hours, we anticipated soon seeing some artillery of this description.

The principal occupation, or rather the serious business of the day, in camp, was the preparation for a meal of some sort. Directly you awoke, human nature at once required some sustenance; you craved for a good hot cup of tea, especially if you found yourself exposed all night to what Virgil calls *placidus imber*. The dry sticks which you had taken to bed with you to keep dry were produced as soon as day broke, and a hot tin of coffee without sugar or milk helped to pull you together. The business of the day then commenced. A rush was made for the nearest 'Marketender' wagon that had come up from Gorze. In the following of almost every regiment there is attached to each company an individual called a 'Marketender.' Half soldier, half publican, and wholly thief, he is a curious mixture of cunning, courage, and dishonesty—terms, I am aware, that are strangely discordant, but which are all represented in the character of the Marketender. His occupation is, with his wagon, covered with canvas and drawn by two wretched-looking horses, to rob, plunder, or buy provisions at any of the villages he passes through, and to sell the produce to the soldiers of the particular company to which he is attached, the number of which is painted on his wagon and carried on his cap.

Very often the Marketender has his better-half to help him—a virago who outbrazens the sins of her husband, bullies the soldiers, and cringes to the officers. Mrs. Marketenderin is by no means an engaging-looking person. The one I had to do with wore a costume sufficiently ludicrous. A French soldier's cap covered her grizzled hair, the peak shading a face which, from exposure to the sun, looked like a piece of badly-tanned leather; a voltigeur's jacket enveloped her body, and a large red bandana was wound round her waist, where she carried a huge knife, with which to cut the hard black bread into the pieces she dispensed to the soldiers; her arms and hands were brown-black, partly from exposure and partly from dirt; whilst, to complete her semi-military costume, the shortness of her petticoat revealed her feet encased in a pair of long boots that had once been the property of some Prussian soldier, whose bones in all probability were lying upon the plateau of Gorze.

They both dispensed their commodities in eager haste, and were not particular as to the change they gave for a thaler. The appearance of these *vivandières* since the invasion of French territory had wonderfully improved, at the expense of *la belle France;* and the money they made has, without doubt, enabled them to eat their 'Kartoffelsalat' and drink their 'Zeltinger' for the rest of their days in peace and quietness on the banks of the Moselle, or wherever else they might please to settle down. If you were in favour, madame produced a piece of meat from the recesses of the wagon, and perhaps an onion, a piece of bread, and a glass of schnapps, for which you paid the moderate sum of one thaler. With these valuables one rushed off to one's shelter, wherever it might be, and, if the rain had not put your fire out, you improvised a meal, which, if not very *recherché*, was at least filling.

The band was really the luxury of the day. It played in the afternoon, and the delicious airs of Beethoven, Mozart, and Meyerbeer transported you in imagination far from the surrounding scenes.

About this time I witnessed a horrible sight. It appeared that some men of the 60th regiment had gone into a wood close by for the purpose of collecting fuel; one of them heard a groan, and upon searching, he discovered a soldier of the 3d voltigeurs, who had been wounded in the action of the 18th. His foot had been nearly carried away by a bit of shell, and, to protect himself and lay *perdu*, he had managed to crawl into the wood. He had eaten all the food he had in his pocket, as well as bits of leather straps, all the time suffering the most intense agony from his wound, and had positively existed in this state for seven days. When I saw him he was a perfect skeleton, although, to all appearance, suffering no pain whatsoever.

The 2d, 4th, 7th, and 8th army corps still occupied the same position in front of Metz up to the 24th of August. By the 26th the blockade of Metz was fairly completed, and the devoted city was entirely surrounded by a cordon of troops. And now commenced a series of manœuvres which has thrown a new light upon modern warfare. The sieges of Metz and of Paris have taught us that against the artillery of the present day no fortified town has any chance of resistance, unless protected by detached forts. The melancholy remains of Soissons, Verdun, and Peronne too surely attest to the truth of this assertion, and we learn that a town commanded by eminences at three English miles is uselessly defended unless protected by detached fortifications at some distance from the body of the works.

Now too commenced the hard work, the dull, uninteresting, wearying duty of outpost in front of a large army enclosed in a fortified city. There is, perhaps, no duty so onerous or so exciting to the soldier as outpost work in front of a vigilant and active enemy. The dull routine of camp life goes on from day to day devoid of anything interesting, except the eager search after daily subsistence, and the proud moment when anything approaching to a meal is safely secured. I say 'safely secured,' because it was not by any means improbable that the forager would be lightened of his load by some hungry party of half-starved soldiers on his way back to camp, who asked for bread with that sort of not-to-be-denied look which meant that they wore sword bayonets, and were likely to use them.

On one occasion the 2d battalion of the 33d fusiliers furnishing the outposts of the 8th army corps, I determined to avail myself of the opportunity, and see for myself the system upon which they worked. To do this I must quote from my diary.

'Just as the gray dawn was breaking, the adjutant roused me from my bed of straw, and after washing in a cooking pot, and putting a fresh lot of bullets in my revolver, I repaired to the head-quarters of the regiment. I have already told you their severe loss. I need hardly relate what were my feelings upon joining them once more in the service of danger, the last time being when we went into action on the 18th, and attacked the French at St. Hubert. The head-quarters of the regiment were now, as indeed they always were, at the tent of the colonel. There too was he, much the same as ever, clean-shaved, well-dressed, a bright and polished gentleman; and if a sad expression flitted from time to time across his features, it is scarcely to be wondered at, seeing that not a single field officer was there to take his orders, that captains commanded battalions, and subalterns companies. Meantime, hot coffee has been made, and we partake of it with gusto, grateful for the warmth that keeps the chill air of dawn out of our ill-clad bodies. I always imagined that this place enjoyed a mild climate; but the intense cold of the last few days made me think that, after all, there are other countries in the world besides England which have cause to complain.

'The battalion is formed up in quarter-distance column of companies; the word is given, "Right section, to the front; remainder, left shoulders forward," and we leave the camp for at least twenty-four hours, some never to return. The outposts in front of Metz were from a mile to a mile and a half distant from the camps, those of the 8th army corps occupying a position from the left of Malmaison to the right of the village of Rozerieulles. This village was at one time occupied by the French, and at others by the Prussians, being at all times within easy range of the French guns upon Mont St. Quentin. All along the ridge facing the French works, between which and the Prussian position there was a deep ravine, the latter had strengthened themselves by throwing up small earthworks and rifle-pits, together with some batteries.

'On a spur of the ridge which advanced considerably into the plain above Rozerieulles on the Prussian side, was the most exposed outpost. The battalion marched to that portion of the road where you get the first view of the valley of the Moselle, with Metz nestling, as it were, in its bosom. The point where the regiment halted to tell off the outposts was one which afforded a grand view of the principal positions occupied by the contending armies. To our left front, situated upon a lofty eminence, frowned the batteries of Mont St. Quentin, about two miles distant, whilst the slopes of the work itself and the hillsides were covered with busy workmen in red trousers. As the steep ascent met the plain of the Moselle, two little villages raised their red-tiled roofs above the luxuriant foliage with which they were surrounded—these were Moulins-les-Metz and St. Ruffine. Carrying the eye farther still, the first object that attracted your attention was the fine old cathedral, situated nearly in the centre of the town; then came the Hôtel de Ville, the melancholy white flag with its red cross flying over it, and then the beautiful bridges over the Moselle. On the slope above the cathedral a crowd of tents showed the situation of a large camp, whilst away to the right stretched the now devastated valley of the Moselle. It was a magnificent panorama, to which the haze of an autumn morning lent a sort of dissolving-view appearance, as the breeze scattered the mists from different points, revealing new landscapes almost every moment. In the foreground, deep down in the ravine at our feet, lay the village of Rozerieulles, the continual bone of contention between the French and Prussian outposts, whilst the clink of the shovel on every side told that the Prussians had taken to the defensive.

'By the time I had noted all this, the battalion had separated to their different posts, and I took my way with the officer in command to the spur of the hill I have already mentioned. When we got to the outpost I found that a small wood just fringing the edge of the spur concealed us from view, and that to our left a stone quarry made a comfortable sort of shelter. Into this stone quarry we descended, two bundles of straw making it sufficiently comfortable. After settling down a little and getting my traps in order, I took my glass and climbed one of the trees close by, from which I got a capital view of what was going on round about. I could see the French advanced sentries and our own, although I could not make out the exact position of their outposts. I could see the soldiers in Metz bathing in the Moselle, and the cavalry patrols going their rounds. I could also see the tramways moving up and down from Mont St. Quentin, carrying what appeared to be stones to strengthen the works, or make fresh ones.

'Whilst looking at these things with considerable interest, the sharp report of the chassepot, followed by the ping of a bullet to the left, made me turn my glass in that direction, and I saw a small patrol of the king's hussars cantering away towards Malmaison with one empty saddle. I found out afterwards that it was unfortunately the officer commanding the patrol, who had ventured somewhat too near the French works, and had been shot through the head. Poor fellow! he was an only son, and the head of an old family. In order to illustrate the fearful range of a chassepot bullet, I may say that Captain von Loè, the officer in question, dropped from his saddle, the men thinking he had swooned, as they none of them *heard any report*, so far off was the man who fired. I also am intimately acquainted with an officer who was wounded three times consecutively, and had never *seen* a French soldier.

'About eleven A.M. breakfast was brought, consisting of black bread, pork, some potatoes, and a bottle of wine; and down we sat in the quarry to a not very tempting meal. The French, however, were determined we should not enjoy it peaceably; for scarcely had I got a piece of bread into my mouth, when the report of a gun, followed by the whistling of a shell, made me scramble to my feet. Bang it went, bursting in the air some hundred yards short of our party. About a minute after came another, this time going clean over us. I now scrambled out of the quarry, and made for a tree just in time; for a shell dropped right into the quarry we were sitting in, and burying itself in the straw, exploded in the midst of the officers. Of course I expected to see nothing but their dead bodies; so you may judge of my surprise when I heard a hearty laugh from the officer in command. Not exactly comprehending how the bursting of a shell could have caused so much merriment, I hastened to ascertain the cause, and I must confess the scene was sufficiently ludicrous. The shell had exploded in their midst, without touching one of them, but it had blackened their faces as though they had been so many Christy minstrels. One young subaltern still remained flat on his stomach, a piece of pork in one hand and a bottle of wine in the other; an old lieutenant was cursing the ill-luck that had broken the cherished china bowl of his pipe; whilst the captain in command was endeavouring to wipe the powder out of his eyes. The French now commenced shelling in earnest; so much so, that we were forced to seek some other shelter, unfortunately not before we had lost six men killed and two wounded. After about half an hour they stopped, and we returned to our quarry.

'The rest of the day was passed much in the same

way until the evening, when I went into camp to get something hot if possible, no fires being allowed on outpost duty. When I got to the colonel's quarters, I found great rejoicings over a tin of potted salmon and a box of sardines that had just been discovered in some Marketender's wagon, and after a hearty meal I returned to the outposts just as the sun was setting. On my way I met about 100 men in the uniforms of various hussar, lancer, and cuirassier regiments, without arms or horses, and looking in a most dilapidated state. Upon questioning them, I found that they had been prisoners in the hands of the French, but that, there being next to nothing to eat in Metz, they had been turned out to shift for themselves. This did not seem to tally with the accounts the correspondents of the *Times* and other papers gave of the provisioning of Metz.

'On reaching the outposts, I found that an order had been received to occupy the village of Rozerieulles during the night, for the purpose of making a requisition for wine and spirits. This was certainly more entertaining than going the round of sentries in the dark, with the chance of a bullet through your body. Accordingly, as soon as it was dark, we marched down the steep road leading to the village, with an advance guard thrown well forward. We gained the village without any interruption, and marched through it, posting a strong guard and double sentries on the side nearest to the enemy. The next thing was to find what we had come for, and for this purpose the quarters of Monsieur le Curé were at once beat up. At first the worthy man pretended to understand nothing, and declared positively, by all the saints, that he could not speak a word of German; but when it was put to him, through my interpretation, that if he did not at once show the way to his cellar the house would be set on fire, he immediately got a lantern and preceded us down some very slippery steps, where we discovered two large casks of very fair *vin du pays*. After this the holy man's larder was ransacked, and a first-rate supper of bread, cheese, and cold chicken put us all in good humour. The curé, I suppose, got accustomed to the situation; for after a time he joined us in his own wine, and became quite communicative.

'During the night nothing occurred, with the exception of a sufficiently ridiculous circumstance. A loose horse had made his way over from the French lines, and, being anxious to get into the village, he had trotted round and round without success. The night being dark, the sentries fancied that it was a French patrol, and continually challenged, but of course received no answer. At an early hour this morning we were relieved and marched back into camp, where, on our arrival, we heard the news that the French had endeavoured to cut their way out of Metz through the investing forces on the right bank, but without success. The Prussians lost 500 men.'

The foregoing extract sufficiently illustrates the sort of daily routine that characterised the long weary duty round the capital of Lorraine. But whilst on this subject, I cannot leave it without a few words as to the Prussian method of detailing and working outposts, not in front of an enemy in an open country, but in front of an army shut up in a blockaded city.

In the Prussian service a company furnishes three or more piquets or posts of from thirty to forty men each; the remainder of the company is the support: the second company of the battalion furnishes the piquets on the right or left, and the remaining two companies of the battalion form the reserve. The employment of cavalry and infantry on outpost duties before Metz was as follows: Outposts were formed of the brigades told off for keeping the line of circumvallation, and were composed of one or more arms, according to circumstances and the nature of the ground. Cavalry, being particularly well adapted to watch this kind of ground by day, if judiciously posted, was always employed. Infantry, being more suitable for night duty and for ground that was impracticable or dangerous for cavalry, relieved these at nightfall. In foggy weather and on clear nights the duty was performed by a combination of the two arms, the cavalry being able to keep up communication more quickly. The business of the cavalry was to watch in the distance and reconnoitre, giving information of any attempt at a sortie. Artillery was never employed on outpost service, except on special occasions, and there being but little or no water to protect; beyond the ordinary duty they were never employed, except in case of a sortie.

The rules to be observed by the officers commanding the piquets supplied from the outposts were as follows:

1. On the least alarm to get as quickly as possible under arms, without noise or talking of any kind.

2. The lighting of a fire or smoking to be regulated according to circumstances and the judgment of the officer in command.

3. No one to leave the post without special leave, and the men to sleep in turns, with their knapsacks on.

4. If cavalry, never to be unsaddled; no compliments to be paid by the sentries.

5. The sentries always to be double, and when attacked by an enemy's patrol, to form into skirmishing order, and if pressed fall back upon the supports.

6. A patrol should keep up a continual communication with the sentries, the piquet, the support, and the main body of the support.

7. The piquet to be relieved before daybreak.

Finally, reserves for the support and reinforcement of the piquets should be handy. They should be placed at cross roads and always under cover. They will mount by day or night, according to circumstances.

One sentry is placed over the arms, and look-out sentries are placed at suitable places. Constant communication is kept up with the main body of the outposts and piquets by patrols. A regiment furnishes the outposts for three days, but at Metz they were relieved every week only by brigades. Thus the duties, although arduous, were simple, practical, easily understood, and combined safety with the greatest comfort that could be permitted to the men.

Referring to my letter to the *Daily Telegraph*, I find that portions of the country in the neighbourhood of Metz about this time, and a further detail of the miseries in Gorze, are thus described:

'*Pont-à-Mousson, August 28.*

'So many rumours had reached the camp within the last twenty-four hours, that I determined to ascertain, if possible, their correctness. The difficulty of doing so is something indescribable, inasmuch as, each *corps d'armée* being utterly isolated, and the telegraph and posts kept rigorously closed, except for the transmission of telegrams from the higher military powers, and of letters through the Feld-post, one is entirely dependent upon the information brought by new comers. This was of so unsatisfactory and inconsistent a character, that I ordered my horse to be ready in the evening, and decided to ride to Pont-à-Mousson—the "key to France" in the present war. Before I left the besieging army two events occurred, one of considerable importance. The first was the sudden orders received by the 3d army corps at once to march to Verdun; and the other the taking of a French work before Metz by the 7th army corps, with the loss of 250 killed and wounded. It was the precipitate removal of the 3d army corps that chiefly influenced me, for it tallied with the reports I had heard of a Prussian reverse in the neighbourhood of Commercy.

'Accordingly, I started from camp on the 27th, at about 11 A.M., arriving at Gorze at twelve. How shall I describe to you the state of misery in this little town! for, in addition to the starvation of its population, they are, as I expected, afflicted with two fearful diseases—cholera and typhus fever. This has arisen from the quantities of wounded who still remain there, and whose miserable state taints the atmosphere, together with the badly-buried dead on the plateau above the town. Men, women, and children clung to my knees, begging for a morsel of bread; haggard-looking doctors stalked about the streets, doing their work almost mechanically. So fearful was the state of things, that I was only too glad to get out of the town as soon as possible.

'Towards evening I arrived at the village of Pagny-sur-Moselle, where the same state of things, with the exception of sickness, existed. I called upon the mayor, who, after he knew who I was, at once invited me into his house, and paid me the greatest civility. I am happy to say that, while I was there, I was the means of protecting him and his family from insult. Whilst we were at supper, a Prussian soldier belonging to the 7th army corps knocked at the gate; when it was opened, he walked into the house, and desired to speak to the mayor. Accordingly the mayor went down, and, after about five minutes' time, a maid came rushing into the room to say that the soldier was going to shoot her master. I endeavoured to calm the wife's fears, and proceeded downstairs into the kitchen, where a sufficiently curious scene presented itself. The soldier—a coarse brutal-looking fellow—stood with his back to the fireplace, a drawn sword in one hand and a pistol in the other.

On the kitchen-table sat M. le Maire, smoking a cigarette, whilst the rest of the domestics were huddled into a corner.

'Upon my entrance, the soldier turned his pistol upon me, and demanded who I was. My answer was brief—that I was an English officer attached to General von Göben's head-quarters, on my way to the King's head-quarters; that he should at once put up his sword, and lay his pistol down on the table; and farther, that he should stand aside, and remain silent until I asked him to speak. The man, being a bully, was at once cowed, and left the kitchen, remaining in the hall until I called him in. The mayor then stated that he had come with a requisition for two pigs, or a pig and a cow; that he had procured him the two pigs; but that he was not content, and required him to produce six sheep and some wine, and a dinner for himself. This the mayor told him was impossible, inasmuch as there was no such thing in the village; if he doubted what he said, he might search for himself. The man then drew a pistol, told him he would give him ten minutes to produce his dinner, and twenty minutes to find the sheep, and that if they were not forthcoming, he should shoot him through the head.'

Such was the common state of things in all the villages, although I must confess I had never before seen such conduct on the part of any Prussian soldier. On the contrary, their requisitions were made, especially by the officers, in as quiet and inoffensive a manner as it was possible to perform such a duty;

but the Prussian army was in great want of provisions, and France must find them. During the time I spent at Pagny no less than forty unfortunate peasants came to beg for bread, as they were starving. The "commune" could not receive them; money would not buy what existed no longer — bread and meat. Their cattle have been slaughtered before their doors, their horses taken into requisition, their barns pillaged of corn and hay, their poultry killed in the streets, and their gardens ravaged until there was nothing left.

The state of things at Pont-à-Mousson is thus described:

'I arrived at Pont-à-Mousson at about 4 P.M., and had the good fortune to meet the Grand Duke of Oldenburg and his staff, on their way to join the 10th army corps before Metz. We put up at the Hôtel de France, where everything seemed to me to be a luxury. In the first place, I got a bedroom to myself; secondly, I absolutely found clean sheets on the bed, and could undress myself; and lastly, I was asked what I should like for dinner. The question seemed to me so ludicrous, that I burst out laughing, much to the astonishment of the *garçon*. Pont-à-Mousson is in a strange state of ferment. The French portion of the community have it that Marshals M'Mahon and Canrobert surprised a Prussian army corps that were besieging Toul, a fortified town near Commercy, and completely routed them, killing 15,000 men; whilst the Prussians declare that Toul was never besieged, although they do not deny the fact of an action. That the French have thrown themselves between the Prussians and Paris is almost a certainty; for an action took place yesterday at the village of Chambord, in the neighbourhood of Châlons, which neither side denies. Had the Prussians gained a victory, the town would have been placarded; but the hasty march of the 3d army corps from Metz has left the impression on my mind that the Prussian arms have sustained a reverse.

'Whilst at dinner, there was an arrival which took us somewhat by surprise—no less a personage than Madame Pauline Lucca, whose husband is an officer of the 62d regiment. He had been wounded, and his wife had come to look after him, lucky fellow! There are many such, unable to move from their beds of pain to the comforts and care of their homes.

'The Grand Duke received a telegram in the course of the evening; and if I am to believe what his servant tells me, "the war is at an end." He informed me M. Thiers was at the head of the French ministry, and that the war was virtually over. This I have put down as another shave. Whilst smoking a cigar on the Place after dinner, I saw a battalion of Garde Mobile, 850 strong, marched in under an escort. The men were dressed in blouses, wearing no uniform at all. They were, however, all armed with breech-loading rifles of some sort, though of what pattern it was impossible for me to ascertain. This valiant body of defenders of their country had been taken by two squadrons of dragoons without firing a shot, the officers being in the uniform of the French line. Intelligence has just arrived that the French and Prussians are fighting at Metz. I shall therefore return to camp as soon as my horses are rested.

'I was very much amused with two old English newspapers which I picked up here, but I shall refrain from mentioning their names. The Special Correspondents seem to have a wonderful talent for the imaginative, inasmuch as they create armies and divisions that do not exist; they have made movements to the right, movements to the left, and have carefully inverted the position of two army corps. According to their account, the 8th army corps has been in two actions which I have not had the honour of seeing, and which must have taken place when I was asleep, as I have never left the head-quarters of that corps for twenty-four hours since the 1st of August. The fact is, that some of these gentlemen are compelled to obtain their information from any one who may happen to come to the rear; some have their credulity preyed upon by young officers, who think it a good joke to tell "the Special" a lie, whilst others good-naturedly try to do their best by telling him what they have heard. I would recommend these gentlemen to be truthful as to the behaviour of Prussian officers and soldiers, if they wish to return to England with their ears on their heads; for although in so large an army some exceptions must be found, the Prussians, in the way of discipline and good conduct, are inferior to none. If these gentlemen are unable to get to the front, which I know is impossible unless they are British officers, they should be careful how they attempt to relate certain atrocities of which the Prussian army is utterly incapable. If they get to the front, they do so at their own peril; and if discovered to be correspondents, they will bitterly repent the day when, not certain of their information, they put their pens to paper. The Prussian army, beaten or victorious, looks only for justice and truth, and people who know nothing of military matters should not attempt to write about them.'

The King's head-quarters were now at Commercy, where it was believed he would remain. The weather was abominable—cold and heavy rain, the worst enemy the Prussian army had to contend against; and if the war was not definitely settled one way or another, it was impossible to see how the troops were to last against such violent exposure. Some of them had now slept for three weeks on the wet ground, in potato-fields or under hedges. They had no blankets—nothing but their cloaks, and, up till then, some straw; the scarcity of forage, however, denied them even this luxury. Disease was beginning to make itself felt, and it was hard to think that the survivors of Spiecheren, Colombey, Mars-la-Tour, and Gravelotte should succumb to such an enemy.

On the 30th of August I again wrote, describing the movements of the German army before Metz, in the following words:

'As I was leaving Pont-à-Mousson, I met another batch of Gardes Mobiles, 185 in number, who were being marched into the town as prisoners, their arms packed in a couple of country carts, and under the escort of a troop of Landwehr hussars. Surely these cannot be the descendants of those peasants of Lorraine who in 1814 threw themselves into Metz, Thionville, and Verdun, and withstood the repeated assaults of the Prussian troops with success? If so, either the peasantry of France care no longer for their hearths and homes, or they prefer Prussian rule to the present state of affairs. In passing through Pagny on my way back to Metz, I was subjected to a somewhat severe cross-examination by a smooth-shaven, oily-tongued priest, who did everything in his power to obtain information as to the position and number of the Prussian troops around Metz. So disagreeable became his importunities, that I was at length forced to inform him that I could not possibly conceive how one of his cloth could expect an answer to his questions from a person in my position.

'As I was passing through the village of Novéant, I met some heavy ordnance, that will, no doubt, shortly open upon the town of Metz, and a little farther a train of Hessian artillery. The unfortunate horses are now beginning to suffer severely, the heavy fall of rain of the last two days having made the roads in a fearful state. Yesterday one battery lost sixteen horses. These troops (Hessian) are by no means so well horsed as the Prussian artillery, for they are altogether smaller and less serviceable-looking animals. The horses everywhere are suffering dreadfully from mud-fever, in addition to the usual casualties of wrung withers and sore backs. What will become of them in ten days' time?

'On my arrival in camp, I found that two army corps instead of one had been sent to reinforce the Crown Prince. In consequence of the weather nearly everybody was suffering from dysentery, while here and there was a case of cholera. The spirits of the troops were by no means good, the inactivity of the last few days, varied only by working parties and outpost duty, being far from conducive to happiness, and the camp one sea of mud, through which you waded your way with difficulty. Head-quarters were established in the only habitable room of a house which had been occupied by the French on the 18th, and had consequently suffered severely from shells. I arrived just in time to hear the news of what had been going on during my absence. Our supper I need not describe; but it was an unusually good one, as I had supplied my saddle-bags pretty well before leaving Pagny, a bottle of punch-essence furnishing us with something wherewith to wet the after-dinner pipe, and a candle stuck in a bottle giving us all necessary light.

'It appeared that on the 28th the French made a sortie in force along the valley of the Moselle, in the direction of Thionville. A division was supposed to have cut their way through, but the remainder were obliged to retire once more into Metz. There had been some affairs of outposts, but no news of the Crown Prince. At an early hour two soldiers came in, spread the room with straw, and put the table out of the window. Nine of us then rolled ourselves in our cloaks, and disposed our wearied bodies as well as we could. Just as daylight was breaking an officer woke us up with the pleasing intelligence that all our forage would be sent on at once to the Crown Prince.'

On the 31st of August I again wrote as follows:

'At an early hour I rode to the front, to see if anything had taken place during my absence. I found the works thrown up to protect the 8th army corps complete, and a battery to the right of the road to Metz, towards Mont St. Quentin, in a fair way towards completion. It is needless to say that it is not the intention of the Prussian army to place any siege guns, or rather guns of heavy calibre, on this side. This battery will, however, be a sort of check upon the guns of Mont St. Quentin, and will protect the patrols entering the villages at the base of the mountain—viz. Rozerieulles, Sey, Longeville, and St. Ruffine.

'Whilst reconnoitring the former works a somewhat interesting outpost affair, between a patrol of the 60th regiment and some French chasseurs, took place close to Rozerieulles. The French chasseurs lined a vineyard just outside the village of Longeau, whilst the patrol of the 60th regiment were posted about the gardens of Rozerieulles. The chasseurs had evidently stolen a march upon the Prussian patrol, for the first three shots killed one man and wounded two others. This loss was, however, quickly repaired by the sergeant of the Prussian patrol, who had wormed himself into a place where the walls of two vineyards joined; a convenient hole gave him his opportunity, which he did not fail to use. The first shot wounded the officer in command, the second killed a soldier who was in the act of taking aim, and the third wounded another. At the distance they were shooting—some 500 yards—the needle is infinitely superior to the chassepot; but from 600 to 1000 and 1200 yards the chassepot is the better weapon. I make this assertion fearlessly, inasmuch as I am convinced every Prussian officer will bear me out. At short distances the trajectory of the chassepot is too high; the bullets go over your head. For instance, at the battle of Mars-la-Tour I lay in a small gravel-pit about 400 yards from a battalion of the Garde Impérial, almost every shot went over the Prussian infantry, about one in fifty taking effect. After hammering away at one another for about an hour, the French patrol withdrew, and the Prussians reëntered the village of Rozerieulles.

'I then rode to the left of the line of outposts, where I found that the village of Lessy, hitherto unoccupied by the French, was now held by a strong force. The Jägers of the 8th battalion had stolen through a wood to the left of Châtel, an outpost occupied by the 28th regiment, within 500 yards of a double French outpost; the Jägers, being protected by a wood, could see the French soldiers chatting and smoking their pipes, apparently quite unconscious of their proximity. The major in command was anxious to obtain leave to try and cut them out; but, fortunately for him, I had my telescope with me, and I pointed out two guns some 1200 yards off, posted evidently in case of an advance out of the wood. The officers of the Prussian artillery and engineers are very ill-supplied with field-glasses—the majority of them have none at all; whilst the other arms of the service trust mostly to their eye-sight, which, as a rule, is anything but good, for in a regiment you will probably see from ten to a dozen officers who wear glasses.

'Some better arrangements have lately been adopted for the preservation of health. The men who are told off for working parties are not permitted to drink water, but each has a portion of cooked wine or hot spirits-and-water served out to him on his marching out and on his return; he has also a ration of properly cooked meat *without potatoes* prepared; and these wise arrangements have done much towards reducing the rapidly increasing sick reports.'

On my return to camp I found that orders had arrived from the Crown Prince to the effect that 4000 wagons should be dispatched daily for the maintenance of his army. Where the provisions were to come from was a thing which no one knew. The country for miles round was quite destitute; but the Rhine provinces supplied the necessary provisions by means of the railroad opened to Ars-sur-Moselle. So little had the Prince in the way of provisions, that he was forced to send one army corps to the rear.

I got some German newspapers to read one afternoon; in one, the *Kölnische Zeitung* of the 23d, I perceived a gross misstatement respecting the battle of Gravelotte. It said that the 33d regiment, after taking St. Hubert, the hamlet to the left of Malmaison, was driven out by the French, and that the 8th Jägers came up and retook it. This is a gross injustice to a fine regiment: for from the advance of the brigade behind Gravelotte to the end of the action they never retired one step. The 8th Jägers were, however, guilty of unpardonable stupidity; for they absolutely fired upon the 33d regiment, who were far in advance, supposing them to be French. So much for the veracity of correspondents who trust to hearsay for their information.

I had a long conversation with the head doctor in charge of the wounded at Gravelotte. He informed me, that in no war upon record had the wounded recovered so rapidly and been able to return to their duty. This he accounted for by the very small and clean wounds that the chassepot bullet inflicts. In nine cases out of twelve where the bullet had touched a bone, it had been diverted from its course, and had taken a diagonal direction. A splintered bone was a case of rare occurrence. On the other hand, the needle bullet made a fearful wound, and the Prussian shells, cased as they were with lead to take the grooves, still worse.

A letter from Marshal Bazaine, commanding the French army in Metz, fell into the hands of the Prussians. It was addressed to his wife, and is sufficiently interesting. In it he said: "As far as I am concerned, I shall await the course of events. My army is entirely with me; and as soon as Napoleon shall have been dealt with as he deserves, I shall be prepared to disclose certain propositions which he has made to me that will at once place me in a proper position with the new Government." So much for French gratitude.

The state of affairs at this moment was one that was not a little puzzling. The Prussian army surrounding Metz were prepared to bombard it and if necessary reduce it to a heap of ruins. They knew that the French army, in number some 160,000, were dying of disease and hunger, that typhus and cholera were raging in the town; and yet the army corps lay perfectly inactive around, not a single gun in position. Add to this, the curious inactivity of the army of the Crown Prince, who, it was said, was doing well, but in great want of provisions, and there was grave food for thought. Was it that diplomacy, that procrastinator of everything, had commenced to exert its influence, and that soldiers were to starve to death or die of disease, whilst politicians quibbled over the stops of a sentence or the phraseology of a paragraph? or was the world not yet content with the carnage of the last five weeks?

Bazaine's extraordinary conduct with regard to his transactions at Metz remains still unexplained; but I venture to assert that no one who followed the blockade of Metz step by step, and saw the magnificent army that marched out of it as prisoners of war, can entertain other than one opinion. The French army that surrendered at Metz was numerically stronger than that of the Prussians: it is useless to argue that they were rendered unserviceable from disease and want; because the answer to that is, Why were they ever exposed to it? Had the same number of Prussian or English troops been placed in a like position, there can be but little doubt that they would have cut their way through—with loss perhaps, but to a certainty; and the opinion of every one conversant with the question is, that the finest army in the world was sacrificed to the intrigues of a grasping soldier of fortune.

Meanwhile the blockade continued until the 28th of August, when Bazaine made an attempt to break out. In my letter of the 2d of September it is thus described:

'*Vaux, September 2.*

'The day before yesterday, the 31st ult., I was aroused by heavy firing in the direction of Grigy, on the other side of the Moselle. I swallowed a cup of coffee, and by the time I reached the advanced post opposite Mont St. Quentin, the action going on to the east of Metz seemed to have become general. The heavy roar of the Metz guns, together with the incessant rattle of the mitrailleuse, told me that something more than an affair of outposts was going on; accordingly, without waiting to take writing materials, I rode off, intending to cross the Moselle at Ars, in the hope of being in time to see some of the engagement. As I galloped across the bridge at Ars, an officer of the 13th, who had charge of the piquet, warned me to keep to the right, as the French piquets on the road between Metz and Nancy had been considerably advanced, and they shot indiscriminately at civilians or men in uniform—especially at those who were mounted.

'After crossing the river I took, as I thought, a road which would bring me to the right of Marly *viâ* Augny, and immediately upon General Manteuffel's army corps, whose head-quarters were at St. Barbe; but after getting into the valley of the Moselle, I found that it was covered with a dense white mist, and that I could scarcely see a hundred yards ahead. Whilst deliberating what I should do, a couple of peasants came out of a ditch, and advanced in the most suspicious way towards me. I at once made up my mind, and riding straight at them, with my revolver in my hand, I asked the road to Augny in a manner not be denied. Whether they were scared, and took little heed of what they were saying, I know not; but after advancing upon the road they had directed me for about a quarter of a mile, I found myself face to face with a piquet of the Vosges tirailleurs in their gray blouses and black felt hats. If it had not been a misty morning, my correspondence would then and there have been brought to a summary conclusion; but, thank Providence, the distance deceived them, and three bullets whistled harmlessly over my head, followed by three or four more. I then recollected the position of the farm-house where this piquet was posted, and at once turned my horse sharp to the right, and after two hours' hard riding, I arrived upon the scene of action.

'For some little time the mist and smoke from the guns wrapped the conflicting armies in an impenetrable shroud; but as the sun came out, the wind rose, and, the dense smoke being swept away, the position of the Prussians first became visible. The 1st army corps, with the 10th army corps, were briskly engaged with the French, who had taken up a position with their left resting on the fort and suburb of St. Julien, whilst their right occupied the ground between the railroad to Thionville and an earthwork thrown up outside Grigy. The Prussians held a position above the last-mentioned places, General Manteuffel's army corps being opposed to the French right, while the 10th army corps, with whom was Prince Friedrich Carl, was engaged with their centre and left. As yet the action had been confined to artillery fire, and a portion of St. Julien was in flames; but shortly after my arrival the French skirmishers came on in a perfect cloud, and occupied a small hamlet in the centre of their right attack. Against these the Prussians sent a regiment of infantry and a battalion of Jägers, and the fire became hot, though at a somewhat wide range. After about two hours of this work the Prussian cavalry made a feint, as if to cut off the French skirmishers; but they were quickly withdrawn, being somewhat severely handled by the French artillery, who shelled them most unmercifully. The Prussian cavalry were so anxious to come into contact and try conclusions with the French, that they occasionally exposed themselves unnecessarily and injudiciously.

'Whilst this was taking place on the right, the French left had retired from their first position, and had taken up a fresh one nearer Metz, the 10th army corps having advanced a mass of troops and overwhelmed them by sheer numbers. It was quite impossible at this moment to see anything farther in this direction, for the heavy guns in the work of St. Julien now opened upon the Prussians, and covered everything with smoke. Meantime the action was carried on briskly in the neighbourhood of the Prussian left centre, neither of the armies moving an inch, and the guns incessantly belching forth a perfect hurricane of shells, the French bursting in the air, the Prussians on the ground; and so the fight continued until neither party could see. The Prussian loss was considerable, but not so large as it might have been, in consequence of the action being confined more to artillery than anything else. In the evening the Prussians retired to a position on some rising ground behind a line of woods. The French bivouacked on the field. It was evidently the intention of the French to endeavour to force the Prussian army of blockade, in order to make good their retreat towards Thionville, and relieve Metz of the fearful pressure which so large a body of troops was upon its resources.

'The night that was passed was anything but agreeable. The troops slept upon their arms, the outlying piquets were doubled, while cavalry patrols kept moving about the whole night. Through the kindness of a major of hussars, I got half a bundle of straw and a blanket, together with some ham, bread, and schnapps; but sleep was out of the question; nor were fires permitted. With the first gray of the morning the piquets commenced a desultory sort of popping at one another, which gradually increased to a smart fire of musketry at six o'clock. The artillery on both sides opened, and the ground in front of St. Julien was again the Houguemont of the position. So determined were the French on this point, that the Grand Duke of Mecklenburg's division was moved up, and succeeded in driving the French troops back into Metz, after four hours' heavy firing on both sides, Metz joining in with the guns of the fortifications.

'As soon as I could, I started back to the head-quarters of the 8th army corps, as I had brought no writing materials nor anything else with me; but when I arrived at Ars, I found that entirely new arrangements had been made. The 8th army corps had been sent to reinforce the troops engaged yesterday, and the 15th division of the 8th army corps had taken up their position with their head-quarters at the small village of Vaux, a somewhat more amusing place than the muddy plateau where we had sojourned so long. The village from which I write this is one of the most advanced posts of the Prussian army on this side of Metz, the houses being not more than 1,500 yards from the French outposts, who, I find, are taken by my friends the Vosges tirailleurs. The Prussian officers made a somewhat curious mistake about these same troops; for when they first saw them they took them to be French peasants, and were highly incensed at their conduct, swearing that if they got into their village, they would make them pay for firing upon Prussian troops.

'I found our head-quarters comfortably settled in

a château surrounded by a lovely garden, and commanding a beautiful view of Metz and the valley of the Moselle. The officers were perfectly wild with the idea of spending even a few days in, to them, such a paradise, after twenty-eight nights' bivouac in the open. The château is the property of Colonel Viville, a French officer of distinction, who has left as *locum tenens* his servant, a curious specimen in his way. He accompanied his master to the Crimea, where he succeeded in quarrelling with every officer in the regiment, and eventually lost his leg in the attack on the Malakoff. Having to wait upon Prussian officers has not served to improve his temper. He is, however, an excellent cook; and when I told him I was an Englishman, he produced a bottle of Château d'Yquem for my special drinking, upon the understanding that I was not to breathe a word of it to those "coquins de Prussiens."

'The general has just come in with a French officer, and has asked me to interpret. The officer is on General Bazaine's staff, and has come from Metz with a flag of truce to ask for medical assistance from the Prussians. His account of the fearful state of Metz from typhus fever is perfectly horrible. He says that, from the immense quantity of wounded that were lying in the hospitals, and the large number of dead horses and other pestilential matter, typhus of a very malignant character has broken out; provisions being short, the troops have not a sufficiency of nourishment to combat against the attacks of so fearful a disease, and the French medical men being almost all of them laid up, there are not enough to attend upon the wounded and sick Prussian prisoners. To this request the general returned an unfavourable answer. He said he was sorry to be utterly unable to grant such a request; for not only were the Prussian medical men fully employed, but, even if there were any at liberty, he could not take upon himself such a responsibility without the consent of his Majesty, whose quarters were at Bar-le-Duc. The chagrin depicted on the poor fellow's face when he got his answer was quite pitiable; he seemed half starved himself, and swallowed the tumbler of bad wine I poured out for him as if it were nectar. "Sir," said he, as he shook me by the hand, "this is a sad state of things; but the time is coming when we shall be able to teach these relentless men that we are fighting in the nineteenth century. Were the English our opponents, we should perhaps have received a more humane answer."

'I must confess that I think something might have been done, inasmuch as the French sent an ambulance corps out of Metz to Gravelotte, to attend upon their wounded and sick, at the request of the Prussians, and the much-vaunted Juanita corps, or volunteers to nurse the sick, are here in large numbers—in fact, wherever you go, you cannot move about without seeing the well-known red cross on a white band. When I was in Pont-à-Mousson, about four days ago, the cafés were full of them, where playing cards and drinking beer seemed to be their principal employment.

'A telegraphic despatch has just been received from the Crown Prince, in the neighbourhood of

Châlons, giving the news of a victory over General M'Mahon, who, report says, is retreating in the direction of the Belgian frontier.

'*September* 3.

'We had all of us made up our minds to a pleasant sojourn in this neighbourhood, when, to our utter astonishment, the 7th army corps marched back again yesterday evening, and an order came for the 8th army corps to return to their old quarters, the muddy plateau above Gravelotte. It appears that the French have once more retired into Metz, finding the opposition to their forcing their way through the Prussian lines in the neighbourhood of St. Julien a matter of no little difficulty. Accordingly, this morning the 15th division marched out of Vaux, and the 7th army reoccupies their old position. How long Metz is to last out I cannot comprehend; for it has been ascertained that they had provisions for fourteen days only, and to-day is the fifteenth day of the siege. I see a communication in the *Times*, asserting that the French had sent 600 sharpshooters into the mountains about Metz, for the purpose of picking off the Prussian officers. This is simply impossible, as all the mountains, with the exception of Mont St. Quentin, are and have been in the possession of the Prussians since the 22d of August. The French outposts are at Lessy, a village on the slope of Mont St. Quentin, at Sey, also on Mont St. Quentin; whilst the remainder are all in the valley around Metz.

'I am thankful to say that we have got rid of a great many wounded, which has improved the health

CHAPTER IV.

NEWS FROM SEDAN.

AFTER the action in the neighbourhood of St. Julien the blockade of Metz continued with the usual dull monotony that operations of that sort entail. The railway plied vigorously between Ars-sur-Moselle, Pont-à-Mousson, and Nancy, bringing fresh men, stores, and medical comforts. The town of Ars, if I may so call the collection of houses that are built, not very symmetrically, on the left bank of the Moselle, is an emporium of iron manufacture, and is surrounded by large ironworks; its population may be about 1,500, perhaps more, and in its most joyous days I should hardly think it could have been an engaging-looking place. Hitherto the troops that had occupied it, and its importance as a dépôt for stores, had made it to all intents and purposes lively; but on the 3d of September it was more than usually animated. The matter-of-fact, stolid air habitual to the Prussian soldier seemed to have forsaken him; several very stout sergeants were embracing one another in the most frantic manner; privates were throwing their caps into the air, and shouting like maniacs; Frenchmen were gathered together in little knots, talking quickly and gesticulating vehemently; hussars and mounted officers were galloping about in every direction. In fact, Ars seemed to be intoxicated.

At the Café du Lion d'Or, the principal inn in the place, General Barnakov, surrounded by a mob of officers and privates, was reading aloud from a paper. The following official bulletin from the King accounted for all this enthusiasm: 'This day, September 1st, in the neighbourhood of Sedan, Marshal M'Mahon has surrendered himself and the French army of 80,000 men to the Crown Prince. His Majesty the Emperor of the French has also given himself up as a prisoner of war.' The news was so perfectly staggering, that for some moments after hearing it, I sat like one stupefied, until a staff officer touched me on the shoulder, and asked me what I thought of it. The first exclamation that rose to my lips was concentrated in a word very expressive in our language, and I fear that I offended the officer much, for I simply answered, 'What a lie!' 'So I thought myself,' said he; 'but if you will take the trouble to come to the telegraph office, you can see the officer in charge, who will show you the despatch in cipher.' I acceded to his request, and, to my astonishment, found that the statement came from his Majesty the King, with orders to the generals to make it known to their troops. 'The war is over,' cried one. 'We shall see our wives and children,' said another. 'But Metz is not taken,' remarked a third. 'O, never mind; Bazaine will give in when he hears the news; besides, the Emperor has sent him orders to give it up.' This last, I suspect, was a little addition of his own.

When I entered the Lion d'Or the scene was indescribable; the place was crammed to suffocation, every one talking at once, every one calling for wine to celebrate the joyful intelligence. 'Sir,' said a gentleman, addressing himself to me in good English, 'I hear you are an English officer; what do you think of the news?' 'I think it is so extraordinary,' I answered, 'that I can hardly credit it. I can scarcely understand the Emperor having thrown himself upon the tender mercies of the King of Prussia.' 'The King of Germany, sir, you mean,' said he, interrupting me, 'for we are all Germans now.' I thanked him for his hint, and proceeded to add that the hard thing to believe was the fact of 80,000 French soldiers laying down their arms; it was a case without a parallel; and I certainly should await farther information.

The troops, as the news reached them, or was read to them by the generals of brigade, set up a shout that must have gone to the hearts of the wearied defenders of Metz; for miles round the hurrahs of thousands were borne upon the still evening air; staid generals and quietly-behaved colonels lost all self-command in the general delirium of joy that pervaded everybody and everything. The French inhabitants seemed to hail the intelligence as a deliverance from the oppressive burdens they had so long and so patiently borne;—their houses turned into barracks, and their larders supplying the wants of hungry soldiers. Poor creatures! Could one wonder that peace was to them a blessing—were it even bought at that costly and precious price so dear to Frenchmen, *la gloire de la grande nation?* There were some exceptions to this feeling; for instance, the man I lodged with was an old soldier who served through the Crimean and Mexican campaigns. He laughed at the rumour, and declared that to take 80,000 French soldiers you require an army of 500,000 or 600,000 men.

On the other hand, the position of the French army and the intercepted despatches of Marshal M'Mahon to General Bazaine in Metz must be taken into consideration. General von Moltke received the information through these intercepted despatches, that M'Mahon would manœuvre to get round to Metz by way of Sedan, and that Bazaine might expect him about the 28th of August; this accounts for the action of the 29th and 30th in the neighbourhood of St. Julien. General von Moltke, taking advantage of this, as indeed he never failed to do of every chance during the whole of the campaign, throws the Crown Prince of Saxony's corps upon the French right. The Crown Prince of Prussia takes ground to his own right flank, and throws himself between Metz and the French army, who are retreating on Sedan; the Saxons then advance, a battle takes place, and the French retire towards the Belgian frontier, with no hope of escape, except by cutting their way through two armies, or violating the neutrality of Belgium. Marshal M'Mahon was severely wounded, and, I concluded, lost all hope of retrieving his losses. Still, an army of 80,000 men, with plenty of ammunition, and with the fortified town of Sedan to support them, ought to have done something better than lay down their arms like a flock of sheep. I had the greatest contempt for the French generals; but I had the most profound respect for the French soldiers.

At seven P.M. on the evening of the 2d of September a flag of truce was sent to Metz, conveying the intelligence to General Bazaine, and requesting him to surrender Metz without farther bloodshed. The general's answer was, that he did not credit the report; that he should hold Metz to the last; and that if the Prussians wanted the town, they must come and take it. Unprincipled as he was, Bazaine was by no means a bad soldier, although a very indifferent general; his idea, no doubt, was that, being but a soldier of fortune, he would hold out as long as he could, so that he might be able to say that he was the last French general who surrendered, when all hope was lost.

Next morning, upon going to the railway station at Ars, I found the news of the previous day confirmed. The Prussians, anticipating an outbreak from Bazaine on the east side of Metz, sent across a strong force of cavalry. Nothing however occurred. It was reported that Metz was illuminated the previous night; but inasmuch as I was on the batteries at ten P.M. and saw nothing of it, I conclude that the report was only a *canard* got up by the anti-Prussian French party in the town.

At Pont-à-Mousson, whither I went on the 4th of September, eagerly did I look for a proclamation on the walls; but there was nothing more than the old placards of the Prussian victories at Weissenburg, Bitsche, and Mars-la-Tour. Four thousand fresh troops arrived there that afternoon; the Potsdam

Guards and the Jäger Guard battalion from the same place—magnificent troops, and in perfect health.

At Pont-à-Mousson for the first time I had opportunity to study the Juanita corps, or Knights of St. John. This corps was composed of gentlemen, many of whom had served in the army; but the greater number of them were civilians who had undergone their three years' regulation service. It appears that in order to qualify to become a Juanita, you must be able to show fourteen quarters upon your coat of arms, and an umblemished descent of many years; you are then entitled to wear a white enamelled Maltese cross, suspended by a green ribbon round the neck, and a uniform of the same description as the Prussian infantry, except that the buttons have a Maltese cross on them, and the white badge of Geneva with the red cross is worn on the left arm. Under the care of these gentlemen, for the purpose of distribution, were placed all the medical comforts—wine, provisions, and bedding—that were sent by individuals or communities for the use of the sick and wounded; and without a special order from them none of these things would be taken even by medical men. Now, I am not going to say that all were alike; but the conduct of these gentlemen for the most part at this time was beneath contempt. They lived on the fat of the land; they never knew what it was to want a meal, and they took care it was a good one. The medical staff were continually at loggerheads with them because they could not get what had been sent out for the special benefit of the sick and wounded soldiers. They were always in the best quarters, and never where they were wanted. In writing this, I am only expressing the opinions of their own countrymen. There were, however, I am happy to say, some noble exceptions. There is not a Prussian officer or soldier who will not bear witness to the unceasing efforts of Prince Reuss. He was here, there, and everywhere; and his simple and unofficious, though earnest, behaviour won the admiration of everybody.

On the morning of the 5th September I received intelligence that at Novéant, half way, I should have an opportunity of seeing some of the French prisoners taken at Sedan. Seeing is believing, and I could ask for no better proof of the news than this. Arrived at Novéant, the first thing that greeted me was a ghastly train, bearing its mangled freight to Pont-à-Mousson. The wounded of the action in the neighbourhood of St. Julien were here, in wagons, in horse-boxes—in fact, in whatever carriages could be procured for them. Poor fellows! not a murmur escaped them, although an occasional groan told their fearful suffering. The Prussian loss on that day was between 2,000 and 3,000 killed and wounded. Fortunately the train was detained for some time here, otherwise I should not have seen the 750 prisoners from Sedan, who confirmed the victory, and capture of M'Mahon and his army. 9,000 more were expected during the day. A sad and melancholy procession!

I had a few moments' conversation with an officer, who explained to me the facts of this most extraordinary and unprecedented episode. He said that the French troops had been retired into a position which, from his description, must have been more like a deep valley, surrounded on all sides by mountains, than anything else. The Prussians were permitted to take possession of the heights, and they poured down a most murderous fire upon the unprotected French masses, huddled together like a flock of sheep. They were only able to return their fire here and there, and then with no effect whatever. This continued for some time, until Marshal M'Mahon was himself wounded, and then the troops laid down their arms. This was the substance of the information which I was enabled to obtain in the short conversation that was then permitted me.

An extract from a letter to the *Daily Telegraph* will perhaps serve to illustrate the position of the contending armies about this time:

'I started off for head-quarters at Gravelotte as soon as possible after arriving at Ars. Just outside the town I met the 16th division of the 7th army corps on the march, and found they were bound over the Moselle. The 8th army corps having once more shifted its quarters, when I got to Gravelotte I found the staff just on their way into Ars, where they were about to establish themselves, the 2d army corps taking their place on the muddy dreary plateau. There was nothing for it, therefore, but to go back; so I made a détour to the outposts to see what was going on in front.

'As I passed St. Hubert, the Houguemont of the 18th, I found that it had been put into a very strong state of defence—to say nothing of the rifle-pits and batteries erected right and left of it. Moscau, the farm above it, had been treated in a similar manner; so that, should General Bazaine make a move in this direction, he might expect a warm reception. As I moved on to the village of Rozerieulles, the scattered, but constant, fire of the outposts attracted my attention as being more than usually warm; and, when I got to the plateau overlooking Mont St. Quentin, I found the railway and the vineyards above it, lying in the ravine between that fortification and the Prussian outposts, held by an unusually strong force of the enemy, who were keeping up a brisk fire upon our outposts. Why such a severe waste of ammunition was going on, I know not; but it appears that since that morning a very decided movement had been made on this side, as if to force the German position. The piquets and patrols had all been strengthened, and every moment an attack was expected under cover of the guns of Mont St. Quentin.

'Whilst watching the movements of the French troops, I came into contact with an officer who had been the first to obtain the distinction of wearing the old-established and new-revived order of the Iron Cross. This decoration is one of the highest orders of merit that can be bestowed, and, like our Victoria Cross, is given solely to those who have distinguished themselves. Since 1813 it has been in disuse, but it was naturally now revived. The fortunate possessor was the colonel of the 11th regiment.

'I now observed a considerable change in the disposition of the French troops around Metz—a very large camp having been brought over to this side. I remained till nearly dark, when I took my way back to Ars, and rode straight to the head-quarters. I am happy to say that, as far as provisions were concerned, the Prussian army were now in a position not only of comfort, but even of luxury, for they had an abundant supply of good wholesome food. I hear that an attack is very shortly expected, and that this was the cause of the hasty shift of troops this morning. The French Emperor is to pass through Ars on his way to Cassel, which, I am told, is settled as the immediate place of his abode.'

Although I have censured the Knights of St. John, I cannot refrain from speaking of the strong contrast which the unaffected and energetic proceedings of the corps of students from Heidelberg, Bonn, and the larger universities of Germany, presented to the wretched inactivity and mismanagement of the former body. These poor young fellows might be seen in any of the larger towns hard at work from morning to night, carrying the wounded on stretchers with their own hands, without waiting for the assistance of the 'Krankenträger,' hurrying to and fro in the villages near the battle-fields, ministering to the wants of their wounded countrymen with almost womanly gentleness.

I must also not forget to mention two trains that were fitted out and sent by the towns of Stuttgardt and Munich to the assistance of the wounded. They were composed of six large saloon carriages on the American principle, with communication from one end of the train to the other. The first carriage was divided into compartments, the first forming a kitchen, where a sister of mercy, with a perfect cooking range and utensils of every kind, performed the duties of cook. The second division was devoted to a surgery, where medicines and other medical comforts were neatly stowed away in shelves, with a hot-water pipe laid on from the boiler for immediate use. The other carriages were arranged with two tiers of beds, one above the other, placed upon springs and india-rubber bands, in order to obviate any jolting; they were fitted up longitudinally, so that the surgeons in charge could walk from one end to the other of their locomotive hospital. Each carriage held twenty wounded, so that the train took one hundred for each freight. These trains were of the greatest possible assistance in relieving the hospital tents, the villages, and the churches of their wounded. For several weeks all services in the churches in the neighbourhood of Gorze were suspended, in consequence of their being filled with wounded.

At this time there were more rumours about the capitulation of Metz. Some said it could hold out for six months; whilst others affirmed that disease and discontent were doing the work which cannon and bullets would take a long time to achieve. My impression was, that Bazaine would hold on to the last gasp, in the hopes of being relieved by some army or another; but where that army was to come from, was a question I scarcely knew how to answer.

General von Steinmetz had taken up his quarters

in the princely mansion of M. Dreyfuss, brother-in-law to M. Rothschild, of Paris. This gentleman was the owner of enormous rolling mills at Ars, where he employed two thousand workmen; and I was told that they could compete with the best manufacturers of Sheffield. Now these men were starving.

News was received, by means of a spy, of a somewhat summary execution, by the orders of General Bazaine, which took place in Metz, on the morning of the 6th of September. It appeared that two French officers, captains in the line, had refused to obey some order given to them which had reference to outpost duty; upon which the general, without going through the form of a court-martial, ordered them to be shot in the presence of the division; which sentence was almost instantly carried out.

I have said that the French had turned 750 Prussian prisoners out of Metz. Now, the common courtesies of war demanded that a like number of French should be sent in return; but up to the 6th of September no orders had been received. Then, however, Prince Friedrich Carl intimated that 750 French prisoners, chosen from different regiments of those taken at Sedan, should be sent into Metz as soon as possible. The reasons for this were certainly diplomatic, not to say cunning. Bazaine pretended that the news from Sedan was false; but when these 750 prisoners went into Metz and told their own tale—he would be unable to stop their mouths—it was hoped that the moral effect would be of considerable use in shortening the duration of the blockade.

It appears that, when the Emperor of the French

resigned his sword to the King of Prussia, he was so poor, that his Majesty the King of Prussia was forced to lend him 2,000 thalers (300*l.*) This is a fact so strongly asserted by the Prussian officers, that I have thought it perhaps as well to repeat it; although I am free to confess, from my humble knowledge of the Emperor's character, I should have thought him the last man in the world to be found destitute of the sinews of war.

A somewhat novel affair took place at the outposts one evening. An old woman was seen by a Prussian 'Doppelpost,' or double sentry, of the 33d regiment, engaged in an orchard picking up sticks. As her occupation was harmless, their attention was naturally drawn away to a more serious engagement going on in the vineyards. Suddenly the old woman takes refuge behind a tree, disengages a carbine from her petticoats, and, taking aim at the nearest Prussian sentry, shoots and wounds him severely. The action, however, had not been so quick but that his comrade saw it, and raising his rifle to his shoulder, he fired at and killed the supposed woman. He had just time to discover a French tirailleur so disguised, when an advance of the French compelled him to retire, taking his wounded comrade with him.

A proclamation of General von Göben, posted in Ars, informed the French inhabitants that any of them found with arms, either in their dwellings or on their persons, whether they belonged to the Garde Mobile or the Garde Nationale, would be taken out and shot on the spot. The population still remaining in the country were so tired of the fearful life they were leading, that there could be little doubt they would have been glad of peace upon any terms. The manufactories were, of course, all closed, and the men employed in making works for the Prussians round Metz, although they were forced to send patrols to drive them out of their houses and compel them to work at the bayonet's point. The people of France were now in a position to realise the words which M. Thiers made use of when he informed the French nation of what the consequences of a war with Prussia would be. The obloquy with which that shrewd and far-seeing statesman was covered, and the insults that he had to put up with from French officers, many of whom sent him challenges for daring to assert that the French army was no match, in its then state, for the Prussians, have been fully compensated by the results of this disastrous war.

On the 8th of September the army remained in precisely the same position, and assumed no greater activity than the usual daily routine of relieving guards and outposts, dispatching sick and wounded back to Prussia, and trying to pass away the day by inventing some new shelter to keep the incessant downpour out of their leaf-covered bivouacs. Sickness had again broken out, more virulently than before; 350 cases of dysentery in Ars, 470 in Corny, and a large number more in Gravelotte were reported. The Moselle had flooded the valley, and the state of the outposts and the troops in bivouac was really pitiable. The weather so long predicted had arrived, and it was now that the army suffered, especially those men whose constitutions were enfeebled by the scarcity and bad quality of the food on which they had lately subsisted.

Meantime the medical department was indefatigable in its exertions. New hospitals were formed and organised for the reception of the rapidly-arriving sick, and every precaution was taken that the situation would permit. The shops in the town of Ars exhibited a few edibles, but the prices were something fearful. Eggs 6*d.* each; a fowl 7 francs; a salad 2 francs; a small melon 3 francs; a cup of coffee 5 sous, without milk or sugar; hay 3 sous per pound; a kilo of oats 5 francs; a small piece of fillet of beef, about a pound, 3 francs; and so on. Sugar you could not buy; there was no milk and no brandy—that is to say no cognac, but plenty of eau de vie de raisin, the most horrible decoction of alcohol it is possible to imagine. It was, however, drunk by the soldiers in large quantities. Poor fellows! a hard night on duty, with nothing but their cloaks to cover them, rain falling in torrents, and the mud up to their knees—they swallowed large doses of the fiery poison as if it were water. The supplies of bread, meat, and tobacco were, however, abundant; there was also plenty of coffee, salt, pepper, ham, and bacon; and as to wine, there was no lack, though it was of a somewhat inferior character.

The inhabitants of the towns and villages in the neighbourhood were really too well treated by the Prussians so soon as they had time to organise matters. Everything in the shape of eatables was paid for in good money by the officers and soldiers, at whatever price the sellers chose to ask. The requisitions made for forage or wine were paid by a receipt given by the officer commanding, who informed the proprietor that he must present the receipt for payment at the end of the war — a somewhat dreary prospect, but nevertheless a more civilised way of appropriating property than at the bayonet's point or the end of a pistol. It is true that the inhabitants were somewhat pressed, and that many of them lost their all; but that was on the first blush of the invasion; and they had now, considering their position, really nothing of which to complain. Gross injustice has been done the Prussian commanders by the tissue of falsehoods which were published in the English papers as to their treatment of the inhabitants. Foremost amongst these publications was the *Standard*, whose columns were the incessant means of spreading false reports, and did more to prolong a useless struggle than any other journal.

About this time the German papers officially announced the Republic in Paris, the Crown Prince's movements were shrouded in mystery, at least to those around Metz, and nothing was known of what was going on, except in the immediate neighbourhood. Meantime the eye was met by the same dreary view of Mont St. Quentin and the fortress of Plappeville—the villages of Lessy and Moulins, occupied by the French outposts, who daily inflicted some loss upon the outlying piquets and patrols—the frowning fortifications of Metz, crowded with busy workmen—and the tall towers of the cathedral. Spies told of the sad state of things in the virgin fortress: 30,000 wounded were in the hospitals, and 20,000 sick were scattered about the town. The barracks were full, the manufactories were full, and the private houses occupied by the dying and the convalescent. Still, Metz la Pucelle held out firmly against the enemy, nor did her defenders seem at all inclined to give her up until the last biscuit had been devoured.

Melancholy processions of French prisoners daily dragged their weary steps through Ars, Novéant, and Corny to their prisons on the Prussian frontier. The Emperor, it was asserted, was already at Cassel, and France had now to look to her Republic to do what it had once before done—save her from a conquering and powerful invader. Was it not possible that amongst her large military population a general could be found to redeem the heinous, not to say puerile, mistakes of an old and effete system—to introduce a new condition of affairs, in which the camps of her armies would not be *à la* Louis XIV., and wine and women give place to pursuits more worthy of the soldiers of France, the defenders not only of their country, but of their hearths and homes?

The Prussian officers quite turned round in their opinion of the chassepot. It was undoubtedly superior to the needle-gun; but they still thought that their men were better shots than the French. As to the mitrailleuse, it proved itself to be severe upon cavalry, excellent in street-fighting, and undeniably good in a breach; but in the open, a battery of eight-pounders was more efficacious.

On the evening of the 8th of September, General von Steinmetz had determined as soon as night fell to bombard the suburb of Montigny-le-Metz, in order, if possible, to drive the French troops encamped there back into the town. For this purpose the artillery officers had chosen *emplacements* for the various batteries, to which light field-pieces were quietly dragged and masked until evening fell. At 4 P.M. the rain commenced to fall in torrents, turning the paths through the vineyards into little brooks, and making a sort of canal of the much-used roads. I scarcely thought the troops would turn out in such weather, as it blew half a gale, that caught you in every exposed place, driving the cold drops into the openings of your coat, and making you feel inclined to turn back to the fireside; but when I arrived at Vaux, I found my old friends the 33d turned out and waiting for orders; the rain beat down upon them most unmercifully, as they stood exposed in the road. I ventured to suggest to the officer the propriety of putting his men under shelter until it was absolutely necessary to start. 'Ah! sir,' said he, 'my soldiers can stand any amount of French bullets, but unfortunately we are called upon to stand what is far worse—this awful weather. My men are ordered here, and here we must stand, wet or dry.' The answer reminded me very much of that which Sir George Brown returned in Bulgaria when it was pointed out to him that the camp of the Light Division, if pitched at Aleddine, would be in a swamp —'I have said the camp is to be here, sir; and wet or dry, let it be pitched.'

After three-quarters of an hour's waiting, the order came to march. Up the steep road they struggled until they reached an angle of the wood of Vaux, commanding a view of the forts of Plappeville, St.

Quentin, and the south of Metz, with the villages of Sey, St. Rufine, and Longeville. It was near the last-named village that the French had massed a large quantity of troops during the last three or four days, as if they intended making a sortie in the direction of Ars. There in front glimmered the lights of the virgin fortress and her fortifications, against whose maiden walls a storm of shell was about to be launched. The rain wrapped the panorama in a sort of misty, weird-like shroud, whilst the wind seemed to whistle a mournful requiem as it swept through the gorges and ravines at the foot of Mont St. Quentin.

At five in the afternoon I marched as far as the French outlying piquets with 100 French prisoners taken at Sedan. They were escorted by a guard of the 48th regiment, and consisted of a dozen Turcos and a number of soldiers from different regiments. This was following out the programme I already mentioned of sending these men into Metz in exchange for the Prussian prisoners that were sent out, in order that they might spread the news of M'Mahon's surrender. The prisoners were handed over in the usual way, but seemed far from delighted at the prospect before them; indeed I felt certain that, had they had their choice, they would have preferred the road to Coblenz. Poor fellows! they were certainly in a miserable plight, covered with bits of old sacking to keep the rain out, and with little and often no covering to their feet. While they stood in Ars none of the inhabitants were allowed to approach them, and the strictest watch was kept over their movements. Whether the answer returned by General Bazaine was an ungracious one, I know not; but certain it is that, upon the return of the escort, immediate orders were sent to open upon the town and suburbs at 7 P.M.

As the chimes from the clock of the little village of Vaux sounded through the valley, and were replied to by the steeples of Sey and St. Rufine, a puff of white smoke, a flash, and the report of a 12-pounder, gave the signal for the batteries to begin their fire. The first battery that opened was that of Vaux, its shells being directed upon the village of Sey and the suburb of Montigny. It was followed by a battery on the other side of the Moselle, and the fire was taken up by the whole of the 7th army corps guns. On the left, too, a heavy fire was opened by the batteries near Point du Jour, on the village of Lessy and the outworks of Plappeville, until the whizzing of the Prussian shells from artillery of the 7th and 8th army corps became incessant. For a few minutes no sound was heard on the French side. Then a light appeared above the village of Sey, then a flitting to and fro of lights in the village of Longeville, then a flash from Mont St. Quentin, and a 24lb. shell came hurtling into the middle of us—bursting to the left of the battery, but fortunately doing no harm. Plappeville now replied to the Gravelotte batteries, but not a gun spoke from the works of Metz. Mont St. Quentin sent a shot every now and then; but the French fire was slack, and they seemed to treat the Prussian 12-pounders with indifference. The fire, however, between Pont du Jour and Plappeville was much more frequent and severe.

About a quarter to eight the rain swept down in awful torrents, the battery of Vaux ceased firing, and gradually the fire slackened, except on the Gravelotte side, where it was prolonged for another twenty minutes. But then all was once more still, and nothing but the howling of the wind and the patter of the fast-falling rain was to be heard. Thus ended the first bombardment, if I may so call it, to which Metz had yet been subjected. Of the injuries done, of course it was then impossible to speak: but I fancy the darkness of the night, to say nothing of the weather, must have prevented any serious damage. The loss of the Germans was very trifling—one man killed and three wounded.

About this time an occurrence took place illustrative of the reports which at this time appeared in the English journals, and which did much to embitter the Prussian commanders against correspondents. It occurred as follows: One evening I found an orderly waiting at my quarters with a request that I would be so good as to attend at the Chief of the Staff's quarters whenever convenient. Accordingly, as soon as I had swallowed a cup of hot coffee, I repaired to his house, very little prepared for what I was about to hear. On my entering the room I found him alone, with a *Daily Telegraph* of the 1st of September before him. After desiring me to be seated, he handed me the paper—he spoke and read English perfectly—and said, 'This paper has been sent to me by the general, with orders to show it you, as he feels certain that you will take the earliest opportunity of contradicting a misstatement which appears in it respecting the 7th and 8th army corps.' I asked if the letter he referred to was written by me. 'No, sir, I am happy to say it is not, although yours is alongside of it.' The letter referred to was dated Carlsruhe, August 27th, and the passage in question referred to the battle of Gravelotte. The writer stated that the 7th, 8th, and 2d army corps were held in reserve.

Now the 7th, and particularly the 8th army corps suffered the most, and had to stand the brunt of the whole day, the only corps held in reserve being the 2d army corps. Again, the positions of the various army corps in this fearful battle were entirely falsified. The centre of the Prussian army was the left rear of Gravelotte, held by the 8th army corps — not their left, as stated. Their right was composed of the 7th army corps, whose position at the commencement was concealed in the Bois d'Ognons, above Gorze, and to the right of Gravelotte. There was no fighting at Amanvillers, as that was held by the Prussians after the battle of Mars-la-Tour. Again, the French position was *not* taken on the afternoon of the 18th: it was taken by the 2d army corps late on the evening of the 18th. The 8th army corps took the Houguemont of the position — the farms of St. Hubert and Moscau, with the hamlet of Malmaison, which formed the centre of the French line. So much for correspondents who write 100 miles away from the scene of action.

The cannonading of the 8th of September was, fortunately for Metz, and unfortunately for the Prussians, of but little avail. When the batteries were placed, a small mistake of 1,000 yards occurred, and 12lb. brass guns were expected to do execution at 6,000 yards instead of 5,000. It is true that a battery placed at Frascati was within range of the French battery at Montigny, and that the French evacuated this battery—not in consequence of the Prussian fire, however, but from the overflowing of the Moselle, which had flooded their works and compelled the artillerists to decamp with their guns. Beyond, therefore, knocking a few holes in the houses of Lessy and Longeville, the powder expended effected no results. The 7th army corps moved forward to take up a position nearer to Metz, and as the Hessian division were to be relieved in Gravelotte, it was anticipated that the 8th army corps would have to take up a position contiguous to Metz on the east side of the Moselle.

In order to illustrate the behaviour of the Prussians towards the inhabitants, I cannot avoid relating an occurrence which took place at Vaux. We had just finished dinner, and were smoking the postprandial cigar, when an orderly came in to say that a Frenchman desired to speak with the commandant of Vaux. This responsible position was held by Lieutenant-Colonel von Henning, commanding the 33d regiment, on outpost duty in that town; and a kinder-hearted and more noble-minded soldier and gentleman never rode at the head of a Prussian regiment. He came from the 40th, or the 'fighting 40th' as I have called it; and although he had been in command of the 33d fusiliers only since the regiment left Saarbrück, he was as much respected and beloved by his new comrades as he was in his old corps. Wherever the regiment was quartered, the inhabitants of the villages never had to complain of severe measures, and many a time have I seen their miseries relieved by donations from his purse. Strict in the discipline of his regiment, kind and affectionate in his disposition, ever ready to do his duty, no matter when or where, Lieutenant-Colonel von Henning was at once a bright example of a Prussian soldier and a German gentleman.

The orderly ushered into the room a person whose appearance at once took us entirely by surprise; so much so, that, by a universal impulse, we all rose from our seats and bowed. Imagine a tall man, somewhat bent with the weight of years, but still striving to be erect notwithstanding his feebleness, neatly but plainly dressed, with the badge of France's chivalry, the ribbon of the Légion d'Honneur in his button-hole, a face noble in expression, a high commanding forehead, eyes still sparkling with fire and energy, an aquiline nose, a white moustache and long imperial, hair as white as snow, a serious though dignified expression,—and you have before you le Capitaine de la Moricière, late an officer in the army of France. I can do no better than repeat his simple story.

'Monsieur le Commandant,' said he, 'and Messieurs les officiers, I beg of you to be seated; and if Monsieur le Colonel will grant me a few moments, I will not detain him long.' A chair was immediately handed him, when he continued: 'Monsieur le Colonel, I am, as you perceive, an old soldier of France, although I am sorry to say that my years and my hard service compelled me long since to relinquish my profession and to retire to this peaceful village of Lorraine, not too far off for me to hear the *réveillé* and retreat borne to me morning and evening from Metz, reminding me of days gone by. My poor country is in your hands. I am too much of a soldier not to respect orders. I have had the proclamation brought to me, that the inhabitants of Vaux should at once bring all their arms to the guard-house. Mine consisted of a fowling-piece and a dagger. It is on the subject of this dagger that I now come to disturb you. Gentlemen, you all know how an old soldier prizes the relics of by-gone glory, or the presents of some dear comrade who has fought and died by his side. I come to claim your forbearance and your kindness in such a cause. That dagger was given to my father by the Emperor Napoleon the First on the bloody field of Austerlitz. I have worn it at my side in many a hard-fought action, and now I seem to miss my old comrade from the nail where he used to hang; and I come to beg you to give the old soldier back a memento that to you is useless, but that serves to remind him of comrades dead and gone, of hard-fought fields, and lonely bivouacs. If I have asked too much, excuse the trouble I have given you in listening to my story; but if it is possible for you to grant my request, accept the thanks of an old soldier who, like you all, has fought and bled for his country.'

I need hardly add what was the sequel. An orderly was immediately dispatched for the much-prized dagger; the old French gentleman smoked a cigar, and drank a glass of wine; and when his much-prized weapon was returned to him by the Colonel, a tear glittered in his eye, as he drew up his tall figure at the door, and with a '*Dieu vous bénisse, Messieurs!*' he bowed and left us.

On the 10th of September the 15th division of the 8th corps received order to march upon Augny, on the other side of the Moselle, and considerably nearer to Metz. About this time the French seemed to have brought a large quantity of troops over to this side. There were two new camps, one between St. Quentin and Plappeville, on the summit of the hill, and the other close to the railway bridge over the Moselle. The outposts occupied much the same positions as before, nothing indicating a change of any sort; the 'Feldwache' amused themselves by taking occasional shots at the French sentries, which were, however, strange to say, not returned.

Truly we live in high-pressure times. It is with war as with other things, and to express surprise at anything is simply to be vulgar. Marshal Bazaine's idea was a most original, if not a fortunate one. It would appear that he stood in great need of some means of communication with the interior; the railways and telegraphs were closed to him; the Prussian army corps cut off all approach; but he was not to be deterred. Late on the evening of the 13th of September, one of the Prussian advanced posts was somewhat surprised by seeing a dark globe-like shape rise out of the centre of Metz, and, after steadily ascending for some hundreds of feet, float gently away in a north-easterly direction. What it was, they could not determine; some supposed it to be a new machine filled with bullets or shells, which was intended to burst in the midst of one of their bivouacs; others declared that it was the result of some explosion, and that the smoke arising from it had formed itself into this fanciful shape. The matter, however, was soon set at rest; by a night-glass it was discovered to be a balloon, with two men in the car—a truly original, but by no means a bad, way, as a *dernier ressort*, of communicating intelligence. Unfortunately, however, for the success of the scheme, the wind at this moment took it into its head to change, and the disappointed aëronauts were wafted in an opposite direction to that in which they wished to proceed. Finally, the balloon came down in the midst of a Prussian guard in the neighbourhood of St. Wendel, where the intrepid aëronauts—to make use of the usual phraseology—were, with their poor balloon, immediately made prisoners. No papers however were found; and, as it is difficult to make a man speak if he positively refuses, no news of the state of Metz was obtained.

The fortress of Laon had capitulated; but Strasburg, Toul, and Phalsburg still held out the unequal combat, even to the admiration of their assailants. The position of Toul, situated as it was on the railway in direct communication between Pont-à-Mousson and Commercy, made it a severe thorn in the side of the Prussians, and consequently another general bombardment was launched against it. Of Phalsburg there was no news, but in Strasburg the state of the town, it was rumoured, was fearful. There were 300 guns in position; but the place held out, and the Baden troops had much to do before the gallant little garrison of 7000 men capitulated.

Meantime the peasants in the neighbourhood of Metz, undismayed by the fate of those who were hung at Corny, continued to shoot at any Prussian officer or soldier, or indeed at any one connected with the army, who happened to become isolated, or was compelled to go anywhere in the neighbourhood of the suburbs of the beleaguered town. One morning a cuirassier started from head-quarters with an order to an officer on outpost duty. In the evening a sergeant came in to report that, whilst riding through a vineyard, two peasants shot at and killed him, taking his horse into Metz with them. The consequence was, that another general search for arms was made in the villages, and a chassepot was found concealed in the house of a peasant in Augny. The poor wretch was ordered out to be shot; but, fortunately for him, the priest proved that some wounded French soldiers had taken refuge in his house after the battle of Gravelotte, and this evidence, added to the testimony of his master that he was a most inoffensive man, saved him from a short shrift.

On this side of Metz the duty of the outlying pickets and patrols was much more severe than on the Gravelotte side. The French had thrown up some earthworks in front of Frascati and Augny. These were occupied every evening at nightfall, and evacuated in the morning. Whether they eventually intended to put guns into them is hard to say, but in their position, even without guns, they proved somewhat annoying neighbours; for no sooner did the French take possession of them in the evening than a serenade of chassepots commenced, which was repeated at réveil in the morning.

If the horses I saw pass through Jouy, taken at Sedan, were to be considered as a fair specimen of the French cavalry and artillery mounts, I am not in the least surprised at their riders' evident desire not to come into contact with the Prussian cavalry. 1200 of the maimed, the lame, the sick, and the blind, ridden by French prisoners, dragged their melancholy way through the town. They were of all shapes, sizes, and sorts, the best of the quadrupeds being a mule. I confess I had not had an opportunity of judging of the French cavalry since the Crimea. In those days it will be remembered how very remiss they were in the way of horses, with the exception of some few of their crack regiments—such as the Chasseurs d'Afrique and the regiments of the Guard. But fourteen years had given them time to improve, and to have profited by their experiences. Here again, however, were the same faults—no bone, badly ribbed, heavy shouldered, small legs, bad action, and evidently bad doers; and it is to be remembered that the French army had retreated into the heart of their own country, with Paris and the whole of the West open to them for supplies of forage of every sort. What excuse had they, then, for the condition of the animals, which only left Sedan three or four days ago, even supposing that since they came into German hands they had been badly fed? This, by the way, was not the case, inasmuch as the Prussians knew the value of horses too well to do anything of the sort. We have all been told of the great doings in the French *haras*—of how much the breed of horses had been improved of late—of the sums of money spent by the Government to import fresh blood: were these the results?

General von Moltke at length found work for Messrs. Fowler's traction engines, two of which he had purchased. They are to ply between Pont-à-Mousson and Commercy, taking stores for the Crown Prince's army, and bringing back the sick and wounded. The advantage of this movement will be at once seen by a glance at the map, and may be looked upon as an evidence of this great man's powers of utilising everything. The fortress of Toul impeded progress, and prevented the Prussians from making use of the railway; but the road from Pont-à-Mousson was straight, and avoided Toul. These engines supplied the want of the permanent way by travelling with equal ease upon the road, and therefore their services were invaluable.

On the 13th September the head-quarters of the King of Prussia were three hours' march from Paris.

The truth of the various statements respecting the condition of the troops in Metz about this time can be pretty accurately tested by the fact, that a healthy horse slaughtered for the purpose sold in that unfortunate town at two francs per pound. A horse that had died from sickness or disease was sold at ten sous cheaper per pound. Marshal Bazaine still considered himself King of France, and steadily encouraged balloon ascents. He had two experiments of this sort, and highly gratifying it must have been to that august personage to know that in both instances the balloons went in an opposite direction to that which they were intended to take. Evidently they must have had more coal in Metz than the French fleet had; for it was then reported that the war-steamers were completely brought to a standstill for want of that most essential commodity.

A most extraordinary piece of news—like all the news that reached us—arrived on the 17th of September, to the intent that Paris had been declared an open city, that General Trochu had made a virtue of necessity, and was willing to admit the Prussians without going through the farce of a siege, hoping thereby to escape plundering, bivouacking in the Tuileries, cooking in the Boulevard des Italiens, and a stabling of horses in the Madeleine or the Palais Royal. The news was accepted with incredibility, and, as it turned out, was untrue; for an order arrived, dated the 14th, ordering up a siege train. Poor Paris! many of those landmarks so dear to Englishmen were about to undergo a severe trial. There are some we could dispense with; but there are others the existence of which makes that charming city endurable to a somewhat large portion of her British visitors.

The whole of Prince Frederick Charles's army was at this moment in a perfect state of ferment, from the reports that had just reached them of the treatment of Prussian wounded who took refuge in the town of Bouillon after the battle near Sedan; and as this statement appeared in the shape of a protocol, signed by several Prussian officers, and officially published in the papers, I suppose it must be accepted as true. Bouillon is a Belgian town on the frontier: thither, after the fearful scene of Sedan, both Prussian and French wounded dragged their weary steps, in the hopes of assistance and aid. As regards the French, it was readily given, but with the Prussians it was otherwise. The wounded officers were desired to get the best way they could into garrets; food was forbidden to be sold to a Prussian; and the severely wounded could only obtain assistance from their less-injured companions. Meanwhile the French soldiers had everything they required. The hotels were open to them, the shops supplied them almost gratis. Now, what may have been the policy of Belgium I do not for one moment pretend to say; but, putting politics aside—a matter which is rarely brought into question with that of humanity—was it fair or just that a *neutral* State should show humanity to one belligerent and inhumanity to another? The man who goes to help the wounded in a campaign cares alike for friend and foe; if he does not, he abjures his sacred office. Wounded humanity, be it English, French, or Prussian, demands the same assistance.

The dull monotony of sojourn in the valley of the Moselle was somewhat relieved by the intelligence that something was about to be done. That something was to be the shelling of the battery in the course of construction by the French in the neighbourhood of St. Privat. Now, this St. Privat must not be confounded with the place of that name which cost the Prussian Guards so dear on the 18th of

August, at the battle of Gravelotte. A glance at the map will show it to be a small hamlet lying to the south of Metz, and to the east of Tournebride. Here the French had erected a work, and were busily engaged finishing it. The Prussians had also erected a battery to keep this one in order, and it was arranged that a little interchange of shells should take place. It, however, all came to nothing, as the Prussians never fired a shot. As in all long sieges, the belligerents became excessively amiable to one another. In the direction of Pouilly, to the east of Metz, the French in Fort Queuleu used to permit half a company to march about and even to drill; but if two men were added to the number, an immediate discharge of shells testified that the liberty taken was too great.

On the 18th a flag of truce, borne by an officer of rank, came to Prince Frederick Charles's quarters at Corny, from Metz. Its purpose was to ascertain if it was really true that Napoleon was no longer at the head of affairs, and, if so, what was the state of Paris and the ministry. His highness furnished the officer with all the information he required, and also gave him a list of the gentlemen who were then at the head of affairs in poor France. How this suited his majesty of Metz, it is hard to imagine.

It is certain that Bazaine was now well acquainted with the movements of the Prussian troops around Metz, and for this knowledge the Prussians had only to thank their kindness and liberality towards the inhabitants of the villages of St. Ruffine, Rozerieulles, Vaux, and Jussy on one side, and Augny, Marly, and

Pouilly on the other. The plan of operation was a simple one. A pass was obtained from the commandant of the town or village, enabling the holder to go to Ars to purchase bread and subsistence. The vineyards were thick, and the undulating grounds specially adapted to concealment. The French and Prussian sentries were but 600 or 700 yards from one another, and spread somewhat broadcast. What, then, was there to prevent a peasant, *who knew the ground*, from stealing through the sentries and getting to the French outposts? If he was caught, his answer, ever a ready one from the peasant of Lorraine, was, 'I have missed my way in the dark whilst returning from fetching subsistence for my starving family.'

One morning an instance occurred which goes far to prove what I have stated. It was made a *sine quâ non*, that every pass submitted to the commandant of a village should first be approved and signed by the mayor of the place, who was held responsible for the good conduct of its possessor. A man obtained a pass, signed by the mayor of Augny, to proceed to Ars for the purpose of buying bread; arrived at Ars, he disposed of his pass to a confederate, who in the early morning, when the fog from the Moselle covered the valley, and made everything indistinct at a hundred yards, tried to crawl through the sentries in the direction of Metz. But, unfortunately for him, the 33d Fusiliers were on outpost, and he was discovered and captured. The mayor was sent for, and told that he alone was responsible; and a fine of 1000 francs was imposed on him, whilst the man was kept close prisoner. Now, if he, taken as he was red-handed in the act, had been shot then and there, he would have richly deserved it; but then the Prussians would have been execrated as monsters.

A severe example was made of three Prussians, who came from the town of Düren. It appears that these three ruffians had disguised themselves, two as Johanniter, or knights of St. John, and the third as a clergyman. On the field of the 18th they were observed by a wounded Prussian officer to lean over the bodies of the dead, and to take an unnecessarily long time over places where no assistance was required. He watched them carefully, until a sharp cry of pain left him in no doubt as to their horrible errand. They leant over a man, who evidently refused to permit them to take from him the things so dear to the dying soldier—perhaps the portraits of his wife and mother—perhaps the few rings that brought to his memory the faces of his children whom he was never more to behold. The wounded officer drew his revolver and hit one of the wretches; the report drew the attention of some army policemen, who, hastening to the spot, secured the three inhuman brutes. Their knives were red with the blood of their victims; but their shrift was short and summary.

Affairs remained in the same state. Nor was it the intention of the Prussian generals to do anything beyond keeping the cordon tightly tied around Metz. Everything now depended upon the Crown Prince and his movements, of which we had but scanty intelligence. Meantime, Toul remained untaken, as also Strasburg, although a breach had been made in the outworks and the citadel was menaced.

CHAPTER V.

THE SIEGE OF TOUL.

I NOW turn for a few moments from the blockade of Metz to a point of interest not very far from the capital of Lorraine, where another act in the drama of the campaign was being played out.

In the deluge of adversity that overflowed France, some little islands of hope appeared amidst the angry billows, raising their heads above the storm, and modifying almost universal disaster. Bright and noble amongst these examples stood that little town of Lorraine, of which history relates innumerable circumstances that have already made Toul famous; but I doubt if this little spot had ever borne a bolder front than at this moment. A glance at the map will show its position on the railroad between Nancy and Paris. It lies in the valley of the Moselle, and by its continued resistance I had been led to suppose that it lay on an elevated position, commanding at least the country in its immediate vicinity. Imagine, therefore, my surprise upon finding a small town defended by earthworks, standing in a sort of basin formed by an abrupt curve of the Moselle, and completely commanded by the surrounding heights. When I say 'completely commanded,' I use the words advisedly, inasmuch as the two hills of St. Michel and St. Maurice overlook the town at a distance of about 3000 yards. I had ridden from Metz quite unprepared to witness a sight so unusual, from a military point of view; and I was still more surprised at what I saw in connection with it.

The little town, at present defended by some 3000 French soldiers, lay in a complete hollow. Rising in its centre is the quaint old-fashioned cathedral. To the right of the edifice, as you approach from Francheville, another church tower is visible. These are all the buildings of importance that meet the eye from any distance. The division of the Grand Duke of Mecklenburg, belonging to the 9th army corps, was the besieging force; and the troops altogether must have amounted to some 20,000 men. It seemed strange that, with their batteries in the position they occupied, one stone remained upon another in the brave little fortress. Referring to my diary, I find the following description:

'As I approached Toul from the side of Liverdun, I could hardly believe that I was advancing upon a besieged fortress, inasmuch as three soldiers were all I saw; and had it not been for a hussar who galloped frantically after me, and told me that I was riding into the suburbs, I believe I should have gone into the town itself. "They have got wall rifles (Wallbüchsen)," cried he, "that carry balls as big as an egg, which they shoot from the church tower at any one approaching." I need hardly say I turned very quickly to the right-about, all the while thinking how strange it was that the church tower, that gave such opportunity from its height to such weapons—if indeed they existed—was permitted to stand under the batteries on the heights of Mont St. Michel. I heard, on my arrival at Gondreville, that positive orders had been received for battering and assaulting the town. Accordingly I determined to wait and see the result; but, beyond a few shots from the batteries on Mont St. Michel, and a little outpost firing, nothing occurred. The railway station had been taken by the besiegers; but this little affected the position of the garrison, who seemed to be unusually well supplied with guns and ammunition.

'From the batteries on Mont St. Michel every street and almost every gun in the town was to be seen; yet Toul still remained in the hands of its defenders. What the policy that dictated such a course was, I know not; but considerable discontent seemed to be prevalent amongst the Bavarian troops, the cause of which was laid far from the right door, I imagine. It had been whispered, but only by Bavarians, that the Prussians made use of their commissariat, and left them to starve. Now, a more unlikely state of things never existed. Nor was it at all probable that, if it had been so, I should not have heard of or known it; but I am sorry to say that at this time there was a wrong feeling springing up amongst the troops, especially Bavarians and Hessians, which was eventually put a stop to. The losses before Toul had been very small considering the length of the siege. To-morrow, I hear, the batteries will open; so I shall pass the night in the village of Gondreville, to be ready for the first movement in the morning.'

'*Gondreville, before Toul, September* 21.

'Last night, whilst sitting on the bridge over the Moselle at this little village, watching the occasional flash of the Bavarian guns as they methodically dispatched a shell every twenty minutes or so into the devoted little town, I was joined by an old French peasant, whose conversation is worthy of repetition. "Ah, sir," said he, "I remember the day when the Emperors of Russia and Austria, with Marshal Blucher, forded the Moselle where we are now sitting, on their way to Paris. It was a grand sight, but Toul was not held by a garrison. When they told me the other day that the Prussians had come, I said it was impossible, *for that none of our troops had been in the neighbourhood*; and, of course, you know, sir, if they had been expected, our village would have been held by an outpost to give notice of their approach."

'The old man's words were but a verification of the manifold mistakes the French generals have committed. In almost every case have they left their front unprotected; nor have they made use of the ordinary precaution of patrols, outposts, or even cavalry patrols. As when, on the 15th of August, Prince Frederick Charles's army lay in the ravine of St. Catherine, only a few kilomètres from Metz, Gorze was not occupied, nor was an outpost or a patrol sent out to scour the country and give intelligence of the advance of the enemy. On the 16th the

French marched out of Metz on their way to Paris, and their first intimation of the presence of the Prussians was their advanced guard becoming engaged near Mars-la-Tour. As at Frouard the Prussian lancers galloped down, cut the telegraph wires, and shot a couple of French soldiers, who were at the station, on their way to Nancy, without a soul knowing where they came from; as at Nancy the first intimation the inhabitants had of the approach of the enemy was the arrival of the Prussian patrol at their gates, so was it at Toul.

'I could mention many more instances of a like deviation from the commonest laws of military tactics. Was it, then, to be wondered at that you heard French officers speaking as they did of their generals, or the common soldiers complaining of having been betrayed? Was it not hard enough, they asked, to be out-numbered, without being out-manœuvred, and led like sheep to the slaughter? What they said was, alas, but too true, as we all of us witnessed. Spies were hard at work in the neighbourhood of the town; nor did I observe that they had much difficulty in effecting an entry or an exit through the sentries.

'One morning I received information from a staff officer, which induced me to leave the dull monotony of the camp before Toul, and return to Metz, *viâ* Nancy. I can only conclude that the idea was to starve the garrison into submission, and thereby save the destruction of the little town; but Toul seemed to me a point so valuable for the purpose of opening up the communication for the Crown Prince, that I could not understand such a seeming want of energy in the reduction of a fortress that ought to have been knocked to pieces in a few hours.'

Nancy *la Coquette* was well named in every sense of the word. After the French towns and villages in which I had been sojourning, it was not surprising if I was struck with admiration at the contrast this little gem presented to the badly-built, irregular, dirty towns of Lorraine. It is not my purpose—nor, indeed, is it my province—to describe the town; suffice it to say, that in the possession of Nancy the Prussians retained one of the brightest jewels forming the circlet of the French frontier. That the inhabitants were in the last stage of despair, and that their despair had found vent in deep muttered vows of vengeance against a person or persons unknown, is a fact which may be gathered from what occurred to me at the mairie one morning. After applying at the commandant's for quarters for myself, my orderly, and two horses—as to the hotels, there was no hope, all being packed from garret to cellar with noisy Bavarians—I proceeded to the Hôtel de Ville, and was ushered into a long room, very narrow and very lofty. Placed upon a table were two candles, whose flickering light scarcely tended to make the large room look more inviting. Seated at a table in the centre of the room were three gentlemen, and, were I disposed to do the thing *à la* James, I should proceed to describe them. This is, however, not necessary.

Upon handing my order, the eldest of the trio—I conclude the mayor—said to me, 'Monsieur, I see by this paper you are an officer; how is it you are in plain clothes?' 'Monsieur,' I answered, 'I am an Englishman, and in this sad war my country has thought it best that we should remain neutral. It is, therefore, strictly forbidden for any of us to wear uniform.' 'An Englishman!' exclaimed all three, with a chorus of intonations. The old gentleman then rose, and, in an imposing manner, with his arms crossed upon his chest, said, 'Monsieur, were you in the Crimea?' 'I had that honour,' I replied. 'Did not the French come to your assistance at Inkermann, without which you would have been eaten up?' 'Monsieur,' I replied, 'the French arrived when the battle was nearly over, and they did what the Turks or the Sardinians would have just as well effected—they produced the moral effect upon the Russian soldiers which fresh troops, brought up at the end of an engagement, usually do—they caused them to retire. I am, however, deeply grieved to see my old companions in arms in the bad hands of those who lead them. They have been sacrificed by their generals in a way which none but French troops would have endured so long: I am here to watch the events of the war; for no other purpose,—were it otherwise, I should wear the uniform of my country.' 'But, sir,' continued the mayor, seemingly still unconvinced, 'you are attended by a Prussian soldier.' 'The kindness of the general,' I replied, 'has directed that I shall be waited upon, and shall have some one to look after my horses. I trust,' I added, 'this sad state of things will soon be over.' 'I hope not, sir,' cried the chorus again; 'I hope it will go on. France has now an opportunity of retrieving what she has lost. France is aroused; her people will fight for her to the last man, and she will yet be victorious.'

The feelings of these gentlemen was a fair criterion of those cherished by the inhabitants of Nancy. They called the Prussians a set of robbers, no doubt from the repeated levies of money which were then wrung from the hitherto prosperous town. Only a few days before I arrived another demand for cash was sullenly complied with; but Nancy was a volcano, from which at any moment might burst a disagreeable eruption of discord and rebellion, that it was well for the sake of humanity was nipped in the bud. To show how easily the people were excited; amongst the prisoners released by the Prussians at Sedan upon parole was a certain General Boër, formerly in command at Luneville. This wise and discreet officer, together with two others, rode into Nancy with their swords on, in full uniform, and galloped through the town from one end to the other. Imagine the effect: the townspeople thought the French troops had arrived; a universal moving to and fro, a shouting and hurrahing took place; the shops were shut, the troops were called out, a message was sent to Pont-à-Mousson by telegraph to send up another regiment, and the whole town was thrown into a state of ferment.

Meantime the inhabitants of Nancy kept their shops open, the hotels were doing a brisk trade, and the cafés were crammed to overflowing. The peasants were gathering their grapes, and the farmers were ploughing land with what horses the Prussians had left them. As to cattle, rinderpest and the butcher's knife had almost exterminated them.

I must now pass on to a subject which, from the complete success of the trials, will form for the future a most important point in modern warfare. I allude to the employment of steam for the purpose of conveying forage, stores, ammunition, or heavy guns from one place to another in an enemy's country, where the railroads are either broken up or in the hands of the foe. We have for many years been employing traction engines for agricultural purposes, particularly for steam-ploughing. Messrs. Fowler and Sons, of Leeds, are very large manufacturers; and employing, as they do, a Prussian engineer, is it remarkable that at the time when the war broke out, two engines were found to be lying in the dock at Geestemünde, consigned to a certain Saxon farmer who had been called to take his place amongst the ranks of his countrymen? I take the opportunity of mentioning this, because Prussia in no way violated any law of neutrality by the appropriation of these engines; and when it was proposed to General von Moltke to employ English workmen to drive them, he at once and distinctly refused to commit what he considered a breach of the neutrality which England had imposed upon herself.

The engines were placed under the direction of a Mr. Töppfer, and sent to Pont-à-Mousson after successfully achieving a preliminary trial at Magdeburg. At Pont-à-Mousson they were unloaded, and as soon as they were ready they started with a train of twelve wagons, tied together by chains, heavily loaded with bread and oats, for Commercy. The journey was accomplished in eighteen hours without any mishap, and the engines were driven over a road where the gradients in some places were 1 in 8. The distance was about thirty miles, and no one knew where either water or coal could be procured on the road. A wagon filled with water-casks obviated one difficulty, whilst wood and refuse did duty for the other. The engines were now employed in taking locomotives in pieces, to be put together at Commercy, so as at once to set up railway communication between that town, Sedan, Rheims, Bar-le-Duc, Verdun, and Châlons. Under these circumstances it will be seen that, as far as the fortresses of Metz and Toul were concerned, their efforts to neutralise or prevent railway communication were rendered entirely abortive by the employment of two steam-ploughing or traction engines.

Military and railway men cannot but be struck with the importance of this new and simple feature, and I took care to make myself thoroughly acquainted with the working and details of a matter which should at once engage the serious attention of our Government. The engines were constructed as follows. They were of 20-horse power, and were built upon the locomotive principle. There were two cylinders of 9-inch diameter inside placed upon a multi-tubular double-riveted boiler, capable of working at 150lbs. pressure on the square inch. A steel crank shaft of 14-inch stroke, having a slit pinion keyed upon it, by means of three intermediate shafts and gearing, all in steel, communicated the power to the driving hind wheels of the engine. The power was reduced from 150 revolutions per minute of the crank shaft to 7 revolutions per minute of the driving wheels. The latter were 6 feet 6 inches in diameter, and 24 inches wide in the tire—thus presenting a considerable frictional surface to the road. The front end of the boiler rested upon an axle, and two wheels of 3 feet 6 inches diameter and 20 inches in breadth. A cup joint at the place where the boiler took its bearing allowed the fore carriage to adapt itself to any irregularity on the road, and to facilitate the steering gear.

This latter was of the simplest description. Two long rods extended from the fore axle to the extreme back of the engine underneath the boiler, ending in a pitch chain which passed round a small corresponding wheel. This was fastened to a spur wheel of 2¼ feet in diameter, and, by means of a hand wheel attached to an upright shaft and small pinion, the steersman, who stood on a small platform attached to the outside of the tender of the engine, obtained enough power to move the leading wheels into any angle sufficient to guide the engine round a corner.

The most important and the most useful addition to these engines lies, however, in the winding apparatus. Under the centre of the boiler, exactly in the middle, and revolving upon a strong stand, is placed a drum, capable of holding 500 yards of seven-eighth steel-wire rope. By means of an upright shaft and bevel gearing direct from the crank shaft this winding drum can be put into motion, and is ready to haul, at a distance of 450 yards, a load equal to 3½ tons strain upon this rope. This winding gear is really a most essential adjunct to a traction engine, for by means of it heavy guns can be dragged up steep acclivities. The engine weighed about 17 tons when empty, and the driver standing in front of the fire-box had every handle within reach of his arm. The cost of each such engine was, I believe, 1,000*l*.

I was unfortunate enough to have to write this description without the advantage of aid from Mr. Töppfer, who had gone with one engine and train to Commercy, and whom I never again saw. I was therefore forced to trust to what little mechanical knowledge I possessed, and to the help of a Prussian engineer; but, from what I have seen of the engines and their trial, I am more than convinced of their immense importance in times of war, and also of their practical and enduring usefulness. I would, however, suggest that the tender be made somewhat larger, in order to carry more fuel and water than are required for the purpose of ploughing a field.

Once more we turn to the weary blockade of Metz, and describe the second attempt of the French to cut through the army of blockade.

The village of Mercy-le-Haut lies south-east of Metz, within range of the strong fortress of Queuleu; it was occupied by the Prussian outposts, who had received stringent orders to prevent the French soldiers digging potatoes. His Royal Highness Prince Frederick Charles was naturally anxious to bring Metz into a state of submission; and I conclude he supposed that vegetables, especially potatoes, were likely to prolong the siege. Be that as it may, the French had been in the habit of coming out of Metz, and of digging potatoes in the fields in the neighbourhood of the villages which form the suburbs of the town of Metz.

This was the first time they had been prevented; for no sooner did they make their appearance than the Prussian outposts, who had been previously strengthened, opened fire. The French then withdrew; but only for a few moments. In half an hour's time the French, much to the astonishment of the Prussians, opened a smart fire from the earthwork of St. Privat. This was the unfinished work of which I have already spoken, and which the Prussians had once thought of destroying; but inasmuch as there were no guns in it, and it was merely occupied by the French outposts during the night, it was not deemed worth the risk. The work was situated about 3,000 yards from the suburb of Montigny, and 3,500 yards from the village of Augny, occupied by the Prussians. Into this work the French had brought some field artillery, and they opened a heavy fire upon the village of Augny, the Prussian foreposts in that direction, and also upon the village of Marly, to the left of Augny. Whilst this was going on the enemy, evidently determined to have potatoes, made an advance, supported by cavalry, in the neighbourhood of Mercy-le-Haut, driving back the Prussian outposts, and occupying that village and the village of Peltre, both under protection of the guns of Queuleu. They were, however, after some sharp skirmishing, driven out; and, having no doubt accomplished their object of foraging, they retired into Metz by way of Le Sablon.

The cordon was now drawn tighter than ever; the best shots, supplied with French chassepots, did duty on the outposts close to the beleaguered city. The general health of the troops round Metz was considerably improved, although fever and dysentery, especially the latter, were still very troublesome. They had also been very much annoyed with boils, and, what was worse, carbuncles; which the doctors assigned to eating fresh-killed meat.

In a very interesting conversation with a Prussian Protestant clergyman, who had been a prisoner in Metz for a month, he described Metz as being in a state of the most perfect order and discipline. The hospitals were well regulated and carefully attended to, and the wounded were rapidly recovering. Sickness was, however, still in the ascendant, typhus, diarrhœa, and dysentery being grievously frequent. As to provisions, horseflesh was the staple commodity in the shape of meat, but there was no lack of bread, biscuit, coffee, wine, &c. Each soldier was allowed 1 lb. of meat, ½ lb. of bread or biscuit per diem. The inhabitants pursued their daily avocations as usual, whilst all the large cafés and hotels were doing a good business, at enormous prices. It was only the small cabarets that were closed. The general in command, Bazaine, had informed the officers and men that he was expecting a French army, which would sweep the Prussians out of France like chaff; that they must be patient and watchful, for that a million of French soldiers were arming for their relief.

On September 23d intelligence arrived that the army of the Crown Prince had completely surrounded Paris, and had taken a small earthwork, although at a heavy cost of life. The 7th regiment of Guards had suffered severely. A siege train of heavy guns was not far distant from the French capital. General Boër's mad escapade of galloping through Nancy with his staff, which I have spoken of, had its fruits. Upon the arrival of a number of French officers at Courcelles—all of whom wore their swords, and who were on their way across the frontier on parole—a Prussian officer received instructions to take their swords from them. Upon his delivering his unwelcome message with all possible courtesy, a French colonel flew into a desperate rage, and, drawing his sword from its scabbard, threw it upon the floor at the officer's feet, exclaiming, '*On ne nous laissera pas la chemise.*' The Prussian officer with admirable coolness replied, 'Monsieur, in our service it is the duty of an officer to obey orders; I have obeyed mine, and you insult me by throwing your sword at my feet.' Then, turning to a French general—also a prisoner—he requested him to be good enough to order the officer to pick up his sword and hand it to him, which was eventually done. The general then expostulated with the officer upon the apparent injustice of the proceeding, stating that it was entirely a breach of the conditions of surrender made after the battle. With this, of course, the lieutenant had nothing to do, and the unfortunate sufferers for other people's folly were left to chew the cud of bitter reflection, and perhaps to brood over the harsh fact that this was not the first occasion that the folly of a French general had tarnished the honour and sacrificed the proud position of the soldiers of the Empire.

The more I saw of the French officers the less was I surprised at the rapidity of events that had hurried this great military nation into the misfortunes that encompassed it. Education, that chief element of military supremacy, seemed to be found but in certain branches of the service. *Good social position, that mainstay of discipline which secures for the officer the respect and attention of his subordinates, seemed to be considered unnecessary. A gallant action demands its reward, but should be tempered with judgment. Bravery is not the only thing required in an officer. Let the common soldier for one moment fancy that he is as well able to perform the duties of his officer as that officer himself, and all confidence is gone, all respect has vanished, especially in an army where the line of demarcation between the soldier and his officer is so thinly drawn as in the French line regiments.*

With the Prussian army it is entirely different. Their officers are educated men and gentlemen. They command the respect of their subordinates, and *every man of them knows his duty.* The examinations he has to go through are severe; and until he has satisfied his superiors of his proficiency, there is no hope of promotion for him. Experience is added to the military education of the officer, who looks upon his profession as a profession, and not as an amusement; and I am confident that the success of the Prussian arms has been mainly due to the thorough organisation and proficiency of their officers in every grade. As to their bravery, the unprecedented average of loss in officers is a sufficient proof of the way the Prussian regiments have been led; at one time the average was one officer to every five men. In addition to this, the Prussian soldier is no mere machine. He has education also; he thinks for himself too, and he knows when a mistake is committed; the soldiers help one another, they assist their officers, their discipline is of the strictest, and, gentlemen themselves, they are commanded by gentlemen.

The state of things about this time may be summed up in a few words. The Baden troops were battering and shelling Strasburg. The division of the Grand Duke of Mecklenburg was *looking* at Toul—they must have known every chimney-pot in the place by that time; whilst the 1st army kept vigorrous watch over Bazaine and Metz. It was hard work this—always on the *qui-vive*, the outposts unsheltered, and exposed to the most harassing and dull routine of duty; every day a chance of your being picked off at any moment, with little glory for recompense. We had, however, plenty to eat and drink, although, of course, luxuries, such as sugar, butter, eggs, beer, or good brandy, were not to be got for love or money. There was also very little hay.

On the 25th of September the official intelligence of the fall of Toul appeared in general orders.

After a brave resistance of some five weeks, this little stronghold of French chivalry succumbed to the irresistible arguments of want and bombardment.

The peculiar position in which the town was situated materially tended to increase the horrors of the bombardment, which the 13th army corps opened upon it from the surrounding heights on the 23d inst. Before the little garrison, commanded by Major Hack, finally succumbed, but a small portion of this once joyous town remained to be seen. In the universal *débris* of houses, of falling walls and burning rafters, men, women, and children alike suffered.

To those who live in security in London it would, indeed, appear strange, if the boy who should have brought them their *Daily Telegraph* were found under the *débris* of a fallen house, if their milk did not arrive because a bullet had gone through the can, and if the butcher did not call for orders because *no horse* had been killed that morning, the stock being exhausted. Can you imagine a family going to bed in security, and waking up to find several of its members gone to that home from which none return to tell the unfathomed secret? Can you, who take up the daily papers and read them as a *bonne bouche* after your comfortable night's rest and plentifully supplied breakfast-table—can you picture to yourself the fear of starvation, of death at your door, of disease all around you, of aggravated suffering for those who form your family circle, from the bursting of a shell in your street, from the want of food in your neighbourhood, from the disease-laden atmosphere arising from the untended and putrefying wounds of your neighbours?

And yet, but a few short weeks before, the town of Toul lay more peacefully in the valley of the Moselle than London does now on the banks of the Thames. Toul surrendered to want, disease, and starvation. *Requiescat in pace.* May the brave defenders be consoled by the reflection that, although isolated in that small spot, without hope of assistance, their noble conduct has been the admiration of their enemies and of the whole world! The defenders of this brave little town, scarce 2,000 in number, surrendered at discretion. They offered to surrender some fourteen days before, provided they were permitted to march out with the honours of war; but this was denied them, and so they fought, and starved, and suffered on, until no hope was left them. The railway communication to Paris was now completely open.

The state of things round Metz was however not long permitted to remain in the peaceful way which had marked the last few weeks. At 3 A.M. on the morning of the 24th of September, the alarm sounded. Now, an alarm at so early an hour in the morning, although a thing of common occurrence, was by no means a pleasant thing on a cold, rainy, autumnal one. First comes the sharp bugle-note, then a galloping to and fro of hussars and aides-de-camp, then the steady roll of the drum, which summons the half-sleepy battalions from their bundles of straw. Out they come, poor fellows; the rain falls in torrents; in a few minutes they are soaked through. Nevertheless, they fall in, and in ten minutes the whole division is under arms. There, however, they must wait until the order comes directing them where to go. Some try to light their pipes, but the rain puts out their matches; some suck peppermint drops; and some take a mouthful of that abominable *eau de vie du pays;* but all are ready. What should prevent them? They lay down in their cloaks, their rifles beside them; and their haversacks contain food for the morrow.

Let us for a moment glance at what the Prussian infantry soldier has to carry on this wet and cold morning. His knapsack contains the following articles: one shirt, a pair of boots, a pair of new soles, a bottle of grease for his boots, a bag of salt and a bag of rice, a pair of calico trousers and a calico jacket for fatigue, and some linen bandages or cloths, with a bottle of tallow, for the feet. I think I hear our commanding officers exclaiming at this last article. Nevertheless, I do not believe that in a whole Prussian infantry regiment fifty pairs of socks will at this moment be found. They wrap these linen cloths, first of all smeared with tallow, about their feet, and then draw their boots on, and I find from experience that this plan answers admirably. I marched from Saarbrück to Gravelotte with the Prussian regiments, and I can confidently affirm that this somewhat primitive sock answered admirably, effectually preventing sore feet, and the inconvenience arising from new boots, with which the greater portion of the army were then supplied. Add to what I have above stated forty rounds of ammunition and a camp-kettle with a lid, in which is placed a coffee-grinder, and you have a soldier's kit in his knapsack. In addition to this, in fine weather he carries his cloak rolled up across his shoulder, a haversack containing his rations, fifty rounds of ammunition on his belt in two pouches, and his water-bottle—the last being the most unserviceable article of the kit, inasmuch as it is made of glass covered with leather. This is all. Let my brother officers take note of this, for with this simple but serviceable kit has the German army performed the marches, and gone through the privations and exposures of the campaign.

But now an aide comes galloping along. "Gewehr über! Bataillon marsch!" and the whole division moves silently off in the direction of the outposts. Arrived outside the village of Corby, the men are halted, arms are piled, and there they remain till eight P.M., when they are marched back. This is an occurrence without results that occurs daily. So much for being in a position where you have to keep sentry upon a large army placed in a strongly fortified town.

Shortly after this, the potato battle, as it was then called, commenced briskly in the neighbourhood of Pouilly. Fort Queuleu again came to the assistance of the *pot au feu* by setting part of the village on fire. Then a somewhat brisker engagement took place in the direction of St. Julien, which terminated in a heavy cannonade on both sides, the Prussian shells setting some of the houses of Metz on fire. Finally the fire slackens; and whether the potatoes for the *pot au feu* were obtained or not remained a matter of uncertainty; but some dead, and a good many wounded, attested the severity of the encounter.

Five hundred chassepots, with ammunition, were

now served out to the Prussian outposts, which they were to use at long distances upon the French foragers—a sufficient proof of the Prussian opinion as to the superiority of this weapon over the needle-rifle. The ammunition, however, remained a great stumbling-block in both weapons. The weather, if at all damp or rainy, had the greatest effect upon both chassepot and needle-rifle cartridges, more particularly on the latter, inasmuch as they are still less protected than the chassepot. I have seen a Frenchman on a damp day load and let off his rifle three times successively without result.

Prince Frederick Charles had a levee, for the purpose of distributing the order of the Iron Cross to some of the staff. His highness is not in the habit of making great speeches, consequently the ceremony was by no means imposing. I heard, however, a story in connection with the Prince which goes far to speak for the interest and affection he has for those who serve under him. Major von Schmeling, of the Fusilier Guards, was killed at the taking of St. Privat, on the 18th of August. His brother, Captain von Schmeling, of the Artillery of the Guard, was aide-de-camp to Lieutenant-General Schwartz, commanding the artillery of the 1st army, and on his receiving the Iron Cross at the hands of his Royal Highness the Prince said to him: 'I have desired my daughter to send to your mother a sketch of your brother's grave, which I have had made, and I have written to her myself to tell her how deeply I regret the loss of so good an officer and so true a friend.'

The first serious change in the command of the army before Metz now occurred. General von Steinmetz was ordered to hand over his command to Prince Frederick Charles and to take the governorship of the Prussian fortress of Posen. That General von Steinmetz is a good soldier, not even his worst enemy can deny; but that he was often failing in the courtly demeanour and behaviour of a gentleman was a fact that even his best friends have not failed to admit. It was, perhaps, this unfortunate bluffness carried a little *à outrance* that caused him to be removed from the command of the first army, and placed, as it were, upon the shelf. His unfortunate misunderstanding with other generals of superior rank and position to his own are facts so well known that I need not repeat them; but certain it is, that the stern unbending nature of the old soldier caused him to be removed from a position which gave him the opportunity of making himself obnoxious in high quarters.

To General von Steinmetz must be attributed the credit of many of the brilliant and resolute attacks which have led to Prussian victory; but he had a fault of attacking somewhat too rashly, and permitting his battalions to advance too far unsupported. To mention one instance only: the advance at Spicheren, and the storming of those terrible heights, was intrusted to three regiments, 9,000 men without supports, who were at first compelled to retire from sheer loss; and had not the 2d line been very handy, the carnage would have been still more severe. General von Steinmetz would not, however, wait until that second line was formed, but ordered the advance immediately. Where, however, there was danger, or that the Prussian army received a check, the first man in the breach or at his post, through good or evil report, was General von Steinmetz. He left the first army commanding the respect of every one—the friendship of but few.

The exact quantity of material and men that fell into the hands of the Prussians upon the surrender of Toul was now ascertained. I have put material before men, because when the two are compared the immense superiority of the former over the latter is obvious. 140 guns, 45 of which were rifled, a very large quantity of ammunition, 150 stand of arms, 500 sabres, rations for 2,000 men, 200 horses, one standard, 190 officers, and 2,240 men. The railway communication between Toul and Nancy being reëstablished, the unfortunate inhabitants, who had undergone this prolonged siege, with all its attendant horrors, and the eight hours' bombardment at the end, obtained that assistance of which they stood so fearfully in need, namely, food and medical attendance. The state of the town, as far as sickness was concerned, was something too dreadful to contemplate—the children crying in the streets for want of food, whilst their parents were dying in garrets of typhus and dysentery.

Nor need I, in thus stating the sanitary condition of Toul, and its want of sustenance, exclude the towns and villages that lie in the neighbourhood of Metz. I am speaking of the French inhabitants. This state of things is easy of explanation. Metz had now been surrounded by a very large army for more than five weeks. Previous to the arrival of that army, every village and town in its neighbourhood sent in its quota of provisions, leaving the inhabitants a bare sufficiency to last them through the winter—for your peasant of Lorraine is by no means a careful person about such matters. These provisions were of course appropriated by the invading army. At first the inhabitants gave freely of everything; that is to say, in most cases, because they all expected that the siege of Metz would be but a matter of a few days, and that the vast army then quartered upon them would move on elsewhere. But as day after day went by, and fresh requisitions for wine, cattle, sheep, wood, and forage came pouring in, the fact that Metz might hold out for a very considerable time began gradually to dawn upon them, and that during that time they would have to endure the tribe of blue-coated locusts who were gradually but surely eating them out of house and home.

The consequences were fatal to both parties. The father who at first received the invaders of his country, and tried to make the best of the situation by keeping on good terms, naturally felt poignantly the sufferings of his starving children. 'I gave you all I had,' he cries, 'and now my happy home is desolate; my children are starving; I cannot earn my bread; my wife is dying of fever; and yet you ask me for more: you make me work at your batteries, and I have no hope for the future.' The only answer to this sad, but too true, lamentation was, that it was the result of war.

The Prussians did everything in their power for the inhabitants; they were kind and lenient to a degree totally at variance with the policy of other armies when in an enemy's country; they paid for everything. But what is the use of money to him who cannot purchase food? Kindness will not save his wife from the grave, or his children from starvation. The shopkeeper, who had hitherto been all politeness, and ever ready to sell his wares or drive his trade for Prussian thalers, now became morose and insolent. He, too, found that all his gains, all the high prices he had compelled the Prussian soldier to pay, would not keep him from starvation. Then came the awful question. What was to become of them in winter? where was the food to come from, or even the wood to cook it? The prospect was too fearful to dwell upon; yet such was the state of affairs in the once fertile province of Lorraine.

Meantime the Prussian army corps surrounded Metz, where it was becoming more plainly visible that hunger had also commenced its fearful inroad. The French troops in Metz no longer fought in order to burst through the iron cordon that hemmed them in. Were they even to achieve the task, where would they have gone to? They now fought for food. Daily, hourly, they struggled for forage, for potatoes, for anything. The hitherto silent batteries now incessantly fired either on one side or the other. Hour after hour the fighting had been on the side of Mercy-le-Haut; in fact, such hot work had been going on in the neighbourhood of this little hamlet, that its name became a perfect byword, and if you thanked a man even for a light for your cigar, you said, 'Merci, le Haut.'

The incessant fighting gave one not a moment's repose; sometimes we slept in a house, sometimes in bivouac—sometimes we ate and sometimes not. One day a feast like a king—that is to say, bouillon, roast beef, and potatoes; the next, biscuit or black bread and bacon, but always wine. Sometimes by night, sometimes by day, but every day from eight to ten hours in the saddle we wend our weary course from one fight to another.

At a quarter to nine on the morning of September 27th, the guns from Fort Queuleu opened upon the village of Mercy-le-Haut. Shell after shell came hurtling in, bursting in the street—if you can dignify it by the word—and the outhouses. In a few moments the place was in flames. The alarm sounded, the troops turned out, and every man was at his post. Then, too, the village of Peltre, to the left, was on fire, and a heavy infantry fire was going on with the outposts in that direction. Happening to turn my glass towards the railroad which leads to Nancy, you may imagine my surprise at seeing a locomotive with full steam up, and dragging a train of wagons, coming slowly forward out of Metz. Between the railroad and Queuleu I also observed an infantry regiment with some cavalry advancing upon Peltre. Just then a heavy musketry fire opened from the hedges and woods in the neighbourhood of the hamlet, and the outposts retired upon the 69th regiment, which had just deployed in rear of the burning houses. Meantime the Prussian artillery had not been slow to come into action; a battery between Marly and Pouilly opened upon the advancing enemy, as also some batteries of the 14th division 7th army corps, to the right and left of Mercy-le-Haut.

The smoke having cleared a little, a line regiment was observed advancing straight upon the hamlet, evidently intent upon its possession, about 600 or 700 yards off. But the steady fire of the Prussians checked the advance; the enemy commencing the usual tirailleur tactics, and keeping up a heavy fire, with, comparatively speaking, little loss. The train had approached near to Peltre. Some said it had gone into the village; but as I did not see it, I cannot vouch for the assertion. One could only conclude that the French anticipated getting some provisions, and that the trucks were for the purpose of taking them back to Metz. At 11 A.M. the French entered Peltre and Mercy-le-Haut, notwithstanding the hot fire of the Prussians, but their time of remaining there could not have exceeded ten minutes; fresh regiments came up, and a perfect storm of bullets was rained on the unfortunate villages. The French then retired, and the train steamed back into Metz. At 11.45. A.M. all was again comparatively quiet.

It appeared that the regiments who attacked were the 70th and 84th regiments of the line, supported by a battalion of chasseurs. They had just come on outpost duty, and were determined to give as much trouble and as little peace as possible; this was heard from some prisoners. The fight of this morning was on a somewhat larger scale than we had lately been treated to. In fact, it was the heaviest action since that of the 30th and 31st in the neighbourhoods of Grigy and St. Julien. The French must have had at least 8000 troops engaged, and the Prussians about the same number. What the loss on the French side was, I cannot say, but it must have been considerable; for during their retreat they retired across some very open grounds, which the Prussian skirmishers and artillery took immediate advantage of.

I observed the French working parties busily engaged at the unfinished fort of St. Privat, of which I have already spoken, and I thought at the time that this same fort, when complete, would be a thorn in their sides which the Prussians would bitterly regret having permitted to grow up there. This battery is but 2500 yards from Augny, and about 3000 from Marly, and had they got a 24-pounder into it, why good-bye to a peaceful night's rest, even in Jouy-aux-Arches.

And now the same old story greeted one at every corner. Every one wished Bazaine individually, and Metz collectively, at the bottom of the sea. His Royal Highness Prince Frederick Charles was suffering from the usual malady, dysentery; and sickness was rapidly on the increase. The German papers teemed with a fresh stock of aggravated abuse against England, who they again most positively declared had just dispatched 500,000 chassepots to France. Indeed, the position of an Englishman before Metz was by no means pleasant, especially if he was a military man. I have had the greatest difficulty in convincing Prussian officers that the Government had done everything in their power to prevent such transactions; that the law respecting this matter had not, as yet, been legislated for by continental governments; and that the belligerents themselves were those who should take the matter in hand. In vain I explained to them that it was almost an impossibility to prevent private individuals from occasionally escaping the vigilance of English officials, and running a cargo of material at any cost. A very wrong view of the matter was taken by a great majority of the Prussian officers. As far as I myself was concerned, I never received anything but the greatest possible attention; but it was decidedly unpleasant to hear, even from one's friends, that your country had committed the 'grossièretés' that the German papers would have had one believe.

Paris was said to be in a state of siege without and revolt within. An official telegram arrived stating that the people were fighting against one another in the streets. M. Jules Favre had had another interview with Count von Bismarck. It was said that in the first interview at Rheims the Prussian Minister, in speaking of the fortresses, said, 'Metz we must have, and Thionville also; of Strasburg we will say nothing at present;' but that, much to M. Jules Favre's disgust, the Minister's words were afterwards, 'Metz we will have, Thionville also; and most unquestionably Strasburg.'

The fall of Strasburg and of Toul naturally affected the position of things before Metz. Serious thoughts were entertained of getting up heavy ordnance from Strasburg, and Generals Schwartz and Biehler, accompanied by their staffs, started on a tour of inspection round the fortress. This looked very much as if a change were meant; probably the guns that have been used at Strasburg would arrive, and then we might expect a second Sebastopol, with the attendant horrors of a winter campaign.

About this time a general shift of quarters amongst the various corps took place, which, to a certain extent, inconvenienced many of the army corps, whose regiments had with considerable labour and ingenuity hutted themselves against the already cold and frosty nights. The huts were for the most part made upon the same principle as those which the Sardinian army employed in the Crimea. They held from 100 to 120 men each, and were warm and comfortable. The manner in which they were constructed was as follows: about a dozen upright posts formed of the trunks of trees are sunk into the ground in a line, leaving a height of eight feet from the surface; along these a strong longitudinal beam is placed, from which sloping rafters are brought down to the ground on either side, forming the roof. The frame is then thatched with fir boughs and other leafy material, and finally the whole is covered with earth thrown up from the outside. A ditch is formed round the hut, which carries off the drainage from the roof. The inside is then dug out to a depth of about one foot, and the building is complete, with the exception of a window at each end, and a door in the centre.

Sickness, particularly typhus, was now on the increase. A very melancholy occurrence, resulting in the death of a distinguished engineer officer, took place one morning, from the effects of that dreadful epidemic. Captain Calman was a young soldier of great experience and ability. He was a universal favourite amongst his brother officers, and highly valued by the generals in command. A few days previous to the event which closed his career, he was attacked with typhus fever in bivouac, and was sent into hospital at Jouy-aux-Arches. One night delirium commenced, and his father was telegraphed for. His servant slept with him in the same room, with positive orders not to leave him. Suddenly, at four in the morning, he awoke his attendant, and asked to be dressed. He should immediately, he said, go to the front, as the French were about to attack. The servant foolishly complied; and they both left for the outposts, Captain Calman taking his revolver with him. Arrived there, he desired his servant to wait whilst he inspected some works in course of formation. Soon after the report of a pistol was heard, and upon hastening to the spot whence the sound proceeded, the attendant found that the unfortunate young man had shot himself through the head with his revolver, under the influence of typhoid delirium.

It has been said that soldiers become hardened by war; that the scenes through which they pass, and the constant contact into which they are brought with violent deaths in various ways, tend to obliterate their softer feelings, and make them indifferent to the sufferings of those around them. All I can say is, that no man promulgating such an opinion could have been a soldier. It is true that in the moment of battle, when the blood is on fire, and the action is hot and determined, one is apt for a second, perhaps, to forget the sufferings of those who lie around; but the moment the action is over there is no woman more tender-hearted, no nurse more gentle, no attendant more watchful, than the man who has just been rushing forward to the destruction of his fellow-man in the ranks of the enemy.

If you could have seen how gently and tenderly that Prussian soldier wiped the blood from the face of his officer—how he raised his poor body in his arms and bore him away to a shelter, whilst the tears poured down his sunburnt cheeks—how he threw himself on the ground, and gave way to a burst of manly sorrow, that spoke more eloquently for his feelings than can any poor attempt of mine—and how, when the first sharp grief for the loss of his master had passed by, he bent reverently on his knees, and, with uncovered head, prayed to Him who is the Author and Giver of life, whilst every soldier around stood bareheaded—I say, if you could have seen this, as I did, you would have said that no more tender-hearted being could exist than your true soldier.

Let me, however, turn from this sad scene to describe one of more stirring interest. Scarcely had daylight lit up the usually dull and uninteresting plateau on the Mercy-le-Haut side of Metz when the customary morning salutation of rifles between the outposts commenced. On the line which, beginning at a sugar-manufactory, ended at the village of Peltre, the fire from the French outposts was unusually severe—so much so, that when it ceased, the outposts of the 15th regiment of the 7th army corps, commanded by General von Zastrow, which held the village, were of opinion that no farther attack would take place that day. The head-quarters of the regiment lay in the village of Peltre, while the outposts were at some little distance.

Now, close by there was a pond full of carp; and I need hardly say that fish was a luxury not a little prized in a place where provisions, although perhaps plentiful, were but little varied. Accordingly everybody set to work to catch the wily carp; but the wily carp are not so easily laid hold of. They bury themselves in the mud when hard pressed; and, inasmuch as the soldiers had no hooks or lines, they took off their boots, and, amidst shouts of laughter from their comrades, tried to catch a fry for their breakfasts. In the midst of the amusement the outpost suddenly opened fire, and came running back towards the village, driven in by a column of French infantry. All was now in confusion: some stuck in the mud, and could not get out; others rushed into the village for their arms, only to find themselves prisoners in the hands of the French. But in a few minutes succour was at hand. The regiment was promptly supported, but not before the French had taken 180 prisoners, the whole of the regimental staff bureau, and its baggage wagon, and, making use of a train that had brought them out of Metz, retired by the railway under shelter of the guns of Queuleu. So much for carp-fishing on outpost.

The French, evidently tired of inactivity, or acting up to Marshal Bazaine's orders—a copy of which, being found on the person of a prisoner, came into

Prussian hands—meant to weary the Prussians by constant attacks on every side. Hitherto they had beat up their quarters, more particularly on the side of Mercy-le-Haut; but new batteries had opened of whose existence they were not aware, and the idea that the French were short of ammunition in Metz was proved entirely fallacious. They had—rightly or wrongly I must leave others to judge—unmasked many of their guns; and the Prussian lines received the benefit almost hourly. No doubt Marshal Bazaine found that time passed heavily for his pent-up legions; and as the French soldiers suffer more severely from *ennui* than anything else, he found that the best cure for the disease was to keep them continually employed.

One morning, at four o'clock, I accompanied a patrol of the 33d regiment, belonging to the 8th army corps, which was sent forward towards the work of St. Privat, for the purpose of ascertaining, if possible, with what force the French held it, and of gleaning any intelligence about the enemy that could be picked up. The patrol was composed of six men and a sergeant, all old soldiers and fine fellows. This work of St. Privat I have already described, and I will merely remark that it was still unfinished. It was situated upon a perfectly level plain, which extended from the suburbs of Metz to the heights above the villages of Augny, Marly, and Pouilly. Between the advanced post and the work there was no shelter whatever, the plain being under cultivation. We had, consequently, to advance with the utmost caution, not speaking above a whisper.

Spreading out to a distance of twenty or thirty paces from one another, and occasionally halting to look about, we gradually neared the slope of the work. The sergeant in command was to the left of the party, the man next him being a tall fusilier, of some six feet two inches in height. This soldier was excessively anxious to distinguish himself and obtain the Iron Cross — which, like our Victoria Cross, is the summit of the Prussian warrior's ambition. I whispered to the sergeant that there seemed to be rifle-pits in front of the work, and he immediately made a sign to the men to lie down.

In this position we remained for some minutes, trying to catch any sound that would indicate the presence of workmen or outposts. The man to my left at last rose, and, speaking in a loud voice, said to the sergeant, 'I don't think the work is occupied; I will go forward and see.' Scarcely had the words left his lips when a dozen chassepots blazed at him from a rifle-pit not fifty yards away. The unfortunate man immediately fell, crying out to his sergeant that he was lost, and begging him, in tones that wrung one's heart, to write to his mother. To go forward to recover his body was impossible, as the fire from the rifle-pits was hot and frequent; we were forced, therefore, to crawl back on our hands and knees, and leave our luckless companion to his fate. Episodes like this were of daily occurrence; and these outposts cost the Prussian army many a good man, for all were anxious to distinguish themselves, and the men were often imprudent in their movements.

Out of this affair there arose, however, a great difficulty. It was necessary to ascertain whether the man was dead or only wounded. If dead, would the French bury him? and if wounded, would they take him in and care for him? These questions, one would think, could have been easily answered; but unfortunately it was not so. To ascertain the fact it would be necessary to send a flag of truce; but, inasmuch as the French fired upon a flag of truce when it approached from this direction, the general would not permit one to be sent. The Prussian dead have lain for days before the French lines without burial; and as for the wounded, the French put them into empty wagons, and pushed them along the railway towards the Prussian lines as far as they would go, and there left them. The same patrol were therefore told off to ascertain the fate of their comrade; and they found that his unburied body still lay in the spot where he had fallen.

On the 2d of October the villages of Mercy-le-Haut and Peltre were re-occupied by the German troops, and their outposts held an advanced position before Fort Queuleu. The fire from the French works was continuous; the enemy commencing at an early hour in the morning by setting on fire the picturesque little village of Jussy, which lies some 800 yards in front of Vaux. Not satisfied with driving the unfortunate inhabitants from their homes, and destroying the little property that was left to them, because a patrol of ten men and a sergeant had taken up their quarters there, they set to work to destroy the remaining houses in Peltre and Mercy-le-Haut on the other side; so that, while Quentin thundered on the one side of Metz, Queuleu growled on the other. In the afternoon the forts to the right and left of Montigny took up the tune, and in the evening St. Julien joined in the concert. The French were evidently determined not to leave one stone upon another in any of the villages around Metz that could afford shelter or protection to the German troops.

This is, alas, one of the melancholy necessities of war; and the unfortunate inhabitants, already deprived of food, were about to have their dwellings taken away from them also. The poor creatures had been endeavouring recently to reap some of the abundant harvest of grapes that loaded the vineyards on every side; but in this work they met with considerable difficulty, for the gathering of the fruit was not the only thing they had to do: the grapes had to be put into the vats and pressed. This, except in a few cases, at least in this neighbourhood, was almost an impossibility; for every wine-press had for the last six weeks been used as a stable for horses, and the Augean filth must be cleansed away before the process of wine-making could commence.

As if to throw more impediments in their way, the Francs-tireurs again appeared in the neighbourhood of Pont-à-Mousson, and their performances by no means tended to improve the position of the Lorraine peasantry. And such was the state of the country, that one dared not ride alone, especially after dark, and more particularly through woods, anywhere in the neighbourhood of Metz. This feature in a deplorable war naturally had a most damaging effect upon the feelings of the German army towards the French peasantry. Hitherto, pity for their unfortunate position, sympathy with their sufferings, and assistance in a solid shape, had marked the dealings of the German soldiers with the inhabitants; but now this state of matters had given place to anger and disgust, to antipathy and contempt, which were visited upon the heads of the innocent as well as the guilty.

The prisoners taken in the affair at Peltre were sent out of Metz to be exchanged. They described their treatment as of the best. They were served twice a day with excellent soup made from horseflesh, and also a sufficiency of bread. The only thing that seemed to be wanting was salt, which they said was served out only to the officers. They described the French troops as being in excellent spirits, and said that the soldiers talked, laughed, and joked with them in the most friendly way. They were not subjected to any examination respecting the disposition of troops, or anything at all connected with the arrangements of the German army; nor were they ever visited by any general officer; but quarters were immediately assigned to them in the suburb of Le Sablon, where they were exceedingly well treated, and eventually sent with a flag of truce to the nearest Prussian outpost. Their report only tended to confirm the opinion I had already expressed, that Metz la Pucelle would not be taken before winter should have tried the resources and constitutions of the German army.

The inhabitants of a village in the neighbourhood

of Châlons, with the aid of a French engineer, had recourse to another method of testifying their displeasure at the approach of German troops. Immediately before approaching Châlons there is a sharp curve in the railway. Commencing at one end and finishing at the other, they had carefully unscrewed the bolts that attach the rails to the sleepers of the permanent way; the consequence was, that on the approach of the first train from Commercy it was impossible to see any impediment in the way; but no sooner had the engine and the first few carriages advanced than they were precipitated over the embankment into a deep ditch. Fortunately no one was killed, although the engine-driver was dreadfully burnt, and several officers and men were more or less mutilated. Truly a humane way of destroying one's enemies!

To give you an idea of the patriotism that actuated not only the men and women, but even the children of Germany, I must relate what occurred to me as I was riding to my quarters one evening. I met certainly the smallest soldier I had ever yet seen. He was completely equipped in uniform, helmet, knapsack, and side-arms, but no needle rifle—the poor little fellow could scarcely have lifted it. He was nine years old, and by no means tall for his age. He stopped me, and, in the most matter-of-fact way, asked me if I could direct him to the town commandant's office. I asked him what on earth he was, and what he wanted with the town commandant—so completely was I taken aback by the Lilliputian apparition. Drawing himself up to his full height, and saluting in the stiffest manner, he informed me that he belonged to the 61st Pomeranian regiment, which had just marched in, and that he wanted quarters. So absurdly ridiculous, and at the same time so thoroughly military, was the whole proceeding, that I burst into a fit of laughter; and, lifting the little manikin into my saddle, I carried him off in triumph to the head-quarter mess, where, I need hardly say, he was well taken care of.

The poor boy's story was a melancholy one. Of his parents he knew nothing. His early recollections were of the barrack, where from day to day the sympathy, hospitality, and kindness that are part and parcel of the soldier's character were never denied to the poor helpless outcast. His manly, amusing, and attractive ways soon made him a favourite, and the men, out of their pay, saved a sufficient sum to buy the clothing of a Pomeranian fusilier. The boy's home was with the 61st—the first words of kindness and encouragement he heard were from the rough soldiers who surrounded him. Bold and manly in his conduct, he found the true road to the soldiers' hearts; and when their country bade them go forth to fight, the little outcast was the first to bind his slender all upon his shoulder, and go with his friends to meet a soldier's fate.

CHAPTER VI.

THE PROGRESS OF THE BLOCKADE.

STILL the same dreary prospect, still the same wearing, wearying vigil round the devoted fortress. After the battle of Gravelotte, every one stoutly affirmed that Metz could not possibly hold out for more than fourteen days: these fourteen days expanded into twenty-eight, and eventually stretched into two months up to the 4th of October. Bazaine knew that there was now no hope for him or his five corps of French soldiers; and yet he made no positive attempt to break through the circle of troops that surrounded his splendid army. In the mean time bands of Franc-tireurs began to make their appearance in the neighbourhood of Metz. They committed some horrible murders at the very moment when the German authorities were using every means in their power to assist the population towards the amelioration of their position, by clearing the wine-presses in order to give them a chance of reaping their harvest of grapes.

On the same day when relief for the unfortunate and starving peasantry was occupying the earnest attention of the Prussian officers, a certain shoemaker of Pont-à-Mousson was seized with a fit of patriotic enthusiasm. He imagined that he was suddenly called upon to do a great deed. The murdering an officer in cold blood, especially if he was Prussian, would immortalise him in the annals of his country, considerably assist in saving France from the invader, and induce Count von Bismarck to listen to the overtures of M. Jules Favre. Accordingly he sallied forth, provided with a weapon which he had secreted, and in a retired spot he saw a cavalry officer in Prussian uniform riding towards him. Now, according to his self-imagined programme, he should have stepped boldly forward as man to man, and, avowing his intentions, have shot the officer in an heroic way. But suddenly the valiant shoemaker recollected the possibility of the officer's carrying a revolver, and estimating the precise amount of his courage, which, Bob Acres like, gradually oozed out at his fingers' ends, preferred the safer method of shooting at him from behind a wall. The hero was hung up as high as Haman.

One evening I had occasion to ride from the headquarters of the 1st army corps to those of General von Göben, commanding the 8th army corps, when I myself had the misfortune to become the mark for another of these gentry. Crossing the river Seille, below Verny and to the left of Corny, over a bridge that had been erected by the German army, I found myself opposite a small wood. I stopped for a moment to light a cigar; and whilst in that anxious state of uncertainty in which a man finds himself, when he strikes his last match, as to whether or not it will burn, the sharp report of a rifle and the whistle of a bullet over my head caused my horse to start forward, and considerably upset my equanimity. The white smoke from the explosion still hung over the place from which the shot had been fired, and drawing my revolver, I rode to the spot; but I might as well have avoided the risk of losing my horse, for I found the wood so thick that it was impossible to advance, while I could hear hasty footsteps retreating through the undergrowth. Riding round to the other side of the road to Verny, I fortunately met with a gendarme, who, with the aid of his comrade, eventually succeeded in making a prisoner of the man. In fact it now became a matter of the greatest uncertainty, when one went 500 yards from a bivouac into the interior, whether the destination was ever reached or not.

It may not be amiss here to say a few words upon the Prussian field gendarmerie, the organisation of which is not the least of their admirable arrangements. The force is composed of old soldiers who have served their time. They are chosen principally for their good conduct and their aptness for such work as an army gendarme must be prepared to do. They are commanded by old and experienced officers, who have served in campaigns and been seriously wounded. To each army corps is attached a troop of 45 men and one officer—the staff of each army being supplied with a lieutenant-colonel and a captain, with five or six men as orderlies. It is the duty of these gendarmes to maintain order in the villages or towns through which the troops pass, or which are taken possession of by an army of occupation. They precede the advance of a division, and prevent plunder or theft. I have seen them stop the troops from even digging potatoes until an order had been given permitting them to do so. Their duty is very severe, inasmuch as they must be prepared at a moment's notice to proceed to any place where anything like disorder goes on, more particularly between the troops and the inhabitants—the latter being placed specially under their protection. They have also to patrol the battle-field after an engagement, and to prevent as much as possible the plundering of the dead. In addition to this they are used as orderlies, and are constantly exposed to the fire of the enemy's outposts. Altogether the duties of the 'Feld Gendarmes' are by no means light or agreeable. It is needless to add that they are mounted, and excellently well; very much of the good order that existed in the towns and villages was due to their exertions. I need hardly add they are the terror of the Marketender, and the *bête noire* of the camp-follower.

The state of things in and around Metz still continued unchanged, with the exception that the French commenced making infinitely more use of their batteries. The hitherto peaceful repose of the villages in front of Ars was now continually disturbed by Mont St. Quentin. Not satisfied with this, the French heavy guns opened upon the town of Ars and the railway station, inflicting considerable damage upon the large ironworks belonging to M. Dreyfuss. A shell burst in the middle of the station, injuring several people; and another came through the roof of the house where an officer was quartered, and, exploding in his room, severely wounded him. The extreme distance that any shell was pitched was 6400 yards by the measurement of a Prussian artillery officer. It now became evident that the object of the French army, following out the programme laid down for them by Bazaine, was to give no rest to the troops that kept them so closely hemmed in; and I very much feared that the beautiful bridge over the Moselle, between Ars and Jouy, together with those two towns, would suffer severely from the fire of the batteries of Mont St. Quentin and Montigny.

The position of the French troops remained the same. They occupied three camps: the first situated in the hollow below Plappeville, and extending to the villages of Devant-les-Ponts and St. Eloy; the second covered l'Ile de Chambière; the third was placed in Basse and Haute Montigny, Le Sablon, and behind St. Privat. By this arrangement it will be seen that no troops were quartered in the town of Metz; but that they occupied the suburbs in every direction, under the protection of the outworks of St. Quentin, Plappeville, St. Julien, Queuleu, and Montigny. Why these camps were permitted to occupy these positions, or to remain in peace and quietness, was a mystery that I have been unable to solve.

No doubt the policy that guided the German generals was one best calculated to save bloodshed; but I heard complaints on every side that, whilst the French batteries gave no peace day or night, the Prussians seldom replied. Artillery officers cried out for those short 24-pounders that had done such tremendous work at Strasburg. Engineer officers fretted and fumed at the apparent apathy that seemed to exist; for it was obvious that, if these camps were regularly and persistently fired upon, the troops would ultimately take refuge in the town. The consequence would be an increase of disease and mortality which would soon force Bazaine to surrender. This, at the first glance, seems an inhuman course; but it is, after all, no worse than the plan of reducing the town by starvation. So long as Metz and Bazaine's army remained, so to speak, confronting the invader, so long would false hopes be raised in other parts of the country, which would only lead to more bloodshed and misery.

The French had still a very fair number of horses. I noticed that some of their cavalry patrols and batteries of field artillery were in excellent condition, considering the state of affairs. Meantime, wherever there was a chance, their infantry, always on the alert, made a dash; but they could do no more, and, beyond keeping the army of Prince Frederick Charles constantly on the *qui-vive*, there were no other results.

I had a melancholy duty to perform one day. Mr. Annesly, British consul at Hamburg, sent a gentleman from that town, in the hopes of discovering the grave of his son, who fell before the village of St. Privat-la-Montagne when it was assaulted by the Prussian Guard on the 18th of August. He was, it appears, an ensign in the regiment, and was known as the Herr von Annesly. Poor young fellow! after some trouble we discovered his grave. He lies in the churchyard of St. Marie-aux-Chênes, close to the spot where he fell, gallantly leading his company. In the same grave are buried eleven other officers of his regiment—the 2d Guards; and it will be at least a consolation for his relatives to know how much he was beloved both by officers and men, and how, under that fearful fire, he upheld the honour of his country by setting a brilliant example of intrepid courage, together with a coolness that has seldom been witnessed in so young an officer. The picturesque little churchyard contains all that was mortal of an Irish gentleman who has found his grave, whilst fighting for Germany and right—in the same soil where his forefathers have many of them lain before him, in the good old days when the Irish Brigade was a terror to the soldiers of the Empire.

A very gentlemanly system of making war was about this time resorted to. If I recollect aright, it was at Charleston that one American general sent his compliments to the other to say that his flag-staff was shot in two, and he would abstain from firing until a new one should have been put up. Much the same sort of thing happened here. One night, commencing at seven and continuing until ten o'clock, Mont St. Quentin sent a shell into the town of Ars every twenty minutes. The fire was principally directed upon the railway station and the splendid ironworks of M. Dreyfuss. These buildings were severely injured—the greater portion of the workshops being entirely destroyed—but with little injury to human life. The next morning a letter was dispatched, *viâ* Moulins-les-Metz, with a flag of truce to the commandant of

St. Quentin, to inform him that the fire of the fort had last night been directed upon a spot where the hospitals of the French wounded and the International Society's tents were placed, and begging that he would be good enough to fire upon some other spot for the future. Now, inasmuch as the white flag with the red cross waved over almost every house in Ars, Jouy, Vaux, Augny, Marly, Pouilly, and the towns and villages surrounding Metz, the French would have had some little difficulty to avoid firing on a spot which flew for its protection this emblem of sickness and disease—if, indeed, they paid any attention to the request, which I greatly doubted. They would naturally say, 'You have the railway; send your wounded and sick to the rear.'

Talking of Moulins-les-Metz, I should have mentioned that it had been arranged between Prince Frederick Charles and Marshal Bazaine that for the future no flag of truce should be received from either side except at this particular spot. This will perhaps account for the various reports that got into circulation respecting the firing upon Prussian flags of truce by the French. The little amusement of three hours' shelling every evening cost the French about 50*l.*; but what was this when we consider the daily cost of the German army to the nation, which was estimated at more than a million thalers per day? In revenge for the affair of Ars, the German batteries in the neighbourhood of Point de Jour opened upon the village of Lessy, which lies immediately under the fort of Plappeville; and, after an hour's shelling, it was set on fire. Whilst this was going on, the batteries near Rozerieulles opened upon the villages of Sey, Longeau, and Moulins-les-Metz, all of which more or less suffered.

On the morning of the 7th of October a smart affair took place between outposts on the Montigny road. The French had started in the fog towards the outposts of the 2d Jägers, in the Château of Frascati; and as soon as daylight permitted they opened a tremendous fire of chassepots, driving in the advanced chain of sentries, and alarming the main body. The wood held by the Jägers was soon wreathed in smoke, while the outlying piquets of the 61st Pomeranian regiment, situated to their right and left rear, came up at the double to the support of their comrades. I had had the good fortune to dine with the 54th regiment at Augny the evening before, and was consequently close to the scene of action.

I got there about ten minutes before the outlying piquets of the 61st came up, and it was really grand to see how splendidly they did their work. Two companies advanced in column of sections, right in front; one company took ground to the right; the other deployed from the right file in skirmishing order, with the two rear sections as supports, covering the road between Jouy and Montigny, and occupying the broken ground, rifle-pits, and garden-walls to the left of Frascati. The other company, when clear of the wood, came to the front turn, halted, and formed column of subdivisions; the left subdivision then advanced at the double, and extended from its left file, while the right remained in support. All was done as if on parade, although the continual whizz of the chassepot bullets made you duck the head perhaps oftener than military dignity would have. I confess to a strong *penchant* for picking out a good thick tree upon such occasions, rather than run the unnecessary risk of having a bullet in my stomach, instead of the matutinal cup of coffee. After about three-quarters of an hour's hard shooting the French retired; the 61st fell back with the loss of two men killed and seven wounded, the Jägers having also suffered a loss of nine wounded. Altogether the affair was very spirited, and the French showed a determination to beat up the German quarters whenever there was the least chance that they would be caught napping.

All sorts of extraordinary things were sent through the feld-post from Germany for the officers of the army round Metz. It was an amusing sight to see the regimental post-office orderly distribute his budget of letters. In one a cake of chocolate; in another, a square flat tin case filled with the best schnapps; in a third, a pair of warm socks, knitted for the father by his youngest daughter; in a fourth, a packet of tea; lastly—*mirabile dictu!*—a square cake of fresh butter, wrapped up in lead paper, and most beautifully preserved. All these came through the feld-post. The organisation of this excellent branch showed with what ease and regularity a large army on the march in an enemy's country can receive and dispatch letters to any part of the world.

Perfect, however, as the organisation of the Prussian army is in most respects, one portion seemed to require a most thorough remodelling. I refer to the medical department. In time of peace the medical establishment of each regiment, consisting of three battalions, is six medical officers. In time of war there must be an addition; and, Prussia being a purely military nation, the call for medical assistance to supply the wants of its huge army is naturally great. Medical men, old or young, competent or incompetent, are gladly taken; and the consequence is, that as it *was* in our service, so it *is* here—many an officer would rather endure pain and suffering than send for his 'regimental persecutor.' First and foremost, the Prussians have no nucleus from which to form a thoroughly efficient military medical staff. They possess no college where the student can study those branches of his profession which will eminently fit him to take his position as a regimental assistant surgeon.

In order that he may learn to erect 'a field hospital,' to practise field surgery, to know what should be the diet of a wounded man under the peculiar circumstances amid which, from the scarcity of material, the army surgeon must find himself in a campaign—that he may be acquainted with the best arrangements with regard to water—the organisation of temporary hospitals in towns and villages, sheds or barns, railway stations or tents—the best methods for supplying the deficiencies of good old linen, bandages, or lint—with a thousand other minor details that are necessary to the peculiar education, so to say, which the army surgeon requires—for all these good schools are needed. The French, and we ourselves, have such institutions, though still susceptible of much improvement. It is of course but seldom that we can learn from experience—that rude schoolmaster—where the shoe pinches; all the more need for us to take warning and improve when we have the opportunity; for, although we are far in advance of Germany in this essential detail, we have yet much to learn.

The Prussian medical man, to qualify himself for service, must spend five years in the medical schools; afterwards, before he can reach the grade of regimental surgeon, ranking as a captain, he will in nine cases out of ten have to serve twenty-five years or more in the army, and will then receive only half a captain's pay. He is now an old man, and for the declining years of his life no provision is made—he receives no pension. The usual salve to a soldier's wounds, privations, and sickness, in the shape of a medal, is denied to him; that is to say, he receives his decoration with the ribbon of a non-combatant attached to it; whilst the orderly who holds his horse —for all medical men ride—receives that of a combatant.

His position is doubly uncomfortable under fire; he has not the excitement of the fight to carry off that nervous feeling of which the best soldier cannot deny the possession when he first goes into action. He must witness the fearful effects of shot and shell upon the human frame, while those same missiles are flying thickly around him; for it is a great mistake to think that a surgeon is never under fire. I contend that he is continuously exposed; if he is not, he does not faithfully perform his duty. In the late war I have seen Prussian surgeons in the foremost positions quietly and dexterously performing their duties, while shot and shell have been flying all about them. Is it therefore surprising that those possessing medical skill, or aptitude for their profession, prefer going into private life and practising as civilians, where they can obtain a better livelihood and lay up something for the future—leaving the comparatively inferior members of the profession to care for the wants of the unfortunate soldier? It is true that during this war many eminent medical men from Berlin and all the towns of Germany flocked to assist their country; but I am sorry to say that the want of good and efficient medical men was deeply and fearfully felt.

I must now say a few words about the traction engines before mentioned. About this time they succeeded in taking to Commercy some locomotives, and, by General Moltke's orders, they were immediately dispatched to Nanteuil-sur-Marne, where it appeared the French had blown up a tunnel and impeded the railway communication. The Germans succeeded in reëstablishing it in the same way as they did between Pont-à-Mousson and Commercy, when Toul lay in the way. The fact was therefore now thoroughly established that these traction engines can transport the heaviest weights, by means of the winding apparatus, at the rate of *twenty miles* per diem, with inclines up to one in eight. Not the least difficult part of their performance was accomplished in the town of Commercy. Here, with a wagon upon which was loaded a locomotive engine weighing thirty-five tons, a truck containing the tender of the locomotive, and another truck containing a quantity of implements, they steamed through the narrow streets of the town, turning *six* corners at right-angles, one corner being of thirty-five degrees. The thing was, of course, done slowly, but without stopping or touching the pavement. Judge, therefore, the effect which this performance had upon the people of the country.

Still the blockade of Metz proceeded slowly but surely towards that fatal result which let two other armies loose upon *la belle* France. In a letter dated the 9th of October I have described the state of things then existing:

'If the troops which blockade Metz have any peace or quietness, it is not Marshal Bazaine's fault. Since yesterday evening, not ten minutes have elapsed without a shell being dispatched from the town in some direction or another. To-day I took up a position overlooking the valley of the Moselle, and just behind the Prussian batteries at Augny. The heavy damp atmosphere of an autumn afternoon held the white smoke hanging in fantastic clouds over each spot from which a gun had been fired, and enabled me to perceive that the French have made two new batteries in rear of the railroad embankment skirting the suburb of Montigny. These works are to the right and left rear of the original earthwork of St. Privat, which still remains without guns; and the armament of these new batteries will, I fear, give the Prussians holding the position south-east of Metz a great deal of annoyance.

'Riding on towards Mercy-le-Haut, I met an escort bringing in some French prisoners that had been taken in an engagement on the preceding Friday night by Woippy. The fight seems to have been a bloody one, the French attacking force numbering 18,000 men. The Prussian loss is 600 killed and wounded; the precise French loss is of course unknown, but it could not have been short of 1000 *hors de combat.* The prisoners were excessively uncommunicative and sullen, refusing even to answer when spoken to, so that I was unable to obtain any information from them. They looked in excellent health, and far removed from starvation.

'It seems to me that the position of the contending forces is gradually changing. Instead of the German troops attacking, they are being attacked, and, instead of plying the French works with shot and shell, they find it difficult to hold their own. It is to be hoped that some of the heavy guns from Strasburg and Toul will find their way here; for, in the present state ot affairs, the German troops are under fire at a distance which none of their guns are of sufficient calibre to reply to effectually. To-day I met two Russian officers of rank—one a general, and the other a lieutenant-colonel—who are busily employed in picking up information for their government. They told me that Sebastopol was nothing to Strasburg, and that the bombardment was something so stupendous as to be scarcely describable.'

Alluding to the above engagement at Woippy, I wrote as follows:

'I have just gone over the ground before Woippy, where the engagement of the night before last took place. Some of the French dead remain still unburied, and mark the places where Bazaine's troops advanced. The position held by the Prussians on the wooded and hilly ground in the neighbourhood of Norroy and Semecourt is a natural fortress, owing to the peculiar formation of the ground. Nature has, however, been strengthened by art, for these villages have been turned into perfect fortresses in miniature. The ground in front and facing Woippy has been cut up into a regular honeycomb of "Schutzengraben," whilst behind every wall a tread has been carefully erected, and the masonry pierced for rifles. The Prussians have become so accustomed to fortifying the small villages they occupy, and have besides had so many opportunities of observing the dexterity with which the French make such places tenable, that in a very short space of time a battalion will put a farmhouse, a garden wall, or a hamlet, in such a state of defence that nothing but artillery will dislodge them.

'The French, after carrying the village of Norroy, were advancing on Semecourt and Fêves, with the intention, no doubt, of penetrating towards Thionville by way of Marange, when they were attacked in flank by the troops lying at Amanvillers, St. Privat-la-Montagne, and Roncourt. The fire from Plappeville assisted the French so long as they were in the neighbourhood of Saulny; but no sooner had they got clear of their own outworks and carried Norroy than Plappeville was of no farther assistance to them. Here an obstinate fight continued for many hours, and here I saw many wounded men. The French then fell back towards Saulny and Woippy, fighting every inch of the road. The night being excessively clear—for the moon was shining brightly—the big guns had no difficulty in opening fire. Plappeville, the works in Devant-les-Ponts, and some heavy pieces of the town itself now took part in the action; but the Prussians seemed to have been determined upon taking Woippy, which they eventually did at nine in the morning. They were unable, however, to hold it for any length of time. When, at about eleven P.M., the action ceased, the French had gained Woippy, and the Prussian troops held Saulny.'

On the 10th of October despatches arrived at the head-quarters of General Manteuffel, bringing intelligence of an action at St. Die, between Epinal and Luneville. Imagine, then, the surprise of the Prussians at finding another army in the field. It appeared that General von Werder, after forming the new army corps known as the 14th at Strasburg, received orders to march upon Lyons. On the 6th inst., when in the neighbourhood of Rambervillers, to the north-east of St. Die, his advance brought intelligence that a French division was marching upon them in the direction of the town of Rambervillers, and coming from the side of St. Die. The action soon after commenced, the French attacking the German division with a force of 15,000 men, together with cavalry and artillery. Being repulsed, the French fell back upon St. Die. This new French army had evidently been formed by concentrating at Epinal all the garrisons to the south of Strasburg quartered in Mulhouse, Langres, Vesoul, Dijon, and Besançon. The French general in command had no doubt been informed that General von Werder was marching upon Lyons; and it was to delay this advance that he attacked him with his small force. I had been quite prepared for such a movement; and was only surprised that we had not heard of French troops in this direction before.

The position of the 1st army corps before Metz remained unaltered. General Manteuffel's head-quarters were in St. Barbe, whilst the Prussian troops occupied the villages of Failly, Servigny, Noisseville, and Flanville. St. Julien was as energetic on this side as Quentin and Plappeville were on the other—the same continual worrying fire of outposts, which wore the men out with constant alarms. The weather, too, had changed. The rain poured down in torrents, and the regiments still unprovided with huts had a piteous time of it. This sort of exposure is, however, one for which every soldier must be prepared.

It has been stated by various writers and correspondents, that Englishmen had great difficulties thrown in their way, and that they were forbidden to follow the Prussian armies. It is true that General von Göben attached me to the army corps he commanded under very peculiar circumstances. He did so before the King's positive order was issued that no English officer was to be permitted to join the German army; but General von Göben gave me my 'legitimation' simply because he trusted to my honour as a British officer and a gentleman. He was good enough to say that, after what I had done for wounded Prussians under a heavy fire—a thing that any one possessed with common humanity would never have hesitated to do—he himself would be responsible to his Majesty for my behaviour; and I cannot refrain from thus taking the opportunity of mentioning the feeling that this distinguished general had for English officers, and to remark, that those who did not succeed in following the movements of the various Prussian corps have only to thank themselves, and the absurd arrogance with which they conducted themselves.

As to the sympathies which actuated Englishmen, we felt as much for the French as for the German wounded. We simply saw one of our own profession, who had well and nobly done his duty, wounded, perhaps to death, and asking us for that assistance which we ourselves might some day require. Did it for a moment matter whether he was French or German? If it did, or if the fact of our having fought by the side of the French in the Crimea could lead to a more decided *penchant* on their side, the conduct of the German troops would have set an example that would put such ideas to shame. They sought to relieve the wants of those with whom they were a moment ago in deadly conflict. You saw the German doctors attending to the French wounded, the German officers assisting the French, and the German soldier ministering to the comfort of the man who would have made his house in Vaterland a heap of ashes.

On the 13th of October, winter, that dreadful enemy, burst upon the armies round Metz in the most sudden manner. The sun rose upon a frosty scene; the ground was as white as snow. Towards the afternoon the wind of the autumnal equinox swept through the valleys of the Moselle and the Selle, bringing with it cold and drenching showers of rain, which wetted the outposts to the skin, and tried the solidity of the huts. It is extraordinary what effect a change of weather will have in a few hours on the health of troops exposed to it. The previous morning the hospital two doors from me contained but seven fever patients:—the next morning there were sixty-two cases of typhus. A staff officer who arrived from Nancy brought the sad intelligence of the death of two officers from typhus; and one morning I myself witnessed a most melancholy scene.

I had gone over to the railway station at Ars-sur-Moselle to see what effect the shelling had had upon it. On the platform I met an old lady, accompanied by her maid; and upon making inquiries from the commandant, I was informed that she had come to see her two sons, who were in the 11th dragoons. The commandment had entreated her to leave a scene utterly unfit for a lady, especially for one so advanced in years. But the mother had come to see her boys; she had travelled far to feast her old eyes, perhaps for the last time, upon all that was left to her in the world. Her husband had been killed in the war of 1866, and she had sent her two children to fight for their country as their father had done before them. Poor lady! sad news awaited her.

Presently she perceived a soldier wearing the uniform of her son's regiment. As quickly as her years would permit, she hastened towards him, and in a mild voice inquired if he knew her sons, and where they were. The man, for a moment taken aback, replied he had no time to answer questions; but upon looking at that old, anxious, upturned face, the rough German dragoon comprehended the whole situation in a moment. Tenderly and carefully he led her to a seat, the tears already standing in his honest eyes; for a moment he turned away to hide his sorrowful confusion of face; and then, brushing the drops away from his rugged countenance with his sleeve, he replied: 'Madame, one of your sons has found a soldier's grave on the field of Mars-la-Tour; the other lies ill of typhus in the hospital at Nancy. Is it possible that you have been kept in ignorance of these facts?'

At his first words the poor mother rose to her feet, and when the soldier had ceased to speak she remained standing, as if carved in stone, looking vacantly into distance. Then, turning towards her maid, she asked, in accents that made one's heart bleed, how far it was to Nancy. Approaching the soldier, she held out her hand, and taking from her bag a small parcel, she gave it to him, saying, 'I had brought this for your lieutenant; but since he has gone to join his father in heaven, take it, and divide it amongst his comrades, and tell them it came from his old mother, who has yet one son left, thank God, to serve his country.' Such scenes were indeed of rare occurrence—for they would have made children of us all.

From this sad accident let me turn to a more joyous one, and, referring to my letter of the 13th of October, give the reader a slight idea of the life of the men and officers round Metz at this time.

'*Before Metz, Oct.* 13.

'I rode to Augny to have a look at things in that direction; for since my old friends, the 33d fusiliers, have left for Courcelles, I have not been much on that side. I found that the French keep up such an incessant fire of shells, that people are requested not to ride too near the battery between Orly and Augny, inasmuch as a single man on horseback is sufficient to draw their fire. The 54th Pomeranians lay in Orly, and I arrived at a moment when they had just received some presents from their countrymen in Colberg. The good people at home, verily, think most effectively of the wants of their soldiers. Here is by no means a large town that sends 22,500 cigars to one battalion, 14,360 lbs. of tobacco, 336 lbs. of chewing tobacco, bread, wine, schnapps, and fish packed in barrels, all in liberal proportions. What a feast we had! I was invited to join in tasting the good things; and if the people who sent those luxuries could only have seen how we enjoyed them, I am sure they would have been amply repaid.

'One old gentleman who accompanied this "gift of love" was particularly amusing. He was seventy-six years of age, and had two sons in the service. It appears that on the previous night his wagons were threatened by some one at a late hour. "Who goes there?" cried the old soldier; and upon receiving no answer he armed himself with two eggs, and again challenged. "If you do not answer, I will shoot!" he cried; and, as the shadow of a dark figure stole away, he valiantly launched his two eggs with great effect and precision. The eggs having come some distance, and, moreover, having been detained on the road, exploded with a loud crack, and hastened the retreat of the would-be pilferer.

'Just as our dinner was coming to an end, and we were anticipating the enjoyment of a good cigar, an explosion in the garden, and a bit of shell through the window of our "Speisesaal," disturbed the harmony of the meeting. Every one rose from his seat, the officers hastily buckled on their swords and revolvers, the bugle sounded the alarm, and the scene of mirth and merriment gave place to the stern realities of war. Happily, the affair turned out to be trivial; the French had perceived some movement of troops, and had commenced shelling from the batteries of Montigny.'

Let the reader now follow me across the Moselle to visit the head-quarters of the Hessian division lying at Gorze. As you entered the place a flood of recollections came upon you. There lay the town, overlooked by the height upon which, in bold relief, stands the golden statue of the Virgin. Here, to the right and left, were the houses that upon the 17th, 18th, and 19th of August were crammed from garret to cellar with the wounded of Mars-la-Tour and Gravelotte. The white flags, with their red crosses, still hung out of every house, but the scene was different. The town was the head-quarters of Prince Louis of Hesse; and, beyond the troops that moved about in the streets, a heavy death-like stillness seemed to hang over everything. The appearance of the Hessian division had considerably improved, principally owing to the indefatigable efforts of Prince Louis and his staff.

The rationing of the Hessian and the Prussian troops is entirely different. In the Hessian army the soldiers are fed in the following manner: In the morning they receive their ration of coffee; at eleven A.M. they have soup and soup meat served out; at one P.M. they dine, and at five they have their evening meal. The Prussian troops have their coffee in the morning; at one P.M. their soup and soup meat; and beyond this they get nothing. The Hessians feed four times per day; the Prussians consider twice sufficient. Is it, then, matter for surprise that the difficulties which prevented and delayed the regular advance of the commissariat trains in the commencement of the war, especially when in an enemy's country, were more severely felt by the Hessians than by troops better accustomed to self-denial? Use is, after all, a second nature, and it affects the soldier quite as much as the civilian. It is well known how our troops suffer when exposed to want; and care should be taken that the soldier should be accustomed to such a quantity of food per diem that he may not complain or suffer when, from necessity, his rations are curtailed. I am perfectly well aware of the privations that our troops can endure without a murmur; but it is a cruelty to expose soldiers to such trials when a less lavish system might perhaps prepare them for what at any time may be their lot.

On the 14th despatches came to hand giving the news that a squadron of Prussian cavalry had been taken before Paris; and it was officially announced that the 1st Bavarian army corps, the 22d division of Prussian infantry, and the 2d and 4th Prussian cavalry division had had an engagement with the army of the Loire before Orleans. They had taken that town, had compelled the enemy to retreat in full flight, pursued by the cavalry, and had captured 3,000 prisoners and several guns. The 21st regiment had a smart affair of outposts at Maison Rouge the night before—one officer killed and 30 men *hors de combat*. The French loss was small, although some prisoners were taken. Captain Hozier passed through, reporting himself to Prince Frederick Charles, on his way to join the head-quarters of the Crown Prince; and great dissatisfaction appeared to exist among the officers of the staff of the 1st army that no English officer was attached here as well. It was indeed a pity that the strategy of the campaign before Metz—to say nothing of the novel movements of troops as a blockading force—was not utilised for the benefit of the British army.

On the 15th of October—so a French officer, taken prisoner at Maison Rouge, informed me—the Republic was to be proclaimed in Metz. As yet General Bazaine and his colleagues had managed to keep the townspeople in ignorance of the true state of political affairs in France; but, by some means or another—probably through exchanged prisoners—the news had oozed out that the dynasty of Napoleon no longer existed. The people of Lorraine and Alsace are nowise Republican; but their dreams of glory and accession of territory had received a rude shock. They had seen the troops who but a short time ago left Metz to conquer, return to its shelter, not disgraced, but yet utterly defeated. They had learnt that French soldiers were not invincible, and that the incapacity of officers will defeat an army composed of the best material in the world. It was thought, therefore, that when they heard that France was governed by a Republic, and that Napoleon III. was no longer Emperor—that there was a chance of their getting out of a pestilential city, and avoiding hunger and starvation—a different state of feeling might, perhaps, spring up; and Metz la Pucelle come to terms. That Bazaine would hold out to the last there was not the least doubt; and that he would do so in no very gentle manner was also certainly the general opinion at that time. He would go to any lengths to compel the obedience of the population, it was said, but the reaction would be trying for him, and Metz might yet open her gates to Prince Frederick Charles, and release his army from the trying, wearying, death-dealing blockade.

As to provisions, the officer laughed when I suggested to him the possibility that famine might compel the bravest army to succumb. 'Ah, bah! nous avons assez, allez!' he cried. 'La farine est là, nous avons toujours des chevaux, et on ne peut pas empêcher la récolte de pommes de terre.' I mildly suggested that salt, although a common and cheap commodity, was yet most necessary. 'On fait la cuisine sans sel, monsieur—voilà tout,' was the answer. In the abstract, this sort of argument, no doubt, was all very well; but, unfortunately, my friend's face was a perfect denial of his assertions. He looked as if he had eaten nothing for a fortnight. I placed sardines, bread, and a bottle of wine before him; and, thinking he could perhaps appease his hunger better alone, or that he would object to show a stranger how hungry he really was, I left the room. In half an hour I returned. The box of sardines was empty, the loaf had disappeared, and the wine was—not. By way of apology, he said, 'Mon camarade, j'ai fait un petit paquet de tout ça pour la route;' but I confess I saw nothing like a packet about him.

One afternoon I rode with the young Duke of Mecklenburg and Prince Reuss towards Mercy-le-Haut, and, as if to refute any hopes that might have been entertained of the surrender of Metz, the batteries were more than ordinarily noisy. Arrived at the camp of the 9th regiment at Orly, six shells welcomed us one after another, killing two men and wounding six. Then came the roar of the big gun behind the railway embankment by Montigny; then Queuleu thundered away; in fact, the fire from the batteries around the town was more severe than ever. The outposts suffered dreadfully, and, if you add to the hardships which they suffered from the town itself those they endured from the miserably rainy, cold, windy weather, you will complete the chronicle of their misfortunes. As I returned, a small batch of prisoners and some horses were brought in from the neighbourhood of Colombey and Ars Laquenexy. Poor fellows! they looked anything but in good condition; and as to the horses, they were nothing but bags of bones.

Some idea of the life that one was leading, and the quarters we occupied, may be gathered from an extract from the following letter:

'*Before Metz, Oct.* 17.

'I had scarcely taken my seat beside a warm fire, when a perfect rattle of musketry made me spring up and ask the meaning of all the noise. Just then an orderly galloped past, and said that the French were advancing by way of St. Privat. In a moment we were in our saddles, and as we clattered through the streets of Jouy, the 61st and 21st regiments were getting under arms. Riding along the road which leads into Metz by way of Montigny, I met a company of the 2d Jägers in columns of sections doubling to the front. A dropping fire was going on in front of Frascati, and as I pulled up in rear of a garden wall, I heard the whistle of a locomotive in Metz. I thought we were in for another bad night; but, with the exception of a little smart shooting before Frascati, nothing occurred; so I rode quietly back to my quarters.

'My quarters, I say, although head-quarters would be the more correct word; for one night I find myself beside a bivouac fire, the next on outpost, the third possibly in the saddle. This night-riding, although necessary, is very disagreeable; one is apt to forget the *parole* for the day, as I did once, in which case you pass the rest of the night with the officer of the outpost, or are sent under escort to the head-quarters of the nearest regiment—at present the house of a rich merchant in Metz. When the German troops came into Jouy, many of these houses were entirely deserted; that in which I reside among the rest. My room has evidently been the boudoir of some young lady. The walls are hung with a paper perfectly in keeping with the red-velvet Louis Quatorze furniture. There is no bed; but a mattress on the ground in a corner is a luxury which not every one possesses—to say nothing of two large looking-glasses, which, no doubt, once reflected some charming little French face.

'Sitting in this room of mine, I often wonder what has become of all the people that but a short time ago filled it—what they are doing, and under what circumstances they were hurried away from their homes. My young lady must have been in love, because, in rummaging about in the cupboards for towels and other articles, I have found most unmistakable signs of such a complaint. Her parents, like all proper parents, seem to have been very hard upon these youthful affections, inasmuch as mademoiselle had evidently been compelled to improvise a sort of lover's lift out of her window, made out of a garden swing. There is a piano in my room, where we have occasional concerts, to say nothing of a dance. We have not failed to make use of the young lady's wardrobe to dress up a German dragoon or a stout lieutenant, and I can assure you that evenings thus enlivened have saved many of us from sickness and disease.

'I must confess I was rather elated to-day while I imagined we were about to have another sharp action, and rather disappointed when my expectations were not realised:—for, truth to tell, the calm which has succeeded to the storm that raged so violently on the 7th is, together with the rainy weather, somewhat depressing. But do not suppose, because a correspondent has little to chronicle, that the besieging army is without occupation. Every moment of leisure that the uneasy Bazaine gives is utilised. The men are constantly employed in erecting huts and breastworks, or in making their positions more defensible. The bad weather of the last few days, the constantly increasing severity of the nights, have really somewhat terrified us. The prospect of a siege extended into the winter is very gloomy. Many of the soldiers are badly in want of good warm underclothing. The erection of proper huts, and suchlike works, the soldiers themselves must do; but have they not some claims for assistance on the German Hülfsverein in the way of clothing, and those other things in which they cannot by any possibility help themselves?'

On the 13th of October, the Prussians commenced the bombardment of Verdun, and the sound of the heavy firing reached the armies round Metz.

The exact loss of the division Kummer in the action of Maizières and Woippy was ascertained: 1800 killed and wounded, and 65 officers, was the fearful sum-total of the few hours. The French loss was about 2400—at least, if one could trust to the information received from the enemy's prisoners. The overwhelming force which the French brought to bear upon this particular point must account for the dreadful loss of life, and the large proportion of officers testifies to that indomitable perseverance and cool courage which will not be restrained. I cannot say too much upon this subject; for the conduct of the officers of the German army is a theme that would fill volumes. The loss of the soldiers may be repaired; but for years to come Germany will feel most accutely the want of those brave and determined gentlemen who have stood their country in such good stead in her hour of trial.

At daylight on the morning of the 17th many an anxious eye was turned towards Metz. The height of St. Blaise was crowded, and if it were possible to wear a telescope out by looking through it, such would indubitably have been the case upon this occasion. I mentioned above that intelligence had been received that on the 16th the Republic would be proclaimed in the beleaguered city. Every one hoped the fact might cause some sort of diversion in favour of those who had for so long gazed upon that plain in the valley of the Moselle, upon that splendid cathedral, and upon the frowning batteries of St. Quentin, Queuleu, and St. Julien; but even these were silent.

The fire from the outposts, usually so brisk at this hour, was also scarcely to be heard, and all were about to wend their way back to quarters—some with the firm conviction that Metz must under any circumstances fall before Christmas, others that French patience had lasted much longer than anybody had ever anticipated, but all apparently satisfied that sooner or later Bazaine must give in—when the well-known rattle of the mitrailleuse made every one turn their eyes in the direction of the earthwork of St. Privat. Out of this work the French advanced towards Frascati with two mitrailleuses, and a strong battalion of infantry; but whether they thought better of their first purpose, or whether they saw that the Germans were prepared to receive them, after firing twice from the mitrailleuses, they retired by way of St. Privat. The town of Metz itself was unusually still. We could hear the church bells tolling, and occasionally the roll of a drum; but, beyond this, there was no indication that anything of moment had taken place.

Intelligence that Soissons had surrendered to the German arms also came to hand; so that, one by one, gradually but surely, the strong cities of France were passing into the possession of the enemy. But at what a cost was this taking place! Did not Germany suffer as well as France? Did not the hospital returns, the lists of killed and wounded, the large number of prisoners she had to supply with food, and the starving peasantry of France whom she would have to assist—at least for the present—did not all these things sufficiently attest that the heart of the nation was bleeding, and that her voice should be raised for peace?

The heavy rain of the previous few days had caused the Moselle to overflow its banks. This had also compelled the French to move their camp from the Island of Chambière towards the suburb of St. Julien. The weather must have had the same effect upon both armies, inasmuch as Marshal Bazaine's troops were all under canvas outside the town.

On the day previous, the first batch of deserters came out of Metz. The effect their presence produced was a good one. They were assembled outside his Royal Highness Prince Frederick Charles's quarters, where they underwent a series of interrogatories, which they answered most freely, and apparently without hesitation. The reason why they had deserted, they said, was, first of all, because the work was too hard and the food too scanty. The next—and what seemed to be the principal—reason was, that Bazaine was organising an attack upon the German position in this direction, for which they had been told off. They had fought enough, they said, especially when they did not know exactly for whom they were fighting; and they preferred a German prison, to want, starvation, exposure, and bullets. One, a zouave, when he heard that Prince Frederick Charles was standing near them, asked that he should be pointed out, and, upon this being done, he took off his fez, and, waving it in the air, shouted, 'Vive la Prusse! vive le Prince Frederick Charles!' The others, however, did not join in the chorus, but muttered, *sotto voce*, 'Vive la France!'

From this incident hopes were once more entertained of a speedy capitulation—indeed, on this particular morning deserters had been coming in from all sides of Metz, and they stated that there was great discontent amongst the inhabitants of the town, which the military had been called upon to put down. The palliasses were being ripped open for straw, which was given as forage to the few horses that remained; the cavalry were dismounted, and acted as infantry; and the allowance of meal was fearfully reduced. The marshal commanding had ordered the meal to be adulterated, in order to make the provision serve longer; in fact, the position of his Majesty Bazaine seemed to be fast becoming actually perilous.

The circular issued by Count Bernstorf to Lord Granville about this time seemed to give great satisfaction to the Germans. There can be but little doubt that there was a very strong feeling upon this subject, although I believe that every Englishman did his best to assuage as far as possible those angry feelings which were entertained towards England. One officer of his Royal Highness's staff, who sat next me at dinner one night, begged that I would impress upon my countrymen, that for the future they should send Martini-Henry rifles to France instead of chassepots, for in that case Prussia would soon be armed with the best weapon in the world. In this he was not far wrong, and I imagine the whole Prussian army will be supplied with these rifles as soon as the occasion offers itself. Simple in its construction, light and handy in use, shooting equally well at short and long distances, easy of repair in case of need, I know of no weapon so well adapted for a military small-arm as the Martini-Henry, except perhaps the Soper—especially in the hands of a young and inexperienced soldier. In the loading of the needle rifle there are five motions, in that of the Chassepot three, and in the Martini-Henry, if I recollect aright, only two.

On the 20th of October, I took an excursion from Metz with a staff-officer, and as my letter to the *Daily Telegraph* of that date explains the state of other parts of Lorraine at this time, I have thought it well to reprint it.

'*Eighth Army Corps, Courcelles, October 20.*

'Has any one ever arrived at that unfortunate period of his existence when he gazes with anxiety every morning into his looking-glass to see how many hairs he has lost during the night, and finds that—being destitute of all the manifold renovating inventions so prolific in these high-pressure days—he has grown balder than he was the day before? Has any one ever eaten for several consecutive days a well-smoked, freshly-killed bit of meat, cut from a half-starved cow, which the facetious butcher chooses to call a "beftek," and eaten it, if not with relish, at any rate with thankfulness? Has any one, who has watched for many weeks a lugubrious-looking church spire rising out of a still more melancholy-looking valley, peopled by half-starved soldiers, been told that there is a chance of a change of quarters, and that he will be permitted the inexpressible enjoyment of viewing the misery of the same soldiers from another point of view? Has any one—heaven save the mark!—ever gone for four or five days without the British bath, so healthful in our eyes, and sometimes so helpful to our nervous systems? If so, let him imagine with what joy I received the intelligence that I was to accompany a staff-officer on a mission of importance.

'It appears that some material necessary to the blockading army had stuck somewhere on the road. His Royal Highness Prince Frederick Charles never permits the grass to grow under his feet. The delay was a matter of importance, and he must know where that had occurred. The wonderful facility which the chief of the first army has for grasping a difficulty was now apparent. Instead of sending off orderlies with official letters, which always entail the receipt of any amount of official answers, he at once came to the conclusion that the delay must arise at Courcelles. Accordingly an officer of rank, who can treat with the authorities—not a subaltern—is dispatched; and I am permitted to accompany him. This morning we started in a sort of phaeton, belonging originally, no doubt, to some rich citizen of Metz, but now "required" for the use of his Royal Highness's staff. Two horses from the telegraph department are attached to it; a non-commissioned officer goes with us as *avant-courier*, and a Prussian soldier sits on the box as coachman. After passing the head-quarters of General von Göben at Cherisy, where we stopped only for a few moments, and learnt that deserters were coming in almost every hour, we arrived in the neighbourhood of Courcelles—I say in the neighbourhood, because it seemed at first utterly impossible that we could wade through the sea of mud which surrounded the village and railway station.

'Any reader who has passed along the line to Paris *viâ* Metz will no doubt remember this pretty little village lying in the valley of the Selle, the neat railway station, the clean-looking peasant women of the country, who offered you fruit or cakes at the carriage-door as the train stopped for a few moments, and the fertile plain by which it was surrounded. But now another slide has been put into the magic lantern. What do you see now?—presto! all is changed. The railway station and the village, it is true, still exist, but they rise like an island out of an ocean of mud. We wade through the sticky, clinging, undrained soil; we struggle, we swear; we are surrounded by *Proviant Colonnen*, by *Marketender* wagons, and by men so thickly covered with mud that it is impossible to tell what they are.

'A final jolt, and we can get no farther. We must dismount, and walk along the line; for time presses, and Prince Frederick Charles is not one who brooks delay. No sooner do I land upon *terra infirma* than I find my foot in a sort of natural bootjack. First, I lose one of my spurs; then one of my boots is half pulled off, and only with very great difficulty do I struggle back into it again. At last I get upon the railway embankment, and finally upon the permanent way. I look with astonishment at the surrounding scene. The embankment right and left of the line is one mass of stores. Hay, oats, flour, barrels of boots, bread, wine, *Liebesgaben* or gifts, with here and there improvised shelters from the now pouring rain. Here I espy a cunning hussar looking, Diogenes-like, out of a large tub into which he has crept for shelter; there, a sentry who has made a sentry-box of flour-bags; farther on is the railway station. Before it stands a train; and as I approach, I can see the wounded and the sick who are lifted by hundreds into the carriages. On either side of the station, some energetic shopkeepers have improvised a sort of wooden house, where they dispense very bad schnapps, not the freshest of German sausages, and hard-boiled eggs, none the better for a long journey. An enterprising storekeeper from Cologne has brought some wine, and thanks to him we breakfasted at three P.M., having had nothing to eat since seven A.M. His wife—all honour to that careful woman!—had packed up six cold chickens for his special use; I demolished one, and my friend another.

'While Major Sieber went to inquire into the matter about which he had come, I had time to sit down and scribble these few lines. The mud of Courcelles is only to be matched by that of Balaklava—the screeching, struggling mass of human beings and horses only by the disorder which reigned when the English first occupied the Crimean port. The atmosphere, never very healthy at this time of the year, is now loaded with a heavy pestilential odour, arising from badly-buried horses, some of whose half-exposed carcasses are to be seen upon the muddy plain around; and I must confess that when my friend informed me we must go on to Remilly, I was excessively pleased at being able to leave so dreary a prospect behind me. One regiment in Courcelles has at the present moment not fewer than 527 men on the sick-list.

'I must, in justice, add, however, that ere we left, the magic wand of Prussian discipline had effected a wonderful change. The confused masses of wagons and horses were now leaving in organised columns for their various destinations, in the charge of non-commissioned officers; the carcasses of the dead horses were being re-buried; and Courcelles began to assume a more orderly and cleanly appearance. It must be remembered that from this place the line goes to Saarbrück, and consequently an immense amount of material must continually accumulate at the dépôt of so large an army, if it is not regularly and properly dispatched.'

'*Remilly, October* 21.

'Last night, at eight o'clock, we arrived at this town. The place is connected with Pont-à-Mousson by means of the railroad—a description of which I have already sent you—well and permanently constructed by the Prussians with infinite labour and cost. By this single line the communication with the Crown Prince's army has been maintained *viâ* Pont-à-Mousson and Nancy, and the resources of Germany have been opened up to both armies *viâ* Saarbrück, in the impossibility of using the line across the Vosges, which the fortresses of Toul and Strasburg for so long a time impeded. In Remilly there existed at least order and method. No trains of wagons blocked the streets, no altercations disturbed the quietness of the town; but as to quarters, that was another thing. His Royal Highness's staff were accommodated with two mattresses in the billiard-room of a café. When we entered our quarters for the night, lighted by a candle stuck into a bottle, I confess I could not help laughing at the absurdity of the scene. Ranged round the four walls of the room, at equal distances, were placed about a dozen mattresses. On being told off to a mattress, you deposit your kit upon it, as a sign that the couch has found an occupant. Blankets there were none, pillows none; these the lodger himself was supposed so bring. On the night in question the room was occupied by two young officers on their way to join the head-quarters of their regiment before Paris, a staff-officer of General Manteuffel's army corps, and a clergyman belonging to the forces.

'Having arranged our effects and secured our mattresses, the next thing was to find something to eat. Yes—there was a café where we could procure something; and accordingly we struggled up a very dark street through a pouring rain, and found ourselves at last in the Café de la France, kept by a matron whom the Prussians had dubbed with the euphonious name of 'Madame Chassepôt,' her name being, to speak correctly, 'Chassepoint.' After a little difficulty and a great deal of whispering, we were served with some mutton, impossible to cut, much less to eat; and some potatoes, so besprinkled with flies that there was no looking at them. This was not encouraging; so I left my friend to battle alone with Madame Chassepôt's viands, whilst I proceeded to analyse the heterogeneous assembly that filled the apartment.

'There were Germans of all sorts—Prussians, Bavarians, Hessians, Mecklenburgers, Hamburgers, and Poles. Then there were Frenchmen, and—need I say it?—there were three Englishmen. One of them introduced himself to me. He informed me that he had just established at Remilly a dépôt of the British Society for the succour of the wounded. From him I heard of the trouble and difficulties with which they have had to contend—troubles and difficulties that might be avoided by a more thorough knowledge of the German language. It is true that one of these gentlemen spoke German, but I could scarcely understand what he said when he spoke it. They have worked hard; and they live a life of privation in order to carry out the objects of the society. But these objects will never be attained—good money will only be thrown away without result, and the stores meant for the use of the sick and wounded will only find their way to the tables of the staff-surgeons or be eaten up by the hospital helpers—unless the society shall appoint a gentleman of position, who thoroughly knows German, and, above all, German character, to superintend the arrangements for the distribution of the stores.

'This gentleman should be officially attached to the staff of the army corps with which he intends commencing operations. His position, I allow, will be difficult; for he will have to combat those prejudices with which every German officer and soldier at present looks upon an Englishman. But, if he is a gentleman and a man of tact—if he will only for the moment forget that as an Englishman he is not the little deity our countryman abroad too often fancies himself—he will find his way considerably smoothed; and when once he has obtained the friendship and respect of those with whom he is brought into contact, he will find no truer friends, no firmer allies and assistants, than the officers and men of the German army. In a word, he must make his position for himself. No amount of letters or introductions from official persons or members of the English Government will secure him the confidence of those with whom he will be associated; they will perhaps obtain the *entrée*, but the coöperation will be wanting. In such a position a man could ask that a detachment of Prussian soldiers or *Krankenträger* should at need be placed at his disposal; and this would enormously facilitate matters. There would be no stumbling-blocks thrown in the way of the quick and safe consignment of medical comforts and stores to the right quarters—to the places where they are most wanted.

'This would also facilitate what is at present a matter of uncertainty—the ready coöperation of other societies, such as the Knights of St. John and of Malta. A staff and head dépôt could be established in some central place, from which other dépôts might be directed; but, until this is done, I fear the efforts of Colonel Loyd-Lindsay and my fellow-countrymen will not prove so successful as they deserve to be. I know that full one-half of the stores sent out have, after distribution, never reached the destination for which they were intended; and for this, I believe, we have to thank the "contraband question." Certain it is, however, that, so far as I know, every Englishman out here has done his best to further the efforts of the society. But every man's capacity is not the same; and where one readily overcomes a difficulty, another fails, or gives up in despair.'

I must now touch upon a question which, if I mistake not, has often proved a source of no little difficulty to officers of much longer experience and of much higher standing: I refer to the method of provisioning an army in the field in an enemy's country. Before entering upon this all-important subject, it may be advisable to enforce the absolute necessity for inducing officers of the army to write upon subjects connected with their military duties and their profession. To this end it is not necessary to possess the *cacoethes scribendi*, or to have gone through the literary training which the journalist or essayist requires; but it is a fact not admitting of denial, that at least four-fifths of our officers, were they asked to write a report of an action, a march, or a tour of inspection, would be sadly at a loss how to begin, and, in all probability, how to finish. 'The sword, and not the pen, is our profession,' I can hear the critics say, in the smoking-room of the Rag and the Junior, when, with frowning brows, they read these lines. I admit it; but, at the same time, the pen is an auxiliary through which the profession is benefited and improved, without making use of high-flown sentences or heart-stirring descriptions.

Such a collection of material from the pens of our officers would form a nucleus of information upon subjects connected with the military profession, which would prove invaluable to our commanding officers and generals. It is from such information, written in the simplest language, that the officers of the Prussian army learn, and correct any mistake in, the discipline or organisation of their troops. And, before any material good is effected in our service, the subaltern will have to learn that, although but a small and diminutive portion of the gigantic military machine, he may assist and improve his profession by writing upon matters other than the daily report which the conventions of the service compel him as orderly officer to send in to his colonel. It was, therefore, with infinite pleasure that I heard that Captain Hozier was to join the head-quarters of the

German army before Paris; and I sincerely trust that every English officer who has had the good fortune to witness this fearful campaign will not fail to remark and note down anything that may be conducive to the furtherance and welfare of our noble profession.

The Prussian military train, or, as it is called, *Proviant Colonne*, is a branch of the service which of late years has undergone many improvements, especially since the wars of 1864 and 1866. To each army corps of 30,000 men is attached one battalion. This battalion consists of two squadrons, and numbers a total of 1000 men and 1500 horses; but from the *personnel* must be deducted the hospital-conveyance drivers and assistants. Each division has a squadron told off from the battalion; and to each brigade in the division half a squadron is allotted for the purposes of the commissariat. Where railway communication is available, a dépôt is at once established at the nearest available point in rear of the main body of the army; and there, first of all, the stores taken by requisition in the neighbourhood are collected and distributed to the various trains as they come in. When the provisions in the neighbourhood of this dépôt are exhausted, resort is then of course made to the home material; and the dépôt from which each army corps, division, or brigade is to draw its provisions appears in general orders; so that no two commissariat trains can come into contact with one another, or no two bodies of troops send to the same place at the same time for their provisions.

In addition to this train, each infantry battalion is allowed to take two wagons, each cavalry regiment one wagon, and each battery of artillery two wagons, which are to be procured at the first available place in the enemy's country. At each of these dépôts the field bakeries are established; although some regiments quartered in villages are permitted, if they have the opportunity, to bake their own bread, and in that case the train brings the same quantity of meal which it would have brought of bread. Each commissariat wagon is drawn by four horses; and the only unserviceable part of the arrangement is, that these wagons have no sort of covering to keep the stores dry in wet weather. The whole machinery is at once simple and thoroughly practical; there is little or no red tape or foolscap connected with its working; and the officers and men had by this time brought the working of their squadrons into such a state of perfection, that the whole moved like a machine, with but rare hitches. The greatest enemy of the system is, of course, the weather; but the field telegraph is also an able assistant, in sending to the head-quarter dépôt for help in any case of need.

The military train, in addition to finding five trains or colonnes, supplies three sanitary detachments, a field-bakery train with baking ovens, a field-bakery train without ovens, and the staff and men for a horse dépôt, to each army corps in the field. This is, of course, the establishment in time of war, not of peace. The staff is commanded in each army corps by an experienced general officer, assisted by six others of different grades belonging to the cavalry, artillery, and infantry branches of the service. There are, besides, six officers and 120 men, who form an escort to the whole of the above-mentioned force. The duty of the five colonnes, or trains, consisting each of two officers, 100 men, 24 draught and 150 riding horses, is to carry the forage for the horses and the subsistence for the troops of their respective army corps from the nearest dépôt to the troops in the field. The office of the sanitary detachment is to superintend the construction of latrines in proper places, to inspect the field and other hospitals, and to look after the cleansing and purifying of the villages or towns in which the different bodies of troops are quartered. The field-bakery trains establish themselves at the head-quarters of the army corps to which they belong, and the bread baked by them is transported by the Proviant Colonne to the troops in the field.

The dépôt for horses is generally established in a convenient farm-house, and in a neighbourhood where forage can be easily obtained. No troops are permitted to take hay, straw, or oats in the vicinity of such a spot; and the dépôt is commanded by an experienced officer, assisted by a staff of three officers, two veterinary surgeons, 93 men, with 66 riding horses, and 100 draught horses. To these dépôts are sent all fresh arrivals or remounts, all horses that are taken in requisition or captured from the enemy, as also all sick horses; so that the cavalry, artillery, and infantry of each army corps can get their sick horses exchanged for sound animals, or be supplied with new ones as they may require them. The whole establishment works like a piece of machinery, and it is one of the principal links in that chain of perfection which enables the German armies to concentrate large masses of troops in échelon upon various spots. The wagons of the Proviant Colonne are strongly built of wood, without springs, the body resting upon a pole supported by four wheels; the body of the wagon is about 12 feet long and about 4 feet 10 inches deep, and is covered neither by a tarpaulin nor by anything else of the kind. This wagon is drawn by four horses, the near-side horses being mounted.

With a few—a very few—alterations, the military train of the Prussian army is as near perfection as any army in the world has yet brought this branch of the service; and from my experience of it I shall content myself by here remarking, that it would be well if Mr. Cardwell were to make some inquiries on the Prussian system of organisation in their military train, from persons who are well acquainted with its working; for I fancy our own service would greatly and materially benefit by such information.

CHAPTER VII.

METZ IN EXTREMIS.

We are now approaching the time when certain indications began to manifest themselves, too surely demonstrating that Metz was *in extremis.* On the 21st October everything was quiet—not a sound was to be heard, not a shot even from those ever-busy skirmishers about Frascati and Maison Rouge. This stillness, so unusual, seemed to portend one of two things—either Metz was about to give in, or else Bazaine was organising some new method of attack; at least, this was the general opinion. Busy conjecture tried to spell out the meaning of things, at first sight inexplicable. Why were those Frenchmen permitted to dig potatoes under the very noses of the German vedettes and outposts? Why had so many flags of truce found their way to head-quarters lately? And why did Bazaine's aide travel post-haste to the King of Prussia, from him to Wilhelmshöhe, thence returning to Metz? Bazaine, we all knew, held his command direct from the Emperor. Would Count Bismarck, weary of a war that was beginning to tell upon German resources, save this invested army for the use of the semi-deposed Emperor? Did he wish that, in case it should be deemed necessary for the welfare of

Europe once more to place a Bonaparte upon the French throne, Napoleon should have the means of holding his position until the troubled seas of political opinion had subsided, and his ever-ready tongue had found an excuse for the misadventure which had impoverished and devastated France?

The strange inactivity on both sides was unaccountable, unless, indeed, the German army was preparing for more formidable operations against the devoted city of Lorraine. Whatever might be occurring in the diplomatic world, of the military this much could be said with certainty—that the French troops were in the forbidden ground digging potatoes, and taking off their caps by way of pleasantry to the Prussian sentries. Another curious event occurred also. The deserters from Metz had hitherto been received by the outposts and sent to the rear; one day 800 were told that they could not be admitted within the German lines, and must endeavour to endure their troubles a little longer. What did this mean? Possibly his Royal Highness deemed, that the more mouths there were to feed, the sooner there would be nothing left in Metz. But the matter cut both ways; for the fact of 800 deserters coming in a body must have had a most discouraging effect upon the besieged.

The Prussian working parties, however, still continued to labour at the batteries, which, it was hoped, would be supplied with guns of heavier metal; for it was the firm belief that, in the then state of affairs, a real bombardment of a few hours would very much tend to bring about a capitulation. Every one lived at that moment in a state of uncertainty as to what was going to happen. This much alone was known, that something important was on the *tapis*. A curious proclamation by the commandant of the garrison of Metz then came to hand. I give you a literal translation:

'LETTER ADDRESSED BY THE COMMANDANT OF METZ TO THE MUNICIPALITY OF THAT TOWN.

Metz, October 15.

MONSIEUR LE MAIRE, — Your municipality has done me the honour to address to me a letter expressive of noble and patriotic feelings.

I hasten to thank you for the expression of such feelings, which did not in the least surprise me, inasmuch as I never for one moment doubted the active coöperation of the inhabitants with our troops, were they called upon to fight for the defence of the fortress; and, with so good an example, you may be confident that we will do our duty in a like manner. But, at the same time, I beg of you to notify to the inhabitants that, in order to obtain this wished-for result, it is necessary that the population should, like men of energy and determination, endeavour to repress any sort of tumult, discord, or disturbance which may occur, and do away with useless proclamations, all of which only tend to promote discord and misery, and have an injurious influence, and tend to destroy the harmony which should, under the circumstances, exist between us.

At this moment a government exists in France, called the "Government of National Defence." We must acknowledge this government and await its determinations; for these, whatever they may be, will be constituted and decreed by the country itself. In the mean time we must adopt their password, and cry, "*Vive la France!*"

You inform me that the inhabitants of the town of Metz are greatly surprised to hear that our provisions and resources are very small. This is a matter easy of solution, when you come to consider that we had to provide for a community consisting of 230,000 souls. I never made a secret of this situation, for, in reducing the rations for the army, the same rule was applied to the town. In addition to this, the general orders published to the different bakeries respecting the supply of bread must have proved to you, M. le Maire, and to the inhabitants, the gradual decrease of our provisions.

Let us avoid recriminations for the past, and let us throw no blame upon one another; but rather let us look keenly at our position as it now stands; and, as you very properly remark, let us bear like men the privations of the past, and seek, from our experience, to derive benefit and counsel for the future.

(*Signed*) F. COFFINIERE,
General of Division, and First Commandant of the Fortress of Metz.'

An additional order of the commandant followed, by which the state of Metz on the 15th October is made clearly visible:

'1. From the 15th instant no bread will be made in any of the bakeries except bran bread.

2. Every baker will daily receive, through the military storekeeper, the amount of meal for which he has orders, and only for a definite number of inhabitants.

3. Children up to four years of age will receive one-fifth of a pound of bread daily; from four years to twelve years, two-fifths of a pound; and every adult, four-fifths of a pound of the above-mentioned bread.

(*Signed*) F. COFFINIERE,
General of Division, and First Commandant of the Fortress of Metz.'

The state of things was hourly becoming more critical. A deserter said *there was no more bread in Metz*—at least, if there was, the soldiers did not get it. Under these circumstances—that is, without bread and without salt—how could the town hold out for more than a week? So certain were the German generals that Metz la Pucelle would shortly be occupied by their troops, that orders had been given that a room should be prepared in the château of Frascati, one of the outposts, where the preliminaries and negotiations for the surrender were ultimately carried out. Indeed, they had already commenced to speculate on their next destination. For five days not a shot had been fired on either side.

But if military operations had for the moment

been at a standstill, diplomacy was not idle. On the 17th Bazaine's aide-de-camp, General Boyer, came to head-quarters; on the 18th he went to King William before Paris, and thence to Wilhelmshöhe; on the 22d he returned, and went into Metz; and on the 23d he came out again, and went on to Paris once more. From his statement it appeared that General Bazaine was perfectly willing to surrender his army, but that the commandant of Metz, General Coffinière, would not consent to give up the fortress. His Royal Highness Prince Frederick Charles very naturally objected to take charge of 80,000 or 90,000 soldiers (the number supposed to be there), still hampered with the condition of having the same battle to fight for Metz. His answer was simply, 'Metz, or nothing at all.' It was easy to perceive that these men must be fed, and that, so long as they occupied a position round Metz, that city must supply them with food. This naturally reduced the amount of provisions, and helped to effect much sooner the reduction of the fortress.

At the same time it was thought that Bazaine's desire to surrender his army as prisoners of war was a mere subterfuge to gain time, in order that the negotiations then pending between the head-quarters of the King of Prussia and the French representatives might come to some definite climax. To obtain this end, no doubt he and General Coffinière had put their heads together, and Marshal Bazaine imagined that by an apparent willingness to surrender, knowing that his terms could not be accepted, he might gain time, and give his people rest, especially during the fearful weather. In this, to a certain extent, he succeeded, for there was no fighting for five days; on the contrary, the utmost cordiality existed between the outposts. They had talked to one another, the officers bowed, the men took off their caps and made signs of friendship; in fact, the same sort of thing existed as existed across the Tchernaya during the armistice; but all this came to an end.

On the evening of the 24th, Bazaine signified that diplomatic arrangements were closed, and that he must have time to deliberate. Count von Bismarck said that he could listen to no more overtures; and his Royal Highness the Prince gave orders for the army to be under arms at seven o'clock next morning. Meantime, the rain fell in torrents, the roads were knee-deep in mud, and the men suffered fearfully on both sides. Eighty more deserters were received, some from the garde impériale—the whole of which was in Metz. They told the same story—nothing to eat; yet they lived on, and I must say the prisoners looked anything but starved. The 24th went by, and Metz was still La Pucelle.

The fact was, Germany was not prepared for the curious manœuvre which France employed for protecting herself. She defended herself in her fortresses. At that moment Phalsburg, Bitsch, Verdun, Thionville, Laon, Metz, and Paris were all in a state of siege. Metz and Paris required a large army to blockade and to besiege; and, although the Germans had more than 800,000 soldiers in the field, the peculiar posture of the enemy compelled her to utilise every man of them. Under these circumstances, it is not surprising that many of these fortresses held out—with the exception of Strasburg, Toul, and Sedan, not one of them had capitulated; and the three that had surrendered were the only ones that had been bombarded. No doubt the German army had taken every available gun to Paris, for there was a lamentable want of heavy artillery elsewhere.

One afternoon I witnessed a very touching scene. A French soldier of the 33d line regiment, belonging to the corps of General Frossard, had been made prisoner at the outposts. He was a native of Jouy-aux-Arches, where his wife and children resided. *En passant* on his way to Corny, where the head-quarters of the Prince were situated, he asked permission to be allowed to see his wife and children. Need I say that the request was immediately granted? The poor woman, half-delirious with joy, asked to be allowed to accompany her husband at least to Corny. This was also acceded to; but then came the difficulty about the bairns. The woman was weak and could not carry her baby, and at home there was no one to mind it; as for the little chap of five—he could toddle along by his father's side. The difficulty was, however, overcome by a great big Pomeranian soldier, who volunteered to act as nurse. This man had been quartered close to the poor woman's house; and the little ones knew him, for he had often played with them. When, therefore, bidding the poor wife be of good cheer, he held out his big strong arms to the little infant, it came to him immediately, and, nestling its tiny head upon his shoulder, seemed perfectly content. So did the Prussian soldier carry the Frenchman's child.

When I first saw the group, the wife was clasped in her husband's embrace, the little boy clung to his father's hand, whilst the Prussian soldier with the baby in his arms stalked along by their sides. Then the Frenchwoman told her husband how, when she had been ill and in want of food, the Prussian soldiers had shared their rations with her, had fetched wood and water, had lit the fire, and helped her in their own rough kindly way; until at last those two men, who belonged to countries now arrayed against each other in bitterest hate—who perhaps a few days since fought the one against the other—embraced like brothers; whilst I stood by, with the tell-tale moisture in my eye. But I was not alone in my folly, if folly it be; several Prussian officers and soldiers followed my example—for we all had wives and children in far-off homes.

On the morning of the 25th, as soon as there was light sufficient to distinguish objects, every eye was turned anxiously in the direction of the town and outworks. The army was under arms, and everything was ready; but the valley of the Moselle lay still and peaceful, the white smoke curled pleasantly upwards in the morning air, the French drums beat the *réveillé*, and the sun rose upon a scene unchanged from that of yesterday evening. A despatch was received by his Royal Highness Prince Frederick Charles, intimating that General Changarnier would wait upon his Royal Highness at twelve o'clock. At the same time the troops remained upon the defensive, and were to hold themselves in readiness at any moment to repulse an attack.

The next day was an anxious one. The fate of Metz seemed to be hanging by a thread, and all sorts of rumours were bruited abroad. Staff-officers stood in little groups of three and four together round the old château, which was the residence, for the time being, of his Royal Highness Prince Frederick Charles. The streets of Corny and Jouy were perambulated by busy politicians and newsvendors, the last not always of the safest description; and orderlies rode to and fro without ceasing along the muddy roads. Aides-de-camp too were more than usually busy. All at once an order was given that the 4th division of the 2d army corps should march for Paris. The trains were ready to receive their freight, the men were ready in a few minutes, and soon Jouy-aux-Arches was minus so many thousand men. At four P.M. it was definitely known that his Royal Highness would meet Marshal Bazaine in the château of Frascati at six P.M.—the former accompanied by General Stiehle, chief of the staff; the latter by General Changarnier. Head-quarters was a perfect *pot-pourri* of opinions. Would the difficulty be overcome? and would Bazaine's surrender of his army outside the walls be accepted without the fortress? The voice upon this point seemed unanimous—Metz, or nothing!

In the afternoon I rode forward to the outposts. Everything was in order. The driving October wind dashed the pitiless rain in the faces of the sentries and vedettes with almost blinding violence. Not a shot was fired, and not a soul was to be seen stirring. The tricolor flag still waved from the ramparts of Queuleu and St. Quentin, and the French vedettes stood like statues in their respective places. I thought that by skirting the four-cornered wood of Frascati, and galloping across to the advanced post by the railway bridge in front of Montigny, I might perhaps get a view of the French camp in this direction; but no sooner did I emerge from the wood than the whistle of a chassepot bullet told me I had gone too far, and, fearing to draw fire upon the outpost, I turned back into the wood, tied my horse to a tree, and climbed into the upper branches, to see what I could make of it. But the rain prevented any view of this sort. I merely mention these facts to show that the same vigilance was kept up to the last moment.

It seems that Prince Frederick Charles did not attend the conference on the evening of the 25th. General Stiehle and General Changarnier being the only two present. The meeting was at first excessively awkward—the Frenchman feeling his position, the German feeling for the Frenchman, but cool, collected, and to the point. After some little hesitation, the same conditions as those accepted by the French troops at Sedan were proposed by General Changarnier; but they were at once rejected by General Stiehle, inasmuch as the French officers had upon that occasion broken their parole—consequently no farther indulgence could be granted them. What, then, were his Royal Highness's terms? General Stiehle laid them before the French general, who requested permission in turn to submit them to Marshal Bazaine; but he felt sure that no such terms could be accepted, and the interview ended.

It was said that an attack had been ordered at ten

o'clock that morning, but that the French troops refused to fight, and consequently nothing was done. However, a despatch was sent requesting General Stiehle to meet General Changarnier at six in the evening, at the same place of rendezvous—the château of Frascati.

I may here mention that I saw it stated in an English paper, dated October the 25th, that Prince Frederick Charles had removed his quarters from Pont-à-Mousson to Metz. I do not know who gave this extraordinary piece of information; but it is fair to his Royal Highness to state that he never left his army corps for one moment. He shared, like every one else, the privations and exposures of the wearisome blockade of Metz—still more wearisome to him, from his energetic temperament. After the battle of Gravelotte, his head-quarters were at Melancourt, in front of Metz, where he remained until the middle of September; he then removed to Corny, a village lying about a mile and a half from the outposts before Metz. The chief of the combined army never spared himself in any way, and was to be seen continually riding about superintending and overlooking every operation. Pont-à-Mousson is ten English miles from Corny, and was never the head-quarters of his Royal Highness except for a few hours.

The result of that eventful meeting, on the evening of the 26th, which lasted from 6 P.M. on the 26th to 4 A.M. on the 27th, was an appointment for that evening at five o'clock, in order to sign the surrender of Metz, and the capitulation of 150,000 French soldiers, commanded by three marshals of France and

4000 officers. Never, perhaps, in the history of the world has one heard of two such occurrences in a single campaign as the capitulations of Sedan and Metz. There was, however, a vast difference between the circumstances which brought about a like result—the surrender of a fortress and the capitulation of an army. At Sedan, the French troops, driven into an untenable position after a great battle, and hemmed in on every side by a ring of fire, like a flock of sheep, were shot down by hundreds where they stood, without being able to defend themselves; until common sense and humanity cried aloud for a cessation of such slaughter, and the tricolor of France gave way to the Prussian eagle. At Metz, after three severe struggles, Marshal Bazaine's troops were driven back upon one of the strongest fortresses in the world, well supplied with ammunition, and well stocked with provisions. Safe under the shelter of those powerful batteries, the corps d'armée of Bourbaki, Ladmirault, Canrobert, Frossard, and Decaen, pitched their camps, sternly determined to do their duty, and if possible to break through that band of iron which surrounded them on all sides.

The Prussian generals, well aware of the strength of the French position—and taking into consideration the frightful losses which they had already sustained in the actions of Colombey, Mars-la-Tour, and Gravelotte—wisely determined to abstain from attacking a place which would entail a perhaps still more severe loss, with the chance of a defeat. Little by little was the line of perfect isolation completed round the devoted town and the French troops. Patiently, laboriously, and bravely did the German troops fortify the surrounding villages, erecting batteries on every side, not for the purpose of bombardment, but merely to prevent an irruption of the French army. The Germans were day and night exposed to privation, without shelter, continually harassed by the fire of the enemy, both from artillery and infantry, without being able to reply to the heavy guns of the French works. Ever on the alert against surprise, they had waited and watched since the 18th of August—just seventy days—for the consummation of an event that filled the world with wonder and surprise. The French troops, on their side, did all that brave men could do. Five times had Bazaine endeavoured to force his way out, three was he driven back with loss. Now, it was urged, starvation and sickness, want of food, and disease, had accomplished — with, comparatively speaking, little or no loss to the German army—what heavy artillery, or bombardment, or the prolonged and murderous operations of a siege, would perhaps have never brought about.

The scene at the château of Frascati is better described in my letter to the *Daily Telegraph*, dated October 28th:

'Yesterday, at four in the afternoon, I rode to Frascati, a château belonging to a M. d'Asnières, which was to be the scene of the capitulation and surrender. This house is situated to the right of the high road leading from Metz to Jouy-aux-Arches. It had always been the most advanced post, and by no means a nice place in which to do duty, inasmuch as it was but 600 yards from the French lines in front of Montigny, one of the suburbs of Metz, and within easy range of their batteries. Five o'clock was the hour at which the French representatives were to sign the conditions of surrender. I had therefore an hour to spare. Walking through the garden of the château, I came upon the advanced line of Prussian sentries, and there I witnessed a most interesting but melancholy scene.

'Immediately in front of the German sentries, not fifty yards distant, were some 200 French soldiers—artillery, cavalry, and infantry—busily engaged in grubbing up, not only the few potatoes that were left, but also *roots* of any description. This was a sad sight; the men's half-starved faces told how remorseless had been the attacks of hunger. The officer in charge of the advance post gave me leave to go and speak to them; and I crossed over to say a few words of comfort to my poor brothers of the sword. They flocked round me, eagerly asking if it was all over. Would they soon be released? They had had nothing to eat for three days, except what they could pick up, and what the Prussian soldiers had given them. I transferred to them my flask, and all the cigars and tobacco that I had; then I walked back. As I was returning, a Prussian patrol of three men and a sergeant came out, and waved the poor fellows back; but it was done kindly and quietly. They were told that, if they remained where they were, when darkness came on they might be shot; so each man, taking up his little bundle of roots, made his way back into the French lines.

'There is a small house, probably for sheltering

cattle, which stands half-way between the French and German outposts. In this little house, every evening after dusk, for the last few days, have the German patrols left of their own accord some bread, some salt, and whatever they could spare from their own rations. Every man of them—the 2d Jägers and the 54th Pomeranian regiment—saved from his bread, from his meat, from his salt, from his little stock of tobacco, something to add to that store left every night by the soldiers of Germany to assist the would-be invaders of their Fatherland!

'Punctually at five P.M. General Stiehle, the chief of Prince Frederick Charles's staff, arrived at the place of rendezvous, accompanied by Captain Stephan and Premier Lieutenant Dieskau. There were two rooms prepared, one for the staff-officers, and an inner room for the generals. In the outer room the Prussian officers had prepared a supper for the French representatives, and everything was in readiness—down to the fatal pens, whose few hasty strokes were about to consign 4000 officers and 150,000 unhurt soldiers as prisoners of war. Slowly the moments dragged on; we spoke to one another in whispers. Half-past five came, and no signs of the Frenchmen. Their approach was to be announced by a mounted orderly. Would they alter their minds? Had they repented of their resolve, and would they endure misery and starvation for a few days longer in that den of typhus called Metz?

'The hasty entry of a staff-officer charged to announce their approach soon put all doubts at rest. A carriage stops before the doors of the château for a few seconds, and then the door of the room is thrown open. Escorted by Major Bagenski of the 54th, Lieutenant von Frier of the lancers of the guard, and Lieutenant von Görz, adjutant of the 3d battalion 54th regiment, the three representatives of the only army that *la grande nation* still possesses in the field enter the room. It was a moment never to be forgotten—the calm demeanour maintained by the Frenchmen, the perfect good breeding of the Prussians; the flickering uncertain light of a wood-fire and two indifferent candles revealing the careworn but still haughty bearing of the one side, the pity and genuine fellow-feeling for their position cherished by the other. To General Charras had fallen the unhappy lot of completing the final arrangements already agreed to. He was accompanied by Colonel Fay and Captain Samuelle. The two generals retired to the inner room, while the officers entered into conversation with one another. After about an hour's conference, the staffs of the respective generals were called in, the scratching of the busy pens told that all had been arranged, and then General Stiehle came out and dispatched two aides to his Royal Highness, informing him that all had been signed.

'The conditions are the same as those made at Sedan. At twelve o'clock to-day the French soldiers are to place their arms in the arsenal of Metz; and at the same hour to-morrow the troops are to march out to the following places without arms—one division to Grigy, one to the farm of Thibault, one to Amanvillers, one to the village of Bellecroix; the corps of the French guard, with the artillery reserve, to Tournebride, close to Frascati; and one corps to Ladonchamps. The fortress will be surrendered at the same hour; two battalions of Prussian infantry, with two field guns, will take possession of each of the forts, and display the Prussian standard upon them. The French officers will surrender themselves as prisoners to the Prussian officers, handing over their swords; the soldiers will remain here for a few days, there being still rations sufficient for six days. Three marshals of France, 50 generals, 500 staff-officers, and 173,000 men, including 16,000 sick, are the total numbers; these figures include the garde mobile of the town. Such are the conditions of the surrender and capitulation; and this morning Prince Frederick Charles has issued a proclamation to the first army, with a copy of which I close my despatch.

'I shall abstain from saying anything farther until I have witnessed the last act which will close the drama of Metz—would that I could say, the last scene of this fearful war!—the march of the French troops out of the fortress, and the surrender of the officers as prisoners of war. I cannot, however, conclude without a few words regarding the feelings of the German army at this moment. As regards the officers, I can only say that, if heartfelt sympathy for their unhappy position, a desire to make that position as little hurtful to their feelings as the customs of war will permit, and sincere admiration for their conduct, can apply any salve to that wound that must now be so keenly felt by the officers of Marshal Bazaine's army, they have it most cordially from every officer of the victorious forces. As regards the men, I can only say that the same feeling is universally entertained. Prince Frederick Charles's proclamation is as follows:

GENERAL ORDER.

Head-quarters, Corny-before-Metz,
October 27th, 1870.

SOLDIERS OF THE FIRST AND SECOND ARMIES,—You have fought battles, and you have invested the enemy conquered by you for seventy days—seventy long days, of which the most, however, made your regiments richer in honour and glory, and none of which left them in these things poorer. You allowed to your brave enemy no escape until he laid down his arms. To-day at last has this army capitulated—this army which consisted of fully 173,000 men, the best in France, of more than five entire army corps, among them the imperial guard, with three marshals of France, and upwards of 50 generals, and above 6000 officers; and with them has Metz surrendered, which was never taken before. While we present this completed work to Germany, we at the same time give her the immense stores in cannons, arms, and war material which have fallen into the hands of the conqueror.

These bloody laurels you have gained by your bravery in the battle which lasted for two days at Noisseville, and in the conflicts around Metz, which were more numerous than those which have taken place in the surrounding districts after which you have called them. I acknowledge gladly and gratefully your bravery, but not it alone. I rank almost higher your obedience and your resignation, your cheerfulness, your devotion in bearing difficulties of all kinds. These are the qualities which characterise the good soldier. The great victory of to-day, for which we ought to be so thankful, was prepared by the battles we fought before we invested Metz; and, let us remember it with thankfulness, also by the King himself, by the army corps which he marched hither, and by all those dear comrades who met their death on the battle-fields, or who succumbed to the sufferings prevalent here. These events it was which rendered possible the great work which you this day, with God's help, see completed—namely, the annihilation of France's power. The wide influence of this event of to-day is inestimable.

But you, soldiers, who, for this end, were united before Metz under my command, you now proceed to different occupations. Bid farewell, then, to the general officers and the soldiers of the 1st army, and to the division von Kummer, and may my wishes for their farther success follow them. (*Signed*) FREDERICK CHARLES,
General of Cavalry.'

About this time a letter appeared in the *Kölnische Zeitung* of October 23d, the Hanoverian paper of the 25th, and other periodicals, containing extracts from a letter written by a special correspondent of the *Daily News*. The letter caused an immense deal of excitement at the time, and as I had the honour of being attached to General von Steinmetz's staff, I can fully appreciate the indignation with which such assertions were received by the officers of H.R.H. Prince Frederick Charles's staff. Nor can I permit so unjust and injurious a report to gain credence, to the detriment—were that possible—of the character and military genius of a man who well and nobly served his country.

The writer proposed to give to the world the solution of a problem: viz. the removal of General von Steinmetz from the command of the 1st army to the governorship of Posen. His reasons were various. I shall, however, only remark upon those with which I am perfectly well acquainted. He stated that General von Steinmetz crossed the Moselle on the south side of Metz against the positive command of his Majesty. This, I am directed to state, was quite untrue; General von Steinmetz never received any orders upon the subject. He went on to say, that had his excellency passed over on the northern side, the combats of the 16th and 18th would have been avoided. Evidently this gentleman had never been on the north side of Metz when he talked of an attack made by way of Saulny; he must also have been equally misinformed as to the events which preceded the operations of the 16th of August, or he would have seen that General von Steinmetz did the only thing he could do under the existing circumstances. He was backed up by H.R.H. Prince Frederick Charles with his army, and the result achieved was all that could be desired.

The troops that were marching upon Châlons to form a junction with Marshal M'Mahon were driven back upon Metz, and a perhaps more bloody field on the banks of the Marne was thereby prevented. Now, by glancing at this manœuvre—that of crossing to the north of Metz by way of Saulny, instead of to the south by Corny and Arry—it will be seen that, had General von Steinmetz done as the writer proposed, he would have found his troops entangled in large woods and in an excessively hilly and difficult country—to say nothing of being immediately in rear of the line of march of the French army, who, on the 15th August, were reviewed by the Emperor on the plains of Mars-la-Tour and Gravelotte. Besides, his left flank would have been exposed to the fire from the guns of Plappeville and St. Quentin, whose shells were at that moment bursting far beyond Saulny. The French army would have immediately marched forward on their way to Paris unopposed, except by the 3d and 9th corps, which were far too weak to hinder their advance. General von Steinmetz therefore seized the opportunity of crossing the Moselle on the south side, and, forming a junction with his Royal Highness Prince Frederick Charles, drove the enemy from their position, by Mars-la-Tour and Rezonville, back to the heights above Metz, thereby cutting off their farther advance on the road to the capital. This was the action of the 16th. The battle of Gravelotte drove the army of Bazaine into Metz, rendering the assistance of these troops utterly null and void for the rest of the campaign, and overthrowing the plans of Marshal M'Mahon.

And now the last act was about to be played out. Metz was no longer in the hands of the French, for on the 29th of October the Prussian eagle floated from every rampart. On that day I witnessed a scene which must have been the lot of but few, and certainly will never occur again in the present century. At a late hour on the previous evening the staff received the order to be saddled at noon; and were my thoughts not so full of the sad and melancholy scenes I witnessed that day, I could tell you, perhaps, how the head-quarter staff rejoiced, soberly and in a German way, over the second event of this truly 'sensational' campaign. The morning broke most unpromisingly. The sky, like a leaden sheet, deluged all around with that straight down-pouring rain which has not about it the honesty of a good shower—that says, 'If you go out, I wet you through'—but a nasty cunning thin downpour, that soaks through and through. Even such a fall ushered in the eventful day when three marshals, at least 50 generals, 6000 officers, and 173,000 French soldiers were to surrender as prisoners of war to a German army numbering, all told, some 175,000 effective men and officers. Early in the morning the streets of Corny and Jouy-aux-Arches were crowded with a curious medley in the shape of proprietors of houses and shopkeepers, who on the approach of the German army had fled for protection to Metz; and they certainly found their dwellings somewhat *bouleversés*.

At 12.30 precisely his Royal Highness, accompanied by General Stiehle, and a staff of forty officers, rode through Corny and Jouy to the place of rendezvous, where the French guard were to defile before the victorious army. The place was well chosen. To the left of Frascati, between it and the railway embankment, is a level plateau, upon which was drawn up the 4th division of the 2d army corps, consisting of two brigades; on the heights above Frascati, between it and Orly, a strong body of infantry, with two batteries of artillery, had taken their position; while the straight road from Tournebride to Jouy was left open for the march of the French troops. On the plateau in front of the farm of Polka—to the left of the road emerging from Jouy, and about half a mile distant from that town—were placed, at regular intervals, heaps of firewood; and the ground was marked out into squares by means of poles decked with straw. This was to be the bivouac of the French guard; here they were to remain, surrounded by two battalions of infantry, and guns; here they were to be fed by the German troops—rations for six days having been provided for them—until they should be marched away in detachments to Pont-à-Mousson and Nancy, where the railways would take them to their German prisons.

The usual order of the Prussian arrangements seemed upon this occasion to have outvied itself. The troops were in their appointed places, and the arrangements for the reception of the prisoners and the commissariat departments had been all reported to his Royal Highness as completely in order before he left head-quarters.

As we rode along the road towards Metz, we met a curious assemblage of all sorts. These were the population of the surrounding villages, who were now making the best of their way back to their dwellings, and who had been unable to leave Metz in consequence of the rapid irruption of the Prussians. Some of them walked, carrying upon their shoulders such of their household gods as the war had left. One held a chair in the right hand, on the seat of which, with the ingenuity of a Frenchman, he had packed some of his baggage; in the left he held an umbrella, the blankets of his bed serving him for a greatcoat. Here you saw a party of ladies packed into a well-made, English-looking carriage, which struggled through the mud, assisted by a mule on one side and a skeleton horse on the other. Then came a farmer, dragging a half-starved, wretched-looking horse, doing his best to stop at every bunch of grass by the wayside to appease his hunger. '*Voilà le dernier, mon capitaine,*' he cried. '*J'en avais six; les autres ont fait du bon bouillon. Allez!*'

As we entered the road whence we could see the battery of St. Quentin, every eye was turned in that direction; for there, on the highest point, waved the black-and-white flag of Prussia. Here too some four or five soldiers of the imperial guard passed us. They were immediately arrested for having broken out of the town without waiting for their regiments. As we approached, we found the brigade of General

Hartmann drawn up on the left of the road, and comprising the 54th and 21st regiments, with the 3d dragoons. At a signal from the general, 8000 good strong Pomeranian pairs of lungs shouted a welcome to the victorious Prince, who, with his staff, galloped up the front of the line and down the rear. His Royal Highness Prince Frederick Charles then took up a position to the right of the first regiment, and, surrounded by his staff, awaited the arrival of the French troops.

It was half-past one o'clock, but yet there were no signs of them. Eagerly every eye was strained in the direction of the bridge which with a single arch spans the railway, to catch the first glimpse of the red trousers; but nothing was to be seen, and the rain descended in torrents—the heavier showers wetting all to the skin. Presently the scream of a railway engine, pushing before it a single first-class carriage along that line of railway that had so often proved the scene of outpost fights, came into view. The carriage contained Marshal Bazaine and staff, going to the residence of his Royal Highness, also to surrender themselves. Slowly the moments dragged on, still no appearance of the French advanced guard. It was now whispered that the officers had lost all control over their men; that there was no discipline; and that this was the reason they had been compelled to give up their arms before marching out of Metz. But a greater libel against the discipline of the French guard was never circulated. The Prussian troops piled arms, and stood at ease: and so they waited and speculated, watching the inhabitants of Metz as they straggled along the road in detached parties.

At three P.M. an aide-de-camp came galloping up to say that the troops were coming; the soldiers stood to their arms, and presently, over the railway bridge, appeared the long-waited-for prisoners. Riding at the head of the first detachment was the town major, a colonel in the French army, attended by a mounted orderly in full uniform, wearing his sword. Approaching General Franseky, he took off his cap, and reported the arrival of the guard to surrender themselves prisoners of war. I was not near enough to hear all that he said; but he was evidently so much affected, that he could scarcely give utterance to a word. General Franseky replied courteously—his Royal Highness being some forty yards off, to the right. The first regiment then marched by; they were the hussars of the guard. The colonel of the regiment, riding up to General Franseky and saluting, handed to him the effective strength of his regiment; then he rode off, followed by his officers, all still wearing their swords. The Empress's dragoons came next; then a regiment of chasseurs de la garde; then the artillery; all, of course, on foot.

As each regiment approached, the commanding officers went through the same formula, presenting the 'states' of their regiments. I never saw more perfect order, or a more quiet soldier-like demeanour, than that exhibited by this splendid body of men, as they marched past in perfect silence. Not a word was spoken. All that could be heard was the measured tread of thousands of feet, as they splashed along the muddy road. The officers, some of them with tears in their eyes, some with haughty and bold countenances, silently shook hands with their soldiers; for the order was, that so soon as the officers had marched their regiments to the quarters assigned for their bivouac, they were to ride back to Metz, and there await farther orders.

Immediately following the above-mentioned regiments came the premier grenadiers de la garde, so well known to Englishmen—so familiar at the gates of the Louvre, at the Palace of the Tuileries, and before the principal buildings of Paris. Poor fellows—how I pitied them as, with a steady, soldier-like demeanour, they strode past, as if they were going to a field-day, and not to prison! The Prussian officers gazed with wonder and surprise upon this fine body of men, most of them between 19 and 23 years of age; and as regiment after regiment, to the number of at least 30,000, filed past, the soldiers whispered to one another, how fortunate it was that they had no longer to fight against such men. The horse artillery and the 4th voltigeurs of the guard particularly attracted attention, the last regiment that marched past being the zouaves of the guard, and a truly splendid regiment they were. It was quite dark when the last troops had filed by.

As each regiment marched past, it took up the place allotted to it for bivouacking. The men pitched their little tents, lit their fires, and commenced cooking their provisions. During the whole time that the melancholy procession went by, not a man opened his lips, either in the French or the Prussian ranks, except to speak in a whisper. The last occasion on which the Prussian troops came as near the imperial guard was on the field of Vionville, on the 16th of August. Night put an end to the surrender. The same scene might have been witnessed at five different points around the fortress of Metz. At each of these points a French corps was marching before the German army as prisoners of war.

I had expected to see the men looking dreadfully ill and 'pulled down;' but, on the contrary, the imperial guard looked exceedingly well, and by no means in a starved state. I do not know what the other corps may have looked like; but it is a curious enigma, which requires explanation, that Marshal Bazaine, with such an army, could not break through the Prussian lines. It is a question which German officers put to one another, and added, 'If Bazaine had really tried to come out of Metz, we could not possibly have prevented him.' Why did Bazaine retire after his advantage gained at Mercy-le-Haut and Peltre? The road was open. Why did he withdraw his troops, after having beaten back the division Kummer and cleared the road to Thionville? These are curious questions, which can only be met by the explanation that has accounted for previous blunders of the French generals—let us say incompetency. And to this incompetency a brave army, composed of the finest soldiers in the world, was sacrificed. Bazaine will, no doubt, try the excuse of famine; but why should he have remained in a spot provided with subsistence for only a certain number of men, when the way of exit was by no means difficult, and very far from impossible?

The French officers remained prisoners of war in Metz, and retained their swords upon parole.

And now General Manteuffel assumed the command of the 1st army, and Prince Frederick Charles received orders to hold himself in readiness with his command, the 2d army. At the same time he is made a field-marshal, and General Kummer becomes Governor of Metz. The first fortress in France fell, the finest army that ever trod were prisoners of war; but yet, alas, all was not over.

Let us turn for a moment to Metz after the surrender. It may easily be imagined with what curiosity and anxiety I made my first journey into the town I had so long looked upon from the heights around it. I could scarcely help thinking, as I rode over Tournebride, that at a line of demarcation which had hitherto always seemed to say, 'Thus far shalt thou go, and no farther,' I should hear the familiar whiz of the chassepot bullet. It was certainly not a nice day; for the rain poured down in torrents upon the unfortunate French prisoners of war, bivouacked in an open field, with no other shelter than their little tents. A curious effect, in that dreary landscape, had those huge red-and-white cloaks of the cavalry regiments belonging to the imperial guard, as they stood in groups, longing for the order that should release them from such dreadful exposure. Poor fellows! this was what awaited them after doing as much as diplomacy permitted. The German sentries even commiserated their position; and you could see them gently remonstrating with the unruly or anxious groups who tried to press across the line of demarcation. Here, seated on the muddy ground, with pools of water all around them, were to be seen those men who had taken the Mamelon and stormed the Malakoff—the heroes of Magenta and Solferino—the tried troops of many an African campaign. It was a sad, sad sight, and one I was glad to leave behind.

As I rode along the road to Montigny, I looked with almost anxious eye at the dreaded fortress of St. Quentin: but now no white puff of smoke made the passer-by hurry to a shelter; all was still, except the incessant patter of the rain on the streaming muddy road. After passing Tournebride you arrive at that little brown house so conspicuous as the French advanced post. '*Maison à vendre, avec jardin,*' was all that could be seen upon the dismantled and loop-holed walls; where the *jardin* lay was a matter that, no doubt, had been left to the imagination. Immediately in rear of Tournebride you came to the first line of the French rifle-pits. They were made principally with fascine-shaped baskets, so that the soldier standing upon the 'tread' could shoot through the baskets, which were disposed something in the shape of an eel-trap, without exposing his head above the parapet.

Farther on, the railway embankment that runs from La Porte de la Citadelle round to Le Sablon formed an earthwork of no ordinary dimensions; whilst immediately in front of this, at unequal distances, small lunettes were thrown up for field artillery. Passing under the bridge, you enter the straggling suburb of Montigny le Metz, and through the long street, meeting here and there a French officer or a French soldier. Chassepots lay everywhere, but absolute order prevailed. The greater portion of the houses seemed to be hospitals, and the number of men who struggled along on crutches, with only one leg—to say nothing of those who had only one arm—was cruelly great. Here General Frossard had commanded, and to his shattered corps had been intrusted the defence of this portion of Metz.

Emerging from Montigny, and riding across an open space—defended, on the left hand of the entrance, by the Lunette de Montigny, and on the right by that of D'Arçon, you approach the Porte Serpenoise; but as the map herein supplied treats of the fortifications, I will only say that I was perfectly awe-struck by the strength of the defences. The first thing in the town that spoke of the trials a blockaded city has to endure was the appearance of the Place Royal. It was literally full of railway vans, drawn up in lines. What did these vans contain? The door of the nearest carriage was open; let us approach and peep in. It contained six sick and wounded soldiers, and every wagon of the crowd that stood there in eight lines, covering the whole Place, had the same kind of occupants—to say nothing of a perfect camp of tents pitched in the gardens in front of the Palais de Justice. The hospitals, it seems, were all full, so were the barracks, so were many of the public buildings. As you entered the Rue Serpenoise, you were still more astonished at the crowds of French soldiers and officers that thronged the streets; but when we come to consider that 6000 officers were prisoners of war, and that each must have a servant, there was, after all, nothing so wonderful.

I rode through the streets straight to the head-quarters of General Kummer, who is the commandant of Metz, and who, for the time, has taken up his residence at the Grand Hôtel de l'Europe. Here we found a vast amount of disorganisation, as may easily be imagined. Every officer wanted to get away from the scene of disaster and misery; and they would fain go, not by ones and twos, but by batches of six and seven. Many had estates in the neighbourhood that they wanted to visit; and this, being a private matter, and not affecting the mass, had naturally to be arranged in a distinct way. Then there were all the ambulance mules to take over—to say nothing of the post and field telegraph train, the cattle for which must now be fed by the Germans. There were the doctors applying for medical comforts and instructions as to their sick; there were the police; and, last of all, the clergy. Such a horrible *mélange* of wants and necessities never, I am sure, before embarrassed the head of that quiet, orderly, and not-to-be-flurried staff of officials.

These matters struck me as I entered the hotel, and where, thought I could not do better than test the alimentary resources of the town. Accordingly I made my way into the *salle à manger*, and calling a waiter, I ordered dinner. You may imagine, therefore, my astonishment when I was served first of all with soup; this I ladled out with such evident misgiving, that the *garçon* came to my assistance with a '*N'avez pas peur, ce n'est pas du cheval.*' If it was, may I never eat worse! Then came an excellent beefsteak—certainly not horse—and then *Krammersvögel*, followed by an excellent omelette. The bread was certainly brown, but it was good and wholesome. Very curious this: for it was utterly impossible that these provisions could have been introduced in such a short time. In fact, I was thoroughly disappointed with my dinner. I wanted to eat horseflesh. I wanted to play at being shut up in a famished city; and I could not, because there was plenty of everything—to say nothing of salt, which most certainly was there.

We must, however, seek the *dénouement* of this strange inconsistency somewhere else than in the dining-room of the Hôtel de l'Europe; accordingly, we sally forth into the streets. The first thing that meets the eye is a placard, written in a bold hand, upon a wall, '*Bazaine et Coffinière sont des traîtres et des lâches.*' Strange, but very significant; so we stroll into the Place Napoléon. All along the shops are open, and pretty shops they are too. We pass several butchers'—there is plenty of meat. We pass bakers' and confectioners'—all are well supplied. The enigma remains unsolved.

We walk into the Café Français, and there I meet with a French officer of the grenadiers de la garde, who had served with me in the Crimea; it is fifteen years ago since we met on the banks of the Tchernaya. We sit down to a table with many others, to whom I am introduced, and naturally we begin to talk and to compare notes. 'Have you suffered much?' 'Not as much as we could; we might have held out three weeks longer,' was the answer. 'The town seems well supplied,' I ventured to remark. 'O, yes; but with us outside it was a different affair.' 'You have many sick?' I added. 'Of course, where so many men are huddled together, this will naturally occur; besides, we have the wounded of the 16th and 18th of August, to say nothing of the other affairs; and Metz lies low.' So many officers were sitting round us, I could not ask all I should have desired; but the truth seemed to ooze out despite this. The officers were anything but satisfied with the conduct of Bazaine; they considered themselves to have been all *sold*—that was the expression; the more so when they ascertained that the German army consisted of but 158,000 men, absolutely 14,000 fewer than they had, with scarcely any heavy guns.

I do not know what the people of England will think when they read this; but I imagine they will agree with me that the surrender of Metz was premature, and that nothing speaks such volumes for the discipline of the French army under the command of Bazaine as the orderly, soldier-like, and quiet behaviour with which they laid down their arms simply because they were commanded to do so by their general. The issue of that long resistance is to be the more regretted, looking at it from a military point of view, because the men who could go through the ceremony of that day with such discipline would have fought like demons had they had the opportunity. Every German officer knew perfectly well that had Bazaine really wished to force his way out of Metz, the blockading forces could not have prevented it.

Leaving the Café Français, we proceeded to make our way through a crowd of all sorts into the cathedral, the spire of which had so long been a landmark. Of the architecture I am not going to speak; but in the long and lofty aisles I could see no wounded or sick. 'Had the cathedral been used as a hospital?' I inquired of a Frenchman. 'No, sir; certainly not,' was the answer. Here I met a Prussian soldier who had been wounded on the 7th of October, and had been a prisoner in Metz ever since. He informed me that his treatment had been of the best; that, whatever rations the French soldiers had received, he had obtained an equal share. In fact, he was hobbling along on the arm of a wounded Frenchman. How does this agree with the inflated absurdities that the *Standard* gave birth to? Leaving the cathedral, we wandered through the streets, and entered into conversation with several shopkeepers and proprietors; but the same story was retailed everywhere. They had never wanted food. They had been rationed, of course, because they anticipated a much longer resistance, and they had eaten horseflesh; but anything like starvation had never occurred.

I had appointed to meet some French officers in the evening, in order to hand over to them some melancholy souvenirs that had been given to me by mortally-wounded comrades on the 16th and 18th of August; and, from what these gentlemen told me, I am inclined to believe that Bazaine's army outside the walls of the town *did* in the last few days suffer from want of bread, and that the imperial guard was by far the best off as to quarters. It appeared that Bazaine was doubtful whether he could rely upon his men, and it was believed that he depended upon the guard to enforce obedience if necessary; hence their better condition. Under any circumstances, I was fully impressed with the conviction that the French army had not arrived at that point of starvation to which an army of 173,000 men should be reduced in order to warrant capitulation.

All the charm, all the poetry of Bazaine's heroic resistance had now vanished into the air. We had hitherto been led to believe that the French army round Metz had suffered inconceivable hardships, and that thousands had died of starvation; that the inhabitants had fed upon all sorts of curious things; that want had filled the town with disease. This turned out, however, not to be the case; had Bazaine wished to hold Metz a few days longer, and to give his soldiers a chance of marching to the assistance of their comrades in arms in other parts of France, an officer and detachment told off from each regiment would have procured from the inhabitants the subsistence necessary for such a movement, even if it had been necessary to do so at the point of the bayonet. The inhabitants might have rebelled, it is true; but the army should have been the first thought.

Early on the morning of the 1st of November, the army of Prince Frederick Charles marched, and I had to say adieu to many kind and good friends. My thanks were most specially due to General von Stiehle, chief of his Royal Highness's staff, for all his kindness and civility; also to those other officers of the staff of the second army with whom I had been so long associated.

And now all was over. First of all, a train, containing some 3000 French officers, left Metz at 10 A.M., transporting its burden to the various towns of Germany told off for their reception. The departing gentlemen were naturally very anxious to dispose of their horses, and a great amount of dealing went on. The programme was very simple. You met a French officer in the street, and asked if he had a horse to sell. If he had not, one of his comrades certainly had. The horse was then shown, a bargain was struck, the money was paid, and the thing was finished. The price for a good horse varied from 25*l.* to 30*l.* The animals were not in very good condition, for they had been receiving but 4lbs. of oats daily; and this ration had been given only to the horses of officers commanding regiments, officers of the staff, and generals. Those who bought oats had to pay six francs a pound.

A touching incident occurred as I was walking down a street. A veterinary surgeon of the ambulance corps came up, and said: 'Monsieur, my horse is dying for want of food; I have ridden him for four years; he has shared my rations, and latterly my bed; for three days I have had nothing to give him to eat. Give him something; save the poor thing's life, and take him for your own; he is a good and faithful beast; you will never regret it.' I immediately accompanied the man, and on my way I bought two loaves of bread, which we cut up as we walked along. Arrived at the shed where his horse stood, the poor beast turned his head towards his master, and neighed out a welcome, though so weak that he could scarcely move. The man rushing up to his horse, threw his arms round his neck, and, whilst the tears stood in his eyes, cried out, '*Tu es sauvé! tu es sauvé!*' The horse belonged to the staff of the French army, and being branded, it was of course the property of the conquerors of Metz. I was therefore reluctantly obliged to hand him over to the proper authorities—at the same time assuring my friend that all possible care would be taken of his dumb but affectionate friend.

As I was returning, I was again stopped—this time by a distracted father, whose son, one of the garde mobile, was lying in the delirium of typhus fever. Raising his hat, whilst his white hair streamed in the wind, he implored me to assist him. 'You speak French and German, sir; perhaps you too have a son; and if so, you can feel for me.' I went with him to the man who could deal with his case, and when I left him, he was showering blessings upon a head that never deserved them.

Notwithstanding the peculiar situation of Metz, people had time to make mischief. That day the *Metz Indépendant*, a professedly unpolitical journal, was suppressed in consequence of two scurrilous articles; but more order was gradually finding its way into the town. The 7th army corps and the division Kummer occupied the city. I read a somewhat amusing placard stuck up over a post-office: in large letters was printed, 'Deutsche Lothringen Post-Amt.' Already was the fair province of Lorraine told off to the conquerors.

On the 1st of November at noon, the muddy bivouac of the French prisoners was entirely deserted; they had all marched off to their German prisons. Another twenty-four hours of such exposure would have decimated the host. The inhabitants were returning to the surrounding villages, and great hopes of a speedy termination of the war were entertained on every side. The French army was said to be rapidly increasing upon the banks of the Loire.

And now the time had come when we were to leave the desolate country that surrounds Metz; for the army of blockade was breaking up in every direction. The 7th army corps and the division Kummer alone remained. Most of the second army—that which at the opening of the campaign was under the special command of Prince Frederick Charles—had already marched, and by the evening of the 1st of November all had evacuated. Prince Frederick Charles went, with his staff, to Nancy for a few days, with the intention of joining his army three or four days' march beyond that city.

Ever mindful of the catastrophe of Laon, the German engineers were busily engaged for the last few days in exploring the fortifications and the outlying works for mines; but their researches were resultless. Captain Schulz, of gunpowder renown, took over the powder manufactories and the arsenal; and under his energetic supervision, immense improvements and fresh supplies of materials were produced for the benefit of the various armies, who, by means of the railway communication, were now able to be more easily supplied. Meantime we had intelligence of bands of Francs-tireurs, who prowled about in every direction, hanging on the outskirts of the advancing troops, and doing as much mischief as they possibly could. Those who were caught received a short shrift, in the shape of a rope and the nearest tree.

One morning, at an early hour, I determined to see as much as possible of the French positions outside the town of Metz as I could before leaving. Accordingly, riding over the bridge of Ars-sur-Moselle, I took the road to Moulins-les-Metz, the point chosen by the belligerents at which flags of truce were to have been received. Like the suburb of Montigny, Moulins-les-Metz is nothing more than a straggling, ill-built village, rendered still more repulsive at that time by the havoc which the French around it had committed. All the gardens, vineyards, and pleasure grounds were now but a sea of mud, plentifully interspersed with dead horses. In the long irregular street leading to Longeville-les-Metz, dead carcasses were to be seen in every direction. The village was defended by a long line of rifle-pits, the houses having been loopholed, and small works for field-guns having been thrown up across the roads. The position was by no means strong; but inasmuch as it lay at the foot of Mont St. Quentin, the work of strengthening the place would have been only wasted labour. Longeville-les-Metz was but a repetition of Moulins; and the state of these two villages showed that the troops must have certainly suffered a little.

Riding through the little hamlet of Ban St. Martin, which nestles at the foot of St. Quentin on its south-west face, I took the path leading to St. Quentin and Plappeville. To the right and left of the road lay the same desolate scene—the air simply laden with putrefaction from dead horses and half-buried carcasses. Ascending the road which leads to the fort, I stopped to gaze upon a spectacle too shocking to be passed by unnoticed. To the left of the road were the remains of an orchard, which had been turned into a slaughter-house. In little heaps everywhere lay the legs and heads of slaughtered horses; hanging to the branch of a tree was the carcass of a horse, evidently placed there for the purpose of being cut up into rations. The ground, trampled and gory, was strewed with entrails and offal; while, attached to several trees, and lying where they had been tied, were the bodies of seven dead horses. A French soldier passing afforded the opportunity of asking for an explanation. '*Ma foi!* that was our butcher's shop; and pretty dear the meat was latterly, I can assure you.'

Passing on, I remarked that the slopes of the hill lying between the village and the work of Plappeville were regularly honeycombed, each hole serving as a shelter for some half-a-dozen soldiers. The range of hills in this direction formed a sort of horseshoe; the end nearest Metz and the highest portion being occupied by Fort St. Quentin, the opposite end by the fort of Plappeville. The bend of the shoe presented its front to the German position, whilst the reverse side sloped steeply down to the valley of the Moselle. Here it was that the French troops suffered most. Arrived at Fort St. Quentin, the whole panorama of the blockade, with every position, became distinctly visible. The centre of the picture was occupied by the town of Metz, surrounded by her mighty fortifications, environed by desolation and devastation; rising out from among the gray and white red-roofed houses, the grand old cathedral proudly reared its mass of wondrous architecture. Immediately opposite were the forts of St. Julien and Queuleu, covering the whole city on the south and west side.

Entering Fort St. Quentin, you find the work very much smaller than at first anticipated; but from its commanding position, and its proximity to Plappeville, one considers it utterly unassailable. A thousand resolute soldiers could there defy an army; while if Plappeville, with the works which connected the two fortresses, were properly garrisoned, you feel convinced that no army in the world could storm the position. When I entered the outer works, the whole road was encumbered with chassepots, sword bayonets, belts, pouches, swords, and drums. Here had been deposited the arms and ammunition of the French division that lay upon the slopes under St. Quentin. Rifles lay in piles, cartridges were scattered in every direction; splendid musical instruments of brass were kicking about in every corner; the music belonging to the bands also lay scattered about. The huge brass guns that had sent their tremendous shells 4000 yards into the Prussian position stood grimly in their places, muzzle in air, by reason of the great elevation they were compelled to use. I did not see more than a dozen guns altogether, and one small mortar; they were all muzzle-loaders.

The shape of the fort was a parallelogram; it was built of masonry, surmounted by strong parapets of earth, and protected by lines of rifle-pits, together with a mass of small field lunettes, thrown up along the ridge and bending outwards towards the German positions of Vaux, Rozerieulles, Point du Jour, and Chatel. It was on this side that the French troops must have suffered more than on any other, in consequence of their elevated position, without shelter of any kind when exposed to the stormy winds and drenching rains of the autumnal equinox. The poor fellows, with the ingenuity of their nation, had endeavoured to make the best of their bad bargain; huts and holes of all descriptions marked the places where the regiments had their encampments.

Plappeville was a work of much larger dimensions, and infinitely stronger, than St. Quentin, although it did not hold so commanding a position. I had only time to remark that it also was encumbered with war material of every sort, when my watch told me it was time to return to Metz. Accordingly I turned my horse's head down that road that had been so often trodden by the weary, heart-sick, half-starved soldiers of France for seven long weeks; and riding across the Pont des Morts, I entered the fortress of Metz. There were a great number of French officers still in the town, who strolled about the streets, dined at the tables-d'hôte, and frequented the cafés, in a manner which did them no credit. It would have been far better if they had remained in their rooms, and lived upon bread and water, until it was time for them to leave the scene of their disgrace, than to swagger about as if the world belonged to them.

On the day that Marshal Canrobert, with General Coffinière, quitted Metz, General Ladmirault distinctly refused to leave with them in the same train. He requested the officer in command at the railway station to dispatch him by any other train, inasmuch as to travel with such people would be a still greater disgrace. Strange words these, but full of meaning! His majesty Marshal Bazaine seemed also to have had a *mauvais quart d'heure* on his way to Wilhelmshöhe. At Pont-à-Mousson he was received with yells, and was compelled to go to the German commandant to procure quarters. At Nancy he was pelted with stones; in Metz his name was execrated.

Wandering round the fortifications, I came upon a place that gave me some idea of the sufferings that the poor horses had to go through. Immediately in front of the Porte des Allemands is a barrack which was occupied by the garde mobile. The square was on one side planted with trees, and to each of these were attached three, and sometimes four, of the most wretched horses you can well imagine. The living numbered 120, the dead 54; the latter had died during the night. So emaciated were the poor creatures, and so weak, that they could not eat; they were past feeding, and only awaited the moment when they were to sink down and die where they were bound. Immediately in rear of these animals, as if in mockery of their dumb suffering, was established a line of baking ovens, for the employment of which these unfortunates had dragged in the flour.

The poor creatures had received only two handfuls of oats per diem for the previous ten days.

I am now relating these circumstances in the hope of finding an excuse for the premature surrender of Bazaine, and for his apparent unwillingness to leave the shelter of Metz. But, grievous as these things may appear to the uninitiated, want and privation are, after all, to a certain extent the lot of a soldier. The French army under the walls of Metz was never exposed to the privations or to the exposure which the British troops suffered during the winters of '54, '55, and '56. The French troops were there also. Is it possible that the conquerors of Solferino and Magenta have deteriorated?

On the day that General Manteuffel took command of the 1st army, he gave a dinner to Prince Frederick Charles and the officers of the staff, together with the generals of divisions. Eighteen generals and a number of staff-officers had the honour of dining with the Prince, who said that when he received his patent of field-marshal it was the happiest and proudest moment of his life, inasmuch as that was the one thing for which he had always hoped and striven.

And now for a parting glance at Metz, for the long weary blockade is over. The first campaign, so to say, is past, and we commence that curious and instructive combat which characterised the struggle of the mobile guard, or the reserve forces of France, during the second campaign.

On the 4th of November, I accompanied General Schwarz to view a portion of the fortifications. I found the fort of Plappeville to be of even larger dimensions than at the cursory glance I had estimated. It mounted eighty-seven guns, and in point of commanding position was little inferior to St. Quentin. But it was unfinished, at least on the side towards Metz. The traverses and the parapets were of immense thickness. The groundwork was of solid masonry, with a much narrower ditch than fortifications of a like sort are wont to have. The scarps and counterscarps were at a more acute angle, and had much more material in them; whilst the whole of the upper works were composed of earth. The fort is irregular in shape, flanked by six bastions, the enceinte being sunk, and the cavalier unfinished; but the peculiar situation of the work, and its aptitude for resisting an attack, were well made apparent by the natural glacis which sloped gently away from it on every side, except the rear, to a distance varying from 3000 to 7000 yards. This glacis was on all sides strengthened by positions for field-guns, and also by rifle-trenches; so that an attack upon Plappeville was utterly out of the question. The same might be said of St. Quentin, which commands Plappeville at a distance of 2000 yards, and at an elevation of seventy feet.

Immediately below Plappeville is a deep ravine, leading towards the heights above Amanvillers. This part of the country is thickly wooded, whilst towards Saulny the same sort of ground is to be met with. Emerging from these two ravines by a simultaneous attack, the French troops, massing a large force, and aided at first by the guns of Plappeville, could have effected their escape. The plateau of St. Privat, the weakest portion of the German position, where the French masses could have deployed right and left, strengthening their front, would have been at their mercy. They could then, by a series of forced marches, have taken up a position on the Meuse, relieving Verdun with a division, if necessary; or by marching on Thionville, concentrated with the Army of the North.

On the other hand to have attacked Metz on any side with the army which Prince Frederick Charles had at his command would have been pure madness; for even supposing, as has been suggested, that St. Julien, then unfinished, had been taken after the action of the 31st of August and 1st of September, the work was completely flanked by Plappeville and St. Quentin. The last was simply impracticable; and, when even all these were disposed of, there would have remained Metz itself to take, defended by the magnificent forts of Bellecroix, Moselle, and the works to the south of the citadel protecting the Porte des Allemands. Metz was captured by one of those lucky incidents that make a campaign famous. Had 50,000 troops been in Metz instead of nearly 200,000, I do not think that even another six months would have seen the black-and-white flag waving from the ramparts.

Most of the prisoners had left Metz, and sad had been the fate of many, but certainly through no fault on the German side. War is war, and there was nothing for it but to supply the vast army of French prisoners with food and firing. This was done most lavishly and heartily, but shelter was not to be had; and so many poor fellows suffered and died from the dreadful weather that was experienced on the 29th, 30th, and 31st of October.

Having returned to Jouy, I found everything in a state of transition. On my way back, indeed, I had seen bodies of troops moving in all directions: one division on the road towards Thionville; another in the direction of Verdun, which, notwithstanding three days' bombardment, held out to the last. I found, also, an invitation from General von Göben, asking me to join his staff, as he thought that the operations of the right wing of the first army at this moment would be interesting to me. Accordingly I made my preparations for departure; and at 7 one morning I proceeded to join him at Ban St. Martin, to which place he had marched from Cherissy. General Manteuffel and his staff left the next day early for a reconnaissance in the neighbourhood between Thionville and Verdun; and the whole of the troops of the first army were put in motion in a westerly direction.

We heard that Garibaldi's advance had been delayed, because there was no more red flannel with which to make shirts! People will have their jokes even in war time. Meantime Francs-tireurs were very much to the fore, and they could not well have had a better opportunity than the present moment; for rifles, ammunition, and pouches lay in every direction around Metz. Forty thousand chassepots were inside the work of Plappeville alone, and I should say quite 10,000 lay scattered about outside also. The worst of it was, that these adventurous gentlemen were no respecters of persons, and they were just as likely to fire upon a *bon citoyen* as upon anybody else.

One was then quite accustomed to packing up; my kit had certainly increased, and I had a mule from the division of General Ladmirault to carry it. This particularly mild-looking animal—chosen on account of his apparent docility—I purchased from a French soldier for 10f. and a bottle of brandy; and he was to carry my little all for me next morning, notwithstanding that my servant, a soldier from the artillery guard, informed me, with tears in his eyes, that the 'Maulesel versteht kein Deutsch.' Maps were being vigorously studied, schnapps were at a premium; and as to warm clothing, the intensely cold weather of the previous few days made it imperative that woollen jackets should be procured. Everything was frightfully dear, bread particularly, although the daily stream of inhabitants from Metz, glad to escape typhus, flowed outwards in all directions, making the supply more plentiful.

The army had suddenly taken it into its head to be photographed; not collectively, of course—but individually you could see Prussian soldiers in all sorts of attitudes staring at you in the most grotesque way from photographic-studio windows. Dogs, too, had been bought up in every direction, and followed their new masters most unwillingly, dragged about with pieces of string tied round their necks. The horse fair was over. What remained for sale were those animals that had been stolen; and if an unlucky wight purchased an animal without first carefully seeing that it was not marked with the government brand, he was likely to have his new acquisition taken away by the first gendarme that met him.

The citizens of Metz had already begun to taste the difference between an occupation by a besieged and that by a victorious army. Provisions had all at once become plentiful, and delicacies were now obtainable by those to whom necessaries were formerly but too welcome. Bread, which during four weeks had been wanting, was now to be had in abundance; for the Prussian authorities caused a plentiful supply to be brought from Saarbrück and Ars. But the change in the position of the fortress must have been particularly a source of comfort to the sick and wounded. What with the terrible conflicts of the 14th, 16th, and 18th of August, and the exposure to the dreadful weather which for a long time afflicted both besiegers and besieged at Metz, the number of those requiring medical aid was dreadfully large. The German authorities used the most praiseworthy exertions to supply the sick with both the doctors and the medicines of which they stood so much in need.

The fall of Metz closes that period of the campaign which brings me to the end of the first volume of my narrative. If my descriptions have been imperfect, it is because I have had recourse to my own observation of events as they occurred, and have not employed any hearsay evidence: the account being confined simply to the operations of the 1st Prussian army, which I never left from the commencement to the end of the war.

There is, however, much to be learnt for our own instruction and guidance, even from the humble narrative contained in these pages; at a time, too, when continental discord has roused from apathy and fancied security the Government of this great country, and that army reform and reorganisation is about to put the profession of the soldier in the place it ought to occupy—*that of a profession, and not an amusement.* In reviewing the events of the campaign up to the fall of Metz there are certain points which cannot fail to arrest the attention. It has been said that the numerical deficiency of the French troops at Wörth and Weissenburg was one of the principal causes of their defeat: if so, the same cannot certainly be said of Mars-la-Tour, where the Prussians were very considerably inferior in numbers. But even supposing this to be the case, have not our own troops in the Peninsula, and indeed in almost every other war, been continually opposed to superior forces, and that with success? What inferences, then, are to be gathered from this series of defeats which the French arms suffered, and are we to look upon the cause of those defeats as attributable to the physical as well as moral superiority of the German over the French soldier? From my experience of the late war I utterly repudiate the latter idea; inasmuch as I believe the material of which the French army was composed to have been, and still is perhaps, the finest in the world. It is to the higher ranks of the service that we must go to look for the solving of this much-argued question. It was undoubtedly owing first to the incapacity and want of genius on the part of her generals; secondly, to the mal-administration of the administrative units, in the shape of *dull, lazy, self-sparing officers;* thirdly, to the injudicious and pernicious method of officering regiments with men who could not command the respect of their soldiers, although they may to a certain extent have had a smattering of military matters, or have upon some occasion done a gallant action, but whose *education and manners* placed them in the same sphere of life as the soldiers they were given to command; and, lastly, to the injudicious ranking of the common soldier, which, when properly administered, is the certain preventative against mutiny or insubordination. It is to these four heads that we must look for the utter collapse of the French army, and the series of disastrous defeats that have plunged France into such an abyss of misery: and I contend that the question of army reorganisation in this country is not a party question; it ought never to be a trial of strength between Liberals and Conservatives; it should not be made use of by either as a question which should oust the one from power, and reinstate the other; but it should be argued for by both sides: Whig and Tory should go hand-in-hand in this great and important step, and military matters should be legislated for by military men. It is my firm belief that until full powers are vested in the Minister of War, and that that Minister of War occupies the same position as General von Moltke, the War Office and Horse Guards being combined under one head, we shall never succeed in establishing the military organisation of the regular and reserve forces of Great Britain upon a safe and advantageous basis, for the protection of the country, or the upholding of our military prestige.

CHAPTER VIII.

THE MARCH OF THE FIRST ARMY.

THE first march into France of the first army which the surrender of Metz had set free from its bondage commenced on the 7th of November 1870. Every day succeeding the eventful 28th of October did the position of Metz improve. First of all, the superfluous, in the shape of those who sought refuge in the blockaded town upon the advance of the German troops, disappeared; they returned home, probably to find their household gods somewhat upset; but this was in a great measure their own fault; for had they remained to take care of their property, beyond the nuisance of having some men and officers quartered upon them, they would have suffered comparatively little inconvenience.

Truly, war, like everything else in these high-pressure times, is assuming curious features. If we revert to the history of warfare, either in modern or ancient times, I think I may safely assert that its pages will rarely record the siege of a fortress by

X

cavalry. Nevertheless, such was the case at Thionville. Infantry were there, but in small numbers; whilst a whole cavalry division, without any guns, formed the blockading force. On the 5th of November, a train for the aid of the sick and wounded wished to enter Thionville. The officer in command of the troops in that direction advanced with a flag of truce even up to the glacis, where the trumpeter, after three ferocious blasts—no light matter, for the instrument of this messenger of peace is harder of inflation than the trombone of the small German bands that haunt the neighbourhood of Brompton—managed to make a surly garde mobile hear. There was a most unsatisfactory parley, and eventually the train was *not* admitted.

About this time the sudden rise of the Moselle caused much inconvenience in the neighbourhood of Thionville—absolutely isolating bodies of cavalry upon little islands during the night. At Verdun fresh troops had now arrived, the batteries were completed, and the bombardment was again commenced.

Before leaving Metz I had a very interesting conversation with General Battaille, who commanded a division under Frossard. Hearing that I was in Metz, he sent his aide-de-camp to ask me if I could conveniently pay him a visit, as he wished to thank me for certain little services I had rendered to French officers at Gravelotte and Mars-la-Tour. I repeat the conversation most fearlessly, in order to rob any scandalmonger of his opportunity. Speaking of the Emperor as a soldier, when I asked him what could have induced the French army to march from

Gravelotte towards Vionville and Mars-la-Tour, on the 16th, without ascertaining the position of the German army by means of cavalry patrols, he said, '*Que voulez-vous?* My division lay at Rezonville. The cavalry returned, and reported that there were a few troops in the woods, but nothing of importance, and then went to breakfast. Almost immediately afterwards the engagement commenced. If the Emperor had not assumed the command, if he had left the matter in the hands of Marshal Bazaine, all might have been well; but he insisted on doing so, and the result was that his orders, even before leaving, were strictly carried out.'

Another account I heard from a gentleman who was with the Empress at Chislehurst about this time. He informed me that every possible persuasion was used to induce the Emperor not to join the army, but that he persisted in doing so. Regarding Spiecheren, General Battaille assured me that General le Fouchecoupet had only 8000 men engaged the whole day; and when I suggested that this was quite enough to hold such a position, he said, '*Ah, mais oui, ça c'est vrai; mais nous n'avions pas de munitions à la fin.*' As to Metz, '*C'était une chose bien mal arrangée.*' Altogether, I left Metz with the most profound impression that Bazaine was execrated, and has utterly and for ever lost his prestige with the French army.

On the morning of the 7th of November, the first army marched for the interior of France. Not a single man but left the dreary scene, where every tree and stone was too familiar, with infinite satisfaction. Our route lay through the famous plain of Gravelotte. All was now changed: the leafless trees were thickly covered with hoarfrost, and the whole landscape was wrapt in a wintry mist. I sincerely trusted that, as we penetrated into the interior, General von Göben would march a little better attended than he was on that day. So far as the staff was concerned, we numbered some thirty officers; but the escort was slender enough to leave one of the best generals in the German army an easy prey to the first roving body of Francs-tireurs we might happen to come across.

Arrived at Gravelotte, there was a halt of a few minutes, during which old quarters were visited and respects paid to Madame the hostess, with whom, *bon gré mal gré*, you had lodged. Notwithstanding the severe famine, the good dame was as fat and as witty as ever. She was exceedingly jocose, and her badinage was of that peculiar character in which the French peasants of the better sort are so apt. 'We are all starving here,' she said; 'everything is dreadfully dear; just give me some of the money you paid to Bazaine for Metz.' She objected to such 'villany,' as she called it, but hoped that the German officers would bring their wives and families to see Gravelotte—Heaven save the mark! It was mildly suggested by somebody that, as she had a room in the house where the Emperor had slept, she should charge so much a head for every one that looked at it. But the '*Ah, le monstre!*' with which she answered proved that his Majesty was in no higher favour than Bazaine. The country between Gravelotte and Jarny was in a miserable state, well worth the attention of Colonel Loyd-Lindsay, or any one else who wished to do really good and noble deeds. Famine stared you in the face on all sides, and as to the cultivation of the land, it was absolutely at a stand-still.

A description of the first halt of the first army in France after the fall of Metz I take from my diary:

'We reached the Château de Moncel about one P.M. The building was an elegant modern residence, the property of a rich French "rentier" of Metz. But what a scene of desolation! The rooms had been locked up; the doors had therefore been broken open. The park and gardens by which it was surrounded remained untouched; but the walks were covered with weeds, and the flower-beds choked with rubbish. Inside, the rooms were lofty, but furnished in that scanty way which makes French houses so comfortless. No sooner had we stabled our horses than far the greater portion, to say nothing of the nobler part, of the staff set busily to work gathering fir-cones for firing. A prince, two counts, and a baron, of the best families in Germany, were busily employed in this operation. Then dinner had to be got ready; this had been, of course, brought with us, for in a land of want there was no hope of anything to eat. We had a great struggle for a table-cloth; but I found some white bed-curtains in my room, which did excellently. Our horses fortunately came in for some straw, of which there was plenty; but hay was not to be got for gold uncounted.

'At dinner some of the old battle-fields were re-discussed, and I then became acquainted with a circumstance which I had never known before, but which serves to illustrate the character of a man who will, if he lives, be among the greatest generals of his country. The rapid movement which assisted his Royal Highness Prince Frederick Charles on the 16th August, and turned the French flank, was attributable almost entirely to General von Göben—who, by his rapid advance with the 16th division of the 8th army corps through the Bois de Gorze, completely altered the fortunes of the day. It is true that General von Göben was under the orders of General von Steinmetz; but upon this occasion he acted entirely upon his own responsibility. Whatever Spiecheren may have done towards producing a moral effect, the battle of Mars-la-Tour clinched that effect beyond a doubt; and when these two conflicts were over, the French soldiers knew that their opponents were men who would not easily give way.

'At Metz we were quartered at Ban St. Martin, in the same house that Marshal Bazaine occupied with his staff; and there we found some curious relics—such as maps of the Rhine Provinces and Prussia as far as Posen, with the routes marked upon them; there was also a strange abundance of ladies' wearing apparel, to say nothing of pearl powder and rouge. Marshal Bazaine took seven cartloads of baggage away with him, Canrobert ten.'

On the 8th of November the news reached us that another French fortress had capitulated. Verdun had fallen. Some of the details are interesting. The first commandant of Verdun was General Guerin de Walspath; the sub-commandant—whose name France should never forget, if her history ever relates the incidents of the present campaign—General Marnier. Verdun was bombarded, it is true, by two strong batteries, the one situated due north, the other east, of the place. On the 13th and 14th of October a perfect hurricane of shells was poured upon the devoted town; but with no effect, at least so far as the ardour of the garrison was concerned. Then General Marnier, putting himself at the head of some 3000 men, made a sortie in a north-easterly direction. At the point of the bayonet, without firing a shot, he drove back the German advanced posts. He then attacked the batteries, and carried them by assault, destroyed the works, dismounted and spiked the guns; returning safe to Verdun, where his small but brave force of 7000 men had held out ever since. The German generals, intent upon the capture of Metz, could spare but an inadequate force for the siege of Verdun. General Marnier no doubt received excellent intelligence about the German forces around Verdun; and profiting by this information, he made the vigorous sortie I have described.

The German troops acknowledged the bravery of Marnier and his garrison, and took off their forage-caps to him with respect; for none can value and respect a brave and determined enemy more than the officers and soldiers of the Prussian army. The officers belonging to the garrison of Verdun refused to give their parole, and were consequently made prisoners; the men shared the same fate; but the garrison marched out with all the honours of war, colours flying and bands playing. The immediate cause of the surrender is not precisely known. In a conversation with the Prussian officer sent to treat with him, Marnier expressed himself as follows: 'Since the capitulation of Metz and Sedan, and the destruction of the French army, I do not see what good it would do my country to hold out any longer, exposing my men to sickness and the heavy fire which no doubt you will shortly open upon us. Political affairs also induce me to surrender Verdun, although I know that I can hold out for many days longer against all your efforts. I have saved my honour and that of my officers and men; more I cannot do, especially when I do not know for whom or for what I am fighting.' Some fragments of the Sedan army were said to be in Verdun. The artillery fire was especially good and well directed. The German loss in the sortie made by the French was severe—officers, as usual, suffering most; in the artillery alone two were killed and seven wounded.

General von Göben and his staff were now lying in the village of Fresnes, some six miles from Etain. These villages had suffered to no great extent from the invading armies. The principal inhabitants seemed on excellent terms with the German officers and soldiers, and readily supplied them with whatever they had. Provisions were, however, dreadfully dear, and luxuries scarce, the people having had no means of replenishing the old stock. The country through which we marched was desolate in the extreme, little or no cultivation going on anywhere; and it was impossible to tell what the people were to do next year. The first army was advancing in a westerly direction.

Leaving the hospitable roof of the château of Moncel, General von Göben marched with the 8th corps upon Samognieux. There was a rumour that there was just a chance of our riding through Verdun, and I need hardly say how anxiously such a chance was looked forward to. Confidential staff-officers whispered that it might be so; but their whispers were so frightfully confidential, that we mistrusted them. However, when we should have left Verdun to our left, General von Göben signified his intention of riding through the place.

Verdun, as every one knows, lies in the valley of the Meuse. It was fortified by Vauban, and remains an immortal monument of the genius of the days he represented. But since that time things have changed; and Vauban must give way to guns that carry a little farther than he ever calculated upon when making his designs. The situation of Verdun is by no means secure or strong; for, like Toul, it is completely commanded by a high ridge called 'St. Michel' on one side—while on the other, immediately opposite the citadel, is an elevation, at a distance of 2500 yards, which also entirely commands the town. Entering by the gate leading into the town from the road of Metz, you come upon the first line of defence —a simple Vauban fort, with a couple of small cavaliers, the rounded bastions telling at once of its ancient construction. Not many guns were mounted on this side, and those were mostly old siege guns of an ancient pattern.

Following the ramparts round to the Meuse, you come upon the Jardin de la Fontaine, which lies immediately under the citadel. Standing upon a gun-carriage, I obtained from this spot a splendid view of the town. Shouldering itself high above a mass of buildings whose architecture seemed to date from before the Flood towered the old cathedral—a splendid specimen of old Norman architecture, the roof of the west aisle having been completely destroyed by a shell. To its right stands the Church of St. Michel, also a very old building; whilst the Meuse flows through the centre of the town, dividing it into two equal parts. The streets of Verdun are certainly not handsome, nor are the houses by any means such as would please the eye of a modern architect; but then Verdun is an old town, and antiquity often serves as an excellent excuse for ugliness. The inhabitants had covered their cellars with bark, to make them as nearly bomb-proof as possible; while many of the poorer classes were obliged to spread manure over the traps, not being able to afford the more expensive luxury of bark. I need hardly add that this device did not improve the purity of the air. A good many of the *bons citoyens* were very drunk—so were three or four soldiers who had remained; whether to drown their sorrows or to testify their joy I know not. The town was filthy and dirty; shattered window-frames, slates, and chimney-pots, dead cats and dogs, dead horses and mules, lay about on every side. I confess that I rode through the streets with a certain uncomfortable feeling; no Prussian troops had entered the town, and our escort was of slender proportions.

The inhabitants scowled at us as we rode by—some of them even going so far as to express their feelings in the very choicest of *patois*.

Entering the citadel, we found the ditch, and the drawbridge leading over it, white with the flour which had been recklessly destroyed, the sacks having been cut open and their contents scattered about in every direction. Inside the citadel—especially on that side which faced the German batteries upon St. Michel—nothing but the bomb-proofs remained standing. Such a heap of ruins as the mass of rubbish into which the barracks and storehouses had been knocked, I have seldom seen. A small chapel—probably designed for the use of the soldiers—was a complete ruin. That portion of the town lying towards the citadel, especially the Rue St. Pierre, had suffered severely; in many houses the shells had gone through two and three stories, demolishing the windows, and breaking down the staircases. To the left of the cathedral stands the palace of the bishop, then a hospital full of wounded French and German soldiers. I took the opportunity to visit some of the Germans who had been brought in there from the sortie of the 25th of October; and they one and all spoke most favourably of the treatment they had received at the hands of the French garrison.

Leaving the citadel, and following the Rue St. Pierre, we quitted Verdun through the gate on the Châlons road. Immediately outside the ramparts there appeared to have been a suburb, containing some 300 inhabitants; but not a house remained standing, not a wall even, to mark the place where perhaps, for many years a happy family had lived together: all was a vast desolation of bricks and mortar. Immediately outside the town we met some 2500 of the prisoners. It appeared that the 57th French regiment of the line, together with the dépôt of the 80th, and a few artillerymen, had been the only representatives of the regular army in Verdun; the rest of the garrison were composed of gardes mobiles; but all marched out in first-rate order, looking extremely well.

The state of Verdun was a proof positive that the old system of fortifying towns without outlying forts must give way not only to the new method of blockade, but to the superiority in point of range possessed by the artillery of the present day. It will be clearly understood that, unless the heights in the immediate neighbourhood of a fortress are occupied by strong earthworks, they will be turned to account by an enemy. It was thus that Toul suffered; and it was thus that Verdun was knocked to pieces by a couple of batteries—one at 2500 yards, and the other at 3000—mounting 24-pound rifled guns.

The road, after leaving Verdun, ran along the valley of the Meuse, flat and uninteresting enough—the more so, that the land on either side lay fallow and uncultivated. At three P.M. we reached the village of Samognieux. The village was by no means large, and, as usual, excessively dirty. Three hundred souls had existed there, had cultivated the land, had gone to mass, and on market-days to Verdun, from time immemorial. I do not believe that any one of them knew why the Prussian troops were in their village;

and assuredly none had ever heard of Bismarck or Moltke. As for the Emperor, he existed in their imaginations as a sort of deity, as much to be worshipped as the wooden Madonnas that decorated their walls. And in this wretched place, made still more wretched by the war, were quartered a general and his staff, a battery of artillery, a regiment of infantry, and a military train.

Advancing by steady marches, with a halt every third day, the army of General Manteuffel on the 10th of November reached the town of Varennes—famous as the place where Louis XVI. was stopped in his flight by the postmaster of the town, was arrested, and sent back to Paris and his beloved subjects; so that General Manteuffel and General von Göben occupied the same town with their respective staffs. Referring to my diary, I find the following description of the halt of the 1st army at Varennes:

'My quarters were excellent, inasmuch as I found my name upon the door of the Hôtel du Grand Monarque, with those magic words inscribed beneath, "General Commando 8 Armée Corps." The house was thenceforth sacred to the staff, and none dared enter. My horses enjoyed quarters quite as good; for the magic white chalk had written my name over the door of a house, the principal room of which was for the nonce to be my stable. A large mirror at the end of the room considerably astonished my mare, who had, no doubt, never seen herself in a looking-glass before; but with the usual failing of the sex, the habit seemed to grow upon her, and soon she stood and stared at herself with evident satisfaction. Two blood-stained mattresses in the corner showed that Varennes had been one of the halting-places of the Sedan army, and farther examination told that the house had been used as a hospital. While I was looking about me, the proprietor entered, and hat in hand begged of me upon no account to remain in the house; it had been a typhus hospital, a perfect sink of disease, he said, and it was fit for no officer to occupy. When I told him it was for that reason that the horses occupied the saloon, he asked me if they also were not liable to infection.

'Having seen my horse comfortably "bedded down" and fed, I strolled into the street, with the intention of seeing something of the town. Upon the door-step I met an old friend, aide to General Manteuffel. We embraced after the German fashion; and then, tucking my arm under his, he marched me off to his quarters. Said he, "I am superbly quartered. I live with the judge of Varennes, one of the best old men you ever met; full of anecdote, and has some excellent old wine." I was speedily introduced to mine host, who immediately whispered in my ear, "Monsieur, all Englishmen like good wine. I have a bottle of '46 in my cellar. I will go fetch it, for it is not every day that I have the honour to meet an English gentleman." The wine was excellent, and the judge amusing; he told me the tale of Louis XVI.—how he had been recognised by the postmaster of Ste. Ménéhould; how the postmaster's son had ridden across the Forest of Argonne, and arrived before the King; how the King's carriage was too high to go under an archway; and how the stoppage enabled the postmaster's son to inform the mayor of the King's flight. By this time we had got to the end of the second bottle, and I was anxious to visit the scene of the royal disaster. Arrived before the house, I was shown the room through the window of which the King looked. The house, I am sorry to say, has been rebuilt; but immediately opposite was a grocer's shop, in which the unfortunate Marie Antoinette was reported to have sat upon a sack of coffee, begging the grocer's wife for mercy.

'Upon my return, my room was a picture which Maxwell would have liked to draw with his imaginative pen. The staff of Manteuffel and Von Göben were there, sitting upon beds, washstands, chairs, stools—in fact, on everything on which it was possible to sit. We were in the land of champagne—why should we not drink the vintage of the neighbourhood? And we did it. Two hundred francs was the little bill which welcomed us into the heart of France. Delightful was it—while it lasted; toasts, healths, and good wishes passed round, which I am sure were not "writ in water." But the last bottle came, there was absolutely no more; and so we retired, to dream of Rheims, of our farther advance into France, and of its consequences. As I looked from my window, the snow was falling in heavy flakes. To-morrow the 8th army corps marches through the Argonne—the favoured and favouring resort, it is whispered, of the Francs-tireurs.'

On the 13th of November General Manteuffel's

head-quarters were at Suippes, whilst General von Göben lay at Vienne-le-Château on the borders of the Argonnes, said to be the resort of a numerous and determined band of Francs-tireurs, who had made use of its large extent and leafy shelter as a sort of head-quarters whence to dispatch small bodies to cut off any German stragglers, or stop the field-post as it lumbered along the heavy cross-roads by which the forest is intersected. Through this wood we marched on that day; and as the long line of troops entered the unwelcome-looking defile through which the artillery horses were struggling, with mud up to the axles of the gun-carriages, I must confess that nobody at all liked the aspect of affairs. The snow, which had fallen during the night, lay to some depth in the woods; while the slush it occasioned in the road reminded me of the route to Balaklava in 1854.

The 33d regiment had been sent on some two marches before, with a cavalry regiment, to clear the defiles, and, if possible, to rout out the band of miscreants whose name of Francs-tireurs was only a pretext for committing outrages upon helpless women and children, robbing wherever they had a chance, and murdering any unfortunate sick soldier who might fall in their way. That our little advanced corps effected the purpose for which it been sent, was proved by the fact that the march of the 15th division was uninterrupted, and that in a heavy shower of snow they came into Vienne-le-Château. Here the intelligence of the defeat before Orleans first reached us; but on so large a field of operations it is needless to say that the German generals never expected to get off without a misadventure here and there.

Referring again to my diary, I find the following extract, which may be interesting to the reader:

'This little town, on the borders of the Argonne and the fertile province of Champagne, was not exactly prepared for the reception of so large a body of troops. My quarters were with a *soi-disant* dentist, who, poor man, did all he could to make me comfortable. His rooms, two in number, were at my disposal—one was for my servant, who, assisted by my host's deaf mother, was to prepare my dinner; the other was to be my saloon and sleeping room. Now, before leaving the neighbourhood of Metz, I had purchased a veritable English gridiron—which had been the constant wonder and admiration of everybody wherever I had gone. It had also been a trusty friend, and with many a good breakfast had we been supplied from its hospitable bars. My rule was, that every man who breakfasted with me should bring his rations, a knife and fork, and a tumbler. I undertook the rest; and often, amid various exclamations of delight, mingled with friendly shakes of the hand, have I converted the "Rindfleisch" into a succulent and nutritious morsel.

'My host informed me that his profession, as he styled it, had been that of a tailor; but so infatuated had he become with the charms of tooth-drawing, that he had abandoned the needle and thread for the tweezers. Without any assertion of the enthusiast's, the fact had already sufficiently demonstrated itself;

for horrid cries—enough even to frighten my stolid orderly—resounded from the next apartment; and when any peculiarly combative tooth drew forth the energies of the "tailor-dentist," he would rush in, and triumphantly holding the trophy on high, would dilate upon the battle he had fought and the task he had successfully accomplished.

'Still the snow fell fast. I had a breakfast; his excellency's staff were my guests. Was it a bad breakfast? First of all, I had prepared beefsteaks *ad libitum;* then Count Eulenburg brought a *pâté de foie gras;* Prince Salm contributed a wondrous production of fowls; the commissary-general a dozen bottles of Rauenthaler; the Count Westerholt—whose beautiful castle is the resort of so many English tourists on the Rhine—yet another delicacy. In fact, the staff had an extraordinary repast; after which we drank all sorts of toasts, and smoked cigars as long as bowsprits—also gifts from the commissary-general; and then we went to bed, to prepare ourselves for the morrow's march.'

And a miserable march it was, in cold, wet, driving sleet, snow; in fact, all the wintry elements seemed to have made a *pot-pourri* of it. But as, getting clear of the broken country, we opened the level and beautiful plains of Champagne, a ray of sunshine broke upon us; and under the favouring beam we approached the villages of Mourmelon, and the works of instruction belonging to the camp of Châlons. We were about to ride over the ground on which the soldiers of the Empire were supposed to have learnt and indulged in those manœuvres that were eventually to have given Napoleon the Rhine provinces.

So far as the movements of large masses are concerned, there can be but little doubt that the plain of Châlons is among the finest in the world. But is flat ground really the best upon which troops may learn the evolutions of modern warfare? Is it there that the difficulties of an advance through a broken country, interspersed with woods, and full of obstacles to artillery advance or cavalry attack—the difficulties, for instance, of such ground as that which has witnessed the military operations and sanguinary conflicts of the late campaign—can be estimated and encountered? For the organising of regiments into brigades, and brigades into divisions—for giving generals an opportunity of becoming accustomed to the handling of large bodies of men—even for ascertaining the effect of the movements of heavy masses of cavalry against bodies of infantry—Châlons is superb. But only in the abstract. Practically speaking, in real warfare no such opportunity occurs; because no troops are likely to seek out a battle-ground like the plains about Châlons. And yet it is curious to think, and very difficult to imagine, how the French generals, with such opportunities, could have sacrificed so fine a material, either through absolute incompetency or through sheer carelessness. How often do we see that the man who can command a regiment is lost when he tries to manœuvre a brigade, and he who handles a brigade with perfect ease is utterly bewildered with an army! But here at Châlons

ance upon the evacuation of the troops. Let me rather describe the military position of affairs, and the manœuvres which threw the first army upon the Somme, occupied the line of that river from the Seine to Laon, and isolated the French army of the north in the Pas de Calais.

The reverse of General von der Tann at Orleans gave fresh life to the levies of troops which, under the command of General Farre, were massed in and about the town of Amiens, where they were concentrating for a march upon Paris *viâ* Beauvais. It is true that by this march the left flank of the French army would have been exposed; but the Saxons at La Ferr and Laon were in such small numbers, that they could have done nothing but make a demonstration. In order to prevent this, General Manteuffel, instead of lingering at Rheims, and hearing that no time was to be lost if he wished to intercept the march of General Farre and throw himself between the army of the north and Paris, gave directions at once to march upon Soissons, in order that by so doing he could come into communication with the Saxons, in case General Farre made a movement southwards. It would have been easy for Manteuffel with his cavalry to ascertain his exact movements, and force him to an action somewhere half-way between Paris and Amiens. But General Farre, finding his quarters very comfortable at Amiens, and hearing of Manteuffel's approach, instead of at once throwing his troops upon the road to Paris, lingered there upon the off chance of beating Manteuffel behind the works which he had thrown up to protect that town.

For the rapid advance of General Manteuffel's army, I must refer my readers to the following extracts from my letters to the *Daily Telegraph* at that time:

'On the evening of the 17th of November I found an order to the effect, that we were to march for Fismes next morning at eight o'clock. I sent off my despatch, and went to ascertain the cause of this somewhat sudden order, inasmuch as we had contemplated remaining in the town some two days. The mystery soon received a solution. The French, it seemed, had at length made a movement. An army had suddenly appeared in the neighbourhood of Orleans, some 80,000 strong; hence the sudden movement in advance which compelled Manteuffel's army on the one side, and Prince Frederick Charles's on the other side, to assume a position between the enemy and the blockading army of Paris. Time is money, and in this case time was also fortune; for if a combined movement from Paris on the one side, and the army of Orleans on the other, had been made, there would have been nothing for it but to break up the blockade of Paris. The chess-board was neatly strewn with the contending parties; and if discipline had nothing to do with it, I should say that France had then the best position she had ever yet held in the war.

'On our arrival in Fismes we received intelligence of bodies of Francs-tireurs in the neighbourhood; but the inhabitants were most friendly, all with the same cry, "Is there no chance of peace?" To-morrow we march upon Soissons. The German troops were never in better condition to meet an enemy, or to confront the exigences of a campaign, than at this present moment. The artillery and cavalry horses, no longer sustained on the stinted provision doled out before Metz, are in splendid condition. Sickness has gradually disappeared from the troops, through change of air, exercise, and a good commissariat; and everything is hopeful. It is true that the following of regiments, brigades, and divisions has somewhat increased; but that is of no moment. The baggage-wagons are mostly all French, and to look at the train you would think ours was a French army on the march, if you did not remark the uniform. We are in the heart of the far-famed land of Champagne; but I confess I have drunk but few good bottles of the "glorious vintage."

'Passing through Sillery, I stopped at the château of one of the principal importers. He was, strange to say, a Prussian by birth, and came originally from Potsdam; but by an odd freak of fortune, he is now burgomaster of the town of Spa, in Belgium. The château, like most others, had suffered somewhat severely from the billeting of troops as they passed on their way to Paris; and, affording accommodation for a large number of horses, it had been perhaps a little more used than would otherwise have been the case. However, a bottle of Sillery was here at my disposal; and to have passed without drinking a glass would have been sheer heresy. At Rheims I lodged in the house of another wine-making firm; and there the staff emptied not a few bottles of "dry monopole." But the fair plains of Champagne are a desolate waste; the inhabitants of the villages have left their homes a prey to the invader, to risk their lives in a useless conflict, which, notwithstanding M. Gambetta's high-flown proclamations, can end but in one result.

'*Head-quarters, Vauxbuin (near Soissons), Nov. 19.*

'Gradually, as we approach the destined scene of the struggle which is to decide the fate of Northern France, the position becomes more interesting. The action in the neighbourhood of Orleans has shown us what men of determination, willing to be disciplined, can achieve. Marching through the towns of Braisne and Sermoise, we approached the ancient city of Soissons, so famous in French history. Soissons, it will be remembered, was taken by the Grand Duke of Mecklenburg after a bombardment of four days—a bombardment which would never have occurred, if the French commandant of the place, General de Nouet, had for a moment considered his position. There can be no excuse for the useless destruction of property and valuable lives which this officer brought down upon the unfortunate town. Soissons lies in the valley of the Aisne. It is a town fortified upon the Vauban system, and, at the time when it was attacked, was defended by 4000 troops, with some artillery. Meagre as the system of Vauban is when opposed to modern siege operations, the engineer who planned the defences of Soissons seems to have endeavoured to make them still weaker; for, beyond a cavalier lying outside the reëntering angle of the bastion of St

John, and a very useless hornwork covering the Faubourg St. Christophe, there is absolutely no protecting structure of any kind to the town.

'The place was shelled by the Prussian batteries from the ridge of Vauxbuin on the west, and from the heights of Belleu on the south side, at distances of 2500 and 2700 yards respectively. From the elevated position of these batteries, firing into the town was something like shooting into a tea-cup. As if to make his ignorance more palpable, the commandant commenced operations by shelling one of his own suburbs—that of the Faubourg of Rheims, situated on the Rheims road—because a few dragoons had ridden into it in quest of provisions. The result has been the destruction of all that part of the town which is situated in the neighbourhood of the magazine. In this direction, by the way, is the church of St. Jean, an excellent mark for the German twenty-four pounders. This fine old building is a mass of ruins, its two unequal but beautiful spires being the sole remains of its former beauty. The cathedral is also pitted with shells, and the large hospital is entirely destroyed; in fact, from the gate of St. Christophe round to that on the Rheims road, the town is nothing but a heap of ruins.

'An affair very much resembling that of Laon was very nearly happening here. Upon the capitulation of the town the engineer officers went to the church of St. Jean, in order to take over the powder and other materials. When they endeavoured to open the door, they found it fast closed against them. The French soldier who was sent with the officers had meanwhile mysteriously disappeared, and could nowhere be found. The suspicions of the party were at once aroused. By displacing a stone near the door-post, a sergeant was enabled to pass his hand round to the back of the door; he there found that a piece of twine fastened the catch; this he immediately cut, and the door was at once opened. Fortunate indeed was it that the absence of the French soldier had been observed, for a truly diabolical scheme had been laid for the destruction of many innocent people. Attached to one end of the string was a gun fuse, which had, by means of two sticks, been made fast in a sack of gunpowder nailed to the ground; while the other end of the string was attached to the door-latch —so that if the door had been burst open, the fuse would have exploded. The floor was knee-deep in powder, every cask and sack having been sprung. This was the way in which *la grande nation* made war under the auspices of Gambetta and Rochefort!

'In Soissons provisions are plentiful. The inhabitants had been greatly elated by the news from Orleans; but upon the arrival of the first army their rejoicings were wonderfully hushed. Leaving Soissons, I rode on to Vauxbuin, where General von Göben had his head-quarters for the night. I found his staff in the château of the Comte de Vélard; a residence made famous by the visit of "Henri Quatre."

'I have read a great deal about German depredations, and the wanton destruction the invaders have committed; but here is a telling case in point to the contrary. The room in which the monarch had slept, together with the furniture, had been carefully preserved, and handed down from generation to generation. A large collection of curious old tapestry covers the walls; and in the room, the lamp, the china, the furniture, everything is antique and historical. All these remain in their places unstirred, and not a single officer or soldier has slept or sat for any time in the apartment. The key is in fact still kept by the person in charge of the house. Does the civilised world, then, believe that the German nation is not refined enough to appreciate such things? I say the German nation, because, in speaking of its soldiers, I necessarily speak of the nation. Every family, every trade, every profession is represented in the army. The German soldiers, from the highest to the lowest, are keen appreciators of all that is historic, talented, and useful. The officers are *not* mere machines, with no other thought than beer and pipes; they are gentlemen of education and refinement, keen observers, and, above all, stern preservers of the old landmarks.

'The nearer we advance to the enemy's positions, the more interesting becomes every hour of the day. All sorts of luxuries must now be dispensed with; boots cannot always be taken off; and, as the weather is getting cold, coats will be no great disadvantage in bed — or in whatever must serve as such for the future.'

It was thus that General Manteuffel advanced, and by the rapidity of his movements completely paralysed the astonished and incompetent French general. The usual stretch of these marches varied from fifteen to twenty English miles per day, with the cavalry well to the front—that is to say, the divisional cavalry; and in order to explain this, it may be as well to touch briefly upon the order of the line of march of the Prussian corps.

In the first place, all parallel roads were made use of, so as not to crowd one division upon the other. Each corps consisted of two divisions, and each division of two brigades. The first army, under the command of General Manteuffel, was composed of the first army corps, the eighth army corps, the cavalry brigade of General Graf Göben, and the reserve artillery. The army corps were made up to their full complement, viz. in each division four regiments of infantry, one of cavalry, and six batteries of artillery. This force was divided into two brigades, each brigade consisting of two regiments of infantry and three batteries of artillery.

If there is a more arduous duty to perform than others, it is the work that divisional cavalry has to do on the march. In the first place, this divisional cavalry consists of one regiment formed of four squadrons. In addition to covering the advance of a line of march and keeping up the communication between brigades and divisions, this regiment has to supply two orderlies to each infantry regiment, an escort to the field-post, a covering party for the field-telegraph corps, and, if necessary, a post relay. The consequence is, that the officer commanding the regiment frequently finds himself with only a squadron or a squadron and a half at his disposal.

When it is ascertained that the country is not

occupied by the enemy, the quarter-masters, from the staff down to the military train, ride forward, and upon entering a town the houses are apportioned off by each, commencing in seniority, from the general down to the military train; so that in marching into a town or village there is no hurry or confusion; each name, regiment, brigade, and division is conspicuously marked up upon the door. In the present instance the cavalry was either on the one flank or on the other, inasmuch as the country having already been occupied, there was nothing to apprehend beyond Francs-tireurs, and of these the divisional cavalry were well able to give an account. To each army corps, in addition to what I have mentioned, was attached a battalion of Rifles, or Jäger battalion, and each division had its own separate field-post with its postmaster and staff of secretaries.

In the present instance the march had hitherto been one of simply going forward, unattended by any impediments from an enemy; but now we were nearing the scene of action, and more caution was the order of the day. It was now definitely ascertained that three, or at the most four, days' march would bring the first army into contact with the enemy; and it is astonishing that all this while, with 70,000 or 80,000 men at his command, the communication on the left bank of the Seine open, and with the seaboard behind him, General Farre never made a movement forward upon the road to Paris.

CHAPTER IX.

THE ADVANCE OF THE FIRST ARMY.

I CAN still recollect the time when, yet a young soldier, I pored over the stirring events of former campaigns, so romantically depicted by Grant, Maxwell, and Lever. How I prayed then that it might be my good fortune to encounter the like! How I dreamed of a campaign on the Rhine—of a battle on the plains of central France—of all sorts of romantic adventures and stirring deeds! Little did I think that in years to come I should witness the stern realities—without the romance. As we advanced farther into the heart of France, along those beautiful roads, fringed with well-grown poplars, bounded on either side by a rich and undulating country—as we passed châteaux and country residences, formerly the abode of happy families, the scene of joyous autumn gatherings, or exciting parties met for sport—the closed windows, the dull silence, the grass-grown approaches, told that here war had already set its relentless foot—that here it had left the imprint of desolation. The eighth corps marched along the valley of the Aisne upon Compiègne—the 16th division by way of Cuise la Motte, Couloisy, St. Etienne, and Pierrefonds; the 15th division by way of Attichy—where General Manteuffel had his head-quarters—Berneuil, and St. Crépin.

General Manteuffel, in assuming the command of the first army, still retained the command of the first corps, which was destined to form a junction at Compiègne with the eighth corps. The whole of the first army would then be together, and would at once march to meet the French army of the north. Where that army really was, no one seemed to have the faintest idea; for the Prussian commanders never credited General Farre with the stupidity of remaining at Amiens, and permitting them to throw themselves between him and Paris. Meantime, north of Paris, and immediately in our front, the cavalry division of the first army had got as far as Clermont; the patrols of the blockading army and our own had met, but still no news of Farre. The next two days it was supposed would give us some certain intelligence of his force; unless, indeed, he should have marched southward to form a junction with the army of the Loire.

We had been told in Soissons that the bridges over the Aisne had been destroyed, and that communication between the two sides of the river was therefore impossible. This, like many other reports, was false; for we found that heavy trains were passing the bridge at Attichy as we rode into Couloisy. Referring to my journal, I find the following extract:

'*Cuise la Motte, Nov. 20.*

'I took up my quarters at Cuise la Motte, with four other staff-officers, in the house of a maiden lady who had gone for a few days upon business to Compiègne. She, poor soul, never for one moment anticipated that her establishment would be honoured by the visit of five dashing officers of General von Göben's staff, and had left her house in the primmest order.

'In the evening I visited the church, an old Norman structure, wonderfully preserved; in fact, Monsieur le Curé informed me that it had ever been a place of resort for archæologists and lovers of the antique. The interior was certainly marvellous; the dome of the chapter, formed of well-preserved Roman arches, its graceful architecture surrounded by the rude sculpturings of former days, gave to the chancel an air of delicacy, refinement, and richness seldom met in country places. M. le Curé was a dapper little man, "not too young, and not too old." He was *vif* in the extreme—bursting with intelligence, and dreadfully anxious for information—one of those curious people who want to tell and be told everything at the same time. "Had German troops ever been here before?" "O, yes! But the German troops were so good. What a difference"—and the little curé lifted up his hands, turned his eyes upwards, shrugged his shoulders, and took snuff—"what a difference," he said, "would there have been if three hundred French soldiers had been here! Just imagine, sir," he continued; "not one woman was insulted—and, by the way, we have some pretty women." These closing words were spoken with the satisfied air of a connoisseur. As to the opinions of his congregation, why, he had told them from the pulpit that they richly deserved all they got; while as to Garibaldi, it was a crying shame that France in her extremity should ask help from such a quarter.

'To-morrow we march upon Compiègne, through those preserves in which his Imperial Majesty used to spend his autumn months just at this time of the year. On our way we pass by the famous Château of Pierrefonds. This, but recently one of the greatest ruins in France, was by Napoleon's orders restored in the most magnificent style to its pristine grandeur—another memorial of a reign which, if not without many faults, fairly claims that a few of them should not be passed unnoticed.'

On the 22d of November General von Göben marched from Cuise la Motte upon Compiègne, where the first army was concentrating for immediate operations against the army of the north. Leaving that little village at nine o'clock, we took the road called La Rue des Bois, passing General de Failly's pretty little shooting-box, situated on Mont Bleu, and leaving the picturesque village of Genancourt to our left. After a sharp ride of half an hour, we entered the Bois des Rochers. Here the remains of an ancient Gallic town detained us for a few moments. The ruins had been, to a certain extent, laid bare by excavation; and most of the walls of the dwelling-houses remained in a high state of preservation. The streets could easily be made out; while the shape of the town, surrounded by the usual 'vallum,' was the most perfect I have ever seen.

Leaving these remains, that spoke of times long gone by—of the changes that have come upon this unruly land so fast and furiously that the pages of her history can scarce contain them—we reached the hamlet of Fontenoy, a suburb, as it were, to the larger village of Pierrefonds. As we turned an angle in the road, we came suddenly in full view of the castle. I shall not easily forget the scene. The November morning had been dull and gloomy; but now the sun broke out from behind a thick black cloud, throwing a flood of light upon the scene:

> 'The battled walls, the donjon keep,
> The flanking towns which round it sweep,
> In yellow lustre shone.'

Raised upon a small elevated plateau, the massive walls of the castle, flanked by eight round towers, and surmounted by innumerable smaller watch-turrets, look down upon the little village of Pierrefonds, that nestles at its base in small irregular clusters of white-walled houses. It is, as you doubtless well know, looked upon as the finest castle in France. The architecture is Norman, of the oldest date; but the roofing in various parts, especially that of the chapel and the large hall, is modern gothic. Time, unfortunately, would not permit us to enter; but we gazed with admiration upon the wondrous and beautiful structure. The bases of the towers and the walls are all old, whilst most of the upper works are new; but the same style has been carefully preserved throughout. In Pierrefonds there is an excellent hotel, with baths—whether mineral or not, I had no chance to ask. The village was small, and very clean;

at that moment the greater portion of the population were at the wars.

Leaving Pierrefonds behind us, we took the direct road through the centre of the forest to Compiègne; and at one o'clock General von Göben and his staff rode into the palace-yard. Dismounting from our horses, we ascended the great staircase in the centre of the quadrangle, and entered the magnificent hall, embellished by those two grand efforts of the Prince de Talhouët. His excellency's staff occupied the left, that of General Manteuffel the right, wing of the palace. In the centre are the chambers of audience, the magnificent ballroom, the famous Don Quixote gallery, and the imperial apartments. The last were unoccupied, and remained only open to view. Every care had been taken of the furniture and other belongings, and not a single article had been damaged in any way. Twenty servants of the imperial establishment still remained, who took charge of the house. The chiefs of the staff found themselves quartered where ministers of state and marshals of France had lived before them; aides-de-camp revelled in the boudoirs of the court ladies; while other officials were surrounded by objects of art, refinement, and taste, with which a soldier but seldom meets during a campaign. 'Did I see the Empress's rooms?' I hear a lady ask. Of course I did. Her Majesty's boudoir, hung with pale blue satin, was charming. Mirrors were on all sides of you—here, there, and everywhere.

In the Emperor's library I found a copy of his own *Life of Cæsar;* not emblazoned with the imperial arms, but bound in a very matter-of-fact commonplace cover. There were other reminiscences there, too painful to mention; and I was almost glad when I passed into the China drawing-room, *le salon Chinois*, where the Emperor and Empress used, in the 'fall,' to pass many happy hours. It was now denuded of many of those landmarks that have made it familiar to English eyes. Most of them had gone to Tours; but the heavier portion of the furniture, the pictures, and most of the glass and china, remained. The mention of the latter reminds me of the dinner we partook of that night. We ate off a cloth bestudded with N.s; our plates, plain white and gold, were marked with the imperial cipher; the glasses too, each delicately cut with the imperial crown and monogram, almost seemed to forbid us to lift them to our lips without the old toast of '*Vive l'Empereur!*'

As I wandered from room to room through those gorgeous apartments, gazing at the works of delicacy and art with which each room was adorned, I could not help letting my memory wander back to the last time that I had seen the same scenes—the last time I had, gun in hand, passed a happy day in the woods that there surround me. Then, the palace, the Avenue de l'Impératrice, the town itself, was a joyous scene, where each one, from the highest to the lowest, found amusement. How changed was all that now! The striped sentry-boxes where the Cent Gardes used to keep watch were empty, the quadrangle resounded only to the music of '*Die Wacht am Rhein*,' and the streets were deserted; while, as to the woods, they furnished sport and amusement to the staff of Generals Manteuffel and Von Göben. To be sure, it was rather a curious battue, for out of fifty or sixty officers only five or six possessed guns; but then they shot with chassepots, needle rifles, and carbines, and one day they managed to kill with these somewhat curious fowling pieces about eighty head of game, chiefly pheasants. The two principal hotels in the town furnished us with excellent dinners, the imperial cellar with Lafitte, Château Margaux, La Rose, Château d'Yquem, and plenty of champagne. If we had not the romantic surrounding so pleasantly depicted by Maxwell, we had at least one of the pleasures of life —'good eating and drinking.'

On the 22d the outposts were at Villers-sur-Coudon, Margny, Rojallieu, and southwards. The enemy, in the shape of Farre, was supposed to be somewhere between Amiens and Rouen. The first corps marched that morning to Noyon, and from it we anticipated receiving intelligence regarding the movements of this ghostlike army, about which no one appeared to know anything. Under the existing state of things, I thought it highly probable that our next movement would be upon Amiens; as, from all I could gather, Bourbaki's army seemed to lie with its right resting upon Forges, and its left extended a little beyond Amiens. Beauvais and Noyon were now held by German troops; so that, unless the French took ground to their right in the direction of Elbeuf, they must either retire towards the sea-coast, or risk an action somewhere in the neighbourhood of Morieul, having Amiens and Rouen to retire upon in case of need. Meantime the troops, in the excellent quarters which they now occupied, had time to get over the fatigue of the severe marches from Metz, and the horses, up to their hocks in straw, with good rations and good quarters, would in a few days be fit for anything.

Our stay in the royal château of Compiègne was good both for man and for beast; but General Manteuffel was not disposed to permit us to enjoy it very long—in fact, on the 25th he shifted his head-quarters to Bangy. Scarcely had the staff got into their quarters, when an orderly reported *a balloon*. Everybody rushed out—and there, sailing away in the direction of Lille, floated the aeronautical postman. His course was not allowed, however, to proceed in peace; a section of men loaded with ball-cartridge, and commenced firing at the unfortunate aeronaut. Fortunately for him, the distance was too great; and, after six shots had been fired, he was permitted to float on without farther molestation. Here we got intelligence of the enemy's whereabouts, the cavalry division having pushed their reconnaissances as far as Neuville and Beaufort. This intelligence at once settled the question as to the advance of the 8th army corps; and General von Göben was ordered next morning, the 25th, to march upon Montdidier.

On the afternoon of that day, after a fatiguing march, we arrived there, and heard precise news as to the enemy's position.* The cavalry of the first army had been engaged at Moreuil and Mézières, and a Jäger battalion had lost some eight or nine men. We also learned that small bodies of the enemy had been seen in the neighbourhood of Ailly. Bourbaki, it seemed, has given up the command of the Army of the North, and gone to form a new corps, called the 18th corps, the head-quarters of which are at Nevers. The command of Bourbaki's army was given to an engineer officer who, it was said, had escaped in some extraordinary way out of Metz.

The inhabitants of Montdidier received us with anything but satisfaction. Their first experience of German troops was somewhat rough. It appears that the republic, fearing the conservative tendencies of the people of Montdidier, had appointed a new prefect. No sooner was this officer duly installed, than he contemplated resisting the army of the Crown Prince of Saxony with 200 gardes mobiles whom he had at his disposal. In vain the inhabitants, most of them old 'rentiers,' begged of him to desist and to spare their homes. The prefect was inexorable. And as soon as the advanced guard of the Saxon army made its appearance, it was fired upon; and, concluding that the town must be held by a large body of troops, the Germans commenced shelling it at 2000 yards. The first thing that occurred was the rapid exit of Monsieur le Préfet, accompanied by six or seven of his gardes mobiles; the next was the hoisting of a white flag upon the church tower—but not before some thirty or forty innocent inhabitants had suffered for the préfet's stupidity. On the morning of the 26th we left Montdidier to march upon Moreuil, where we intended to remain, if the enemy permitted, until the 1st army corps should have massed at Roye, and the two corps forming the army of Manteuffel could operate upon Amiens.

At Neuville a halt occurred, and the staff of General Kummer—now commanding the 15th division, 8th army corps—and that of General von Göben entered into conversation, and, so to say, compared notes. At Moreuil, General Strobberg reported Francs-tireurs in the neighbourhood of Hailles and Gentelles, two villages right and left of the road to Amiens. General von Göben therefore determined to make a reconnaissance with his staff upon the Amiens road. With the king's hussars in front, and patrols from the same regiment thrown out on both flanks, we advanced at a good trot. We had just got as far as the village of Thennes, when the patrol to our left flank received fire froma small wood on the other side of the river Noye, a branch of the Somme. Then came a halt, and glasses were put into requisition; but the mist hung so thick upon the hills, that it was impossible to make out anything. Just then an orderly galloped up to say that the village of Hailles, some three-quarters of a mile to our left front, was held by a battalion of chasseurs-à-pied. The mist at this moment cleared away, and we perceived a body of men retreating upon Hailles along the ridge of the mountain on the other side of the river.

We then moved forward as far as the entrance to the village of Thennes. Here we again halted, until the second battalion of the 68th regiment and a battalion of artillery moved forward. These troops then marched through the town, and we followed. As soon as we were clear of the houses, the cavalry took ground to their right flank, and occupied the heights.

Scarcely a mile outside the town we perceived the enemy's first line of skirmishers. A company of the 68th regiment was immediately detached, and, advancing in skirmishing order, drove the enemy through the wood upon the bank of the river to the high ground crossing the Amiens and Roye road. Here the enemy appeared to be in force, for a heavy fire was opened upon us, and the whole of the battalion in front became engaged. A battery of artillery then came up at the trot, but did not come into action. Meantime heavy firing was heard in the neighbourhood of Gentelles, to the right flank, where it appeared three battalions of the enemy made an attack upon a company of the 68th, but were driven back with loss. The Prussian loss in this reconnaissance was three officers and eighty men killed and wounded.

We then returned to Moreuil—that is, the staff; but the 16th division held the ground they occupied, the enemy retiring in the direction of Amiens. Next morning, the 27th, at eight A.M., heavy firing was heard in the direction of Gentelles. The whole division immediately marched.

The battle of Amiens was fought on the 27th of November, and is thus described in my letter to the *Daily Telegraph:*

'*Head-quarters, Eighth Army Corps, St. Saufliеu, Nov. 27.*

'Although I address my letter to you from the above-named place, you are not to suppose that the eighth army corps holds this position. On the contrary, after a hard day's fighting, the 16th division, under General Barnekow, occupied Dury, and the 15th division, Boves—both of which places have been this day taken from the enemy. At nine this morning, the 27th, the staff of General von Göben left Moreuil, where it had passed the night, and taking ground to the left flank, the corps marched upon Ailly. Here we found General Kummer and the 29th brigade of the 15th division—the 30th brigade, under General Strobberg, having marched upon Thézy by the opposite bank of the river Avre. It was a raw misty morning, such a one as that 5th of November on which the Russians attacked at Inkermann. The little town of Ailly-sur-Noye was full of artillery and infantry when we entered it. There was a slight pause, to give time to the 16th division to clear themselves to the left flank through Grattepanche and Rumigny. This was soon effected, and the 29th brigade, 15th division, marched in the direction of Estrés. Scarcely had we left Jumel, a sort of suburb of Ailly, when heavy firing to our right told us that General Strobberg was engaged. In the village of Estrés we halted for a short time. No sooner had the troops piled arms than the houses began to be visited, but with little luck so far as bread was concerned; for the Francs-tireurs had been there the evening before.

'Whilst on the subject of Francs-tireurs I must not forget to mention that, notwithstanding M. Gambetta's high-sounding proclamations, few of the peasants of Picardy have joined these anything but organised bands. My experience, I am sorry to say, of Francs-tireurs is anything but pleasant. The French seem to think that any one who can get a rifle and ammunition is at liberty, having attached himself to the nearest band of miscreants he comes across, to commit any atrocity he or they may deem fit. For instance, in the affair of yesterday by Thennes and Gentelles, when a patrol of the 9th and the king's hussars approached the village of Hailles, the inhabitants waved pocket-handkerchiefs to them, and showed white flags. The unsuspecting Germans advanced; but when at thirty yards from the village, a murderous fire was poured in upon them, severely wounding Count Wermitz and emptying several saddles. Can the world be surprised if a severe and merited retribution followed such deeds?

'I had gone into a house, in which the poor woman gave me some hard-boiled eggs, one of which I was just enjoying with some salt, each grain the size of a pea, when my orderly came to tell me that the general had mounted. From Estrées we rode to the town of Sains. Here two battalions of the 33d and two batteries of artillery, leaving the road to St. Fuscier, marched on a farm called Cambos. Meanwhile the 65th regiment, with some artillery, marched upon St. Fuscier, to keep up the line of communication with the 16th division, already engaged before Dury. By this it will be seen that the French left rested on Villers Brettonieux, whilst their right was in Dury, and their centre in Boves. Accompanied by his staff, General von Göben, hearing the sound of heavy firing to his right rear, went in the direction of Fouencamps. As we rode across the open ground towards Boves, an aide-de-camp brought intelligence of the movements of the 16th division. The 9th hussars had charged a battalion of marine volunteers at Herbecourt, and completely cut them to pieces, with the loss of the Prince Hatzfeld; the 70th regiment had stormed the village of Dury, and the artillery had five officers *hors de combat.* The enemy was falling back upon Amiens.

'With a smile upon his face, the general rode forward until he came opposite the French position, whence we could see the French troops retiring upon Boves before General Strobberg from the wooded ground above St. Nicholas. Here the staff awaited the advance of the troops. The 33d regiment—that is to say, two battalions—marched forward to the ravine between St. Nicholas and Boves, to storm the village and the French position; whilst a battery of artillery stationed themselves at a distance of 2000 yards, about a quarter of a mile in front of the farm at Cambos. No sooner did the 33d deploy, and covered by half a company of skirmishers advance to the attack, than the enemy opened the most determined fire. They, however, were but weak in artillery. After the lapse of half an hour the French were driven from their position, the 33d storming the village of Boves, and taking 300 prisoners, losing, however, many men. The Prussian batteries punished the French columns severely as they retired by the road to Amiens; but the battle to the right still went on vigorously.

'As evening fell the French brought out some guns from Amiens in order to cover their troops, who were making an anything but orderly retreat into the town by way of the Roye road. After the taking of Boves, General von Göben rode to the right, where General Strobberg, commanding the 30th brigade of the 15th division, was still engaged with the enemy. This brigade had been fighting since nine o'clock in the morning. We found the French in an intrenched position between Gentelles and St. Nicholas, with two guns; and it was deemed advisable not to attack them, as night was fast coming on, and we could scarcely see. In the evening, at six o'clock, General von Göben left the battle-field, having thoroughly reconnoitered the position of the enemy, and rode to St. Sauflieu, on the Amiens and Dunkirk road.

'It is impossible at this moment to state the German loss; but that they have suffered, and, as usual, much in officers, there is but little doubt. When we rode into St. Sauflieu, we could see the occasional flash of the guns from Amiens as they shelled the bivouacs of the 16th division. Had the 1st corps come up, as was anticipated, they would have inflicted an irremediable loss upon the French, and turned their right flank; but up to ten o'clock to-night we have no news of their whereabouts. General von Göben has gone to see General Manteuffel, whose head-quarters are at Moreuil—no doubt to make arrangements for to-morrow, when I fear daylight will usher in another day of blood and massacre.'

The extraordinary evacuation of Amiens is again thus described:

'*Head-quarters, Eighth Army Corps, Amiens, Nov. 28.*

'You will perceive by these lines that my prognostications of last night have, to a certain extent, been realised. We have taken Amiens, but, I am thankful to say, without bloodshed. Little did I think, as I sat in my far from comfortable room at St. Sauflieu, that we should march into Amiens with so little resistance. The town of Amiens, where the army of the north was to have made that stand which would turn the fortunes of France, and drive the Prussians from Paris, where the wonderful commanders were to establish military discipline, and, so to speak, supply, in the short space of two months, ready-made soldiers fit to drive the Prussian veterans of Gravelotte back in confusion—this town has now surrendered without a struggle. You have had so many letters describing their preparations, that no doubt you anticipated great things from the army of the north; but all that can be said is, that, after fighting for two days in the neighbourhood of the city with 45,000 troops against 15,000—who were, after all, only making a reconnaissance—they abandoned, at four this morning, the town and the earthworks they had erected, without firing a shot. It was not a retreat; it was simply a disorderly, drunken flight, headed by General Farre, the commander of the army of the north, and brought up in the rear by the prefect of the Somme. Before leaving the town, the following proclamation was addressed by the latter to the inhabitants:

"PREFECTURE OF LA SOMME.

FRENCH REPUBLIC.—LIBERTY, EQUALITY, FRATERNITY.

To the Inhabitants of the Department.

CITIZENS,—The day of trial has come. In spite of the incessant efforts made by me for three months, to the feeble extent of my means of action, the chief town of the department falls in its turn into the hands of the enemy. The council of superior officers has just determined on the retreat of the army of the north and the disarmament of the national guard. I am absolutely obliged to leave you, but in the firmest hope of an early return. Calmness and confidence! France will be saved. Vive la France! Vive la République!

THE PREFECT OF LA SOMME, J. LARDIERE.

Amiens, November 28, 1870."

The mayor, poor man, left to his own devices, immediately followed with another:

"The generals intrusted with the defence of Amiens have suddenly departed with the troops, and, considering them too feeble, have abandoned us. The military committee has not been consulted. The prefect quitted Amiens to-night. As for me, I remain with my municipal council in despair, but without forces against the enemy. Devoted to my fellow-citizens, and ready for all sacrifices in their behalf,

THE MAYOR."

'At five P.M. yesterday the 70th regiment had been relieved by the 40th regiment, which occupied the cemetery immediately opposite the French lines between Dury and Amiens. The unusual stillness and non-appearance of sentries in front of the spot in which the French were supposed to be induced the commanding officer to send a patrol forward to reconnoitre; the distance was some 300 yards. You may imagine their surprise when, entering the works, they found nothing but the cannon and the dead bodies of those slain in yesterday's combat. Intelligence was immediately sent to General Barnekow, who at once ordered an advance of the troops. They, without opposition, entered the town; and thus ingloriously fell the good city of Amiens.

'When the news reached General von Göben, he could scarcely credit it; nor, indeed, could any of us; and, in fact, orders had been given to remain on the defensive. We awaited an attack from the enemy, whose numbers were too great to admit of our attempting a forward movement until the first army corps should have had time to deploy to the right beyond Gentelles and Cachy. In order to satisfy himself if the extraordinary news were a reality, the general rode to the front.

'Leaving St. Sauflieu, we took the road through Hérbecourt and Dury, the scene of yesterday's fight. No sooner had we left Hérbecourt than the road on both sides showed signs of the battle. The way was strewn with military accoutrements and dead horses; while here and there lay the body of a chasseur de Vincennes alongside that of a Prussian fusilier. Leaving the wood of Dury, we came upon an undulating plain, bounded by the town of Amiens. On the highest ridge of the undulations the French had thrown up long lines of rifle-pits; and the road was defended by a battery mounting two howitzers and two 16-pounder rifled guns. All these remained in the hands of the victors. Right and left of the road as we advanced the barracks of the troops came into view—plain wooden huts, on each side of which were raised platforms covered by straw mattresses. Half way between these lines and the town were two *emplacements* for guns, one to the right, the other to the left. The position was a strong one, and if resolutely defended, would have been no easy matter to take.

'After a great deal of delay we entered Amiens, accompanied by the three battalions of the 40th regiment, and two batteries of artillery. These filed past the general in the principal part of the town, and then we retired to breakfast in the Hôtel de France. Amiens was captured, and the 45,000 Frenchmen that should have held it were in rapid retreat upon Arras, Doullens, and Rouen. The citadel had not, however, surrendered, and the commandant refused to give in upon any terms. The railway station bore sufficient proof to the disorganised state of the French troops. They had shot the clock to pieces, broken their rifles, and strewn the whole place with cartridges.

'Most of the rifles were Remingtons, a fact which accounts for the extraordinary range at which the French fired yesterday. To give you an instance: the general and his staff took up their position on the left flank of the right battery that was playing upon Boves. This battery was covered by two sections of the 33d regiment. That in front of the staff were told to lie down; one man, however, preferred kneeling—he was about ten paces from where the general stood. I was just going to caution him, when a bullet fired at a quite extraordinary distance passed clean through his body. The whole staff were forced to dismount, and the horses were sent to the rear; for the fire during the first twenty minutes was anything but agreeable. General von Göben, notwithstanding the remonstrances of his staff, always insists, no matter how heavy the fire, upon taking up a position where he can see everything and direct the movements of his troops. It is quite impossible to keep him back.'

Much has been said of the exportation of arms from England; but the fall of Amiens threw a new light upon this vexed question. Seven hundred and fifty thousand Remington rifles and five million cartridges had within the last few weeks been imported from America, through the exertions of General Lafayette, 40,000 of which found their way to Amiens. The population who but yesterday shouted '*Liberté, égalité, et fraternité!*' '*Vive la France!*' and '*Mort aux Prussiens!*' to-day received with open arms the troops who had saved their town and property from a lawless soldiery. Many of those who the day previous wore the uniform of Francs-tireurs now appeared in plain clothes, and attached themselves to the French ambulance corps; so that it was anything but safe to walk about alone in unfrequented quarters. The shops were all shut; for, before they left the town, the French troops pillaged right and left, leaving not an ounce of tobacco or a bundle of cigars in the whole place.

Although the citadel had not surrendered, General von Göben determined not to bombard it until the last moment. The mayor, poor man, with tears in his eyes, begged the general to persuade Captain Fogel, an old line officer, who commanded, to capitulate, and thus to set free 300 gentlemen belonging to the best families in Amiens, that were only aggravating misery by a useless resistance; but at 12 noon, the citadel opened fire upon the town, and the 'gentlemen of the best families' did their best to destroy their own homes and kinsfolk.

Meantime reports of the Francs-tireurs continued to come in. That morning eight wounded Prussians were found hanged in a wood near Boves. The inhabitants of several of the villages had taken off their uniforms, hid their arms under the mattresses, and shot through the windows when they got a chance. It was most horrible to contemplate the tragedies that were going on round Amiens—wounded men slaughtered or having their eyes put out, and innocent people suffering for the guilty.

The citadel had not surrendered; what the commander meant by so useless a resistance is beyond comprehension. The Prussians were long-suffering, patient, and humane; they were commanded by one of the kindest-hearted gentlemen in the world; but General von Göben was also one of the best soldiers of the day—and, hard as it may appear, he could do nothing else, unless a foolish and useless opposition were discontinued, but destroy a place which he could not possibly leave behind him.

On the 30th November, however, at seven o'clock, the citadel of Amiens surrendered at discretion. It fell thus. I have already mentioned the fact that Captain Fogel, an old line soldier, steadily refused surrendering when called upon to do so by General Barnekow. Accordingly, two companies of the 40th regiment took possession of the houses in the immediate neighbourhood of the glacis, and opened a fire upon the place, which was returned by the garrison with artillery and chassepot fire. All day long this sort of guerrilla warfare continued, the German troops using no artillery. On the evening of the 29th it was determined to shell the disobedient earthwork into submission, and eight batteries marched out at three in the morning, taking up their positions right and left of the citadel at 2000 yards. But, as day dawned, the white emblem of submission was seen waving from the ramparts, and the melancholy fact was ascertained that the commandant had been killed during the night.

The citadel was much stronger than was supposed. The garrison was composed of 400 men and twelve officers, with thirty pieces of ordnance. The height of the *revêtement* was eighty feet from the ditch to the rampart, so that it would have taken some little time, and no small loss, to capture the place; but the death of the commandant—killed while superintending the training of a gun—put an end to farther resistance. The loss of the defenders was four killed and thirteen wounded. Within the citadel were found one officer and sixteen men of the 4th Prussian regiment, who had been taken prisoners the day before in the fight at Gentelles; I need hardly say, they were agreeably surprised when their countrymen knocked in the door of the room in which they were confined. Thus fell the capital of Picardy after an inglorious resistance, and the next operations bid fair to meet with the same result, unless the invaders were opposed by different material.

Most pitiable reports continued to arrive from the scene of the conflict on the 27th. A village was discovered by Captain Uniacke of Colonel Loyd Lindsay's society on the extreme left of the French position, in which, huddled together without medical assistance, without comforts of any sort, lay 600 wounded Frenchmen, many of the injured limbs requiring amputation. The French seemed to have made no provision whatever for their wounded; and, were it not for the British Society and for the exertions of its agents, under the command of General Sir Vincent Eyre, I know not what would have been the result.

The loss of the German army, in the affairs of the 26th and 27th November, was twenty-six officers and 500 men killed and wounded; the French loss, 2700.

A telegram from the King arrived, announcing the complete rout of the Loire army. On the 28th instant they were attacked by the 10th division. The French were utterly defeated, and left 1100 dead and wounded on the field of battle. The Prussians took 1600 prisoners, and lost 1100 killed and wounded. On the same day the garrison of Paris made a vigorous sortie upon the 5th and 6th army corps, in the neighbourhood of L'Hay; fighting lasted for several hours, when the French troops were repulsed with severe loss. Such was the text of the telegram published in general orders.

On the 1st of December the 1st army, leaving Gröben's cavalry in Amiens, marched westward, and for the next few days it was believed there would be but little fighting, as no troops had been heard of in the neighbourhood. So much has been written about the town of Amiens, that it would be superfluous for me to add to any of those lively descriptions which were published at the time; suffice it to say, the population were agreeably surprised to find that, after all, the Prussian soldiers were not so *méchants* as they anticipated. In fact the people began to say that they were *forts gentils*, and a most cordial sort of arrangement seemed to exist.

The soldiers grumbled a little at the price of articles, and had a somewhat novel plan of altering it to suit their own idea of the article's value. For instance, while I was in a shop one day a German soldier entered with his comrade to buy a purse. The comrade's French was exceedingly limited, not to say select. First of all, squaring himself before the somewhat frightened shopwoman, he pulled out a handful of money, and, holding out his hand, said, '*Portemonnaie.*' '*Oui, monsieur, mais je pense qu'ils seront trop chers pour vous.*' This sentence was a puzzler; so out came *Der Deutsche Soldat in Frankreich*, a small book of sentences, with French on one side and German on the other. But, unfortunately, the present exigency had not been provided for. Accordingly there was a consultation, and then came the result. '*Nous voulons portemonnaies.*' '*Oui, monsieur; mais trop cher.*' '*Nicht cher, donnez à nous vite!*' '*Eh bien, monsieur, celui-ci est de six francs.*' '*Six francs! Donnerwetter! das bei uns kostet zehn Silbergroschen,*' cried the indignant fusilier, throwing the unhappy portemonnaies on the counter. I then came to the rescue, and eventually a bargain was struck, by which the purse became the possession of the soldier for three francs—exactly half what was first asked. The shopkeepers tried to impose in really a scan-

CHAPTER X.

THE MARCH WESTWARD.

Not long were the troops permitted to remain idle. The line of the Somme must be occupied, and the town of Rouen, if possible, also. The fertile departments of the Somme and Seine Inférieure must feed and clothe the invader whilst they kept watch upon the French army of the north. Accordingly on the 1st of December, the 8th and 1st corps, leaving a garrison in the citadel and General von Gröben's cavalry to watch the movements of the enemy, marched from Amiens, to Poix—a long and fatiguing journey, made endurable, however, by the frosty weather. As we left Amiens, I could not help thinking that by this time the French people must have learnt that, after all, *la belle France* was neither a sacred nor a holy land. This had, of course, been carefully fostered and nursed by Gambetta and Company, who still sang in the ears of the unfortunate people the theory of the 'last cartridge and the last man.'

I found a book whilst I was in Amiens which went very far to prove what were the prevalent notions; it was called *The French Soldier in Germany*, and consisted, like the German book of the same description, of a number of useful sentences, the French on one side and the German on the other. At the end there was a form of prayer which the soldier was to use, ending with the following sentence: '*And now, O Almighty One, do not forget that France is the land to which all other nations of the globe look for instruction. Do not forget that Frenchmen are your own chosen people; and bless our arms in this just war!*' People would not be inclined to believe that the matter had really gone so far as this; and had I not read the above lines with my own eyes, I confess I should have felt a doubt as to their authenticity.

There are some incidents connected with the action before Amiens on the 27th that I have neglected to describe, and now take the opportunity of doing so. The French right rested in Hérbecourt, a village in front of Dury. It was against this place that the 16th division was sent, and to them was intrusted to oust the enemy from their position, and drive them, if possible, back upon Amiens. Here it was that the 9th hussars made the charge I have already described. Here also the 70th and 28th regiments fought, together with the 40th. After driving the French out of Hérbecourt, the village of Dury was stormed. Both these hamlets lie on the Amiens and Dunkirk road. About three-quarters of a mile beyond Dury were the French works, with a battery of four heavy guns placed upon the road itself. Immediately in front of these works, at a distance of three hundred yards to the left of the road as you go into Amiens, is a small graveyard, surrounded by a hedge. For upwards of two hours this graveyard was held by two companies of the 70th regiment, *in the face of this battery and at the distance above mentioned*, to say nothing of the long line of rifle-pits running right and left of it. The only cover the men had were the gravestones, of which there were very few, the greater portion of the monuments being iron crosses.

A more courageous deed was certainly not performed in the campaign, and it goes to show with what dogged determination Prussian soldiers will hold a position of which they have once got possession. In every action hitherto, they had always attacked, and the French always received them in a chosen position, where they had burrowed themselves into the ground like so many rabbits, Mars-la-Tour being the only exception. In the affair of Dury the Prussian batteries took up a position at 1200 yards, and, although they lost five officers and half their horses, nothing would induce the commandant to retire to 2000 yards. It was principally owing to their fire that the French troops were driven out of the works and retired into Amiens.

One more episode, and I have done. I have already mentioned the attack of the 33d regiment upon the village of Boves, and the French position to the left of it. The scene I, of course, described as I saw it from where I stood, about 1000 yards from the French rifle-pits; but it appears that an English officer witnessed it from the French side, having taken up his position in a church tower in rear of Boves. He told me that when he saw the regiment advancing he never witnessed anything so fine in his life. They only wanted red coats to make them an English regiment; and when they stormed the position and drove the French into the village, and from that into the Amiens road, forgetting the lofty observatory upon which he stood, he took off his hat and threw it into the air, and had consequently to trudge back into the town without one.

Previous to marching out of Amiens, the gardes nationaux, having given up their arms, were permitted by the Prussians to return to their homes. This was anything but a good system, for it placed the men in a position to form themselves into bands of Francs-tireurs in their rear, who might annoy the postal communication very considerably. We heard that the enemy occupied Grandvillers and Formerie, so that when we marched that morning we fully anticipated an action before we came into our quarters. Our expectations, however, were not realised. The French troops retired during the night, and we entered peaceably, without firing a shot.

At dinner-time the post usually arrived, and the *Mittagsessen*, as the Germans call it, over, the letters and papers were distributed. It was amusing to watch the anxious faces that spoke of intense desire for news from home, and the disappointed looks of those to whom the post brought none. How notes were compared, and what curious things were produced from various packages! A father shows with pride the photograph of his child, a husband that of his wife, a lover that of his *fiancée*. A rush is made at the newspapers; and when these are digested, the unlucky French correspondence that has been intercepted is handed round, to see if anything is to be got out of it, or if it conveys intelligence to the enemy. This done, the letters are carefully sealed up and dispatched on their way. Some of them were sufficiently amusing. One was from a distracted young lady to her lover in the garde mobile. So full of endearing epithets was this dainty epistle, that two of the aides made a bet upon the number of *bien cher ami's* to be found in two pages. The one said twelve, the other fourteen; the latter won.

The French force before us was definitely ascertained to be composed of 42,000 men, with 74 heavy guns and 32 light field-pieces. The question now was whether they would fight in their present position, or retire upon Rouen and make a fight for the old town. The general seemed inclined to think that, after the severe way in which they were handled at Amiens, the last was the course they would adopt. Had they done so, they might have given some trouble, for the ground was well adapted for the purpose to which no doubt it would be devoted. The sailors, too, were almost sure to fight well, and at the time I fully expected a battle at or in the neighbourhood of Rouen.

As we advanced, the same cry for peace met one's ear everywhere; but, by dint of the lies in the papers and the heroics of M. Gambetta—who, by the way, was thoroughly detested in these parts, except by the Reds—the unfortunate assemblage of men called an army was kept on foot, to be decimated and slaughtered like so many sheep. '*Que voulez-vous, monsieur?*' said a French baron to me one day, 'France suffered for

Napoleon, and is now being tortured by *sansculottes* and newspapers.' As a specimen of the latter, I quote a paragraph from the *Journal d'Amiens* of the 29th. Seeing that the place surrendered and was in the possession of the Prussian troops on the 28th, the account of the action on the French right at Dury is somewhat astounding:

'Notwithstanding the insufficiency of the numbers, to fill in which at a proper time so many useless demands have been made, in spite of the defective organisation of the armament, the legion executed punctually the instructions that had been given to it for its order of battle, and did not flinch under the shower of shells which the Prussian batteries fired against our batteries at Dury, and which, passing beyond the latter place, fell in the fields to the right of the road on which were deploying the national guard.'

The state of the town is more truthfully depicted in the following paragraph:

'Soon the crackling of the fusillade in the streets, on the boulevards, sounded the alarm in the centre of the town. They are fighting in the streets, it was said. It was only the detonations of the guns that are discharged—not always with sufficient precaution, since balls penetrate into several houses. When day breaks a lamentable spectacle is seen in all parts. *Gamins* run through the streets with arms that they have found or stolen. These they are breaking, careless that the greater part are still loaded. Sometimes the shot goes off, and the ball strikes some surprised person or the façade of the houses. A considerable crowd hurries to the barrack — St. Jacques—which it sacks, throwing to the four winds or appropriating all the military articles which were contained in it.'

So much for the papers. The commandant of the citadel of Amiens was buried on the ramparts in the place where he fell, a fitting spot for a soldier's grave. His funeral was attended by a numerous body of the townspeople, whilst the 40th Prussian fusiliers supplied the band and a firing party to perform the last honours for this brave old soldier.

On the 2d of December the cavalry sent in intelligence that Forges les Eaux and Formerie were occupied in force by the enemy, and accordingly, leaving Poix, we marched through Grandvillers, and on the 3d reached Gaillefontaine. Early on the morning of the 4th the eighth corps marched upon Formerie, which we found deserted by the enemy; but almost immediately after the advanced guard and cavalry came upon the enemy, who had taken up a strong position on the heights of Maquency and Bose Bordel, on the Rouen road. From this position they were driven by the fifteenth division, retiring upon the village of Buchy, where, for a few moments, they made a stand, in order to enable their troops to get into the trains that were waiting for them. In fact, they made but a poor and shameful resistance, relinquishing a strong position defended, as we afterwards ascertained, by 35,000 troops.

The troops were almost entirely composed of the reserve forces or garde mobile, sent from the various camps of instruction, where, for some months, they had been in training. As I reserve my comments on reserve forces for a future occasion, I shall not pause here to note the organisation and discipline that rendered this fine material of so little use in front of tried troops, and which, indeed, furnishes a good lesson to ourselves, upon which our Government could act with advantage: suffice it to say that on the 5th of December—the anniversary of the battle of Leuthen—that glorious victory in which Frederick the Great captured more prisoners than the strength of his own army—again witnessed an achievement by the Prussian arms. The fourth town of importance in this distressed and devastated land was left to the mercy of the invader, and was occupied without firing a shot. Rouen was entered on December 5th at three o'clock by the troops of General von Göben.

The events which immediately led to this extraordinary piece of good fortune are soon told. After the skirmish on the heights of Maquency and Bose Bordel, the 16th division followed up the retreat of the flying army under General Briand as far as Vert Galant, on the road to Rouen. Here darkness put an end for the day to farther operations. The strange manner in which the French troops, evidently strong in numbers, had abandoned position after position from Gaillefontaine all along the road to Rouen, induced General von Göben to make one of those rapid advances which have so often led to triumphant results. The troops under his command, with that confidence in their general which military knowledge and success can alone obtain for an officer, received with their usual enthusiasm the order to advance upon the road to Rouen; and, notwithstanding the severe marching of the last few days, every man strode along the road to all appearance as fresh as on the day he left the banks of the Rhine. The army felt that something must happen that day; they anticipated a battle before Rouen; they believed that the French army was strong in numbers, well armed, and possessed artillery, with the advantage of occupying a fortified position. Every officer and man of the infantry regiments made up his mind to a severe day's work, while every cavalry soldier sat down on his horse, hardened his heart, and caught hold of the bridle.

With the ice on the hard-frozen road crackling under the horses' feet, the staff left its anything but comfortable quarters at Buchy as the clock struck half-past eight on the morning of the 5th—the red rays of the frosty December sun throwing a rosy light upon the frost-bespangled trees on either side of the way. General von Göben had received instructions to make a reconnaissance upon the Rouen road, and not to attack the enemy if he found that they had taken up a position behind earthworks; while General Manteuffel, whose head-quarters were at Argeuil, should make a reconnaisance with the 1st army corps, in the direction of Boos, having occupied the line of the Andelle. Arrived at Quincampoix, we there found General Barnekow with the 16th division. The advanced guard had brought back an old gentleman taken prisoner as he was driving out of Rouen in his gig. He turned out to be the mayor of Quincampoix, and from him intelligence was received that 35,000 French troops had camped at Quincampoix on the previous night. They had, however, only remained for an hour, and then continued their retreat upon Rouen. There were no troops between us and the town; and, from what our informant had heard, Rouen intended making no resistance.

So astounding was this intelligence, that at first it was believed to be only a *ruse*, to induce the already wearied soldiers to advance upon a strong position defended by fresh troops. But the general, accustomed to find himself in all sorts of difficult positions, divined more accurately. He went into a small room with Colonel von Witzendorf, the chief of his staff, and Major Bomki; and after a short consultation his mind was made up. A despatch was sent to General Manteuffel, and the troops were ordered to advance, feeling their way carefully, on both flanks. Just at this moment the omnibus from Rouen arrived, having been sent back with an escort, in order that the driver might give his information to the general in person. His statement was almost incredible. In the morning the French troops had all retreated upon Havre. The town had subscribed 10,000,000 francs as a contribution, which General von Göben was invited to come and take. Everything was now boot and saddle; the 40th and 70th regiments, forming the 31st brigade, with the 9th hussars and two batteries of artillery, advanced along the road to Isneauville, and the staff waited in Quincampoix, to permit the infantry advance.

Meanwhile the village of Quincampoix was having a rough time of it. In front of the Mairie were strewn a quantity of weapons deposited there by the garde nationale and mobile. These were at once destroyed, and the houses were then searched for arms or ammunition, that any unlucky occurrences might be prevented. Those doors which had been unwisely left locked by the owners were at once forced; while those which remained open were left untouched. The mayoress, wise in her generation, and thrifty as a good housewife should be, had not only locked the doors of her mansion, but closed the windows, and barricaded them with furniture. Upon the approach of the searching party with a demand for admittance, the poor woman put her head out of a hole in the roof, telling the officer that there was no one at home, and that he had better be off about his business. The answer was a crash of broken glass in the kitchen-window; upon which the good lady surrendered at discretion. The mayor by and by appeared, and was informed that all barricades on the road must be removed within three hours, failing which a heavy fine would be imposed upon the village. The good old man then supplied us with some excellent cognac, presenting me with a special bottle for my services as interpreter.

By this time the general had mounted, and we rode forward on the road to Isneauville. Arrived at that place, we came upon the first lines of the French works. In the middle of the road lay two heavy ship guns—24-pounders. Their position explained at once that the French troops had retreated, leaving Rouen a prey to the advancing army. General von Göben, by his rapid advance upon Rouen, had taken the French general completely by surprise; indeed, before even he had had time to organise defence, or complete his intrenchments, the 8th army corps had vigorously attacked and driven back upon the main body the troops he had dispatched to watch the movements of the Germans. Another rapid march of the German line, and the discomfited Frenchman, with his wavering troops, decided at once to retreat. Rouen was left to take care of itself. The 24-pounders lying in the road attested the want of preparation. The French had not had time to put them into position. The batteries were unfinished; while, on either side of the road, the Prussian troops actually marched among the still burning camp-fires of the hostile army.

What, then, had Generals Briand or Farre been doing for the last two months? They had had more than ample time, money, and material—to say nothing of their close proximity to Havre, Dieppe, and Boulogne—to establish a line of defence before Rouen that might have altered the face of matters most effectually. They had done nothing but abandon every position which, with immense labour, their troops had constructed between Isneauville and Gaillefontaine, where every village might have been made a fortress—all the more easily because their army did not consist entirely of mobiles, but included several line regiments, and the 5th hussars, with thirty-five guns.

Riding through the suburb of Rouen, on the north-east side, among the luxurious villas and summer residences of the rich citizens, we arrived at that bend of the road from which the traveller gets the first glimpse of the old town. Rouen lies in a basin, surrounded on all sides by high hills. Through the town flows the Seine, then unusually full. No troops had yet entered, beyond a patrol of hussars; and, as we stood upon the height overlooking the city, strange sounds were carried to our attentive ears. Here and there a shot, a discordant shout, then a hollow rumbling noise as of a huge body of wooden-shoed men in movement—these different sounds followed close upon each other; then a shriek, as of some one in terror; until at length there came a dead stillness. Meantime, the smoke of the town curled tranquilly up through the frosty air, its course dreamily watched by the Prussian troops resting on their arms.

Presently a magistrate made his appearance—a tall thin old man, with the ribbon of the Legion of Honour on his coat. Would the general send some troops into the town as quickly as possible? The square of the Hôtel de Ville was in the hands of the *gamins* of Rouen, who, armed with the weapons thrown away by the national guard, were trying their best to shoot the mayor. They were firing upon the Hôtel de Ville—firing in that sort of drunken, miserable way in which a French mob delights. Already the façade of the Hôtel de Ville was pitted with bullets, the windows were broken, and the members of the Commune, huddled together in a back room, were, to use their own expression, *au désespoir*. The German troops were, fortunately for the mayor and the town, soon upon the spot; and marching into Rouen, they halted upon the Place Cauchoise. Here one battalion of the 40th, with two guns, took up its position; while the other two battalions, with the 70th regiment, filed in different directions through the town. The general then rode to the Place de l'Hôtel de Ville, and, standing beside the statue of Napoleon I., who seemed, hat in hand, to receive him (the statue represents the Emperor in this position), he saw the 16th division, with bands playing and colours flying, march past. Henceforth everything seemed to shake itself into its place. The shops, it is true, were closed; but Rouen was safe from anarchy and disorder.

And now let us for a moment consider what General von Göben, by his manœuvres and by his decision, won for the cause of Germany, as well as the price at which that gain had been purchased. In Rouen the German army of the north found all that it wanted; for this town, besides supplying fresh horses, 40,000 pairs of boots, 10,000 blankets, 2,000 shirts, 20,000 pairs of socks, and 10,000 cigars, furnished an amount of specie which considerably strengthened the sinews of war. Here the army could remain in secure and comfortable winter quarters, in direct communication with the Crown Prince of Saxony and the army of Paris; and from this point, unless the communication *viâ* Amiens should be disturbed, a great military movement could be organised. The cost of all these advantages to the army of the north was attained with 11 men killed and 50 wounded, without the loss of a single officer. The French lost five officers killed and 18 wounded, 45 rank and file killed, 100 wounded, 600 prisoners, and 27 pieces of heavy marine artillery, together with the city of Rouen.

Whether the good people of Rouen slept what is called the sleep of the just on the night of the 5th, I am not prepared to say; but their awaking must have been uncomfortable. Strange noises sounded in every house. In the corridors the people meet strange soldiers, smoking uncommonly strange pipes, and not always very good tobacco, who in their rough kindly way greet their host with a '*Guten morgen*,' followed by a demand for *café*. The matutinal cup is supplied; the soldier cleans his beloved rifle, brushes his clothes, polishes his accoutrements, and goes out to his duty. The owner of the house wonders—begins to feel himself all over, to ascertain if he is really awake. Are these, then, the brutal Prussians he has been taught to look upon as the assailants of women, the lawless destroyers of property, the drunken maniacs of an ill-disciplined army? At twelve o'clock they return for the *mittagsessen;* and dinner finished, they light their pipes, and try to talk French, to the infinite amusement of both themselves and their entertainers. Once more the house is left in peace. At night they return; perhaps some of them may have drunk an extra glass of wine. Can you blame men who have marched from Amiens to Rouen in five days, fighting on the road; who have been so short of tobacco—a necessary of life to them—that they have chopped the withered vine tendrils into a semblance of the fragrant weed, and smoked the bitter mixture, if not with relish, at least with contentment? Is it marvellous that, in an army of some 100,000 men, you find one here and there committing an impropriety in a moment of drunkenness? I will, at any rate, answer for one thing: had any other army, not excepting our own, found itself in a similar position, the guard-houses would have held ten soldiers for every one of Manteuffel's that has found his way thither.

And here let me remark, that if English people chose to remain in a country occupied by French troops, upon whom they knew perfectly well the

Prussians were advancing—if they chose to risk the unlikely contingency of the Prussians being compelled to retire—they must also take all the chance of having Prussian troops quartered upon them in the event of French defeat. The fact that residents in a foreign land, inhabiting houses which they rent from French proprietors, were English subjects, did not exempt them from having troops billeted upon them. The very infliction of such a burden protected their individual property—and woe to the unlucky man who did not respect it; but here the privileges of the foreigner end.

A case in point came under my especial observation; that of a Mr. Colbeck, who had a cloth-mill in the neighbourhood of Rouen. Notwithstanding his statement to a Prussian officer that he was an Englishman, that functionary refused to look at his papers, and treated both himself and his family with unusual severity, committing many outrages and doing much damage. Mr. Colbeck reported the matter to me. I investigated the alleged offences, and found them to be, though only half as bad as they were represented, still of sufficient moment to warrant me in laying the circumstances before General von Göben. The whole matter was at once put under a strict examination; but it appeared that the circumstances could not justify the general in taking any notice of it.

On the morning after the surrender the members of the municipality of Rouen had also a *mauvais quart d'heure.* At eleven o'clock the intendant of the 8th army corps had an interview with M. Nion, the representative of the mayor. The latter, poor man, what with the fright of the day previous and the multitudinous requisitions on all sides, had suddenly collapsed or gone into a mad-house. M. Nion was one of those dried-up, withered specimens of humanity, in whom, at first expecting nothing, you on farther acquaintance often find a great deal. The mission of the intendant was to say, that at ten next morning all the horses in Rouen must be paraded in the square of the Hôtel de Ville; furthermore, that 40,000 pairs of boots must be got ready within six days, according to a pattern which would be supplied. '*Ah, mais, monsieur, c'est impossible!*' cried the unfortunate man. Next, his excellency the general would be obliged by 20,000 pairs of socks being supplied within three days. '*Monsieur, je vous assure, ce n'est pas possible,*' was the answer. 'Pardon,' continued the immovable intendant; 'after this I shall only trouble you for 2,000 flannel shirts, 10,000 blankets, and 10,000 good cigars.' At the last demand M. Nion, who had been carefully noting the various items, threw down his pen in despair, pulled off his glasses, glanced at the ceiling, stretched his legs to their full extent under the table, and groaned once more, '*Monsieur, c'est impossible.*' 'I am very sorry to hear it, sir,' answered the imperturbable intendant; 'for in that case his excellency will impose upon the city a fine of three times the value of these articles.' The intendant bowed; M. Nion also bowed, shrugged his shoulders, and said, '*Je ferai mon possible.*' And so the matter terminated, for in the end everything was forthcoming.

The streets of Rouen were covered with snow. Winter had come suddenly and severely, and all were thankful to be in good winter quarters.

On the 8th of December the news of General Mannstein's victory at Orleans arrived. General Manteuffel gave a great dinner at the Hôtel de France—one of those banquets to celebrate a success of which there had been so many. Great was the rejoicing on account of the news, for every fresh success brought the German soldier nearer to a certainty of seeing his home. We sat down to dinner some seventy officers; and I may fairly say, there was not a man in the company but would have been delighted to hear that there was even a likelihood of peace.

As was anticipated, General Barnekow moved in the direction of Dieppe, while other troops were dispatched to the south, marching upon Elbeuf. News arrived that the post had been attacked on the frontiers of Belgium by Francs-tireurs—so we all bade adieu to any chance of getting communications from home for some time.

The inhabitants of Rouen came to the conclusion that the Prussian soldiers were, after all, civilised beings, and were beginning to draw comparisons between them and the French troops lately occupying the town by no means complimentary to the latter. They were perfectly contented with their situation, their only difficulty being the Prussian money, which they avoided taking if they could. One day I went into a shop to purchase a pair of warm gloves, and presented a bank-note of five thalers in payment. 'Monsieur,' said the suspicious Frenchman, fingering the piece of paper, turning it all sorts of ways, and in the end unable to make head or tail of it, 'I should prefer your owing me for the gloves.'

And now let us for a moment glance over the map of France, looking at it from a military point of view. Drawing a line from Dieppe through Rouen, Evreux, and Chartres, and so on to Orleans, you will have the position of the German troops not engaged in the siege of Paris. Against these troops we find the scattered bands who, flying before Manteuffel and Von Göben at Amiens, took refuge in Arras, Doullens, and other places in the north. At Havre, Honfleur, and thereabouts are the fugitives from Rouen; while, farther south, are the corps at Le Mans or Conlie and on the Loire.

Let me for a moment consider the material, and the relative chance, which these scattered bodies of troops had in this unequal contest. The principal, if not the largest, portion of these troops were composed of gardes mobiles. I have hitherto avoided criticising these troops until we had an opportunity of judging them under fire, on the march, or in an emergency. These opportunities I had now had, and I cannot say that my opinion had undergone any material alteration. Armed, disciplined, and led as they were, they could never hope to make head against the invaders of their country. Their want was not so much in point of arms, because, in every town we entered, Albini, Remington, and Snider rifles, with plenty of ammunition, disproved such a view. Nor were the mobiles at a loss for accoutrements; they were as well clothed as armed. And surely they could not be in want of provisions; for France, from the poorest to the richest, would scarcely deny food, shelter, and comfort to those who did their best in the cause of their country.

What, then, prevented this numerous and willing force from accomplishing their desires, or preventing the victorious advance of the invaders? First of all, the leaders; then the material; then the want of artillery and cavalry; and lastly, the blind unheeding confidence which was given to the self-constituted government. If the Prussian armies were destroying the commerce and emptying the rich coffers of *la belle France*, so were M. Gambetta and his colleagues, by their obstinate policy, prolonging a war which, to use a familiar expression, was burning the candle at both ends. In rejecting Bourbaki, the government refused the services of the best soldier left available to France. His post was given to General Farre, who, with General Briand, accomplished the *fiasco* of Amiens and Rouen.

These generals, if I may so call them, commanded troops, the *gros* of whom were raw levies that had never seen a shot fired, had never marched a mile in heavy order, had never beheld a battery of artillery in action, and knew not what it was to starve and fight for twenty-four hours. To encourage these men, the few line troops left in the country were mixed up, in order, if possible, that they might set a good example; but the policy which suggested this course was a bad one, for the old soldier knows when he is supported and when he is not. He was simply told to go into action, and let himself be killed or wounded, as an encouragement and example to a would-be army which had never yet heard the whistle of a bullet or the explosion of a shell. To support and encourage such a system, this jumble of troops was asked, without cavalry and without artillery, to fight against—nay, even to overcome—the finest artillery in the world, supported by excellent infantry, and covered by numerous cavalry squadrons. Is it therefore to be wondered at that Amiens fell, that Rouen was occupied, that the army of Northern France was driven to the sea-coast? But no. Republicanism was not satisfied with the butcher's bill. It was not satisfied that the needle-rifle had taken the place of the much-loved guillotine.

On the morning of the 9th December, intelligence was received of the combined victory won by Prince Frederick Charles and the Grand Duke of Mecklenburg over the Loire army at Orleans; 21,000 prisoners and 71 guns were the sum-total of the takings. It appeared that, after a severe engagement, the 10th corps and that of the Grand Duke of Mecklenburg occupied the suburbs of Orleans and the railway station, whilst the French troops retreated through the town. It was then that Prince Frederick Charles, with the 3d corps, started in pursuit, and took the number of prisoners and guns I have named, driving the flying forces of the enemy in every direction.

Notwithstanding this intelligence brought to General Manteuffel by special messenger from the King at Versailles, the infatuated population of Rouen believed that at that moment Ducrot had shaken hands with Paladine, that the army surrounding Paris was cut to pieces, and that Versailles was on fire. I do not suppose there is one sensible, sober-minded Frenchman who will not agree with me, when I say that if there was one agent more than another which at this time tended to destroy France and to deluge her soil with the blood of her people, it was the French press. How this strange blindness is to be accounted for, I know not. The good people of Rouen knew as well as I did that General von Göben was to move his head-quarters on the morrow for Yvetot, which lies on the Havre road, and they must have seen that he would hardly do this if the army of the Crown Prince were in distress or retreating. But to reason with people wilfully obstinate to argument was useless.

The flying columns sent in the direction of Havre reported French troops to the number of 25,000 in that town, whilst detached parties in the neighbourhood of Dieppe had not up to this time had an opportunity of displaying their valour. Another flying column occupied Elbeuf, to the south of Rouen and north of Evreux, where of course requisitions were made.

The absence of the English vice-consul at Rouen at this time caused great inconvenience and trouble, not only to the English residents, but to the Prussian authorities. I sat patiently and listened to the complaint of visitor after visitor, without the power, beyond the little interest I possessed with the general, to assist them. They one and all protested energetically against being left without official help, and they intended representing the matter in the proper quarter upon the first opportunity. The English residents objected to Prussian troops being quartered upon them; but they forgot that by remaining in a country which they knew was about to be invaded by a Prussian army, they ran the risk of this, from which no international law that exists could protect them. Their property was sacred, and could not be touched, nor were they liable to requisitions; but lodging they must give, and food also; the cost of the latter they could hereafter reclaim from the Commune at the rate of two francs per man per day. Had the British vice-consul been at his post, he would have been able to explain this, and prevented a great deal of trouble and annoyance.

It is somewhat curious, and I believe I am not the only person to whom it appears so, after the magnificent march which the 1st army made—to say nothing of the battle before Amiens and the actions of the 26th of November and 4th of December, finishing up with the occupation of Rouen—that his Majesty the King of Prussia forgot to acknowledge the services of his generals and soldiers who had cleared the north of France to the sea-coast. Generals Manteuffel and Von Göben, as well as their troops, more than 2000 of whom remained dead or wounded on that long road between Rouen and Metz, most certainly deserved that their conduct should be the subject of some public notice.

I made the strictest inquiries in all parts of Rouen as to the conduct of the Prussian troops, and I can safely say that the population themselves were not only agreeably surprised, but even almost contented with their lot. The cry was 'peace!' 'When will it end?' 'How is it all going to be finished?' These were the questions which met one at every corner, in every shop, and in every café.

Whilst the 1st army lay, so to speak, inactive at Rouen, flying columns were dispatched to requisition and quarter themselves in the surrounding country. Through these General Manteuffel obtained intelligence that Havre was strongly garrisoned, but that Dieppe and the seaboard was open as far as the mouth of the Somme; the object being to victual the troops, and send supplies to the blockading army of Paris.

General von Göben was dispatched with the 8th corps to make a feint upon Havre. He was to march upon Bolbec, where he was to mask his northward march by leaving a force to watch the Havre garrison. Accordingly, the capital of Normandy was clothed in a shining mantle of silver as we started on the morning of the 10th of December from before the Hôtel d'Angleterre, to march upon Yvetot. All the staff were on their horses, General von Göben having set the example; however, a hundred yards upon a road of ice showed the impossibility of riding, so we all dismounted and walked.

Shall I tell you that the proprietor of the Hôtel d'Angleterre was sorry to lose us? If I did, I am quite sure you would not believe me; and I must confess that I have inwardly rejoiced at the disconsolate look of mine host as bottle after bottle of Moët was discussed; his horror when a smart staff-officer, to whom he addressed himself with his hands in his pockets, told him that he was not accustomed to be spoken to by any one in such a manner; and his miserable looks when he was told to send his bill in to the mayor to be paid. You, my brother Englishman, who have had to contend with the insufferable pomposity and grasping avarice of the French hotel-keeper, will appreciate my feelings. Never had so much champagne been drunk before, never had so many oysters been eaten, never had so many photographs been bought. 'Only imagine, sir,' said the unfortunate proprietor to me, with tears in his eyes, 'the gentlemen drank 300 bottles of champagne last night.' 'Ah!' said I, 'it was to drown their grief at leaving the Hôtel d'Angleterre.' If a look could have killed me, I should have died upon the spot.

Scarcely had we left the hotel, when General Manteuffel walked up to General von Göben, and informed him that Dieppe had been occupied by the Uhlans the evening before. What a fuss there must be in the English colony there! I thought; and what on earth will they do when they have the Prussians quartered on them? As we left Rouen behind us, and got upon the road to St. Jean, the snow, about a foot deep, enabled us to proceed on horseback with some degree of safety. At St. Jean we found a considerable earthwork across the road, evidently thrown up to protect the retreat of the valiant army of Generals Briand and Farre; and after a miserably cold ride of five hours we reached Yvetot.

I cannot say I was prepossessed with the town, or with the principal hotel, where we lodged; but then it was war-time. Perhaps in days of peace the ill-built pasteboard-looking houses appear less dirty, less comfortless, and more regular. No sooner were our horses stabled than something to eat was the vigorous demand of every one of us. The first café we drew was a blank—plenty to drink, but nothing to eat. So we strolled along, sabre and sabretache clattering about over the ill-paved slippery road, until we lit upon a café restaurant. A particularly inflammable-looking damsel, made still more so by reason of a profusion of crisp red locks, requested to know the wants of Messieurs les Prussiens. '*Ah, messieurs, nous avons seulement des sardines et du fromage, vous savez?*' As if we knew! On such occasions these two words at the end of each sentence always seem to me a useless monstrosity in the French language.

Whilst partaking of our somewhat meagre fare, washed down with some excellent champagne, three or four young Frenchmen strolled in. One of them, a particularly forbidding-looking young man, as old maiden ladies are wont to say, informed us, with the utmost nonchalance, that he had just come from Havre through the Prussian lines. My comrades winked at one another, and commenced a course of badinage which quickly drew from the Frenchman all his information. Had he not heard that Gambetta and Jules Favre had fled to Bordeaux, and that on the way they had quarrelled because Favre had 50,000 francs more than Gambetta out of the plunder, and would not share, he was asked. No, he had not heard that; but then he knew that Generals Briand and Mocquard were in Havre with a tremendous army and powerful cannon—beautiful cannon, mostly American. Then there was a terrible corps of braves, who called themselves *Les Vengeurs du Havre*, who wore a death's-head upon their képis, and who were too awful to behold; and then there were the Francs-tireurs of Mocquard, each one ready to make an end of a whole battalion of Prussians. In fact, so interesting was his news, that all of a sudden he found himself arrested, and marched off by two gendarmes to the 'Wache,' in order to retail any farther information he might have at greater length, and with more precision, to the general. I merely quote this as proof of how the Prussian officers lost no opportunity of gaining information, no matter how slight, that might be of service.

On the 11th of December the 32d brigade of the 16th division of the 8th army corps marched into Bolbec, the cavalry brigade under Count Brandenburg marching out of it on their way to St. Romain and Angerville. With the 31st brigade of infantry, they were to watch the movements of the French army in Havre. It appeared that a cavalry patrol had had a slight skirmish at the village of Eprétot on the previous day, but immediately retired upon finding the place held in force by French infantry. Meantime the 15th division of the 8th corps was away south towards Gournay, and the 32d brigade was ordered the next day to march upon Fauville, unless General Briand should choose to come out and make an attempt to prevent them. Thus, as I have above mentioned, Havre was not to be attacked, but the 8th corps, after having made considerable requisitions in the north-east of France, was to retire upon Amiens, and go into winter quarters.

Meanwhile the first corps remained at Rouen, as a check upon General Briand. Here we had an opportunity of reading a most amusing French account of what they were pleased to call the *battle* of Buchy—a battle in which the Prussians had between fifty and sixty wounded, and not one man killed. In this veracious narrative it was set forth that General Briand, sword in hand, led on the brave troops under his command, and that they, after prodigies of valour, were forced to retire. The latter part of the statement was certainly correct, for retire they did, and in no very graceful way, when they saw a squadron of the King's hussars stealing down towards them. The French had upon that day upwards of 35,000 men in the field; the Prussians had but one regiment of infantry, one battery, and two squadrons of hussars engaged.

On the 12th we marched to Fauville. Before leaving Bolbec, a very peculiar circumstance took place, serving to illustrate the somewhat extraordinary ideas which the French military authorities in the north seemed to possess concerning the ordinary customs of civilised warfare. Just as the staff were preparing for bed after a hard day's work, two French army surgeons were announced, who wished to see the general in command. Where had they come from? was naturally the question asked. 'From Havre,' was the astounding reply; 'under escort.' Their business, as stated by them to an aide, was briefly told. 'General Briand's compliments to the Prussian general in command; two of the surgeons attached to the French army of the north had forgotten a couple of instrument-cases, and other medical comforts, in Rouen; the general had sent them back to fetch them, and would feel obliged by General von Göben passing them on to their destination, without let or hindrance.' I could scarcely believe my ears when I heard this astounding message. Need I add, that these two nondescript gentlemen—whether spies or not, it is hard to say—were immediately sent back to the place whence they came? I can scarcely imagine a more impudent request, and I was only astonished that Prussian forbearance let them off so lightly.

When we set out on our march, the frost and snow of the last three days had given way to a steady drizzling rain, which made the roads, if possible, more disagreeable than ever. The horses of the commissariat, baggage, and ammunition trains laboured with difficulty over the slippery way. The troops marched along with their usual free and elastic step, certainly; but those merry choruses and heart-stirring songs which usually beguile the march of the Prussian soldier had been silenced by the drenching downpour. Luckily for the troops, however, they had but a short distance—about twelve English miles—to travel, and good quarters awaited them at the end.

As we marched through the villages of Normandy I was particularly struck with the English look they had about them. The quaint old houses, the large farmyards surrounding the comfortable homesteads, the labourers' cottages, all reminded a homesick man of his country. I was also struck with the wonderful proportion of old people we saw—I mean those who had far outlived the Psalmist's threescore and ten. For instance, in the Hôtel de Fauville I met a man of eighty-four years of age; and I was told by the inhabitants that men equally old were often to be seen.

The disposition of the army of the north at this moment affords a subject well worthy of study, and one of great interest. I may therefore be forgiven for drawing the attention of the reader yet again to the same subject. Perchance some are not military men; and a little help towards unravelling the intricacies of military manœuvring, and the marching of various bodies of troops apparently in different directions, may not be quite thankless. After the occupation of Rouen, flying columns were dispatched, as I before remarked, in the direction of Havre to the north, and to the east, for the purpose of watching the movements of the enemy, and marking the proceedings of the main body of the French army. The 15th division of the 8th corps, under General Kümmer, then marched upon Totes; whilst the 16th division, under General Barnekow, with the head-quarters of General von Göben, marched upon Yvetot. No sooner was Yvetot occupied, than a flying column, under General Gneisenau, marched upon Goderville and St. Romain, in order to protect the flank of the 16th division in its march upon St. Valéry, and to keep General von Göben informed of the movements of the French army in Havre. Meanwhile the 1st corps, with General Manteuffel, remained in Rouen, whilst General von Göben swept the whole of north-western Normandy. The column of General Gneisenau was destined to retire upon the main body, which continued its march eastward, by way of Dieppe, sweeping the country before it as it advanced, collecting the arms of the national guard, and levying contributions.

A glance at the map will easily indicate the position. The 15th division, having performed its duty to the south and east of Rouen, would march eastward also, and be in readiness to effect a junction with the other division, in case General Farre, with the remainder of his troops, from the neighbourhood of Arras and Lille, should choose to act on the aggressive. By this manœuvre it will be seen that the garrisons of Lille, Arras, and Doullens were reduced to helplessness; for the troops in them were not only isolated, but cut off from all supplies except what they could get by sea. Meantime the French troops at Havre could do nothing in a southerly direction on this side of the Seine, unless they attacked Manteuffel before Rouen. That was scarcely probable; but, if they did, it would only sign the death-warrant of another body of French soldiers. General Briand could, however, make a movement *viâ* Honfleur to the south of the Seine, and, forming a junction with other troops to the eastward, bring a formidable body to bear upon any point east of Rouen. Such, then, was the state of affairs in the north of France at this time.

On the morning of the 13th we marched into St. Valéry, and the troops of General von Göben had the satisfaction of seeing the sea, many of them for the first time in their lives. I hope not to be accused of weakness, if I say that I gazed longingly across the waters to the land of my birth, where, five months ago, I left behind wife and children. Even at the risk of being thought romantic and homesick, I confess that I was deeply moved as I stood upon the end of the little jetty of St. Valéry, and looked across towards old England.

Then I turned round to contemplate the scene that was being enacted inland. Already the beach was covered with Prussian soldiers—some tasting the water to see if it was really salt; others gazing with wonder as the heavy swell dashed the curling wave of the ebb against the pebbly beach; some inspecting the French fishing-boats. Close to one of these a little group was gathered, and I drew near to hear what they were saying. '*Vat is dat für ein Ding?*' asked one in the most approved Platt-Deutsch, eyeing a French lugger curiously from stern to stern. '*Ein Schiff*,' sententiously responds his companion. 'Of course,' says the first speaker; 'but which end goes first?'—adding, 'for on the Rhine both ends are alike.' 'Ah,' says his companion, 'but then, you know, sea-ships have always a square end and a sharp end.' '*Warum?*' inquires the first. 'O, well, because they are sea-ships.'

The little battery on the pier was being manned with Prussian guns, as a precaution against the arrival during the night of any of the enemy's cruisers; and the artillery horses, very unwillingly, were being led into the sea to cool and refresh their legs. They too, like the men, tried to drink the water. The lanterns on the pier-head were carefully put under sentry; not one was to be lighted. The telegraphs were cut, and the signal station of the coastguard occupied by a patrol of hussars. St. Valéry is but a poor little fishing town, and the resources of the inhabitants were now subjected to a severe test; but the march upon Dieppe next day relieved the poor creatures.

The troops of General von Göben marched into Dieppe on the afternoon of the 14th of December, having come from St. Valéry, a distance of twenty-five English miles, in a little under seven hours. Pretty good marching this for men who had made the rapid stretches to which the 8th corps had been subjected for the last three weeks. No time for the garde mobile to burrow in the ground; no time for them even to concentrate on the roads. And this was all done in heavy marching order, with ninety rounds of ball cartridge, over a heavy road.

The English colony of Dieppe had been expecting us for some days; and I am glad to find that my ideas of the discipline and soldier-like appearance of the Prussian troops have been fully borne out by the opinion of several old English officers who resided here. The town of Dieppe, although full of troops from end to end, looked as if not a soldier were in it. There was no brawling in the streets; no cries of drunken soldiers annoyed the repose of the inhabitants; at 9.30 P.M., nothing but the heavy surf on the sea-shore, or the challenge of the sentries, with here and there the footstep of some inhabitant, disturbed the stillness. The English portion of the community — which was, by the way, not a small proportion—had had rather a rough time of it since Count Dohna, with his cavalry, left the previous week.

To cite an instance of the absurd fancies and ridiculous ideas that filled the heads of the inhabitants here: the English vice-consul was seen speaking to a Prussian officer; the conversation was a short one, inasmuch as our countryman only wished to ascertain the name of the officer commanding the troops, which the Prussian kindly wrote for him on his card. The careful and intelligent citizen who, before the Prussian vedettes made their appearance, was going to defend the second watering-place in France to the last cartridge, but changed his mind and received the invader with a smile on his countenance, proceeds at once to the mayor and reports the English officer as a spy—an informer in league with the Prussians. To such an extent had this piece of absurdity been carried, that the French vowed—when I say the French, I mean the lower classes—to burn every Englishman's house upon the departure of the Prussian troops. This was no mere hearsay, for I had myself had ocular proof that, upon the first opportunity, they would do as much mischief as possible. It was therefore as well that her Majesty's Government sent a ship of war over to protect the interests of some 1000 of her Majesty's subjects, who from social and commercial circumstances were utterly unable to leave Dieppe.

The first English paper I took up after my arrival here was one of the 5th December, containing the telegram of General Briand regarding the action and victory, as he calls it, of Etrepagny. In order that my readers may have some idea of the extent of injury which some English papers did at this time by their absurd and wilful belief of what was untrue, I will give you a concise description of this 'glorious victory.' A squadron of Saxon cavalry occupied the town of Etrepagny at about four o'clock one afternoon. The horses were stabled and fed, the guards posted on the outskirts, and the men went to their quarters, and eventually to bed. No sooner had the inhabitants made certain that the tired soldiers slept, than a daring citizen stole to the church, situated in the centre of the town, and opened the door. Immediately from out the sacred edifice there poured a battalion of gardes mobiles. Still and quiet as the dead they loaded, and then proceeded to butcher the unfortunate persons in their beds. A truly glorious victory! No doubt, whilst in the church, these mobiles had prayed fervently to their patron saint, if they had such, to aid them in this dastardly deed; no doubt General Briand chuckled in his sleeve when he covered this work of murder with the name of victory. But it cost Etrepagny somewhat dear; for the Saxon troops were not very long in avenging their murdered comrades, and all that now remains of a once flourishing country town is a heap of smoking ruins.

General von Göben treated the English residents of Dieppe with every kindness consistent with the customs and necessities of war; and I do not think there is a single person who has a word of complaint to make upon this subject. In every possible way the Prussian officers endeavoured to show the respect they had for her Majesty's subjects; and when the men were quartered in an English resident's house, their conduct was beyond all praise.

Whatever part the French press may have had in

the responsibility of prolonging a grievous and disastrous war—no small share, I allow—there was another influence, equally great in its magnitude, and immeasurable in its influence, which induced the people of this country to continue an almost hopeless struggle. This was the gross ignorance and want of education which pervaded the masses of the French people, and which induced them implicitly to believe in almost any man who, rising out of those masses, possessed a certain amount of cultivated talent, that, according to his disposition, might be made productive either of good or of detriment to his country. In politics as in religion the French peasant never allows his mind to dwell upon a subject which he has left, as he expresses it, for wiser heads than his own to determine. As the priest tells his flock that they are not to question or reason upon the subjects of religion, which are only for the elect, so the politician has trained the minds of the masses to accustom themselves to take for granted what their representatives may think fit to promulgate.

The French peasant of Picardy and Normandy, when told to 'mobilise' in the flaming words of Gambetta, never permitted himself to discuss the decree of this supreme ruler. M. Gambetta ordered certain things; that was sufficient. So the peasant sholdered his *tabatière*, went to fight for *liberté, égalité, et fraternité*, received a bullet through the head after having let off his weapon three or four times with his eyes shut—and consequently, in all probability, in the air—and left a wife and little ones to mourn and starve at home. I say the peasant, because you did not find that the middle classes were at all inclined to allow themselves to be killed; they had moved about in the world a little more, they had received a certain amount of education, and they dared to judge for themselves.

When M. Gambetta shouted '*Vive la République! Vive la France!*' from his rostrum, he was no more a republican than I am; for he reserved to himself and his colleagues the right of dictating measures, and of influencing a class of people who, he knew, had not education enough to grasp his motives. If there was to be liberty, then must the peasant, so far as his capabilities will allow, have the liberty of a certain amount of education; if fraternity was to exist, then the brother must not lead or drive the brother to death; and as to equality, when the voices of a few self-constituted persons represented the government of the country, equality could hardly exist, because those who swayed the destinies of the nation were unequally chosen, and maintained a position which the voice of the country had never given, and which reasonable France repudiated.

CHAPTER XI.

THE BATTLES IN THE NORTH.

It will now be seen that the object of the Prussian commanders had been achieved. The line of the Somme was occupied by a sufficiently strong force, with a certain amount of support from the Saxons and what troops could be spared at a pinch from Paris. It was therefore necessary, first of all, to keep General Briand inside Havre, and General Faidherbe, who had succeeded Farre in his command on the north side of the Somme, from making any aggressive movement southward. General Graf Gröben with his cavalry occupied the capital of Picardy, and General von Göben marched with the 16th division to requisition the country north of Rouen, and arrived, as I detailed in the preceding chapter, in Dieppe.

The day before the Prussians left Dieppe her Majesty's gunboat Helicon, Commander Johnson, made her appearance off the harbour. It was a nasty misty morning; there was not even wind enough to blow out the Union Jack on board. Prussian guns commanded the entrance to the harbour, and Prussian infantry were on guard right and left of the ship. As the Helicon approached, there was for some time considerable uncertainty as to her nationality. An Englishman, commanding a collier from Cardiff, went so far as to declare to the Prussian officer commanding that he was certain it was a French gunboat under American colours. The officer, naturally supposing that an English sailor ought to know best, desired the guard to fire in the air, in order to prevent a nearer approach; and there is no knowing what mischief might have ensued, through the Englishman's erroneous information, had not an officer of Prussian engineers recognised in the supposed American flag the Union Jack. I need hardly add that the Helicon came in directly there was water enough to float her, and that two officers immediately waited upon Captain Johnson to offer their apologies for the blunder that had been committed.

Dieppe has some huge tobacco manufactories; these were ordered to produce a certain quantity of tobacco for the use of the 8th corps. It appears, however, that Monsieur le Maire raised some difficulties, and at ten on the morning of the 15th not an ounce of tobacco had yet been given to the German troops. Monsieur le Maire then put in an appearance *in propriâ personâ*, and declared that it was utterly impossible to comply with the German commander's orders. The raw material was in the manufactory, he admitted, but there was not sufficient time to manufacture it. His excellency was very sorry indeed that M. le Maire had not thought of this before, because it now became his painful duty to ask for 120,000 fr., which the town must pay before nine the next morning, else M. le Maire and his colleagues would be marched off as prisoners.

All that evening there was a great deal of running to and fro, but without any result; for at nine the next morning, when the troops were preparing to march, those only excepted that had been told-off for the especial benefit of M. le Maire, but half the fine had come to hand. At nine A.M. the horses were brought round as usual, punctual to the moment. The staff-officers stood in front of the Hôtel Royal in groups, smoking their cigars, laughing and talking. The general made his appearance in the balcony, glancing uneasily at his watch. No sign, however, of the balance of the fine. The authorities of Dieppe then got a respite of an hour. If, however, the fine were not paid by ten o'clock, their fate was inevitable. At length, just at the clock was on the stroke, four black-coated gentlemen, with the Legion of Honour in their button-holes, escorted by a subdivision of the 40th, made their appearance. Having marched up to the hotel, they were ushered into the presence of the general. They brought with them nearly the whole amount, some 20,000 fr. being still wanting. This the general told them they could bring on that evening to Neufchâtel, upon which we were then marching, taking only their words of honour as a guarantee. For the credit of Frenchmen, let me say the promise of the mayor was punctually kept, the intendant of the army receiving the money at Neufchâtel at the appointed hour.

Before leaving Dieppe, I must mention how the brave and valiant Sous-Préfet de la Seine Inférieure kept the promise he made in the high-sounding proclamation with which he prefaced his departure. In this precious document he stated that the rapid advance of the enemy compelled him to leave Dieppe, but that he went to do his duty as a soldier and a patriot in the ranks of the army of the Loire. He left his townsmen, of course, with tears in his eyes, buoyed up, however, by the consciousness that he was about to defend his country elsewhere. That day the English packet took Monsieur le Sous-Préfet to Newhaven, where, for aught I know, he is still to be seen. '*Si monumentum quæris, circumspice!*'

Just before the Helicon left Havre, an American vessel with 50,000 stand of arms came into port. Truly Uncle Sam never lets the grass grow under his feet. I had a somewhat interesting conversation with an American colonel and his family, who were residing *pro tem.* at Dieppe. Referring at that time to President Grant's tendering the services of the American fleet to Russia, in case of another European difficulty, he said: 'I guess it ain't true, 'cause our policy is not to meddle in anything Eu-ro-pe-an.' His remarks anent M. Gambetta were certainly not flattering to that gentleman; and as to the export of arms from America, his only comment was that his countrymen were 'doing a good trade.'

On the 16th we entered Neufchâtel. In these high-pressure days of campaigning, you cannot be very particular as to where you lay your weary bones to rest; you must be prepared to sleep either in a bedroom or a cow-shed. But, if there is one thing that makes a quarter more disagreeable than another, it is an infectious disease. Imagine, then, the feelings of his excellency when he was told that in the particular house appropriated for himself and staff the smallpox raged. O, it was very little use changing, even if it were possible, said an amiable old woman; for it was the same wherever you went. Now, I individually hate smallpox—a feeling, I may say, I extend to all infectious diseases. I not only hate them, but I am very much afraid of them. I had infinitely rather face a battalion of Francs-tireurs than a very little boy with the smallpox. Imagine, therefore, the delight with which I heard that I was quartered in the house opposite. Repairing to my *logis*, I was met, cap in hand, by a venerable schoolmaster, who bored me with bad English while showing me the way to my room. I was just going to open a door, when the schoolmaster threw himself frantically before me, exclaiming, '*Pas là, monsieur, il y a la petite-vérole.*' I did not exactly beat a hasty retreat, but I positively rushed out of the house, and remained standing in the middle of the street, not exactly knowing which way to turn, until I was found in this unhappy condition by the quartermaster-general. It was no use, for the whole town of Neufchâtel was in the same state; so, trusting to vaccination and several bottles of champagne, I managed to sleep the night through in some way or other.

The next morning my orderly brought me a message from an English lady who wished to see me in the Hôtel Dieu. Accordingly thither I repaired, and in a large room, where lay fourteen wounded

Prussian soldiers from the affair of the 4th, I found a quiet, pleasant, ladylike-looking person talking to the Sœurs de Charité that surrounded her. As I entered, she came forward, and, holding out both hands, exclaimed, 'And are you really English?' Kind reader, pardon the bull. 'Very much, indeed,' I answered, 'if Irish will do as well.' I think she would have kissed me, if the sisters had not been there; for she had one of those dear, kind, good old English faces, looking out from under a mass of snow-white hair, that made me think of the hearts and home I had left behind me. She told me she had lived for twenty years in Neufchâtel, and was married to the judge; that she had taken care of the Prussian wounded, and had found the Prussian soldiers orderly, quiet, and well-behaved beyond her imagination. I was then asked if it were really true that the King of Prussia was a prisoner, that Ducrot and Vinoy were advancing against Manteuffel, and that the Prussians were in full retreat upon Metz. Such were the reports that the self-established French Government circulated in order to bring more misery upon their ill-fated country.

From Neufchâtel we marched to St. Samson, on the road to Amiens, leaving the seacoast towards Abbeville and Tréport unsearched, for the purpose, no doubt, of making a junction with the 15th division in the neighbourhood of Amiens. It will be obvious, even to the most unskilled observer, that the manœuvres of the 8th corps tended but to one end. The decisive action of the 27th of November, with the occupation of Amiens, had served to make a considerable impression upon General Farre's troops, who retreated upon Arras. Taking advantage of this success, the 1st and 8th corps marched upon Rouen so rapidly, that General Briand had scarce time to withdraw his troops to Havre; and Rouen, with the exception of the affairs at Buchy and Bose Bordel —which are hardly worth mentioning—fell into the Prussian general's hands without opposition. Meantime the shattered troops of General Farre, now superseded in his command, having received a new general, massed in the neighbourhood of Péronne, Arras, and Doullens. The Prussian tactics throughout had been always to attack—never to permit time for large bodies of troops to concentrate; hence the march of the 8th corps in this direction, for the enemy were threatening Amiens. The French general again made a great mistake; for, had he wished, he could have repossessed himself of the capital of Picardy and regained the line of the Somme during the absence of the first army, inasmuch as it was held by a brigade of cavalry only and two companies of infantry.

It had been the intention of the Prussian commander to direct his troops upon Beauvais, to the south of Amiens, as it was rumoured that General Faidherbe, who had lately assumed the command of the army of the north, intended masking Amiens and marching directly upon Paris. But the large bodies of troops which were concentrating upon the Somme at Corbie induced General Manteuffel to alter his intentions; and on the 18th of December, on a bitterly cold day, instead of marching on Beauvais, as was originally intended, General von Göben received orders during the night to proceed to Crèvecœur. It was rumoured that this change was owing to a threatened movement of the enemy upon Amiens. We also heard upon arrival in Crèvecœur that Poix was occupied by Francs-tireurs, probably a detached party of those who were holding Abbeville. The inhabitants of this ancient town had been in a high state of excitement, in consequence of the sound of heavy guns having been heard the day previous and that morning in the direction of Montdidier; but as no intelligence came, it was concluded that the matter was not so serious as represented.

The little town of Crèvecœur, in ancient days the property of the Sieur de Crèvecœur, was the scene of one of those tournaments at which the Chevalier Bayard, *sans peur et sans réproche*, is said to have assisted. The family of Crèvecœur, it appears, made an alliance with the ancient and noble family of Rochefoucauld, who eventually became possessed of Crèvecœur and its dependencies, and in 1400 built the vast château of the same name, in which General von Göben and his staff were quartered. In a letter to the *Daily Telegraph* the château of Crèvecœur is thus described:

'I write you these lines from the "Chambre des Archevêques"—a large grim old room, with a huge fireplace, and a niche in the wall, where my bed is now being made up. The old judge who has bought this portion of the château, and who remembers the occupation of Crèvecœur by the Prussians in 1815, has been sitting opposite to me, telling me many curious and interesting stories of the old castle we inhabit. It appears that the powerful family of Rochefoucauld were some years ago, after their intermarriage with the Duc de Liancourt, compelled, from straitened circumstances, to sell the old château, where so many barons and bishops of the name had held almost feudal sway. The main body of the building was divided into six lots, one of which was purchased by my host, who for many years filled the office of Juge de Paix. He remembers the visit of the beautiful Duchess of Rochefoucauld-Liancourt, the last of the family that visited Crèvecœur. The old gentleman has just gone to bed, leaving me alone in this large and lofty chamber. As the wind shakes the window-sashes, and comes moaning down the great chimney, I almost fancy that I hear strange footsteps behind my back, that I can detect whisperings behind the ragged tapestry which still flutters upon the walls. But my solitude is unbroken; no ghost of mail-clad warrior or mitred bishop disturbs my peace.'

The feeling in this part of the country (Département de l'Oise) was strangely at variance with that of Normandy. Here we found very strong Bourbon tendencies; whilst the memory of the Citizen King was revered and worshipped. Here the people hoped for the Duc d'Aumale, and sincerely trusted that Republicanism was not to be the form of government upon which the future prosperity and reconstruction of France was to rest.

It would appear that General Graf Gröben had left Amiens almost to take care of itself, in consequence of information which he had received that the enemy were marching upon Montdidier and Compiègne; and, had the 8th corps not been so handy, a very serious misfortune might at this time have occurred. The 15th division was, however, already close to the capital of Picardy, and the 16th on the 19th of December marched up Ailly-sur-Noye.

On the afternoon of the 19th December we marched over the old ground that we had already crossed on the 27th of November, previous to the battle of Amiens. All along the road no intelligence could be obtained respecting the sound of cannon which had been heard; but we were told that Amiens had been reoccupied by a brigade without opposition, although during the absence of the Prussian troops the Francs-tireurs had pushed their reconnaissances up to the suburbs. The citadel was held by two companies of German infantry, supported by the guns in position; but beyond this there were no troops to defend Amiens.

The same afternoon General Barnekow occupied Poix, which had been evacuated the evening before by the Francs-tireurs, who retired in the direction of Molliens-Vidame and Picquigny. The enemy was said to be in force along the Somme, between Corbie and Bray-sur-Somme, to the number of 40,000, with 28 guns and some cavalry regiments—though where the latter came from it was impossible to say. It would therefore appear that the French generals contemplated making a movement in force southwards, by menacing the capital of Picardy from the direction of Corbie. This point was, however, determined by the advance upon Amiens of the next day, and the reconnaissance which took place.

Along the road to the left of which, on the 27th of November, thundered the combats of Hérbecourt and Dury, and to the right those of Boves and Gentelles, General von Göben and his staff rode towards Amiens. Reports continued to arrive during the morning of the enemy's patrols having been seen at Longeau and in the neighbourhood. The long lines of rifle-pits and the batteries on the road to St. Fuscien were being levelled, probably by the very men who had helped to construct them; bodies of discontented, ill-conditioned-looking workmen were scattered over the undulating landscape that, without hedge or wall, surrounds Amiens on this side. It was like a return to old familiar quarters, so pleasant did the sight of the cathedral appear to our eyes.

Early in the afternoon we entered Amiens—not a moment too soon; for as we shook ourselves into our places, and once more opened our portmanteaus—a luxury not always enjoyed—the report of brisk firing in the neighbourhood of Allonville was borne to our ears. The cause was soon explained. A reconnaissance, composed of a battalion of the 4th regiment, two squadrons of cavalry, and a battery of artillery, had advanced to the neighbourhood of Allonville and Querrieux. The village of Allonville lies to the left of the road to Albert, Querrieux to the right. They are both situated upon eminences, and between them is a somewhat thick wood. This was the French position; and so strong were they, that casualties to the number of fourteen killed and fifty-four wounded in the infantry battalion alone were reported this evening.

It is a fatal mistake not to *compel* troops to retire when only a reconnaissance is meant. The task is difficult, I admit, but it is in such moments that the greatest loss is suffered. The fall of each comrade awakens a dare-devil spirit of revenge; and I can quite imagine the feelings of the men of the 4th regiment when they were ordered to retire. The French of course followed nearly to Rivery; when the heavy masses of the main body, and the threatening position of the cavalry, with the fire of the Prussian artillery, sent them flying back along the road to Querrieux. It would appear from the reconnaissance, with the intelligence brought in from other quarters, that the line of the French operations extended from Doullens, through Achieux and Albert, on to Peronne. There were heavy bodies of troops at Corbie and Bray-sur-Somme. The former place was held by four line regiments, one battalion of Turcos, two squadrons of cavalry, and twenty guns.

The enemy retreated from the neighbourhood of Roye and Nesle across the Somme, northward of La Fère, towards Peronne; so that any movement of French troops southwards was, to all intents and purposes, negatived, and the French generals were now confronted by Manteuffel and Von Göben, with the chance of avenging the battle of Amiens. They were strong in numbers, they held a good position, and had ample time to complete their arrangements, in addition to being now commanded by a man who, had he been properly supported, would in all probability have achieved much for his country. In General Faidherbe the Prussian commanders found a brave man and a skilful soldier, nor was General von Göben behindhand in acknowledging his admiration at the way he manœuvred his ill-conditioned army without cavalry and deficient in commissariat. The French outposts were at Coisy, Allonville, Querrieux, Daours, Vecquemont, Aubigny, and Corbie. They had had an outpost in an old mill before Villers-Bretonneux, but it was withdrawn across the Somme. St. Quentin was occupied by the Saxons.

Talking of Villers-Bretonneux, I must not omit to contradict some French statements to the effect, that the German troops were guilty of gross barbarities and useless cruelty after the battle of the 27th of November, in burning some villages in the neighbourhood of Villers-Bretonneux, and treating the inhabitants with dreadful cruelty. I beg most distinctly to affirm that no such thing occurred; and in this statement I am borne out by the English officers connected with the British Society for the aid of the wounded in Amiens, who were themselves present at and after the action. The villages of Villers-Bretonneux, Cachy, Gentelles, and those in the neighbourhood, were all held by the French, and were made as defensible as possible. Naturally, therefore, these villages were shelled by the Prussian artillery, and shelling is a process always liable to set a town or village on fire. In Cachy, if I recollect right, three or four houses only were burnt from artillery fire; but the other villages in no way suffered.

It appears that our arrival in Amiens was none

too soon; for whilst the town was unoccupied the 'roughs' evidently meant mischief. They made a rush in a considerable body upon the museum, a fine modern building, containing much valuable property; and, had it not been for the firmness of the mayor, serious results might have ensued. On the 22d the position of the enemy remained unchanged, the Prussian patrols receiving fire whenever they approached the French outposts. Prince Bentheim, of the King's hussars, was wounded before Blangy—a bullet through the arm. The 8th corps was now reinforced by three battalions from Rouen; and it was determined that the French position near the Somme should be vigorously attacked on every side. There seemed to be a slight disposition on the part of the French to withdraw their troops from so close a proximity to Amiens; but for all that a battle was inevitable.

The great festive season of the year had come. All England was merry-making. Every family had its rendezvous, and bright faces, blazing fires, groaning tables, mirth and laughter were to be seen and heard on every side. So it was in England; let me describe a somewhat different picture in France.

I have already described the position of the armies, French and German, before it had been definitely settled to attack the French forces under Generals Faidherbe and Le Coing. But it is necessary to state that the Prussian troops engaged in this action did not exceed 18,000 infantry. These were composed of the 15th and 16th divisions of the 8th corps whilst the French forces numbered 60,000 men and sixty pieces of cannon.

The morning of the 23d of December was bitterly cold—the frost most intense. As we got upon our horses at eight A.M.—many of us for the last time in this world—the 15th division, under General Kummer, crossed the Somme by some pontoon bridges near Carnon, and, leaving Rivery to the left, formed on the plateau in front of Allonville, with the cavalry of General Count Gröben on the right. The 16th division, under General Barnekow, marched up the road to Rainneville and Pierregôt to the north of Amiens, whilst a brigade proceeded along the Somme from La Motte upon Vecquemont. General Göben's plan was to advance upon the French position of Allonville and Querrieux, and to make a strong demonstration on their centre and left flank; whilst General Barnekow, with the 16th division, after arriving at Rubempré, was to wheel round, and, having first taken the villages along the extreme right, to advance upon the French position, and endeavour to turn their right flank.

Having ridden some distance out upon the Albert road, the general and his staff dismounted, and, sending the horses to the rear, awaited the advance of the troops upon Allonville. This little village is situated upon one of those ridges of hills that lie along the east side of the valley, which stretches from Fréchencourt past Querrieux to Corbie. A magnificent sight truly to behold the troops advancing. The 29th brigade, commanded by Colonel von Boch, and composed of the 33d and 65th regiments, with artillery, and one squadron of the King's hussars, marched forward to the right of the farm of Les Alençons; the 30th brigade, with the 70th and 28th regiments, and two batteries of artillery, advanced upon the left of Allonville, covered by a regiment of lancers; whilst Count Gröben's dragoons moved along the crest of the hill looking across to the heights, on the other side, above Corbie.

Steadily, as if on parade, marched the compact masses of infantry, the skirmishers in front, with their supports to the right and left of the Albert road. They took possession of the woods beside Allonville; in a moment the village was occupied; still not a French soldier was to be seen. Had the enemy, then, retreated? No; an orderly galloped up to say that the village of Querrieux in front was strongly held by the French troops. We mounted our horses and rode straight up the road to that village. At Les Alençons there is a road which leads off to the left through the village of Cardonette and on to the Pierregôt road. Along this galloped Captain Allborn with orders from General von Göben to the 16th division to change front to their right flank, and, marching across between Molliens-aux-Bois and Mirvaux, to storm the French positions in the villages of Bavelincourt, Behancourt, and Fréchencourt. This change was made in consequence of the superiority in numbers of the French troops, and the fear General von Göben had of extending his line too far with so few troops to cover the alignment. Arrived at the château of Bengerie, we saw the French tirailleurs retiring upon Querrieux. The 29th brigade then brought their left shoulders forward, two batteries of artillery took up position on the right, and at ten minutes past eleven the first shot was fired by the French infantry from a windmill to the right of Querrieux.

So the battle of Pont-Noyelles commenced. By twelve (noon) the village was stormed, and the French had retreated upon their position. What a position! Who would have expected nature to have supplied defences better than those of the best engineer? The French right rested on a wood, situated upon the brow of a range of steep hills, whose right spur looks down upon Conty and Vadencourt. Drawing a line from here through the village of La Houssoye, and on to La Neuville, upon which the French left stood, you have along this whole extent an elevated plateau; and the plateau thus situated was held by 50,000 or 60,000 men, and by some sixty pieces of artillery. The position of the Prussians occupying the lower ridge opposite was anything but pleasant. The French batteries all along the plateau, especially that to the right of the village of La Houssoye, kept up a determined and well-directed fire upon Querrieux. Meantime, to the right, the villages of Daours, Vecquemont, and Bussy had been taken by the Prussians, the French retiring upon their intrenched position in front of Corbie. The fighting here was also hard, for both sides appealed to the bayonet to settle the disputed possession of the villages.

At two P.M. the enemy, under a heavy fire of artillery, endeavoured to retake the village of Querrieux. Hard indeed was the struggle between French and Germans. For nearly twenty minutes they fought actually looking into one another's eyes. But the French again retired, and again their five batteries of thirty guns at La Houssoye opened a crushing fire on the Prussian line. Every eye was now anxiously turned to the left flank, but as yet there were no signs of Barnekow's division. The Prussians were very weak before Querrieux, and the reserve was ordered to move up to the left of that village. The 30th brigade deployed in the valley and took a small village, into which the French poured a shower of shell and shrapnel from their batteries to the right of the Albert road.

And now the space between Querrieux and Bengerie commenced to fill with those tell-tales of an action—carts and carriages of all descriptions, bearing ghastly burdens to the rear. The British Society were represented by two wagons, which were accompanied by Colonel Cox, C.B., and Captain Uniacke, with Doctors Leslie and Goodenough. These gentlemen had taken up their quarters in a small house some quarter of a mile from Querrieux. In this house was also the Princess Salm, who, with a large apron tied round her dress, assisted Surgeon-General Busch. Fortunate it was that the English wagons were there; for they supplied blankets to cover the poor suffering soldiers, whose wounds were made still more painful by the keen biting frost and intensely cold winds. They also brought out food, which the Princess had cooked with her own hands.

About this time, 2.30 P.M., the French made a strong demonstration between La Neuville and Daours.

The French guns to the left of La Houssoye took ground there, whence they opened a heavy fire upon our right flank, a considerable body of troops at the same time advancing as if to retake Bussy. But Captain Fuchius's battery of horse artillery galloped to the right, unlimbered, and opened such a hot fire upon the advancing enemy, that first of all the infantry halted, then faced to the right-about, and eventually doubled to the rear, in a most orderly manner, the French artillery quickly following their example.

At 2.40 I rode off to, the heights by St. Gratien, and as I got there the welcome sound of General Barnekow's artillery greeted my expectant ears. Soon I could see his troops advancing on the village of Fréchencourt from the Conty road, and I galloped back to inform the general of this important fact. At 4 P.M. the 16th division had stormed the villages of Bavelincourt, Behancourt, and Fréchencourt; but their farther advance was stopped by the same formidable position which had brought the 15th division to a halt.

The whole Prussian army now held a line of villages in a valley through which flowed a small tributary of the Somme—the Hallu—which tributary formed the line of demarcation between the two armies. On the other side of this stream, a natural glacis extended to the summit of the ridge of hills occupied by the French army. Up this glacis, with 60,000 troops at the top, and fifty or sixty guns, it was both too late and too dangerous to advance; so the artillery pelted away at one another, whilst the skirmishers of both armies kept up an incessant fire, a distance of but 300 yards between them.

Meantime the village of Querrieux was held by two battalions of the 33d and 65th regiments. Again and again had the French tried to retake it, without success. At 4·45 I entered Querrieux for the purpose of bringing some comforts to a wounded friend. Whilst I was in the house in which he lay a furious fire was opened upon the village, and my orderly came rushing up to tell me that, if we did not make haste, we should be taken prisoners, as the French had again attacked Querrieux, and the 65th were retiring. As I got to the street-door, the last sections of the 65th were slowly falling back, whilst at the other end of the village I could see the dark uniforms of the chasseurs advancing. I made a rush at my horse, and scrambled into the saddle; but just at that moment the French chasseurs received a murderous fire from the 33d, who advanced upon them from the cross streets with the bayonet, and once more drove them back pell-mell out of the village.

The 33d and the 65th were now nearly destitute of ammunition, and in this fact is to be found the cause for the momentary retreat by the latter to which I have just alluded; but the gallant fellows would not give up the position so dearly bought at the price of many precious lives, and there they stood, each man in his place, determined to make cold steel take the place of ball-cartridge. It was now dark, the Prussian artillery had ceased firing, and the village of Querrieux was in flames in four places. Six companies of the 33d regiment determined to avenge the last attack made by the French. In the dark they stole out of the village, formed line, and at the point of the bayonet charged up to the French battery on the right of the Albert road. They had spiked two guns and taken the horses, when they were attacked by five French battalions, before whom they were forced to retire into Querrieux, the French following so closely upon them that at one moment I thought the village was lost. By this time, however, the 65th, having received ammunition, drove the French back with a withering fire.

And now it was 5.30. The battle of Pont-Noyelles was over, the Prussians having taken seven villages, 900 prisoners, a lieutenant-colonel, and a post-captain in the navy, who was jocosely asked why he had not brought his ship with him. Their loss was between 1000 and 1200 killed and wounded. The French fought uncommonly well, and great credit was due to their artillery, which was well served; but then it must be remembered they greatly outnumbered the Prussian troops, and, as usual, held a magnificent position. They still occupied that position, and as we got upon our horses, their bugles were sounding the assembly. We rode back to Amiens, our road lighted by the blazing village of Querrieux, whilst a French battery to the left was firing a parting salvo in the darkness. The 23d of December 1870 will long be remembered as the day on which was fought one of the severest actions of the campaign.

On Christmas-day the French still occupied the line of heights from Corbie to Franvillers, whilst the 8th corps held the ground below the French position on the other side of the valley. Each army could observe the position of the other, clearly marked by the lines of bivouac fires that burnt brightly in the intensely frosty atmosphere, at intervals of 1500 to 2000 yards.

The next morning, at 7.30, Generals von Göben and Manteuffel left Amiens for the field of battle. General Manteuffel riding to the 15th and General von Göben to the 16th division. As we came upon the ground occupied by the reserve of the 16th division, the French batteries on the heights of Franvillers were busily engaged in shelling a body of the Sanitäts-corps, who were endeavouring to bring in some of the wounded. These poor fellows had lain out in the plain all night, and many of them died from exposure. You can imagine their sufferings when I tell you that wine and beer were frozen, although in a barrel and packed in straw. The French commander can have no excuse for this piece of barbarity, for the distance was certainly not more than 2500 yards—the French being on the heights, the Prussians in the plain. It is an episode in this action of Pont-Noyelles which will add one more to the already numerous instances of atrocity to be laid to the account of the French Republican army.

As we rode round to Querrieux, through the valley and between the two armies, the curious sight presented itself of 60,000 French troops, with 60 or 70 cannon, looking down upon 24,000 Prussians with 40 guns. There stood the heavy masses of the French infantry, drawn up along the brow of the hill, with their batteries right and left of the brigades, covered by cavalry; there stretched a long line of tirailleurs covering the whole front, keeping up a constant fire, wherever there was a chance, upon the valley below. On the German side all was still. The troops stood to their arms, the artillery was unlimbered, the cavalry kept their bridles over their arms; but not a shot was fired. Why this inaction? The Prussians were too weak to attack the powerful force opposed to them, whilst every moment they expected to be attacked by the French. It had been surmised that General Barnekow would be detached to the French right, in order, if possible, to turn their position—for an attack upon Franvillers from Fréchencourt would have been an impossibility; but the day wore on, and the two armies stood still, silently confronting one another.

About this time we received intelligence that his Highness Prince Albrecht was coming from Paris with a cavalry division of the guard. News also arrived that General Schüler von Senden, with a division, was advancing in the direction of Corbie from St. Quentin. Things began to look brighter; and those who had whispered something about being compelled to abandon our position of the 23d, which had been so dearly bought, began to think what they had said was rather stupid. In fact one gentleman went so far as to tell his friend, whose tone was rather despondent, not to make a fool of himself. At 2.30 Prince Albrecht with his staff arrived, and great was the rejoicing, although cavalry could do but little against such a position; and so the day wore on, evening again falling upon both sides still silently confronting one another.

During the day I visited Querrieux—just below

Pont-Noyelles, after which the battle has been named. In the former village 670 killed and wounded had lain during the night. If one desired to see what some people call the 'horrors' of war, but what men of sense are in the habit of styling the 'necessities' of a battle, you had a good opportunity for doing so in this little village of Picardy. Shell, bullet, and bayonet had all been at work, and their melancholy products lay around. Truly the German adage, 'You cannot cut wood without splinters falling,' was clearly exemplified.

One or two little exploits during the battle now came to my ears, of which I shall give some account, as they prove the unwearying perseverance and cool courage of the Prussian troops. Lieutenant von Knesebeck, of the 7th hussars—better known by English people as the Bonn hussars, or the King's hussars—was on patrol duty on the evening of the 23d, to the right of the Albert road. He perceived a French outpost carelessly cooking round a fire, and at once determined upon the somewhat rash exploit of cutting them out under the very muzzles of their own guns. He accordingly advanced upon the unsuspecting moblots in skirmishing order, and, when within a hundred yards of the picket, he bade his bugler sound the assembly, and rode straight at them. Some six or seven were killed, the rest were made prisoners, and brought into the Prussian lines before they knew where they were. Again, his excellency General von Göben sent a company of Jägers and a squadron of lancers to feel the French left flank by Vecquemont. As I have already told you, the French held a strong position, in considerable numbers, between Corbie and Daours. Nevertheless, the handful of Prussian troops advanced against this position and made a thorough reconnaissance of it. Again, Colonel von Löe and Major Levinzki, the former commanding the Bonn hussars, and the latter one of General Manteuffel's staff, rode alone before their men into the village of Daours, in order to ascertain if the French had really been driven out. As they proceeded down a by-street, they were saluted by a loud '*Qui vive?*' and a whole column of chasseurs immediately after made its appearance, and opened fire upon them. I am thankful to say they both escaped unhurt; for it would have been indeed a severe loss if two such distinguished officers—the former especially, who is as much beloved and respected by the whole army as he is by his own regiment—had been lost to their country.

Nine hundred and fifty prisoners and 19 officers were officially returned as having been taken from the enemy. The Prussian loss was 800 killed and wounded, among whom were 26 officers killed and wounded.

Evening at last came to close this curious day. It has been said that, after a battle has been fought, each ensign could give a better opinion, or make a better movement, than the general commanding; but this is not a question of movements of troops—it is a question of the commonest tactics of one army in front of another. General Faidherbe, at the battle of Pont-Noyelles, commanded forces, taking the computation of his own officers, three times as strong as the corps of General von Göben. He had the most magnificent position nature could give him, and was assisted by a powerful and well-served artillery. But I have to say he permitted the whole of the 24th of December to slip by without doing a single thing, and in the end he retired on Arras. Now, supposing that he had even received intelligence that General von Senden was advancing to his left rear, and that the Prussian army had received reinforcements, he never tried to ascertain this by any reconnaissance upon either flank. Had he made a strong reconnaissance towards the Prussian right flank, or crossed the Somme at Fouilloy with 20,000 men, whom he could have well spared, and marched upon Amiens, the Prussians would have been forced to retire upon that town. But no; he wasted a whole day, permitting General von Senden to advance, and the Prussians to telegraph for reinforcements. The French troops who fought were almost all line troops and marines; therefore he had not even the poor excuse that he could not depend upon his mobiles.

At an early hour on the 26th General Manteuffel received the astounding intelligence that the French had retreated during the night. Everything was, of course, 'boot and saddle'—cavalry to the front. At high noon, the staff rode towards Albert, upon which road a brigade was advancing. At Franvillers we heard that Albert was occupied by the French troops; so that it would be necessary, if they intended remaining, to drive them out in order to get quarters for the night. As we rode through La Houssoye the dead bodies lying about and collected close by the graveyard spoke but too plainly of the carnage of the 23d. The severe frost had stiffened them into all sorts of quaint attitudes; and as we passed the churchyard, friend and foe were being buried in the same grave. Arrived at Albert, we found that General Robin with 3000 men had just left it; so that we were treading upon the heels of the retiring enemy pretty quickly. Many prisoners had been made upon the road, and the cavalry were pursuing in every direction. That evening the Prussian army occupied Bray-sur-Somme, Albert, and Hédeauville, their patrols all in front. The French were in Bapaume, and to the left and right of it.

At Albert the Prussians obtained some curious letters directed to their friends by French soldiers engaged in the battle of the 23d. The best proof of the skill with which the Prussian handful of troops were disposed is the fact that the French, as appeared from these letters, imagined they were 100,000 strong, and I put the strength of the French army down at 60,000 men and 60 guns.

At eleven in the morning the whole of the army advanced on the line of the French retreat, marching upon Bapaume.

CHAPTER XII.

THE BATTLE OF BAPAUME.

On the morning of the 26th of December, the pursuit of Faidherbe's army, who were retreating upon Arras, Douay, and Cambrai, was continued by the cavalry of Generals Mirus and Count Gröben, together with the cavalry division of the guard under Prince Albrecht. The 15th division marched upon Bapaume from Albert; and upon approaching that town, a patrol of the King's hussars surprised a train on the railway near Achiet. This Achiet is the station for Bapaume, and lies about an English mile to the left of the place. No sooner did the hussars make their appearance than the locomotive, which appeared to be waiting for its freight, steamed off to Arras. Several mobiles were, however, taken prisoners in the station, one of whom had the imprudence to fire at the patrol; but he got away without even broken bones. About half an hour before the arrival of the hussars, two trains full of soldiers had left for Arras; and the town itself had been occupied that morning by a considerable body of troops, who had marched at seven o'clock upon Cambrai and Douay. At Pozières, a village about half way between Albert and Bapaume, several prisoners were made, belonging to the 2d chasseurs and the 43d regiment of the line. They stated that, having had nothing to eat for twenty-four hours, they were quite unable to march any farther; and their condition was certainly most pitiable.

The town of Bapaume is an ancient fortress, which was dismantled after the fortifying of Arras, Doullens, and Cambrai. The works appear to have been considerable, and would even then, if defended by infantry and field artillery, have proved sufficiently inconvenient to an invader; but no attempt whatever had been made to defend the place, the French having evidently endeavoured to make the best use of their time, and retire as quickly as possible to stronger positions. The good people of Bapaume did not seem to be impressed with that enthusiastic appreciation of the defence of their hearths and homes with which one would have supposed, from the French reports, this portion of France was inspired. On the contrary, they objected very strongly to the French troops having been billeted upon them; and they still more objected to the Prussians. One unfortunate pork-butcher, who had the honour of entertaining some officers of rank, expressed himself as follows: 'Monsieur, the unluckiest news I can receive is that of a French victory; for as sure as I hear of it, so sure do the Prussian troops enter my house four hours after. I do not believe any more in French victories; and as to the advance of the Prussian troops, it is a painful reality, for they eat up everything I have in the house.'

A party of the Bonn hussars made a somewhat laughable capture. A lieutenant, with his patrol, was ordered to reconnoitre on the other side of Corbie. Whilst riding along the canal, an abrupt turn in the road brought him upon some eight or nine mobiles on the opposite side. As soon as he was perceived, the mobiles pointed their weapons at him; but the lieutenant pulled out his revolver—which, without doubt, would never have gone off—and, riding towards them pistol in hand, he summoned them to surrender and lay down their arms. Whether the moblots had had enough of campaigning, or whether the impudence of the request had the desired effect, I know not; but they submissively inquired where the officer wished them to place their rifles. 'Throw them into the canal!' was the reply. This having been done, he coolly requested them to be good enough to point out the bridge by which he could cross, in order to make them prisoners. With this intensely impudent request they also complied, and under such circumstances these brave and patriotic defenders of their country were marched off to the nearest guard. *Sic transit gloria Galliæ!*

The French military authorities now published a sort of pamphlet of instructions, which they invited every officer of mobiles to study attentively. On the titlepage was a sort of *croquis* supposed to represent the march of the Prussian troops. Had I not known that it was taken from the person of a French officer, and that it bore the impress of the Republic, I could scarcely have believed that such a document could have existed outside of *Punch* or *Kladderadatsch*.

First of all, the intelligent officer was requested to remark that, as soon as he saw three uhlans appear, this was an infallible sign that some twenty or thirty were about 800 yards in rear. Again, when he perceived twenty or thirty, he should conclude that a detachment of cavalry was close at their heels. Finally, should he see a detachment, he was at once to expect the appearance of a division or a brigade. He was farther to read, mark, learn, and inwardly digest the fact, that the Prussian troops always advanced in échelon, and that their flanks were invariably protected by uhlans, who kept up the connection between the various corps, and so enabled them at need to concentrate large bodies upon any given spot. The mobile officer was told to go and do likewise!

On the evening of the 27th the Prussian patrols were fired upon at Bucquoy on the road to Arras, and at Nareuil on the road to Douay. The enemy's rearguard was also engaged by their cavalry on the road to Cambrai. On that day we had a few hours of rest in that desolate place—made still more desolate through the shortness of provisions and the sulkiness of the inhabitants. To follow on the heels of a retreating army is by no means pleasant, especially when they take care to eat up everything in front of them. The night's rest was also disturbed by cries of '*Au feu!*' which were vociferated in the streets. A large factory was on fire, and blazed away, keeping many people warm who would otherwise have been frozen. The snow was falling steadily too, and everything looked dreary and melancholy. Prisoners continued to arrive in small detachments — wretched worn-out-looking creatures, who did not seem even fit food for powder.

The retreat of the French artillery appeared to have been as precipitate as that of the infantry. So badly were the live shells packed in the tumbrils, that this negligence caused the jolting over the uneven roads to explode them in the streets of Bapaume. The French artillery, it appears, thought the Prussian cavalry was upon them; the horses were driven into a gallop, and the shells, from the concussion, exploded in the tumbrils. The explosion of their own shells was supposed to be those of the enemy's, and the infantry commenced a still more undignified flight.

At Bapaume we learned, that General von Senden had arrived at Péronne, and that his troops lay before that ancient fortress. The batteries had been put into position, and had already opened upon the town. A flying column, composed of a battalion of the 33d fusiliers, one battery, and a squadron of cavalry, encountered the enemy upon the Cambrai road. A slight skirmish ensued; the Prussian officer, however, finding the enemy in force, ordered his men to retire after ascertaining the position of the French. Seventy-five more prisoners passed through, all looking in the same state as those I have above mentioned, half starved and ill clad.

By referring to the map, it will be seen that the town of Bapaume is situated at the apex of a triangle formed by the high-roads from Amiens and Péronne to that place, the base of the triangle being the line of the Somme. All the fortresses on this line were in Prussian hands, with the exception of Péronne; and it was therefore deemed necessary, for the more perfect occupation of this base of operations, that Péronne should also be occupied by Prussian troops. This determination was come to by General von Göben, who about this time assumed the command of the army of the Somme, which was composed of the 8th Prussian army corps, the division of General von Senden, the cavalry of Prince Albrecht, and that of General Gröben. To effect this purpose, General von Göben detached the 16th division under General Barnekow to the assistance of General von Senden, who received orders to report himself at Versailles; whilst the 15th division occupied Bapaume, so as to cover the operations upon Péronne; the whole army being still under the command of General Manteuffel.

General Faidherbe's beaten forces had taken up a position on the Scarpe, their right resting on Arras, their left on Douay. The Prussian cavalry was at Fins, with the town of Combles occupied, and the line between Bray-sur-Somme, Cléry, and Péronne held by the troops of General von Manteuffel's old corps. At two P.M. on the 28th, General Barnekow, having duly invested Péronne, commenced the bombardment of that fortress. The Prussian batteries, nine in number, mounting fifty-four guns, were in position upon the heights of Mont St. Quentin, Biaches, and Doingt. That night, as I returned from Combles, where General von Manteuffel had his headquarters, the snowy landscape was lit up by the red glare of the burning town. All night long the batteries poured an incessant fire upon the place, which was defended by 6000 men. Cambrai was reported but lightly garrisoned; and Prussian patrols and outposts were as far as Graincourt and Boursies.

Meantime Lieutenant-Colonel von Pestel had a brilliant skirmish with the enemy on the right and left bank of the Somme, on the road to Abbeville. The forces under his command consisted of one battalion of the 70th regiment and the 7th lancers, with which he attacked a body of the enemy in the neighbourhood of Hangest; and after a sharp fight, he drove the French back, taking prisoners a lieutenant-colonel, two captains, six lieutenants, and 230 men, with three standards. Fifty French dead were left upon the field. The loss of the Prussians was five wounded—three severely. Among the prisoners were twenty-five peasants in blouses, with weapons in their hands; their fate was inevitable.

On the 30th of December I wrote thus:

'*Bapaume, December 30.*

'Since the arrangement of yesterday, of which I have given you details, General von Göben has, so to say, obtained a distinct command. It is true that both he and General Bentheim, commanding the army of the Seine, retain their respective commands of the 8th and 1st corps, and that the whole of the forces, as the first army, are under General Manteuffel; but I prefer designating General von Göben's command as that of the army of the Somme, inasmuch as for the future the achievements of that corps will not be mentioned under the title of the first army. The glorious day of Querrieux was telegraphed as an achievement of the first army. It would have been nearer the truth if 8th corps had been said; for, with the exception of a small detached force, the 8th corps were the only troops engaged.

'General Faidherbe's accounts of that day were most amusing. You will perceive how diffident he was in referring to the storming of the six villages by the Prussian troops, and how delicate was his allusion to the headlong flight of the French troops, which he was pleased to call a retirement upon their cantonments. One part of the statement which holds no water is that in which he mentioned that on the French left Daours and Vecquemont were retaken, as also Pont-Noyelles and Querrieux; whereas after one P.M. not a single Frenchman ever crossed the line of these villages—or, if he did, he never returned to tell the tale. At five P.M.—the hour when, as he states, "*le succès était complet partout*"—six companies of the 33d regiment, with scarcely any ammunition, made their famous charge upon Fréchencourt-la-Houssoye, spiked two guns in the battery, took the horses away, and were compelled to return into Pont-Noyelles for want of ammunition.

'Although three parts of Péronne are burning, the place still holds out. Siege guns from Amiens arrive to-day, with plentiful supplies of ammunition; so that, unless General Faidherbe chooses to abandon his position on the Scarpe, and come to the assistance of the beleaguered town, Péronne must fall in a short time. To-day I did my best to reach the town, to see what advancement had been made. Riding was impossible; so I hired a carriage, thinking, in the innocence of my heart, that I could get to my destination much more expeditiously. Péronne is about fourteen English miles from Bapaume. The mayor of Bapaume had been adjured by all the gods, both German and French, to supply me with a good conveyance by eight o'clock this morning. At that hour a miserable-looking leather box, upon four indifferent wheels, drawn by a venerable white cart-horse with innumerable bells about his trappings, the greater portion of which were held together with string, made its appearance. Nothing daunted, I set out, with two soldiers behind, bearing loaded rifles, and in readiness for Francs-tireurs. I had, however, mistaken the road, across which the snow lay in heavy drifts of four and sometimes even of five feet. After sliding, cursing, and thumping the boy who drove, and finally breaking the whip, I got three kilomètres on my road. Here the harness fell off the horse, one shaft broke, and I thoroughly lost my temper. There was nothing for it but to return; which I accordingly did, inwardly vowing never to try such an experiment again.

'General Faidherbe seems to express a wish to be attacked anew—a thing, perhaps, not unlikely to occur. In this desire the people of Arras do not at all coincide; on the contrary, they are determined once and for all not to be shelled out of their homes even for M. Gambetta. They seem, indeed, almost anxious to see the invader at their gates, which they are prepared to open without hesitation. In this I think they are right; for the force the Prussians can now bring to bear upon General Faidherbe and the French army of the north will require all that general's energies to make head against. It appears that in the year 1815 Bapaume was occupied for three weeks by six companies of the 33d (Duke of Wellington's) regiment. My host, an old man of 71 years of age, remembers not only the circumstance, but the names of some of the men and officers. He informed me that he could speak English, but that the English he spoke was *patois* English, or, as he believed it was termed in that language, "gibberish." I am free to confess that his vocabulary is not very select, inasmuch as there are many very high-sounding and inelegant words which have, since those good old times, gone out of every-day use. When I asked him which he would sooner have quartered upon him, English or Prussians, his answer was, "*Ah, mais, mon Dieu, monsieur, Prussiens! Ces messieurs Anglais étaient si exigeants.*" He also informed me that Messieurs les Anglais wearied very much of Bapaume. They were allowed to work in the fields if they liked; but half an hour of this recreation always seemed to satisfy them.

'There is a marvellous story, derived from goodness knows where, about the Prussians having taken away 100,000 francs from the town of Amiens, and having, for better security, packed the money in a coffin purporting to contain the body of poor Prince Hatsfeld—who fell in the cavalry charge at Dury on the 27th—and sent it back to Germany. One portion of the story is true. One hundred thousand francs were indeed required to be paid by the city of Amiens; but this contribution has never left the town, and was held as a security for the good behaviour of the capital of Picardy when the army should march away. That sum is now in Amiens, and, far from having been confiscated, it remains there as a simple hostage for the good faith of the city. It is a pity that things are not always put in their proper light; for, were the mayor of Amiens himself interrogated upon the subject, he would be the first to laugh at a story so improbable and ridiculous.

'Heavy snow is again falling, and the movement of troops has become almost an impossibility.'

I have often asked myself the question, why people take a festive delight in seeing the old year out and the new year in? Surely, being twelve months nearer the end of one's existence has nothing particularly joyful in it. And yet you are asked to sit up, to drink all sorts of horrors, and eat a frightfully indigestible dinner, because, forsooth! you have approached closer by one year to the grave. Let me attempt to describe the way in which we passed the memorable evening that saw the last hours of an eventful year out, and ushered in the perhaps more stormy days of the new one.

On the 31st of December General von Göben removed his head-quarters from Bapaume to Combles, in order that he might be in the most advantageous spot from which to direct the operations against Péronne, and at the same time to keep a close watch on General Faidherbe's movements. The scene through which we rode was wintry enough to fill with delight the hearts of those who think that without ice, frost, and snow, this season loses all its charms. The wintry triumvirate was strongly represented—the wind blowing the snow in heavy drifts, varying in depth from two to five feet, across the road; icicles hanging from every eave, in long graceful glittering pillars; whilst each pond and puddle reflected the desolate scene upon its ice-bound surface. On our way the dull sound of artillery in the direction of Péronne sang the only requiem to the dying year; and I thought, as I sat shivering in my saddle, of the burning fires, the joyous laugh, and happy countenances to be seen in each hearth and home of dear old England. I was still in the clouds, when the harsh challenge of the sentry to the general's escort woke me to the shivering reality that I was in France, and not at home; that we were in an enemy's land, with 70,000 French hearts but a short distance off, burning to wipe out the disgrace of Querrieux—or, as the French have called it, Pont-Noyelles; and that perhaps to-morrow the new year would open upon a scene of strife and bloodshed.

Combles is not an engaging town—it is straggling, ill-built, dirty, and comfortless—but was not to be despised, especially on such an evening as that of December 31, 1870. In the best house of the town we found that the ever-provident and truly wonderful Captain Baron von Lilien had metamorphosed a dreadfully cold and uncomfortable room into a cheery-looking dining *Saal*. Sixteen plates were laid upon a table which, of course, as an article of furniture, would hardly bear inspection; but then a long white table-cloth covers a multitude of sins. At 5.30 P.M. we sat down, fifteen officers, the number composing his excellency's staff, and one guest—Major von Bronikowski, commanding the Rhenish rifles battalion. In a campaign, eating is a matter so important and absorbing as to leave but little time for talking. No sooner, however, was hunger to some extent satisfied than conversation began on every side, merging at last upon the interesting topic of the battle of Pont-Noyelles, and more particularly upon a brilliant episode by which it was distinguished: I mean the taking and holding of Daours by the Rhenish rifle battalion against a whole division of the French army.

This feat, together with the resistance and charge of the 33d West Prussian fusiliers, under Colonel von Henning, will mark the stubborn fight of Pont-Noyelles as among the most glorious in the campaign of 1870. Who so well able to describe the most interesting points as the commander of the Rhenish battalion, Major Bronikowski? Every mouth was hushed as he told the general how, with this body of 800 men, he waited for the heavy columns of the enemy who came to attack him, until they got within ninety paces—how then every one of his men, who had been waiting for the word with his eye on the enemy and his finger on the trigger, as his commander gave the word, '*Nun! Kinder, schnell Feuer!*' sent such a volley into the ranks of the Frenchmen as to leave upwards of forty dead in one place. With this body of men, a battalion of the 65th, and a battalion of the 33d—in all not 2500 men—was the French left forced back upon Corbie; with this body the villages of Bussy, Daours, and Vecquemont were taken and—still more surprising—held against repeated assaults of the enemy.

Then the colonel told us of the feats of a boy-hero, one of the many who know neither father nor mother, but who from infancy have followed the fortunes of the regiment to which they have attached themselves. This little fellow, seeing a French chasseur lying dead a few yards in front of the line of fire, made a rush out, seized his chassepot, pouch, and ammunition, and with a shriek of joy at the prizes he had made, rushed back to take up his position in the ranks of those who to him were father and mother, sister and brother. Then the embryo rifleman took up his position behind an old tree, and, notwithstanding the furious kicks which each shot from the chassepot dealt his little shoulder, he fired without intermission, and advanced with his company, until darkness and the retreat of the French ended the fight. Next morning, not satisfied with his achievement of the previous day, the boy Jäger steals out in front of the Prussian advanced posts, and comes upon a French lieutenant of mobiles, who, having divested himself of his sword, is sitting under a cornstack, dreaming, in all probability, of the glories that his regiment cannot achieve. Creeping quietly up, our German lad makes a bold snatch at the sword, grasps his prize, and, drawing it from its sheath, turns upon the astonished Frenchman. There is nothing for it. The French officer must return with the German soldier-boy—a prisoner of his sword and spear.

And now the conversation, which has become general, is interrupted by the entrance of the *Ordonnanzofficier*—that is, in other words, the aide-de-camp of the day. He has returned from Amiens, and many and anxious are the inquiries of those who surround the table for news of their wounded comrades of the 23d. By my side sits a captain of the 68th regiment—that regiment which fought at Fréchencourt in the 16th division, under General Barnekow; he is an old friend, and has been on General von Göben's staff since the commencement of the campaign. Fair, tall, and powerfully built, there are few who would like to meet him alone if he were in a determined mood—a good soldier, a kind friend, and a warm-hearted companion: he too has got a friend who, in front of his battalion, had received a severe and, as it turned out, a fatal wound. The two men had been boys, men, and soldiers together; they loved one another as brothers; and I shall not easily forget how, when we sat down to dinner after the battle of Pont-Noyelles, he told me of his friend's wound. As the aide-de-camp, with punctual and rigid military discipline, delivered his despatches to the general, I saw the anxious eloquent look upon the face of him who sat next me. Presently the officer came round and passed behind his chair. A few words were spoken—so few, indeed, that I heard not their import; but as I looked round, the expression on that open manly countenance was unmistakable. The kindly eyes were already full of tears, the great strong arm was rigid as the hand that nervously grasped the table-napkin, the brow was wrinkled and full of thought, the chest heaved with ill-suppressed sorrow. His friend was dead—gone to swell the list of those who had fallen for *Gott und Vaterland*. And so the evening passed on; glasses were emptied to 'hearths and homes,' until the hour when the old year glided out and the new one stole in.

A good deal has been said about Prussian injustice in the north of France. Three proclamations issued by the Prussian prefect of the Somme will go some way to prove that these cruelties and injustices existed only in the imaginations of some would-be 'sensation-mongers.' The first remitted the fine of 20,000 francs imposed upon the town, assigning as the reason for this act of grace 'the impartial and energetic humanity with which the municipality of Amiens had coöperated in the care of the Prussian wounded.' The second abolished all requisitions in boots and the like, and ordered the establishment of a public workshop for the supplying of these articles to the German army at fixed prices. The third proclamation I give in full, on account of the compliments it paid to a useful, but somewhat comical, body of French public servants:

'Prefecture of La Somme.—The devotion and the energetic zeal for the safety of the city of which the Corps of Pompiers has so often given proof, especially during the last weeks, has gained well-deserved gratitude from the Prussian authorities; and it is with pleasure that I bring the present proclamation and exemption from all billeting of soldiers to the knowledge of the inhabitants of Amiens:

"PROCLAMATION.

I am charged by his excellency the general commanding-in-chief of the first army, Baron Manteuffel, to express to the Corps of Pompiers of the town of Amiens his sincere gratitude for the good services rendered during the last two fires. To give, on my part, a proof of this gratitude, I order that 'Messieurs les Pompiers' be all *exempted in their dwellings* from all billeting of soldiers, and that my present order be respected by all soldiers of the Prussian army.

VON RUVILLE,
Major-General, commandant of the town of Amiens.

Amiens, Dec. 23, 1870."

I am convinced that the honourable Corps of Pompiers (*l'honorable Corps des Pompiers*) will show on every other occasion the same devotion for the well-being of the town of Amiens.

SULZER, Prefect of La Somme.

Amiens, Dec. 24, 1870.'

Next morning the guns of Péronne again thundered away, but as the heavy siege artillery from Amiens was not yet in position, the bombardment *à l'outrance* had not commenced. General Faidherbe made a reconnaissance in the neighbourhood of Fins from Arras, but returned without firing a shot; and the first day of the year stole by without bringing with it anything of importance. Intelligence arrived in the evening that a heavy division of French troops had marched towards Cambrai from Douay; it would therefore appear that the French general was not disposed to sit quietly down on the banks of the Scarpe, and allow Péronne to be taken under his very nose, without making an attempt to relieve that ancient fortress. What he had been about during those last few days, was a question which he alone could answer; but his strange inactivity proved only too clearly the utter check to their enthusiasm which the French troops received on the 23d of December.

Be that as it may, the subsequent energetic movements on the part of General Faidherbe clearly showed that it was never his intention to permit Péronne to fall without a blow for its relief.

On the morning of the 2d, General Faidherbe made a strenuous though unsuccessful attempt to turn General von Göben's left flank, protected by the 30th brigade of the 8th corps, lying in Bapaume. The French had lightly felt the Prussian left flank without coming into action; but later in the day their commander seems to have made up his mind to make a still farther trial in that quarter. The affair commenced about noon, the French advancing upon the Prussian outposts lying in Sapignies and Behagnies. These villages were held by the 28th regiment, the 68th regiment lying in Bapaume, Achiet-le-Grand, Bihucourt, and Favreuil. The contest was sharp, short, and decisive, the French being compelled to retreat with the loss of ten officers and 200 men made prisoners. Their loss in killed and wounded was also considerable; but by the uncertain light it was difficult to tell exactly how many. The Prussian loss was small—one officer wounded and a few men. It would appear by this movement that the French intended to occupy Albert, and to make an attempt at cutting off General von Göben from Amiens. This, however, was an utter impossibility, as he possessed the Somme from Cléry to Amiens—a certain and safe barrier against the intruder. Had the French occupied Albert, and attempted to repeat their former advance, they would at once have found themselves in a cleft stick from which it would have been difficult to escape.

That evening the French occupied Achiet-le-Petit, Bucquoy, Ablaineville, Gomiecourt, and Mory. The Prussian cavalry was at Miraumont.

Meantime the news from Péronne was reassuring. The town burned in three or four places—the heavy artillery brought from Amiens having done its work. The French artillery had not been so successful: the mortars were badly served, and did but little good; while the fire of the town was wild, infrequent, and very badly directed. Count Portalais's squadron of the Bonn hussars made a very fine attack in the affair before Sapignies. General Faidherbe lost much valuable time; and, in so doing, permitted the Prussian army of the north to outmanœuvre and out-march him. Had he made the bold push that he ought to have made, and, instead of marching on Amiens, taken the road to Beauvais, matters might have been otherwise; but the bait of the capital of Picardy, skilfully left for him, was a temptation he could not resist.

The news of the capitulation of Mézières now arrived, but without any details; and the next forty-eight hours were big with the fate of the army of the north. That evening the prisoners taken in that day's affair arrived—10 officers and 248 men. It appears the French attempted to take one of the Prussian batteries, and had advanced to within 200 yards of the guns, when the 28th regiment, who had been lying in wait, made a rush at them and took prisoners the number I have named—fine-looking fellows, though dreadfully pinched from cold and hunger. They told me that their corps had suffered very severely in the skirmish of that day; and they expressed themselves as tired of soldiering, and of being led, as they called it, to the slaughter. They wanted peace, but they did not exactly know how they were to get it except by driving the Prussians out of the country. Marching from Arras at six that morning, they had been told they would get quarters in Bapaume; they had neither eaten nor drunk all day. The total attacking force of the French was 10,000 men, with five batteries of artillery; the total defending force of the Prussians was 2800 men.

In the position which the contending armies now occupied, it was but too evident that an action must be fought within forty-eight hours. Scarcely had the days of the old year, fraught with so much bloodshed, been brought to a close, when another scene of misery and carnage has to be recorded. Faidherbe made his effort to relieve Péronne, and to turn the left flank of the army of the Somme. His battalions fought hard and strove bravely for him; but at the moment when success was to a certain extent within his grasp, he retreated before an enemy whom he outnumbered by two to one. On the 2d of January, having thoroughly felt his way on the Prussian left flank, General Faidherbe determined to attack them at Bapaume the next morning. Accordingly, at nine next morning, the 3d, just as General von Göben with his staff arrived at Le Transloy, half-way on the Péronne road between Combles and Bapaume, the enemy commenced the action.

Let me first describe the relative positions of the two armies. Bapaume, with the villages of Avesnes-les-Bapaume, Ligny, Tilloy, and Grevillers, were held by the 15th division, under General Kummer, composed of the 29th brigade consisting of two battalions of the 33d, and the 65th regiment. Two battalions of the 33d held the villages of Avesnes and Grevillers; the 65th regiment the suburb of Bapaume, called the Faubourg d'Arras. The 30th brigade, consisting of the 28th regiment and the second company of the 68th, held the ground towards the Arras road and the wooded heights of Sapignies. Bapaume and its environs were consequently held by about eight battalions, with six batteries of artillery. I must not fail to remark here that at this moment, with the exception of those of the 19th regiment, no battalion could bring more that 600 men into action; consequently the Prussian force at Bapaume may be put down at 4500 infantry, with 36 guns. To their left was the brigade of General Count Gröben, who lay at Miraumont, on the Arras and Amiens railway. The Prussian right was commanded by Prince Albrecht the younger, with the 40th regiment, three batteries of horse artillery, and the division of the cavalry of the guard, whose head-quarters were in Equancourt, at the juncture of the Cambrai, Bapaume, and Péronne roads. The reserve consisted of the 8th Jäger battalion, one battalion of the 33d regiment, one battalion of the 68th, and the artillery reserve. These lay upon the Bapaume and Péronne road between the villages of Beaulincourt and Le Transloy. We have now the position of the Prussian troops—their left at Miraumont, centre at Bapaume, and right at Equancourt. The French right extended beyond Achiet-le-Petit, and lay in the villages of Bihucourt, Achiet-le-Grand, and Gomiecourt; their centre was in Behagnies and Sapignies; whilst their left rested upon Vaulx and Lagnicourt.

The French began by an attack upon the Faubourg d'Arras, and by an attempt to drive the 33d regiment out of the village of Grevillers. In this the French signally failed, being driven back and pursued by the 33d into the village of Biefvillers, which they stormed and took possession of. But the French made the village soon too hot to hold them. Heavy masses of infantry came on to attack the gallant little band, amongst whom the French artillery was making sad havoc. Slowly, and with their faces to the enemy, they retreated upon the suburb of Bapaume, where they found the 65th regiment at their backs, and whence a quick and uninterrupted fire was soon poured upon the French troops. Meantime, the Prussian artillery posted on the Arras road swept the plateau beneath, and poured a plunging fire of shell into the heavy French masses as they struggled across to gain the Faubourg d'Arras. The French artillery was never so well served as upon this occasion. It fairly equalled that of the Prussians, both for rapidity and precision. The 33d regiment, fearfully reduced —I mean the two battalions of that regiment—had now taken possession of the old citadel of Bapaume, situated on the Albert road, and of the windmill to the left. The 65th held a part of the Faubourg d'Arras, while two horse-artillery batteries were sent forward to the left flank, and, taking up a position at Ligny, opened fire upon the French right.

The action now became general. Bapaume was a circle of fire and smoke. The Prussian left, overwhelmed by the numbers of the enemy and the hot artillery fire, was beginning slowly to give ground, when the Rhenish Jägers, with two fresh batteries, deployed to the Prussian left and came into action. Meantime Prince Albrecht had marched upon Bancourt from Equancourt, and had detached two batteries with some cavalry in the direction of Beugny-le-Château; whilst he himself, with the 40th regiment and the remainder of his command, excepting the hussars of the guard, engaged the enemy's left from Fremicourt. The hussars of the guard were sent along the road to Cambrai, to make sure that no troops were advancing on our right from that place. At the village of Boursies, two regiments of French infantry, with a squadron of cavalry, were reported as advancing on the Cambrai road upon the right flank. The officer in command was equal to the emergency. A squadron was dismounted, and took position of the buildings and out-houses of the village. No sooner were the French within range than the hussars opened a heavy fire upon them with their carbines; and the astonished Frenchmen, thinking the village held by infantry, made a hasty retreat.

While matters were going on thus on the centre and right of the Prussian army, General Count Göben advanced against the French right from Miraumont. Making a slight *détour* to his left flank, he suddenly appeared on the enemy's rear, and, opening fire from his artillery, made them imagine he was about to attack them in reverse. This had a very good effect; for it compelled the French centre to draw off some of their forces, and gave a little breathing-time to the gallant defenders of Bapaume. Meantime confusion was supreme in the streets of that town. The inhabitants were rushing off pell-mell in this direction and in that; the shells came hurtling into the houses, the bullets smashed the windows, whilst the town began in some few places to burn. As we stood on the road outside Bapaume which leads towards Beaulincourt, we could distinguish the sound of the heavy guns playing upon Péronne; and I reflected how anxious must have been the commander of that fortress for news of those who were trying to relieve him, and whose fire he could, as we were afterwards told, distinctly recognise.

Towards 1.30 things were looking serious: the heavy fire and superior numbers of the French had told heavily—so much so, that the suburb of Arras was relinquished, and the 29th brigade, under Colonel Bock, retired into Bapaume. The 30th brigade formed up in rear of the town on the Péronne road, and for a short time the French ceased their operations, except on the right flank, where Prince Albrecht was hotly engaged, neither side gaining any advantage. At 5.30 the French entered the suburb of Arras before Bapaume, and commenced erecting barricades at 200 yards from the Prussian forces. At six P.M. they were driven out of all their positions by the Jägers and the 33d, and the combat closed by the French occupying their old positions on the Arras and Douay roads.

This is a point in this action where Faidherbe was severely to blame. The Prussians, notwithstanding their gallantry, were ridiculously outnumbered, and their position was no longer tenable; so much so, that the general in command, finding his losses so heavy, and the enemy so superior in numbers, had determined upon retreating across the river Somme. Orders had actually been given to that effect, when it was discovered that the French army was also in retreat, having been as roughly handled as the Prussians, if not more so. Already had the heavy baggage trains commenced their retrograde movement, when it was ascertained that the French general was withdrawing his troops in a northerly direction, and it became consequently unnecessary to make any retreat.

And thus ended the battle of Bapaume, in which the Prussians had only 10,000 infantry engaged, with 84 field-pieces. The French brought into the conflict at the very least 50,000 men, with 60 pieces of cannon; but, notwithstanding this preponderance of force, they never for one moment drove the Prussians from their positions. That they inflicted severe and heavy losses upon the handful of men who covered the road to Péronne is a melancholy fact which I cannot deny; but that they gained not the slightest advantage on the 3d of January, beyond the effect produced by that loss, is also beyond power of contradiction. Had General Faidherbe waited for the result of the day's action, he would have found that the position which the Prussians held the day before was, from their severe losses, no longer tenable. He would then have been able to advance to the relief of Péronne.

and have partially cleared the left back of the Somme. This would have put fresh ardour and energy into his troops, and have inspired those hopes of success with which General Faidherbe found it very difficult afterwards to imbue them.

Notwithstanding the retreat of the French troops, General von Göben determined upon removing his head-quarters to the village of Dompierre, that he might be nearer to the scene of operations around Péronne. It was late when we reached our quarters in Combles after the battle; while the extreme severity of the weather was far from calculated to promote feelings of comfort, especially in the breast of the tired and hungry soldier. Talking of hunger, our dinner, while it would have amused most people, would have horrified M. Soyer and his constituents. In a farm-house at Le Transloy, after dusk, General von Göben had his quarters, receiving the reports of the various brigades and regiments with respect to the movements of the enemy, and issuing his orders. We were all of us desperately hungry; accordingly, with the assistance of another officer, I set to work to improvise a dinner.

First of all, we killed four hens and a duck; then I found a leg of mutton in the wine-cellar, plenty of potatoes, four frozen heads of cabbage, and a dozen iced onions. Two orderlies soon stripped the fowls, every one gave a hand to the peeling of the potatoes, and I was elected *chef de cuisine*. I cut-up the cabbages and onions into a large caldron, and added thereto the fowls, with salt, pepper, and a piece of bacon. I crammed the leg of mutton into the oven,

of Arras, the enemy continuing in full and hasty retreat.

Again had the French troops been guilty of barbarous cruelty, displaying rather the ferocity of an uncivilised country than the vaunted chivalry and heroism of the defenders of France. *They deliberately and in the most cruel manner bayoneted the wounded as they lay helpless on the field of battle:* my blood boils as I write these words, the simple writing of which is ample condemnation of the act.

Those who have stood with their regiments under a heavy fire of artillery well know how demoralising is the effect which well-served batteries can produce upon infantry in masses or in particular positions. Infantry fire is what every soldier expects and is accustomed to. He does not even listen to the peculiar whistle of the lead as it flies past him or lays some comrade low; but with shells it is different. They try the real steadiness of soldiers under fire more than anything I know; and I may therefore, remembering its conduct in this battle, claim a very large share of *sang-froid* for the 33d East Prussian fusilier regiment. Its men had done most of the hard work, and had the heaviest losses; they were on outpost when the action commenced, and they bore the brunt of the fight both here and at Pont-Noyelles. As I shook hands with the commandant, Lieut.-Colonel von Henning, in the streets of Bapaume, on the evening of the 3d of January, and congratulated him on the way in which his regiment had kept up its prestige, the tears filled his eyes and his voice trembled as he said, '*Dear friend, I have no regiment left;* they are all gone. I have but three officers alive; I can do no more.' Ten minutes after he led his shattered troops against the villages of Tilloy and Avesnes, taking them from the enemy, and gloriously ending a most glorious day for 'his king and his country.'

And now the heavy snow covered the unburied bodies of our comrades; the guns of Péronne were sounding a fitting dirge for the soldier's burial. Many friends lay there, with whom I had camped and lived long dreary months — whose kindness of heart and nobleness of disposition had filled me with admiration. Shall I be thought romantic or absurd if I thus take the opportunity of paying my humble tribute to their memory? If there be any ready to scoff at such feelings, let them go through such scenes and see if their stoicism will carry them through the dangers, the privations, and the sickness of a campaign such as this was, without a friend to help or to cheer them.

Referring once more to the battle of Bapaume, I cannot help thinking that, if the cavalry had been a little oftener employed, more decisive results might have been obtained. There is no use in showing the enemy heavy masses of cavalry, if they are not to come into action; and the laming of a few horses by riding over a frozen ploughed field is no sufficient reason why a whole regiment should not be sent against the enemy.

CHAPTER XIII.

THE SIEGE OF PERONNE.

In the foregoing chapter I mentioned the pursuit of Faidherbe's forces by the Prussian cavalry after the action of Bapaume; and that a regiment of cuirassiers had ridden down some infantry. As this episode shows that, notwithstanding the improvement in military weapons, cavalry is absolutely necessary *as an auxiliary* to an army in the field, I shall repeat the circumstances under which this gallant action took place.

A squadron of the 8th cuirassiers of the Rhine, commanded by Captain von Maré, were ordered after the battle of Bapaume to follow up the retreat of the French troops along the Arras and Douay roads. Just beyond the village of Sapignies, between it and Mory, Captain Maré came upon two retreating battalions of French infantry—one a chasseur regiment, the other consisting of gardes mobiles. At the moment he discovered the French troops he was riding exactly parallel to them, the undulating country having hitherto hidden them from his view. As soon, however, as he saw the position of things, he determined on attacking the enemy. It will be remembered that the greater part of the country in the neighbourhood of Bapaume is arable land, most of which had been ploughed, and the furrows from the severe frost of the previous ten days were frozen into bars of iron. Cavalry officers well know how trying it is to horses to make an attack over such ground, and will therefore understand the difficulties that a heavy cavalry regiment had to overcome under such circumstances.

After some little deliberation, a spot was chosen upon which to attack. No sooner did the French infantry perceive the approach of the Prussian cuirassiers than they formed two squares. The foremost square—that which was first attacked—waited until the cavalry came to within 300 yards before it opened fire. Then, however, a perfect shower of bullets rang against and pierced the cuirasses of the advancing horsemen. The captain was shot through the knee, and his charger through the head; the lieutenant was unhorsed, and suffered a severe concussion; and the troop sergeant-major received a bullet through the heart. Undaunted by the fall of their officers and squadron leader, the men rode boldly at and right through the square, scattering the foe on all sides, sabring and trampling down many. When the Prussian cavalry had thus pierced their way to the other side of the enemy, they immediately spread to avoid any concentrated fire. Unfortunately they were not supported. If they had, in all probability the regiment of infantry would have been cut to pieces; but a ravine of great depth separated them from their comrades, who were unable to cross in time to take part in this gallant action. The remains of the shattered French square were thus enabled to gain the shelter of a village, against which it was of course impossible to advance with cavalry. It was a gallant action, and one that will be remembered amongst the many that have occurred in this most eventual compaign.

On the same day on which the severe action of Bapaume was fought, General von Bentheim on the Seine had a somewhat sharp engagement with the French troops from Havre. These, under their new commander, who, it was rumoured, was received with acclamation, had for some days past been massing upon the left bank of the Seine, threatening Rouen. On the morning of the 3d of January, at five, when, as I need hardly add, it was perfectly dark, General von Bentheim, with a strong division, surprised the French army in their quarters. The attack was short, sharp, and decisive; four standards, 500 prisoners, and two rifled guns falling into the hands of the Prussians. Not satisfied with this result, a company of infantry were immediately placed upon wagons, and, with two horse-artillery guns and two squadrons of cavalry, went in pursuit of the flying enemy, capturing two more guns and many additional prisoners, the force being commanded by Major Preinezer of the artillery; the gallant general commanding the French troops, and his no less gallant forces, taking refuge behind the earthworks of Havre.

The enemy's troops were followed as far as Courcelles, Ervillers, and Nareuil after the battle of Bapaume. Here farther pursuit was stayed.

The day previous we learnt from a Prussian surgeon taken prisoner by the French, but who subsequently managed to make his escape, that the French had received strong reinforcements from Boulogne, Calais, and Lille. All day long the trains were bringing troops from Arras to Boiry, a small village on the Arras and Amiens line; and the enemy had advanced their outposts as far as Ablaineville and Gomiecourt, upon the road to Amiens. Upon this General Count Gröben, who held Bapaume, thought it necessary to evacuate that somewhat important point, and sent the intelligence of his retiring movement to General von Göben. I will not for a moment find fault with this somewhat peculiar abandonment of a spot which had cost the general commanding and his troops so much anxiety and so much blood; but I may venture to remark that the movement was injudicious and unnecessary, especially with the cavalry that General Gröben had at his command. The consequences of this somewhat precipitate change of quarters were to compel General Kummer, who with the 15th division was at Albert, to withdraw upon Bray-sur-Somme, and Prince Albrecht to retire upon Combles.

Meantime the French made a very strong demonstration to the left of Albert. Their patrols had been met at Mailly and Bertrancourt, so that Lieut.-Colonel von Pestel was obliged to retire from Acheux to Albert. By the way, the 7th lancers, Lieut.-Colonel von Pestel's regiment, again distinguished themselves much in the same way as did the hussars of the guard upon the road to Cambrai.

It appears that they came across a reconnaissance which the enemy was making in force, consisting of two battalions and a cavalry regiment, somewhere in the neighbourhood of Courcelles. The Prussian squadrons were immediately dismounted, and took possession of a small hamlet; and when the French infantry had advanced to within 1200 yards, the uhlans began to fire off their pistols. I need hardly say the bullets did not carry a hundred yards; but the smoke was there; and as the uhlans loaded quickly and kept up the noise, the hardy mobiles thought the village was held by infantry, and made a hasty retreat.

As matters now stood, Péronne was the *pièce de résistance*, in every sense of the word. It made the position of General von Göben anything but an agreeable one, and kept the troops continually upon the *qui vive*. The commander of Péronne was a Frenchman who had broken his parole, and knew that he fought with a halter round his neck. It would have been well if he had been the only instance; thirty-two prisoners of the same sort being brought in in one day. To add to the difficulties at Péronne, the thaw which had set in flooded the valley of the Somme, and the rain that was falling made everything and everybody dull and melancholy.

Despatches of General Faidherbe fell into the hands of the Prussians. From these it appeared that the French commander left Lille on the 5th, whither he had gone after the battle of Bapaume, and had arrived in Arras.

Péronne, one of the most important points in completing the line of the Somme, now capitulated. That its garrison had made a brave defence, a brief recapitulation of the particulars I am about to relate will distinctly prove. The valour of his opponents was acknowledged by General von Göben; for the garrison marched out with all the honours of war, colours flying and bands playing.

The town of Péronne is built upon an island formed by the river Somme, which flows round the grass-grown fortifications of Vauban, flooding the fields, and making a natural rampart against an assailant. At that season of the year, when the river overflows its banks, it is quite impossible to approach the town except by the roads from Biaches and Bussies, both of which are defended by heavy and unassailable *têtes-de-pont*. To take the town by assault was therefore impossible. Péronne, however, must fall, or else the Prussian arms in the north would have sustained a very undesirable reverse. After the decisive battle of Pont-Noyelles, on Dec. 23d, General von Göben was enabled, by the rapidity of his advance in the rear of the French troops, to gain a very important point in the town of Bapaume, commanding as it did the Arras, Douay, and Cambrai roads. The 16th division, under General Barnekow, was at once dispatched to form a junction with the brigade of General Schüler von Senden, and complete the investing force of Péronne; whilst General von Göben, with the 15th division under General Kummer, and the cavalry under Prince Albrecht, held Bapaume, and covered the besieging forces.

On the 27th of December Colonel Kameki (now General Kameki) opened upon Péronne with nine field-batteries, there being no heavy guns or siege train of any sort available, and the town was soon in flames. All through the nights of the 27th, the 28th, and 29th the fire continued, answered at times with great energy from the French side. Then some heavy guns which stood in the citadel at Amiens were sent for, and on their arrival were found to be almost next to useless. Meantime General Faidherbe, having rested his troops, suddenly awakened to the fact that Péronne was being bombarded, and that he ought to march to its relief. Accordingly, on the 2d, his advance guard reached Sapignies and the line of Vaulx, to the right of Bapaume, Achiet being to the left. His advanced posts engaged those of the Prussians, and a lively fusillade was kept up for a couple of hours. The next morning, with the sound of the bombardment of Péronne ringing in his ears, General Faidherbe fought the battle of Bapaume, in which 4300 French and 800 Prussians were put *hors de combat*, and in which the 29th brigade of the 15th division fought against the combined attacks of Faidherbe's forces. After the French general had succeeded in occupying the villages of Grevillers, Biefvillers, and Avesnes-les-Bapaume, a portion of his troops actually established themselves in the Faubourg d'Arras, a suburb of Bapaume; but from some unaccountable cause he suddenly ceased firing, and thereby enabled the Prussians to pull their shattered forces together, to come with renewed energy to the attack, and finally to drive him out of all the above places, and compel him to retreat beyond Sapignies, on the road to Arras.

The Prussian general, delivered from a perilous position, once more could breathe freely. All his energy was then turned upon the reduction of Péronne, which capitulated on January the 10th, the garrison marching out with the honours of war, and the officers being released on parole. As we rode along the Villers road, we met the French garrison coming out to surrender. I was particularly struck with the appearance of the garde mobile. Fine, tall, soldierly-looking young fellows they were, who, if they had been only as good as they looked, were just as well on the other bank of the Rhine. The town itself was nothing but a heap of ruins. There was not a house, not a corner, on which a shell had not inflicted more or less injury. Of the beautiful old church, the two lofty Norman-built towers reared themselves alone above the desolation that surrounded them. It is easy to imagine the completeness of the destruction, when I say that the houses of Péronne were no exception to the thin unsolid architecture which characterises most French habitations. The small shells from the 4-pounders had completely riddled the roofs and destroyed the façade of every house, whilst the larger projectiles, when they entered a dwelling, caused it to collapse like a house of cards. The streets were littered with rubbish, and the inhabitants, even after the town had surrendered, were creeping about, popping in and out of cellars or curious holes where they had buried themselves, as if in fear that their lives were still in jeopardy. The number of wounded soldiers in the town was thirty-five, of wounded inhabitants fifty. Add to these twelve soldiers and four civilians dead, and you have the sum-total of the losses of Péronne. The Prussians took 3000 prisoners, two standards, and forty-seven guns, with a considerable quantity of ammunition.

Just as the town had surrendered, General Faidherbe made a movement towards Fins, and was reported to be advancing in such heavy masses upon that place, as to warrant the belief that he intended to relieve Péronne. It was, in view of this news, deemed impracticable to occupy the town, inasmuch as the time allowed would be too short to organise any defence or to get the troops into convenient situations before the enemy should advance. Whatever may have been the French commander's intention, or whether he may have altered his plans upon hearing of the fall of Péronne, I know not; but certain it is that he returned to Bapaume, into which he had marched with bands playing and colours flying, that town having been evacuated by the Prussians as unnecessary after the fall of Péronne.

It will now be perceived that General von Göben had thoroughly carried out the objects of which he made no secret—namely, the possession of the line of the Somme, with the towns of Rouen, Amiens, and the fortress of Péronne. Across this line of demarcation General Faidherbe must, if he wished to reach Paris, force his way; and I have not the slightest hesitation in saying that, judging from what I saw of Faidherbe's troops, he could never have accomplished the task. That he had excellent material in his troops is a fact which no one who was present at the battles of Pont-Noyelles or Bapaume will venture to contradict; but his proceedings were so utterly foreign to the commonest rules of modern warfare, that unless he changed his tactics he could hardly have had a right to succeed. Meantime his head-quarters were at Bapaume, from which place there was little doubt he intended making some offensive movement, either towards Amiens or towards Péronne.

On the 14th January the head-quarters of the 1st army, under General von Göben, were once more removed to Amiens. The enemy held the same positions, and no movement of any importance occurred on either side.

About this time an important change took place, viz. the dispatch of General Manteuffel to command an army that was to operate against Bourbaki, and the assuming the command of the 1st army by General von Göben, the idol of the 8th corps. It would be presumptuous for me to offer any opinion as to the events which brought about this important change. There were, however, reasons for it which may, perhaps, be discussed at a future time: but one thing was certain—that there was no one so little pleased at the important position which had been deservedly bestowed upon him as General von Göben himself—and that none were more thoroughly convinced that in him they had the right man in the right place than the whole army of the north. General von Manteuffel took his leave thoroughly respected and beloved by all grades, and I cannot do better than describe the parting dinner which he gave to his staff, at which I had the honour of being present.

His excellency had taken up his quarters in the princely residence of M. Dubos, in the Rue Neuve, Amiens. At six P.M. in the gorgeous drawing-room were assembled the officers of his excellency's staff, the préfet of Amiens, Count Lehndorf, well known in England as a breeder of horses, and some few other officers of rank connected with the 1st army corps—the corps, it will be remembered, which General von Manteuffel commanded before succeeding General von Steinmetz as general of the 1st army. There was something extremely impressive in this scene—this reunion, for the last time possibly, of those comrades who had fought and worked hard in the service of their country and of their much-beloved commander. The room, too, by its brilliancy completed a *tout ensemble* which was exceedingly striking. The walls painted in panels of white and gold, the delicate manipulation of which was so characteristic of the French artist; the heavy yellow damask curtains, the gorgeous lustres and costly ornaments, the furniture of yellow damask *à la* Louis XIV., and the magnificent hangings of Chinese tapestry which covered the large squares between the panels—these, by the way, were said to have been brought from the Summer Palace of Pekin, and to have been presented to the proprietor by Count Palikao himself—all combined to make the spectacle striking and brilliant.

The officers stood about in groups and spoke in whispers; some of them were still to follow the fortunes of their old commander, whilst others were to remain or to rejoin their regiments. Presently the door opened, and the general entered. Dressed in the uniform of the dragoon regiment he commanded, with the aiguillettes of an aide-de-camp to the King of Prussia hanging from his shoulder, and without an order upon his breast, the old soldier of Germany advanced into the room with that courtly polished grace of which no man is a greater master. A shake of the hand, a kind word here and there, and dinner was announced. After dinner, General Schwarz, inspector of artillery, being the oldest general present, stood up, and, amidst universal silence, proposed the health of his excellency General von Manteuffel. The speech was all that could be desired.

His excellency then rose. He thanked those who had supported him; he glanced at his efforts in the cause of his country, and, in a voice made tremulous by emotion, he said, 'I exist in the 1st army; and although I leave for another command, I shall never forget it. But it is the will of his Majesty. Gentlemen, I ask you to drink to the 1st army and his Majesty the King. Long may he live! *Hoch!*' General von Manteuffel then called his servant, and from a small dressing-bag he took out a few photographs of himself, wrote his signature at the bottom, and distributed them to those around. There were many moist eyes at the table when the fine old gentleman took his farewell. He left with almost the whole of his staff for Versailles next morning, and General von Göben arrived to take up his new command.

It is but right that I should here take the opportunity of congratulating Colonel Loyd Lindsay and the British Society upon the very satisfactory and energetic way in which the charities of the society were administered under the superintendence of Captain Uniacke, who succeeded Colonel Cox in his onerous and far from pleasant post. I do this the more readily because I have had occasion to animadvert upon the waste and disorder which marked the proceedings of other branches of the society. I do not for one moment know what Captain Uniacke's resources were; but I cannot help thinking that he must have often been dreadfully pressed to carry out the energetic and useful line of conduct which he had adopted. The combats of Pont-Noyelles and Bapaume, and the siege of Péronne, must have sorely tried his means, although I took special care to note that in no one instance had goods or stores been given out except in cases of real emergency. It is such efforts as these that the British public should support—not the disorderly, useless, and wasteful proceedings which were, I am sorry to say, too evident in other parts of France.

General von Göben's having succeeded General Manteuffel in the command of the first army, or the army of the north, gave rise to certain changes. His excellency the general, on taking the command, removed his head-quarters to Amiens. This change did not separate me from my old comrades, the firm friends of many a bivouac, march, and battle; for General von Göben, in taking over the first army, still retained the control of the 8th corps, the head-quarters of which were likewise fixed for the present in Amiens. Meantime General von Bentheim commanded the 1st army corps—General Barnekow the 16th division, and General Kummer the 15th division, of the 8th army corps. Prince Albrecht retained the division of General von Senden—who had been sent to the south—and the cavalry division of the guard. General Schwartz commanded the artillery of the first army, and General Biehler the engineers. To assist him, General von Göben had two efficient and talented soldiers in the persons of General von Sperling, chief of the staff of the first army, and Major Bömki: upon the latter his Majesty had conferred the distinguished decoration of the order of the Iron Cross, first class.

The left flank of the Prussian army now rested upon Rouen, and the right upon Péronne, the centre being in Amiens. After the brilliant surprise of French troops effected by General Bentheim at Grande Couronne, the French commanders appear to have withdrawn their forces entirely within the lines of Havre. In this well-known seaport at this moment there seemed to exist anything but that military discipline and combination so necessary for success to the defenders of France's hearths and homes. First of all General Briand tried his hand and failed, to be succeeded by General Le Roy—who, in his turn, was first assisted by General Peletingeas, and eventually gave place to a new man in the person of General Loisel. Opposed to General von Bentheim, who commanded the Prussian left, we find, first, General Mouchez, commandant of the town of Havre, which was defended by 15,000 troops, 2000 of whom were marines; secondly, 15,000 troops on the left bank of the Seine, in a glorious state of indiscipline, under the command of General Le Roy—all these forces, some 35,000 strong, with nine batteries of artillery, being under the chief control of General Loisel, the new commander. Opposed to General von Göben was the army of Faidherbe, whose head-quarters were in Arras, whilst his advanced posts lay in front of Bapaume, and so on to Fins. His forces could not be far short of 70,000 men, and he had besides a powerful artillery worked by marine troops. His right rested upon Bapaume, his left upon Cambrai, and his centre between the two places, distributed amongst the villages. This is a slight sketch of the military position, without diving into details.

The social position of the country, meanwhile, was becoming every day a matter of manifest anxiety. In Amiens there were 35,000 workmen with little or nothing to do; in Rouen, about 50,000 in a similar condition. How were these men to live? How would they manage not only to support their families, but also to find food for the Prussian soldiers who were quartered upon them? The means of replenishing the fast-diminishing resources of eatables in these two large towns were completely stopped, and, unless food came from Germany, it was impossible to legislate for the difficulty.

On the 15th of January all was again boot and saddle; for intelligence arrived that General Faidherbe was advancing in a south-easterly direction in considerable force, that St. Quentin had been abandoned by the Saxons and occupied by him. News also came that an officer of the 10th dragoons had been shot at Bolbec. It appears he was on patrol, and, having done his work, had entered Bolbec for the purpose of breakfasting. Bolbec is a town which had been at one time held by the Prussians, at another by the French. Latterly, however, a Prussian patrol had regularly entered and passed through the town, returning the same way, without let or hindrance. Upon dismounting at the hotel, the officer gave his horse to his orderly, and, not speaking French very well, he took out of his purse a thaler (3f. 75c.), and, laying it upon the table, requested the landlord to give him breakfast. Breakfast shortly appeared, and the hungry soldier, casting aside his sword and revolver, sat down to his last meal upon earth. Scarcely had he begun to eat when the door was suddenly thrown open, four rifles were pointed at his breast by as many men dressed in blouses, and the fatal report rang the death-knell of a young and promising soldier. Was this war—civilised, straightforward, manly war, which so delights the heart of an Englishman? or was it, in plain English, deliberate coldblooded murder?

At Rouen, or rather in the positions occupied by the belligerents in front of that town on both sides of the Seine, a constant sort of patrol warfare was going on. The Prussians had their outposts at Pavilly and Totes on the right, at Bourgtheroulde and Bourgachard on the left bank of the Seine. The Forêt de Brotone was a nest of Francs-tireurs, who never by any chance fired upon a party of Prussians numbering more than three, or at the very outside four; if their enemy mustered in greater strength, he was permitted to proceed unmolested. The town of Rouen itself was quieter and far more contented than the neighbouring capital of Picardy. Distress was, of course, there—and very widely-spread distress, too; but some of the manufactories were at work, and employed all hands, so that the suffering was in some localities alleviated.

Upon obtaining the intelligence above alluded to, I immediately left Rouen for Amiens, and as my train steamed into the station, the platform presented an unusually bustling appearance. Evidently something was afloat; for as I searched among the crowd, I saw many staff-officers, who could be there but for one purpose. As we alighted, I was told I had just come in time—for the general would be on his way to Nesle by the next train; that my horses and baggage had been sent on, and that we were going to meet the advancing army of Faidherbe. How I wished that really hard-working soldier-like Frenchman at the bottom of the sea, and deplored not having eaten a good breakfast before I left Rouen! Count Lehndorf, with his usual kindness, provided me with breakfast; and a flask of good Bordeaux, with the chance of meeting Faidherbe on the morrow, nearly pulled me together.

Arrived at the town of Nesle, there was no news of importance, beyond the fact that Faidherbe was advancing by way of Ham, covering his real intentions by a strong demonstration on his right flank towards Péronne, as if to lay siege to that unfortunate town. Deplorable was the slush, the rain, and misery for both men and horses! Every one tumbled in wherever he could find a place, and at about one o'clock at night the army may have been said to have first tasted repose during the previous twenty-four hours.

On January 17th, at an early hour, we marched upon Ham, that fortress which for so long a period had been the prison of the ex-Emperor. There was a hard thaw, and the roads were in anything but good order. However, bad as the weather was, it seemed to make but little impression on the troops: infantry, cavalry, and artillery marched along as if struggling through mud was really a pleasure. Arrived at Ham, reports came in fast and furious. St. Quentin had been evacuated by the Saxons, and was held by four hostile battalions, the French advance being but three-quarters of a German mile from us. I visited the scene of Napoleon III.'s imprisonment — two miserable empty rooms, where a French colonel taken prisoner at Péronne, who refused to give his parole, had, with his three daughters, passed the previous night upon bundles of straw. So far it appeared that Faidherbe was playing a good and a sound game; the result was in the hands of his troops. This time it would not be the fault of the general; for even his enemies admired the manner in which he manœuvred. Several slight engagements had taken place during the day, which finally resulted in the last decisive action fought in the north of France between the French and German troops, and which commenced early on the morning of the 19th.

Before, however, proceeding to describe the decisive battle of St. Quentin, it would be well to glance at the position occupied by the belligerents. After the action of the previous afternoon, in which General Memerty received a dangerous wound, the detachment under his orders, with the 15th division, and

General Count Gröben's command, held a line through Pœuilly on to Tertry, or exactly west and north-west of St. Quentin. The 15th division occupied the line between Tertry and Ham, the 29th brigade to the left, the 30th to the right. The 16th division, with the head-quarters of General Barnekow, lay in and north of St. Simon, on the east side of the canal running between Ham and St. Quentin; while the extreme right was held by the Saxons under Count Lippe. At seven on the morning of the 19th of January, the Saxon troops, consisting of the Jäger battalion, three cavalry regiments, and some artillery, marched out of La Fère, and advanced along the road to St. Quentin; the 16th division, under General Barnekow, directed itself against the same point through Artemps and Séraucourt; the reserve—composed of the 41st regiment, a detachment of the 33d, and the 2d lancers of the guard—proceeded with General von Göben and staff along the direct road to St. Quentin, through Douchy and Fluquières; the 15th division marched against Savy; while General Count Gröben, with his command, and the detachment Memerty, swung round, advancing through Marteville.

The action was commenced by the 16th division. They found the enemy in a very strong position between and in the villages of Grugis and Neuville. At half-past ten the battle on this side became general; and so strong and determined a stand did the enemy make, that the 41st regiment and two batteries were sent to reinforce General Barnekow. Here the 19th regiment lost 350 killed and wounded, and the division suffered severely, but at length succeeded in driving the enemy from their positions, and occupied the villages. On the left the 15th division, under General Kummer, entered Savy unopposed. The enemy were, however, in force on the opposite heights, and here the 1st regiment, the grenadiers of the Crown Prince, took two guns by storm under fire, but with considerable loss. At Savy, or rather to the right, a squadron of the King's hussars, under Captain Rudolphi, encountered two squadrons of the enemy's dragoons—and for the first time in the north, except at Sedan, were the Prussian cavalry able to measure their strength. The hussars rode them down as if they were standing still—the French dragoons being encumbered with their heavy white cloaks—and drove them back in disorder under the shelter of their infantry, killing many, and taking some prisoners. On the extreme left, at about one P.M., General Count Gröben and Colonel von Witzendorf's advance drove the enemy back, taking the woods in rear to the right of the Vermand and St. Quentin road.

The whole French line, now driven from its original position, had fallen back to a second one, equally commanding. Before the enemy were compelled to abandon this position also, the Prussian troops had to go through a repetition of the fighting by which they gained their first success. At last, however, the French were compelled once more to withdraw their left and centre slowly upon St. Quentin.

Meanwhile Count Gröben's movement on the French right had not been accomplished without danger. The French general dispatched four battalions and two batteries, which, advancing from St. Quentin along the road to Vermand, suddenly appeared on the flank of the Prussians. This was a critical moment, and required all the coolness of the Prussian commander. Ultimately, however, he hit upon the promptest and by far the safest method; for to make troops retire at such a critical moment is not merely hazardous, but too often fatal. The advance was therefore continued as if nothing was happening, and General von Gröben, after taking two small villages, occupied Fayet.

I must now revert to what was passing on the right flank of the 15th division, or, so to speak, on the Prussian centre. It was now nearly two P.M., and the peculiar formation of the ground, in heavy undulating rises, with deep valleys between, enabled the French to assume the defensive upon every eminence as they were driven backwards upon St. Quentin. Half-way between St. Quentin and Roupy, to the left of the road from Ham, stands a windmill upon a considerable eminence. Here the French seemed to be massing a formidable force of infantry, and, with three batteries of artillery, they looked for a moment as if they meant mischief; but Captain Leo's battery and another were so beautifully served, that in a short time the French artillerymen were seen to limber up and retire upon the town itself. Again the Prussian line moves forward, the artillery taking up the position just abandoned by the French, and the slaughter commences afresh.

The French were beaten at all points, and the 8th Jägers occupied a suburb of St. Quentin at six P.M.

At seven the 41st regiment drove the French from their barricades, and entered the town; at half-past the French troops were flying along the roads to Cambrai and Le Cateau; and St. Quentin was in the hands of the Prussians, with 9000 prisoners, six guns, and 3000 wounded in the town. The French loss, roughly computed by their own officers, was between 5000 and 6000 men, that of the Prussians between 2000 and 3000. On the right, the squadron of Count Wachtensleben, belonging to the hussars of the guard, made a brilliant charge, as also the dragoons of the reserve with the 16th division.

The result of this battle, to all intents and purposes, completely crushed the hopes of the French in the north; and the success of the day was principally owing to the wonderful rapidity with which General von Göben moved his troops to the scene of action. At 10.30 on the 17th the intelligence arrived at Amiens of Faidherbe's movement, and at one P.M. General von Göben was himself personally *en route* to meet him. The French artillery was wofully slack, except on the right flank, where it behaved well; but in the centre their shells came singing over our heads, falling 200 and 300 yards in rear of the batteries. In this action the French mobile officers took to wearing cuirasses—that is to say, breastplates made of tin, covered on one side with leather, on the other with paper; I could not make out what I had found when I discovered the first one, still attached to the body of an officer. In this instance, however, it had availed him but little, for a needle-gun bullet had gone through his brain. Next morning the flight of the French army was followed up, and, if an opportunity had occurred, another attack would have been made upon Faidherbe's demoralised forces.

Notwithstanding that General Barnekow, commanding the 16th division, occupied quarters in St. Quentin that night, General von Göben did not enter the town until next morning. The general and his staff lay all night in the next hamlet, and slept the hard-earned sleep of the tired soldier. A glorious victory had been won, and won by sheer hard fighting; and proud and satisfied was the conversation as we sat round the fire and discussed the events of the day. The name of Faidherbe occurred not unfrequently, and was mentioned with respect; for there can be but one opinion on this score—that he was about the best general that France at this time possessed. His failure was purely attributable to the French military system under the new republic, by which undrilled masses were hastily clothed, armed, and equipped, formed into regiments and battalions, and supposed, by this process, to have acquired the steadiness of old soldiers.

If proof were wanting, the battle of St. Quentin was an undeniable demonstration; and that fact General Faidherbe himself does not deny. His difficulties had been still farther increased by the fact that most of his regiments of garde mobile had been raised in the northern provinces of France. These men were surrounded by their mothers and sisters, their wives and children, who, day after day, pitied their miseries, and poured into their too willing ears the assurance that their general was a brute, and that their officers were savages. This sort of thing is not calculated to make soldiers of men taken from the lathe and the loom, the harrow and the plough. Had these men been sent away from such influences, and placed under Bourbaki or Chanzy, their conduct might have been different from what it was.

General Faidherbe had 50,000 men and 70 guns, and of this seemingly large army 25,000 men were all that he could depend upon, inasmuch as, with the exception of the battalions of garde mobile from Brittany and the west, his troops not only *did not* and *would not* fight, but ran away so soon as they came under fire. It was this that saved the left wing of the Prussian army when they were outflanked upon the Vermand and St. Quentin road; for it appears that the outflanking force consisted of eight battalions of garde mobile, with two batteries. The batteries came into action, but the mobiles refused to move. General Faidherbe's losses were 5000 killed and wounded, 9000 or 10,000 prisoners, and six guns; consequently all that remained to him of those troops upon which he could depend was 10,000 men.

The Prussians had 18,000 infantry engaged, with about 3000 cavalry; their loss being 3000 *hors de combat*.

As we rode into St. Quentin, the *Krankenträger* were still searching on the battle-field for the wounded. Poor fellows! they had lain out all night in the mud, with the rain and snow pouring down upon their mangled and ill-clad bodies. One poor fellow had just been found lying in the furrow of a ploughed field; his groans had attracted the attention of some labourers, and they had carried him down in a blanket to a house by the wayside. In this little house, consisting of two rooms, lay the dead bodies of four and the living frames of six Frenchmen. Of the four dead, three would most assuredly have been saved if proper medical assistance had been at hand; as to the six living, there could be little chance for them without immediate medical attention. A Prussian ambulance passing at that moment, I stopped it, and asked the doctor to attend to the man just brought in. He immediately did so, and, whilst employed in probing the wound, a French ambulance, with a French doctor, went by. I immediately ran out, and told him that six wounded men lay in the house, requiring immediate care and attention. The doctor dismounted and entered the house; and then the Prussian, being required elsewhere, left the room, and handed over his charge to the Frenchman.

I was just congratulating myself upon having been the means of perhaps saving one human being's life, when the French surgeon came out hastily, took off his hat, and said, '*Monsieur, il n'y a rien à faire avec ces misérables-là!*' Now, the Prussian surgeon had informed me otherwise; he had even gone so far as to say that there was every chance of recovery for at least three of those who lay there suffering the most dreadful agonies; he was, moreover, a famous surgeon, whose word might be implicitly depended upon. Imagine, therefore, my indignation at the conduct of the French doctor. 'Sir,' said I, 'I do not know who you are, or what you are, whether you are an apothecary or a hospital assistant; but this much I do know, that you shall not leave this house till the wants of those men have been attended to.' Then, taking the bridle of his horse, I gave it to an orderly of hussars, with instructions to remain there until each wounded man had been cared for, put into a wagon, and sent into St. Quentin.

I do not exaggerate when I say that the conduct of the French military medical men here was, with a few exceptions, beyond contempt. In St. Quentin alone there lay 2000 wounded—the theatre was full, the hospitals were full, and they were still pouring in from the villages around; yet you might go into the cafés and find French military surgeons lounging about, smoking, drinking, and playing billiards, whilst their countrymen, who had done their duty like men, lay groaning upon beds of pain.

The theatre of St. Quentin presented, if one may associate the terms, a horrible and interesting sight. The stage was littered with bloody mattresses. In the pit, where the well-to-do artisan had once taken his wife and family, the lover his sweetheart, the groans of the wounded, the uplifting of the hand, the writhing of the covered form, told of the anguish which lay all around. The private boxes, instead of being tenanted by the fashionable *dames* of the locality, were now inhabited by soldiers of the Republic, minus leg or arm; and the dress circle, that ring of demarcation between those who are *comme il faut* and those who are doubtful, was full to the brim of wounded men. The town itself was mournful and dirty, and the inhabitants were more or less drunk. They seem to have a savage consciousness of having been beaten at all points, and of having been shamed by a generous enemy into owning that the dastardly conduct of the inhabitants, when they fired upon the evacuating Saxon troops, had been leniently dealt with.

It appears that when the 1st grenadier regiment took the two guns from the French under fire, they positively harnessed the French troops to them, and forced them, with many a '*Vorwärts, monsieur!*' to drag the guns back into the Prussian lines. A curious capture was made by three hussars and an officer who were riding the previous night with orders in the neighbourhood of St. Quentin. In the mist of the evening they lost their way, and came suddenly upon some sixty or seventy infantry. There was no time to deliberate, so the officer determined upon, if possible, riding through the enemy. Each man sent his tired beast along at as good a pace as he could, but when within 100 yards of the French infantry every man of the latter threw his rifle on the ground and surrendered. And these brave and loyal defenders of their country were marched by four Prussian hussars into a church and locked up, to the number of about sixty!

General Barnekow, with the 16th division and the cavalry, followed in the steps of the flying enemy. It was not a retreat; it was fairly and honestly a rout of the greater portion of the French troops—although how General Faidherbe managed to escape so well is a marvel.

It has been said that one of the most difficult manœuvres is that of withdrawing beaten and disorganised troops from before a victorious enemy without farther losses. This General Faidherbe certainly achieved most marvellously. He removed his long trains of munitions, his artillery, and his infantry in a most masterly and, considering the circumstances, orderly manner. That he so well succeeded was perhaps owing to the somewhat dilatory movements of the Prussian cavalry; for even as it was they were close upon his heels, the tired infantry struggling through a composition that I can only liken to that which was to be found on the Woronzoff road, between the camp of the Light Division and Balaklava, in 1854. The point for which the French general seemed to be making, and which he reached just in time, was Cambrai. This town he placed between himself and the fast-pursuing Prussians, and for a few hours it proved a haven of refuge for his tired, worn-out, shoeless infantry; whilst he himself, with the artillery and cavalry, striking along the old Roman road running north-east from Bellicourt, passed the night in Caudry.

Meantime, Barnekow was in hot pursuit of the French. At Caudry, so near was he to the enemy, that, but for the fatigue of the infantry, Faidherbe would have been attacked on the night of the 20th. Human nature—even Prussian human nature—will, after all, bear only a certain strain. Military prudence dictated a few hours' rest to those who had marched thirty miles through mud up to their knees, whilst the cavalry and artillery wanted a like respite; so Faidherbe was able to reach Cambrai in the middle of the night, and there, with the broken-down, dispirited, worn-out remains of his army, he passed the night of the 20th.

The next morning saw the French on the road to Douay, and the Prussians before Cambrai, making their requisitions actually in the suburbs of the town itself. The Faubourg of Paris and that of St. Druon contributed to our breakfasts. The cavalry meantime spread out to the right and left flank, whilst General von Göben and his staff left Caudry to return to St. Quentin, and on the 22d to Amiens. Here we found the French journals from the Pas-de-Calais. The Lille paper, in speaking of the battle of St. Quentin, says, '*Notre armée vient de recevoir un échec.*' The *Echo du Nord* goes a step farther, and describes Faidherbe's entry into Douay and the state of his troops. This, it would appear, was most pitiable. Very many had no shoes to their feet, whilst their trousers and uniforms were one mass of mud. A regiment of chasseurs, 800 strong when they marched out, now returned 270 of all ranks. The artillery horses were sinking with fatigue, whilst those of the cavalry were for the most part unable to bear their burdens. The roads to Cambrai, as we passed by, especially that between Caudry and Cambrai, beyond the village of Beauvois, on the Cambrai and Avesnes high-road, showed unmistakable signs of the thorough *déroute* of Faidherbe's forces.

Meantime Longwy, on the Belgian frontier, had capitulated. As usual, just before the town surrendered, the commandant issued a flaming proclamation, to the effect that he would hold out until the last house had been bombarded into ruins. News had also come to hand, by telegraph from head-quarters, that Bourbaki was in an unpleasant position, the 2d corps having got into his rear. Strange murmurings were flying about the highways and byways of Amiens, in which the name of Paris was coupled with capitulation. Some said that the surrender of the capital was already under consideration; that the delegates on both sides were hard at work—the French trying to get the best for the gay city, the Germans stern and positive in their demands. Should Paris surrender, would the capitulation bring the beginning of the end? The world had by this time learnt that Paris was not France; and those who had watched narrowly the progress of events in the provinces could be of but one opinion. France was crushed and humbled to such an extent that, by fighting on, she could not make matters much worse; whilst, with Chanzy, Faidherbe, Bourbaki, and Gambetta, she had always the off-chance of at any rate improving her position. This was the prevalent idea of most Frenchmen.

Small as that chance was, useless as the sacrifice of life might appear to be, no one can in his heart blame men like Faidherbe and Bourbaki for their vigorous endeavours to ameliorate the position of their country. I do not for one moment suppose that either of them imagined it possible to drive the invader from the land; but something might be done to improve the terms upon which peace was to be made for the benefit of France. Upon one occasion two Prussian officers saw General Faidherbe upon some business. When the interview was concluded, General Faidherbe's last words to them were, '*Au revoir, messieurs*,' and an aide who was standing by added, '*Oui, à Berlin*;' but the general turned away with a mournful shake of the head.

On the evening of January 29th a telegram from Versailles threw every one into a perfect fever. General von Moltke telegraphed a cessation of all hostilities, pending an armistice, from the 31st inst. at twelve noon. The respective armies and corps halted in those places in which that messenger of peace found them; the Franc-tireur forgot to load his weapon; the mobile got drunk in anticipation; the soldier of France let his memory wander back to the blood-stained fields of Spiecheren, Mars-la-Tour, and Gravelotte, of Wörth and Sedan, where France's honour and France's chivalry were sacrificed to a miserable incapacity. The stout legions of the Emperor of Germany received the intelligence of this chance of 'an end' with their usual stolid reserve; but the glitter of the eye, the heaving of the breast, and the grasp of the hand told that in imagination they were already far on their way back to Fatherland, already embracing the aged parent or the sorrowing anxious wife. How the people of Amiens managed to know that something of this sort was going on forty-eight hours before the Prussian authorities, with their advantage of the telegraph, is a thing I cannot account for; but it showed with what perseverance and intelligence the country managed to transmit news from one place to the other.

Again at this time did the humane policy of the

Germans assist the starving, thankless population of northern France. Want of work, want of fuel, want of food, had hitherto, through the management of Count Lehndorf, the Prussian préfet of the Somme, to a certain extent been staved off, and some of the 20,000 workmen employed in working for the Prussian army. Half of the hostage money, too, which was demanded for the good conduct of the capital of Picardy was returned by the Prussians, and used by them in keeping starvation away from the doors of the unfortunate mechanics and artisans out of employment.

But the evil which the German authorities had hitherto successfully combated again showed itself in a more virulent form. Before, the town suffered from the want of money with which to buy food and coals; now, it was the want of coal, material, and food, which was not to be got for love or money, that threatened the town with serious injury. The manufacturers could do nothing without coal. Their supplies from Dieppe and Abbeville were cut off through the blockade of these places by the French gunboats. The few barges that lay in the canals could get no farther, in consequence of the blown-up bridges that prevented their advance; while from Lille and the Belgian frontier it was equally impossible to draw supplies. Here was a state of things liable to bring about a combination of miseries which would have perhaps eventually led to some horrible deeds of murder, induced by that evil whisperer to man's conscience —hunger. Could the father bear to see his little ones starving for want of bread, while that Prussian

Pickelhaube quietly sleeping in the corner had plenty under his head? Could the husband stand by and see his sick wife drooping and dying before his eyes for want of nourishment, whilst the soldiers quartered upon him were cooking upon his own fire, and in his own kitchen, strengthening soup that would perhaps save her life?

What, however, did this telegram of General von Moltke's portend? Such a man, with Faidherbe destroyed in the north, Chanzy helpless in the south, and Bourbaki surrounded in the east, would hardly grant an armistice except upon a basis very favourable to Germany, and indicative of peace. Then came the still more important news—'The German troops under orders for the seat of war were to remain where they were.' This was a sure indication that we were, perhaps, at the 'beginning of the end.'

'"*On the 31st of January, at twelve noon, an armistice will commence.*"' Such was the short but decisive telegram, and by that time the position of the first army was as follows: The bulk of the army stood on and behind the river Somme. General Gayl, commanding the 1st division of the 1st army corps, would by that time be in and about Roisel, north-east of Péronne. Fins and Le Catelet would also be occupied. The 15th division, under General Kummer, would occupy Acheux, with outposts at Bucquoy. The 16th division, under General Barnekow, would hold Bapaume, and a detachment of the 15th division would occupy Doullens. Count Gröben with his cavalry would advance on the road to Abbeville, and General Bentheim, with the 2d division of the

1st army corps, occupy Dieppe. So that had Gambetta's eloquence prevailed on General Faidherbe to advance, and pay no attention to the armistice in which he had had no voice and had never been consulted—if the ragged remnants of the French army of the north could possibly have been brought to attack General von Göben's position, which was then anticipated, as Gambetta had paid a visit to Lille—they would have found a still harder task before them than any they had yet undertaken.

Curious was the effect this welcome message of peace had upon both French and Germans. The inhabitants rushed into one another's houses, kissed, shook hands, laughed, and cried by turns. The Germans grasped one another by the hand, and thought of their Fatherland, and the hearts that were waiting and yearning after their return. Suddenly, while all this joy and gladness were visible in every street and alley of Amiens, the sounds are hushed, as the slow and measured tramp of soldiers, bearing a coffin covered with its pall of black and white, and surmounted by an officer's helmet, is borne along. He who lies under that velvet pall was every inch a soldier and a gentleman, a comrade and a friend. Major Hohlleben, commanding the 2d battalion of the 40th—the 'fighting 40th,' the Hohenzollern fusiliers—was severely wounded by a piece of shell while gallantly leading his men at the battle of St. Quentin. Amputation was necessary; and two days after he sank under the effects. In him his Majesty the Emperor lost a brave and loyal subject, his general a gallant soldier, and the officers and men of his regiment a firm and true friend. *Requiescat in pace!*

At half-past six, on the 29th of January, the usual serenity of the head-quarters dinner-table was broken by the news that the forts round Paris had been occupied that day—the 29th—by the Prussian troops; that the city had to all intents and purposes capitulated; and that a truce of twenty-one days on land and at sea had been agreed to by the Emperor through Count Bismarck, and subscribed on behalf of France by M. Jules Favre. If his excellency the commander-in-chief had not been present, it is impossible to say what might not have occurred; for at that particular moment I imagine each individual felt desperately inclined to waltz round the room with his neighbour, to throw his glass through the window, or to dance upon his hat. For a few moments there was silence; each watched his neighbour's face, and then turned to the centre of the table.

General von Göben is at no time what can be called a demonstrative man; but those who know him can tell whether the events that are passing around give him satisfaction or otherwise. At that moment his eyes were fixed upon the despatch; the lines of thought which usually marked his brow seemed to vanish, his eyes sparkled, and his mouth relaxed into a smile of deep and intense satisfaction. Turning to Colonel von Witzendorf, the chief of the staff of the 8th army corps, he spoke a few words, and, as if by magic, every tongue became loosened round the table, every glass was at once raised to the lip, and drained with that hearty, silent, deep-felt gratification, so much more real than boisterous exclamation.

I feel confident that of the eighteen or twenty officers who sat round that table there was not one who did not feel more pleasure at the chance which now existed of peace than at the feat of arms which their comrades had accomplished. It was but natural that they should be proud of an achievement the consummation of which never entered their heads at the commencement of the conflict, even in their wildest moments of hope as to the future; for, when Germany went to war, there was not a man or an officer who did not know what a severe struggle was before her. They did not believe that they should win, but they felt certain that they should not be beaten. Is it, then, to be wondered at that when the general retired a fresh supply of champagne made its appearance, and that bumpers were drained to the Emperor, to the Crown Prince, to Moltke, to Bismarck, and to many other worthy chiefs and comrades?

In the midst of our merriment the *Feld-Jäger* from Versailles burst into the room—a *Feld-Jäger* is an officer employed specially as the Emperor's messenger. Truly the evening was to be a 'sensational' one, for he had brought with him the convention entered into between Count Bismarck and M. Jules Favre. This was read aloud; the passages that affected the armies of the north being those which occurred in Article I. We read that 'the Departments of the Nord and the Pas de Calais, ... together with the peninsula of Havre as far as a line drawn from Eretat on the seacoast in the direction of St. Romain, should remain in the hands of the French troops. The advanced posts of the belligerents were to take up their respective positions at five kilomètres' distance from the line of demarcation, so that ten kilomètres should exist between the two armies. Each army reserved to itself the right of maintaining order in the territory which it occupied, and of employing such means for enforcing that authority as the respective commanders might think fit.'

The last shot between France and Germany had now been fired in the north of France, and the soldier waited patiently until the diplomatist had settled the terms which would permit him to return to his home after the trials and toils he had endured.

It is scarcely my province to carry my narrative beyond that time which is marked by the battle of St. Quentin. After that action and the pursuit of Faidherbe's army up to the walls of Cambrai, there are no military movements to chronicle; for the armistice scattered the Prussian troops in various directions over the departments of the Seine Inférieure and the Somme, in order that they might press as lightly as possible upon the impoverished country. This was, however, done with a due regard to speedy reconcentration upon any point if necessary. The conduct of the troops in these outquarters is beyond all praise, and this is more clearly demonstrated by the parting which took place between the Prussian soldier and the French peasant, when the order to march for home arrived.

To those who followed the events which marked

CPSIA information can be obtained
at www.ICGtesting.com
Printed in the USA
LVHW110900020323
740706LV00006B/411

9 783382 113803